SURVIVING

The Uncollected Writings of
HENRY GREEN

Surviving

The Uncollected Writings of
HENRY GREEN

Edited by
MATTHEW YORKE

VIKING

VIKING
Published by the Penguin Group
Viking Penguin, a division of Penguin Books USA Inc.,
375 Hudson Street, New York, New York 10014, U.S.A.
Penguin Books Ltd, 27 Wrights Lane, London W8 5TZ, England
Penguin Books Australia Ltd, Ringwood, Victoria, Australia
Penguin Books Canada Ltd, 10 Alcorn Avenue, Suite 300,
Toronto, Ontario, Canada M4V 3B2
Penguin Books (N.Z.) Ltd, 182-190 Wairau Road,
Auckland 10, New Zealand

Penguin Books Ltd, Registered Offices:
Harmondsworth, Middlesex, England

First American Edition
Published in 1993 by Viking Penguin
a division of Penguin Books USA Inc.

1 3 5 7 9 10 8 6 4 2

LIBRARY OF CONGRESS CATALOGING IN PUBLICATION DATA
Green, Henry, 1905–1973
Suriving: the uncollected writings of Henry Green /
edited by Matthew Yorke.
p. cm.
ISBN 0-670-80476-2
I. York, Matthew, 1958– . II. Title
PR6013.R416A6 1993
823′.912—dc20
92–50355

Printed in the United States of America
Set in Bembo

CONTENTS

FOREWORD

This book has been long in the offing. It was John Lehmann who
first proposed a volume of Henry Green's Uncollected Writings.
'Dig about and see what you can come up with,' he urged Green
in 1971, enthusiastically listing the wartime stories and articles
from the fifties. It is not known whether Green even replied to
the letter – in all probability he did not. Two further attempts
were to founder, one soon after Green's death in 1973, the other
at the end of the following decade.

That nothing came of these three ventures can now only be
seen as fortuitous in view of the fact that a considerable amount
of previously unknown material has come to light, the bulk of
which was discovered in the late 1980s when the Yorkes' house
in Knightsbridge was being cleared. It is therefore from a much
fuller archive that I have been able to select the pieces which
comprise this book.

It has been my aim to arrange the material in strict chronologi-
cal order. Not only does this reveal a strong sense of the development of Green's style, it shows the extent to which he veered
away from fiction after the publication of his last novel *Doting*
in 1952. Where the pieces have been previously published there
have, of course, been no problems with dates. However the
unpublished stories and sketches, many of which were found and
taken from undated notebooks, have been much harder to place.
Letters to and from Nevill Coghill, his close friend of Oxford
days, and Edward Garnett, reader for Dent and Jonathan Cape,
should have provided the clues – unfortunately in some instances
they have failed to do so. Where dates cannot be accurately attributed to pieces I have set out the facts of the matter as I know
them.

[vii]

Disregarding a large amount of juvenilia (carefully preserved by his older brother, Gerald Yorke, the words 'saved from the wastepaper basket' touchingly written in pencil on one of the manuscripts) this volume represents about three quarters of the material in the Henry Green archive. All that remains now are a number of abandoned projects, two plays, and two articles on the craft of writing, published in the fifties, their points covered in more depth in pieces printed here.

In the course of compiling this book I have been given generous assistance, and I should like to thank the following people: Jonathan Burnham and Carmen Callil; Lady Dorothy Heber-Percy; Joan Henry; Alice Keene; Margaret Scrutton; John Updike; and the Yorke family.

INTRODUCTION

BY JOHN UPDIKE

Henry Green was a novelist of such rarity, such marvellous originality, intuition, sensuality, and finish, that every fragment of his work is precious, as casting a reflected light upon his achievement, the nine novels and the memoir that he published in his lifetime. There is not much uncollected Green, really; he was not a worker on Grub Street, piling up copy every week. Through the 1930s he was a man fully engaged in his business at the London office of H. Pontifex & Sons, able to produce only one novel, *Party Going*, in the decade. The forties saw him become an auxiliary fireman in the blitz and its aftermath, with one day in three devoted to his business – in spite of all, his most productive period. In the fifties, growing famous, he ventured out into the world of journals and the BBC, and even managed a few such extracurricular chores as a translation from the French and a paeon to Venice, an obituary tribute to Edward Garnett and a friendly note for an exhibition of Matthew Smith. But, though these peripheral compositions are interesting, and in some cases revelatory, his art and his claim to fame are all but entirely concentrated in his novels. We read these previously uncollected pieces, lovingly marshalled by his grandson, for an answer to the question the editor Edward Garnett posed to the twenty-year-old Henry Yorke after reading his first novel, *Blindness*: 'How did you ever come to write any thing so good?'

In England the literary vocation is usually the prerogative of the middle class, even when, like Evelyn Waugh, the successful writer puts on upper-class airs. The Yorkes enjoyed not only a venerable aristocratic background but owned a Birmingham factory. By Green's own account, in *Pack My Bag* and the autobiographical tidbits he released in later life, he was an unprepossessing, overweight, rather sad and solitary youngster, fond of fishing and reading. At Eton, he did not do as well as his two older brothers, Philip and Gerald, and his beginning a novel while there was, according to his schoolmate Anthony Powell, 'an undertaking not regarded over-seriously by relations and friends'. At Oxford, he was on the billiards team, drank and went to the movies a great deal, and eventually failed to graduate, allegedly because he could not learn Anglo-Saxon and 'for the rest discovered that literature is not a subject to write essays about'. But he did manage, while still at Oxford, to complete his novel, to show it to Edward Garnett, and to get it published by Dent in 1926. He was then twenty-one. We search his juvenile writings for clues as to his possession so young of a defined and venturesome style and an imagination that, in *Blindness*, ranges impressively beyond the mind of his schoolboy hero into the thoughts and feelings of a middle-aged woman, a defrocked and decrepit clergyman, and a young girl wasting away in unnatural isolation.

A tendency toward authorial invisibility and a universal empathy manifested itself early; Green's juvenile effort is to create, as he when mature would consummately do in *Living*, *Loving*, and *Concluding*, a field of characters, mingled with their environment like small creatures coming and going in a meadow. In 'Bees', the earliest published piece here, from an Eton magazine when the author was seventeen, a sunk clergyman – kin perhaps to the miserably eccentric Parson Entwistle of *Blindness* – retreats from the world of men into that of bees, a vision of adult despair carried out naïvely but with a brave completeness, right to the final ironical amorous twist which the school authorities deleted and, Green added in his handwriting, 'so removed all point to the story'. The adult writer's voice, in its compression and obliquity, can be already heard in an admirably pawky sentence like 'He detected an insult in the butcher boy's whistling as he delivered the meat.' And in 'Arcady' from 1925, the style is full at work, its cunningly limp convolutions searching for a simultaneous precision of emotion and sensation: 'the air inside drooped with folded wings at the shut windows & the scent she used, sweeping through the streets that swirled in eddies of

changing light, talking nervously she & I of what was coming.'
It is an exercise, directed to Coghill, and leaves a rather mannered
and priggish impression, yet in its deflationary account of the
deadness of a date of which both parties had unreal expectations
– a barren night at the theatre ('Hysterical laughter when the
curtain came down to cover the emptiness that was left. . . .
Then a scene with a bed upon the stage with the tumult of my
fears storming within me') – there is, remarkable in a nineteen-
year-old, that terrible tender honesty with which Green was ever
to gaze at human romance. 'Adventure in a Room' contains the
embryo of *Blindness*; one would love to know what incident gave
Green, a painterly writer of great visual intensity, his fantasy of
blindness, and what frustration 'exasperated' him, an advantaged
youth of seemingly callow character, 'into a desperate striving
after the beautiful'.

The two stories about giants are quaint surprises, childish and
familial; yet they lead us to reflect that part of Green's unique
effect, as we read his fiction, is the largeness that his diction gives
his characters, a statuesque magnification achieved by the studied
piling-on of some words and the withholding of others. For the
first time, in 'Monsta Monstrous', we see the withholding of
articles, with incantatory, epic effect:

> Mountains are in Wales but he strode over these and often
> knocked over the tops of them, till he came to where they fell
> before plains and sat down on the last mountain and let his
> feet rest in the plain, resting the toes in a river to cool them
> (and they were hot with knocking) and sat there looking at the
> smallness before him. Toes made floods immediately.

'Saturday' extends articlelessness into the sensations of a young
working-class woman and the territory of his great second novel,
Living.

> No blind was over window. Sun came by it. And she turned
> head over from sun towards them sleeping and did not see
> them. She smiled. Head on bolster was in sunshine.
> Life was in her belly. Life beat there.

The growing writer's next venture is again into the mind of a young woman, one of his own age and class, and it failed to become a novel. He discussed *Mood*, with liberal quotation, thirty years later, in the essay 'An Unfinished Novel'. He tells us that he was in love with the model for Constance Ightham, his heroine, and the images with which he furnishes her stream of consciousness have an assurance lacking in the almost comically primitive giant's world of Maggie Cripps, who was transformed into Lily Gates in *Living*. He may have loved Constance but didn't admire her, as he admired the rougher-hewn Maggie, and perhaps admiration for a character is more sustaining than love. At any rate, *Mood* was abandoned and *Living* became his second novel, though eventually and with visible artistic difficulty Green did incorporate in his third novel, *Party Going*, his own social set, which included (his son's memoir tells us) Aly Khan. 'Excursion', with its railroad terminal and crowd confusion, seems a dry run at *Party Going*, on the plebeian level; without any of the gaudy colour and giddy comedy of the upper-class interactions within the terminal hotel, the panorama stays inertly, wanly grey, though Green by this time (1932) has his style and sympathies in place.

These early pieces show, in sum, a self-effacing, broadly empathetic author assembling a style which with a seemingly casual sensitivity can register a wide range of visual, vocal, and emotional nuances. Green is unusual, for his class and nation, in his strong democratic tastes – for football and pub talk, and those experiences of factory and fire fighting that broke down class barriers – and his avant-garde propensities. He was sent to France in 1923, before going to Oxford at the age of eighteen, and along with the language he imbibed there, it seems, a certain continental approach to art: Proust and Céline were high among his artistic heroes, and his novels never give the impression of being merely social news. A certain abstract shimmer, a veil as it were of transcendent intention, adds lustre to all his pictures, and piquancy to his prose. Each paragraph has something of a poem's interest and strangeness. The uncollected pieces of the forties show him functioning at full tilt, bringing to the inferno of blitzed London a descriptive power of almost lurid virtuosity. Fire meets an ice of visual exactitude:

Already it would have been possible to read in the reddish light spread by a tall building sixty yards away, the top floors of which, with abandon, in recklessness, with fierce acceptance had exchanged their rectangles for tiger-striped hoops, great wind-blown orange pennants, huge yellow cobra tongues of flame. . . . There must have been a gas main alight beneath the debris for whitish yellow flames were coming out, as I could now see five yards away round a great corner, in darker blue, of sculptured coping stone, curved in an arc up which this yard-high maple leaf of flame came flaring, veined in violet, then died, then flared again.

The prose is not easy; it must be read and read again, until the picture comes clear. From this decade comes also Green's most considered and passionate piece of criticism, his 'Apologia' for the idiosyncratic prose of C. M. Doughty's *Arabia Deserta*. Green exalts qualities we do not think of him as aspiring to: monumentality, purity, magnificence. Doughty's prose represents 'the magnificent in written English'; Doughty is 'harsh, simple to a point of majesty, and not clear, that is his sentences meander'. Green considers the point that the rhythms of this prose derive from Arabic and says that others who also knew the language – T. E. Lawrence, Gertrude Bell, Wilfrid Blunt – have 'an elegance that is too easy'. Doughty is not easy: 'when he passes on a tale, he treats it as a man will granite that he has to fashion.' 'He is often obscure. He is always magnificent.' As if to cinch this professed admiration for a meandering, majestic, difficult prose, Green ends his essay with one of the most defiantly tangled and impenetrable sentences ever committed by a careful writer to print. This yearning for the majestic surprises us but explains an enduringness, a resistant hardness, a something graven that distinguishes Green's prose from the lucid, efficient, common-reader prose of many of his contemporaries; one such, Anthony Powell, recalled of his old friend Yorke that 'he had a passion for Carlyle (an author tolerable to myself only in small doses), and (a taste I have never acquired) Doughty's *Arabia Deserta*; both indicated a congenial leaning towards obscure diction'. This leaning would seem to be at the opposite pole from his celebrated fondness for demotic speech; but colloquial diction too, as we can see in an orgy of it like 'The Lull', can be obscure, and needs to be reread for the meaning to soak in. Green might be writing of himself when he says of Doughty that in a miraculous way he 'puts words together which, entering by our ears if they are read out loud, or slipping by our eyes if they are scanned in print, express their meaning in our bones'. In his striving for a prose that, coming at us at an unexpected slant, penetrates to bone-deep meaning, Green was in the company of, among others, Ronald Firbank, Rose Macaulay, and Virginia Woolf. But it is Henry James he cites on 'the effort really to see and really to represent, [which] is no idle business in face of the constant force that makes for muddlement'. Though he elsewhere deplores the late James style, it seems truer of James and himself than of Doughty that 'His style is mannered but he is too great a man to be hidden beneath it.'

As Green was precocious so was his decline into silence premature. His last novel, the impeccable but attenuated *Doting*, was published in 1952, when he was only forty-seven. It is difficult, given the oblique invitation of its title, not to take 'The Great I Eye' as autobiographical, and to consider its profoundly hungover hero as a pilgrim on the path of Green's own decline. The muddle of Jim's spotty memories of last night's flirtations, nudity, and drunkenness doesn't quite clear to make a story that stands free; the prose loops out to include what seem stray images:

> When drunk the trouble one caused spread ripples, several dry walnuts thrown at the same time into a water tank hung with green ferns; and where the ripples met, leering faces of his green friends mirrored in the base over and over again in the repeated olympic bracelets; linked arms for false amity, a symbol of old games.

Old games, perhaps, are wearing the player down, 'one's body that did not forgive. Always the same. The feeling it couldn't go on like it, misery, anxiety, death death death.' A dismaying despair flecks Green's multiplying personal statements during the fifties: he told the New York *Herald Tribune* in 1950, 'I write at night and at weekends. I relax with drink and conversation. In the war I was a PFC fireman in London, the relaxation in fire stations was more drink and conversation. And so I hope to go on till I die, rather sooner than later. There is no more to say.' Rather sooner than later! John Pomfret, the hero of *Nothing*, written in 1950, ends the novel by wanting, 'Nothing . . . nothing.'

Yet Green's descriptions of the processes and strategies of writing for *The Listener* show a loving pride in his craft, and the handful of book reviews he consented to do reveal a love of the written word that was broad and voracious; he boasted of reading a novel a day. He undertook literary chores, offering *Vogue* some pages of thrillingly purple prose on Venice, and sharing with *Esquire* some alarmingly tough male thoughts on love. Having come increasingly to believe that dialogue was the best way to carry a story, he was attracted to playwriting. After *Doting*, he spent a great deal of time and energy on a political farce, *All on His Ownsome*, which though it passed through several drafts was never produced; nor has it been included in this collection. Based upon the not unfamiliar conceit of one potent man left in a world of women, it seems at once hectic and static. Even Green's dialogue, without the embedding descriptions of scenes and poses, refuses to kindle into mental pictures and psychological resonance. The two unpublished short stories, 'The Jealous Man' and 'Impenetrability', have a new, slack tone; the teller, so delicately and elusively felt a presence in his best fiction, moves to the foreground. The first story feels like a fable spun in an Oriental bazaar, and the second like a BBC chat. The BBC, which broadcast a number of talks by Green, might have done even more; surely the play *Journey out of Spain*, with a little trimming, could have been broadcast on radio. It is a play of voices purely, with no need of scenery, and charmingly renders one of those near-disastrous yet in the end harmless and even rejuvenating scrapes that foreign travel involves. The device of the monologues is excellent, and the unexpected emergence of the Fixer into the limelight shows a touch of Green's impish social reach: 'English people are OK but they cannot understand. Maybe they do not wish.'

Green's own emergence as a *Paris Review* interview subject deserves its place here among the works of invention. His droll turn as a tall deaf man is carried off with an explosive precision like that of highly honed farce:

> After fifty, one ceases to digest; as someone once said: 'I just ferment my food now.' Most of us walk crabwise to meals and everything else. The oblique approach in middle age is the safest thing. The unusual at this period is to get anywhere at all – God damn!

The interviewer, Terry Southern, seems more deeply deaf than the subject; nevertheless, Green manages to enunciate a number of interesting confidences, from why he preferred to keep his writing side hidden from business associates to the way he carried in his head the '*proportions*' of a novel in progress and reworked the first twenty pages 'because in my idea you have to get everything into them'. His proclamation of the purpose of art is almost hierophantic: 'to produce something alive, in my case, in print, but with a separate, and of course one hopes, with an everlasting life on its own.' This credo returns, later in the discussion, with some specific articles of faith: if the book has a life of its own, 'the author must keep completely out of the picture' ('I hate the portraits of donors in medieval triptychs') and there will be discrepancies, for 'life, after all, is one discrepancy after another'. Though Green gave some later interviews in which he appeared depressed and dazed, he was in good form during that session with Southern, and stated with a beautiful crispness why fiction, in its forms, must keep moving on:

> I think Joyce and Kafka have said the last word on each of the two forms they developed. There's no one to follow them. They're like cats which have licked the plate clean. You've got to dream up another dish if you're to be a writer. . . . It isn't that everything has been done in fiction – truly nothing has been done as yet, save Fielding, and he only started it all.

The interview ends with mention of a book under way, a factual account of the blitz to be called *London and Fire, 1940*. The first section of that uncompleted work, with an opening sentence very like the one Green confided to the interviewer, is this collection's last substantial item, and restores us to the flourishing Greenian universe, with its ingenuously compacted sentences – 'That innocent could never have even guessed how much of a child one fireman he saw before him was swishing past' – and its glowing full palette:

> . . . we saw a parrot-coloured group of rich women and one or two men with rods and waders. The little river dark red with peat tumbled through an emerald field to the slate-dark sea ribboned with white-capped waves as far as a break-out in dark clouds, edged with sulphur yellow, turned a streak of waste waters below to brightest aluminium.

But more than enough has been quoted of the book that lies in your hands. At its highest pitch Green's writing brings the rectangle of printed page alive like little else in English fiction of this century – a superbly rendered surface above a trembling depth, alive not only with the reflections of reality but with the consolations of art. He thought about art with a French, or modernist, concentration, and in the final pages here comes up with an un-Aristotelian statement of art's therapeutic powers: 'Living one's own life can be a great muddle, but the great writers do not make it plain, they palliate, and put the whole in a sort of proportion. Which helps; and on the whole, year after year, help is what one needs.' Help is what art gives us, with its 'sort of proportion', and what Green gave, and gives, in those ten volumes to which this now adds a glinting, uneven, but in part priceless eleventh.

TWENTIES AND
THIRTIES

Henry Vincent Yorke was born in 1905, educated at Eton (1919–24), and Oxford (1924–6). *Blindness* was published under the pseudonym Henry Green in 1926. Apprenticed as an engineer, he worked at The Farringdon Works, the Birmingham branch of the family business, H. Pontifex & Sons, between 1927–9. *Living* was published in 1929, the year he married Adelaide Mary Biddulph, and moved to London, where he was to work as a director for H. Pontifex & Sons in their George Street offices, until his retirement thirty years later. The Yorkes' only child, Sebastian, was born in 1934. In 1938 Henry Yorke joined the Auxiliary Fire Service, and was stationed at the outbreak of war in Davies Street, London W1, *Party Going* was published in 1939.

BEES

(Published in College Days, *the Eton magazine, under the pseudonym of Henry Michaels, in 1923)*

'Bees' was one of three of Green's stories published in *College Days*.

He was fresh from a slum parish in Liverpool. The doctors had ordered rest: and, now that the first flush of his religion had worked itself off, he was content enough to rest. It was his duty now to work for a sleepy, unenthusiastic village; to visit everyone personally – else they would not come to church; to minister to the non-existent spiritual needs of a righteous little colony of country people – or so it seemed to him after the harsh realities of his slum parish. The pettiness of his duties hedged him round. He could not get away from it all, for he never read a book or a magazine. All the endless little squabbles of village life were brought to him, till he was sick to death of them; till he lost his sense of proportion, and it seemed to him, when, for the first and last time, the schoolmaster under extreme provocation swore before the children, that it was a serious thing indeed.

Soon he had become devoted to bees. They had grown to be a reigning obsession. They always appeared to have something to do and they were always doing it efficiently; that was the marvellous thing about them, that was what he really admired. Besides, they did not sting him as they did the rest of his family when they approached the hives, and that endeared them to him. As he never read anything, these creatures were the only means of taking him out of himself: and he used to sit entranced, watching them fuss about. The Church and the village retired into the background. He was taken up with his bees – and why should he not spend a few peaceful minutes in his garden, with his bad

[3]

health and all? So gradually he faded out of village life. The attendance at Church on Sundays dwindled to the few inmates of the almshouses, too near the grave to risk absenting themselves from the weekly service.

The Squire, who did not understand his soul-weariness, was angry with the parson. The Squire saw the Church emptying; he heard complaints that the parson never went near anyone unless they were on the point of death, when he paid them a farewell visit. The Squire's wife found all the village work come on her hands, because the parson's wife was always ill. No one ever saw the parson's wife, she might not have existed. Her duty was to have children and to cook food in the intervals.

Neither the Squire nor his wife could see any fascination in bees. They could only repeat, when asked about it, how they had once lent him a book on bees, and in eight months he had not got through one half of it – 'on his pet hobby, mark you!' So they began to despise him. But then what did he care for dry-as-dust volumes on dead bees? All the summer he watched his bees work and in the winter his bad health and thoughts on bees kept him indoors. So it went on.

Then there was a tragedy. His eldest daughter, aged sixteen, died. 'Little' Grace, who had always been such a help to her mother; who had always been so quiet, and had never disturbed him at his bees. Now she was dead. And in his morbid state of mind he made it all into a terrible blow to himself: forgetting, of course, his poor wife, who really was prostrated with grief. He sank into himself. The funeral was the only time in three months that he left the rectory garden.

Everyone was very sorry for him then. One used to say: 'Ah! poor Wheatley. He has just lost his eldest girl, you know.' One felt sorry for him. But after six months one looked for some sign of life. With the arrival of spring, the Squire (who was in the City) jovially remarked to us that it was high time the man started earning his 'living' – a joke! But the bees had come out of their winter sleep, and he was fondly watching them, marvelling at their activity. With the summer merging into autumn the Squire let fall a kindly but not overtactful hint! 'We haven't seen you about for some time, Wheatley; really the village has almost

[4]

forgotten the look of you,' and so on. Bitterness started, and rankled on secretly within him. His life was so taken up with himself that, when his bees retired for the winter, he sat indoors brooding over his grievances; of the death of his child, who he thought had meant so much to him; of his wife's ill-health; of the nuisance of his other children, 'so unlike poor Grace'; of the way everyone misunderstood him, especially the Squire.

As time went on he became more and more preoccupied with himself. His life he felt was a tragedy, and he had to live up to the tragic in it. All day long he thought of how he was to stand the blow of his daughter's death, and, although it was eighteen months since she had died, he was still composing answers in his mind to the letters of condolence that never came. In the busy buzz of his bees he detected the sympathy he could not discover in the world outside. His wife, whom he always regarded as a drone, could do nothing with him. He was sure that every man's hand was against him. He detected an insult in the butcher boy's whistling as he delivered the meat. So he turned to his bees, who always sympathised, and were so practical, and who were not useless like his family.

His wife called in the doctor, who prescribed baths in certain chemicals. The next day he took the bath prepared for him, and, when he had dried and dressed, he hurried out to his beloved bees again. Unfortunately they disliked the smell, which still clung to him, of the chemicals in his bath. There was a vast buzz and they stung him to death. And he, poor fool, thought to the last that it was but an excessive display of sympathy.

Yes, she married the doctor.★

★ This was censored and so removed all point to the story. [H.G.]

[5]

ADVENTURE IN A ROOM

(Unpublished, c. 1923)

'Adventure in a Room' is clearly a forerunner of *Blindness*, begun at Eton, completed at Oxford, and published in 1926.

He sat in the Windsor chair, gazing about his room. It was his last night at Note. All round were the trifles, the few intimacies of his school life. For six years he had lived with the same old furniture. He had changed his rooms once or twice, but never the wall paper. The small brass figure, talking so severely to his dog, must know him very well by now, he thought. And it was his last night, tomorrow he would be leaving. Those pictures, too, they had looked down on him all the time he had been at Note. The paroquet pictures, the few third-rate prints, his own drawing that Armstrong had said showed such originality, his faithful looking glass – all of them must know him well. His bat he looked on as a pugilist looks on his hands. He had used his bat for so long without its ever having split that he had come to regard it as part of himself. The way it 'drove' made him think it was alive. And his books. Dull school books. God! There was a Badminton he had forgotten to return to the school library. Tomorrow. . . .

He had just said goodnight to the friend he 'messed' with. 'We messed together for years.' Who had said that? He recognised the point in it now, anyway. Mark and he would never feed together again; he was going to Oxford and Mark to Cambridge. There had been the School Concert that evening.

Four cricket and rowing 'bloods' had sung the Vale. The captain of the eleven had sung it very badly. Such a good fellow and quite on speaking terms with him! Why had he himself never done better at cricket or football? Not for lack of trying. Yet there was that fellow Armstrong keen on art and music and all that. He had got endless colours and was in the Note Society, the acme of human desires as it seemed to him, without any effort at all. He had painted that face to please Armstrong, and it was damned good. He ought to go to bed. He had got his House Colours, anyway, and had got into his house library, a community for the dispensation of justice to younger members of the house. Not many fellows – men – got that far. No. It was time to go to bed. Tomorrow he was leaving and it did not seem possible, somehow. All the unpleasantness of his time at school was wiped away. He looked back on days packed with happy incident. He went regretfully to bed, and fell asleep immediately.

The next morning he was up at five, notwithstanding the fact that no one was allowed out of the house before seven. He was also smoking a cigarette, to the well-simulated horror of the tip-scenting maids, and to his own intense satisfaction. He was wearing an ON tie; he was a 'blood' at last – all old Noteians were bloods, on the last day. Everyone who was staying on envied them so. For three short hours, he enjoyed himself hugely, showing off. But when he was in the train, he fell into the blackest depression.

Note was left behind now, for ever. His things, all his pictures, knick knacks, and furniture were following him. Physical connection with Note was cut rudely off, and home life was beginning. An orphan's life at that. Alone with Nanny, for his parents were dead, and he had no relations to speak of. It was terrible his still calling her 'Nanny', now that he was a man – you were always a 'man' after you left a Public School – he must not persist in calling her Nanny. There was a little rough shooting though, and he was great friends with the parson's son, whose sister held open wide the glass doors of Romance. He longed to pull her out of the river just as she had come up for the third and last time, or something.

At that moment a little boy on the embankment idly threw a stone at the train, rushing so impersonally past him. The stone hit the window, which flew into shivers of razor-sharp glass, which, in their turn, buried themselves with extreme speed in his face.

★

[7]

He was twenty-two, and blind. For three years, now, he had been engulfed in a world peopled with sounds and solids. It had been very dreadful at first. 'You may never see again – but of course there's a chance, there always is,' the doctor had told him. For weeks after that the words 'you may never see again' had run through his head, again and again, insensately. But he had come to care less. Blindness had its compensations. He found that everything had a most wonderful 'feel'. He would walk round his room, made just as it had been at Note that he might not be lonely, to touch and caress everything. The feather pictures of paroquets; his old blackbird doll, tattered remnant of nursery days; his Windsor chair; the table with the cuts on it and the neat hole he had burned one winter evening with a red-hot poker. . . .

Sounds, too, he loved. Any bird song was revealed to his delicacy of hearing as something really exquisite. Blackbirds especially – though he always rather blamed himself for this, saying that he should prefer the nightingale; for it was not safe to have wide divergencies from popular opinion. Next to a blackbird's song he put the scream of swifts as they fled past his window. How wild it was, that sound, and free. He used to sit at his window, letting the earth, with all her sounds and scents, come up at him. He gloried in a rainy day, the fragrance and freshness of it were a never-failing joy. Curiously enough, he could not bear the smell of new-mown grass, it appeared sickly and sugary to him.

His blindness had made him terribly shy. There had been a dreadful day when a little girl, eating peppermints, had been brought to see him. She had said, very distinctly, 'I don't like horrid blind boys,' and the smell of peppermint had half choked him. He had retired still more into himself after that episode. Time passed. He lived in a world of suggestiveness, of delicate, fragile hints of things. Speech he considered harsh and unnecessary. You could say all you wanted by creating atmosphere. His was a delicate exquisite nature. He was right when he thought the world was rough.

One summer evening at dinner he ate indigestible food deliberately, that he might dream and see once more the world of light he had lost. When at length night fell, the air was still laden with the heat of the day, oppressively. He fell into uneasy slumber, and a dream, strange and erotic, came to him.

He was seated in the Windsor chair. It had always been hard and uncomfortable. But now the hardness of it seemed to have melted to a soft luxuriousness. The danger of its being so soft never struck him till afterwards. Miraculously he found himself seeing the wall paper of staring roses in watery blue and tired pink on muddy stalks with nameless leaves writhing out at him as he sat. It was not unpleasant. The roses appeared to be real. Coming from them there was a faint, heady perfume. They wreathed themselves around his chair, accommodatingly. He plucked one, to see if it was real. The broken stalk bled out yellow blood onto his hand. The yellow drop of blood immediately grew into a knob of amber, the size of a pigeon's egg; and he thought it very clever of the blood drop.

There was a flutter of wings. The paroquet flew out of the frame that encompassed him. It did not seem very surprising, somehow. Gorgeous in geranium lake, deep violet and creamy white, she settled on an arm of the chair, preening herself, majestically. Then the other paroquets came out, perching all round him. They also glowed in every conceivable colour. When they moved, so dazzling was the sheen on their wings, that it seared the eyes. They talked to each other, shrilly.

The blackbird, torn and tattered, hopped out of the corner which had been his these last three years. He was chuckling happily deep down in his throat. Then he burst into his clear, shrilling pipe, from sheer joy of living. And the little brass figure was jealous. All the years he had stood there, on the mantelpiece, so rigidly admonishing his rigid little dog, he had longed to be able to whistle really well. He had practised silently for ages, and now, at the blackbird's paean, he began to whistle. But it was rather like a railway train, so he had to give up. He stopped, listening. The blackbird went on, gloriously. The little figure could bear it no longer. 'Stop' he said, quite simply, 'it is too beautiful.' 'Yes' said a paroquet. The blackbird, obliging as ever, stopped and began pecking at the real flowers in the carpet pattern instead.

[9]

'Did you ever hear how once I was kissed?' said the little figure as he stretched his legs. 'Yes, I was once, years ago, by a hideous little girl, who had been eating peppermint, it was the romance of my life, yes, she kissed me.' He paused for breath. 'I've always liked you,' he went on, 'you're a good sort, you never clean me, and I like being dirty, yes I . . .' Here one of the pictures on the wall interrupted in a loud voice. 'Come and have a walk in me,' it said. The brass dog yelped angrily, the little figure cried 'Here I say . . .' but the idea of walking in a picture was too much for the boy.

He stepped up and into a picture, finding himself listening to the quarrel merrily progressing after many years' catalepsy. But the man said 'Damn you' and the woman said something worse; so he came hurriedly away. He felt he was on dangerous ground. He walked into the next picture, a street. But it was the least bit out of drawing, and he could not go far in. So he just stood watching the white pigeons for ever circling and settling again; the blue sky; the two dogs for ever fighting over there; the groups of people dressed in blazing colours; the fragile architecture. But the pigeons went on circling in the same way, so did the dogs go on fighting and the figures posing, that he found something sinister in it all. He felt he ought to leave.

He stepped into a Boucher Love Affair, quite a good reproduction in its way, but what the two were saying was a little too intimate, and, like a true gentleman, he left – besides that sort of thing was dangerous. From the Boucher picture he turned to a drawing of his own, painted by him just before he went blind. How proud he had been of it, then. How pleased he had been with everyone's praises of it when he could see it no more. How hollow it had been, that praise, he had never realised till now. It was a portrait, just a head and shoulders. He had gloried in the evil look he had put into the face, and the eyes. And now it was saying, vacuously, 'I am empty nothing, empty nothing, empty nothing, empty nothing . . . nothing.' Just then he glanced into the mirror, that had been so useless for so long. There was there a face he knew not, with empty eyelids rimmed in red. A flabby white skin, black beard and wild hair. It was his own face reflected in the glass, and he did not realise it till afterwards.

At the sight of that face, he gave one strangled cry, to convention. In the room there was a hush. Then they all began to laugh. The paroquets screeched their amusement; the little brass figure shrieked his laughter; and the little dog wagged his tail sardonically. Harsh words dropped from the quarrel; sickly intimacies floated down from the Boucher; fatuous reiterations fell out of the drawing. It was Bedlam. The air was stifling. The perfume choked him with its thick rich quality. How they loved to hurt others, these things. 'Oh, ha, ha, ha . . . . . . ha, ha . . . . . . ha, ha, ha, ha.'

He cried out: 'I hate you all, I loathe you, you aren't nice, oh bother you all.'

And the paroquets screamed with fury and flew at his eyes, and the roses came off the chair, wreathed their stalks round his neck amorously, and began to strangle him. He died slowly – in his dream.

Three weeks later he was seated by his window, listening to, and enjoying the rain which was pouring down so gently and steadily. There was hardly a sound save for the persistent swashing of the rain, and the birds were silent. He had not recovered from the effects of his dream yet. For days his old nurse had had her hands full, so 'nervy' and 'captious' had he been. He had lost faith in himself and in all mankind. Sympathy and kindness seemed to be qualities so rare as to be non–existent. He had suffered acutely and was suffering now, sitting by his open window.

Then a blackbird began to sing, and his song dissolved all the troubles in the world, instantly. He listened, raptly, to the story that never was the same. He lost all sense of personality, he was just a pair of ears and a brain, absorbent as a sponge. But it was not to be for long. A butcher boy started whistling, and the blackbird, of course, flew away out of hearing of such cacophony.

Raspingly, piercingly the butcher boy whistled, and it was agony to the boy in the window. But it served one great purpose, that whistling. It woke him out of the passive timidity that had enveloped him ever since he went blind.

He was exasperated into a desperate striving after the beautiful. His world was so very small, it did not go beyond the confines of his room. And his room had failed him. He had lost all confidence after the dream. The world was now trying to take away his music, to roughen, to cynicise him with its constant irritations. And he, with his infinite romanticism, resisted it, passionately. He was forced into some sort of definite action, for in inaction he knew there was despair. So he determined that he would teach himself to whistle, whistle that he might talk with his birds, and that he might express all that was in him unexpressed, all the longings, the doubts, the fears.

He began practising. Though he had had endless and constantly changing ideals in his life, this one hit him very hard, absorbing all his energies and concentration. For hours together he would try trills and shakes: soft little cadences of sound which he repeated again and again till the very air grew lazy and hung dead and listless round the room. Yet there was a peculiar wistful quality about his whistling, which from the first drew the attention, and, after six months' hard work, with nine or ten hours a day of practice, it became really remarkable. There was a power in it, yet a kind of fairy lightness, also. Each note was beautifully clear and distinct, and soon he learnt to soar higher and higher up the notes till at each one it seemed impossible for there ever to be a higher, yet there it always was, silvery perfect.

At first this practising had been very trying, to everyone near him. Nanny, the eternally impatient, naturally had protested immediately and continuously. Still it came as a big surprise and mortification when the room protested. But the boy had grown, mentally, and the room did not succeed in frightening him into silence. It was in a dream, of course. Again he was seated in the Windsor chair, as suspiciously soft as before. Again everything came out at him, and there was a great silence. Then they all said together, 'We have had enough of it, it really is too terrible this whistling of yours.' And the little brass figure cried 'Why don't you whistle like me?' And he let off a blast like a steam siren. 'Shut up,' said one of the paroquets, 'he ought to learn from us,' and she, in her turn, let off a screech. The roses, tightening round his throat, said, 'Do you see?' tighter, 'Do you see?' tighter, 'Do you see?' tighter still. But the boy sprang up out of the chair. 'No I don't,' he shouted. 'Blast you,' and then he woke up on the u in you.

At length, in a year's time, what with his concentration and his soleness of purpose, he had attained to as near perfection as possible. For it was the whistling of a caged bird, exquisite in its way, but just lacking that glorious, confident freedom that lies at the bottom of all bird songs. It was very wonderful though for all that.

One night, after he had been whistling more sublimely than ever, the dream came to him. The roses curled round him, timorously. The paroquets came out, silently. Only the doll blackbird was at all sure of himself. There was a hush, and then they all whispered, in unison: 'We are sorry.' 'Damn you,' he shouted, and the doll broke into a song gloriously telling of triumph, for he loved the man.

As he woke up a blackbird was welcoming the dawn. He was a man, now.

THE WYNDHAM FAMILY

(Unpublished, c. 1923)

Green regularly visited Petworth House, home of the Wyndham family, during the school holidays. The characters in this play are based very specifically on Green's uncles and aunts. The Christian names of all the characters are unchanged; 'MVY' is Maud Yorke (née Wyndham), Green's mother.

(It is after dinner one evening in June and the Wyndham family, male and female, are all by some strange chance sitting together in the White Library. The windvane has been pointing N then S then N again at regular intervals and so on for some time, but though all have been watching it Violet is the first to speak.)

VIOLET

Charles do look at the windvane.

CHARLES

(Trying to be facetious.)

Bless my soul.

MVY

Charles dear, isn't that very extraordinary.

CHARLES

I have never known the wind like that before.

EDWARD

How very interesting.

(Charles gets up and goes to the window, followed by Hughie and Edward. Humphrey picks up The Times *and begins to read the leading article. Looking out of the windows the others see the head of what is obviously a giant, for while his chin is on the ground a lock of hair rests heavily on the monument. There is a rapt expression on his face and he appears to be watching the White Library. Charles turns purple and goes back to his chair. Hughie after putting on pince nez comes back.)*

HUGHIE
Ha.
(Edward stands looking still.)
CHARLES
(Looking at the tip of his cigar.)
God damn.
MVY
(After she has seen it.)
Edward am I drunk or what?
MAGGIE
My dear, it is a giant.
EDWARD
Well, well.
CHARLES
(Ringing the bell.)
God damn.
HUGHIE
Ha.
MVY
My dear Charles, how very exciting.
(Wickham comes in.)
CHARLES
Wickham, if you go to the window you will see a giant by the monument. Send out to tell him to go away at once or I will have the police on him.
MAGGIE
It is not Sunday.
WICKHAM
(Having looked.)
Very good my lord.
(Goes out.)
CHARLES
I can't understand what the fellow wants. Trust his damned impertinence.
(He rings again. Tiny comes in.)
TINY
My dear Maud this is very interesting. Apparently he has taken up his position by the monument and cannot be dislodged.

[15]

EDWARD

I never remember seeing a giant before.

(Alfred comes in.)

CHARLES

Alfred go and find Ball and tell him to take the hounds away at once, anywhere away from the Park.

TINY

Above all we must keep calm.

MVY

What would the parent have said?

CHARLES

(Labouring under a sense of injustice.)

He would have been very angry and I don't think anyone in the kingdom would have denied him the right to be.

MAGGIE

Edward is he advancing?

EDWARD

My dear Margaret he is stationary.

MVY

He seems to be in an attitude of observation.

TINY

My dear do not let us act hastily, let us review the situation coldly.

HUMPHREY

I am very glad that Mother is not here.

EDWARD

It is a very good thing.

MVY

Charles, what are we going to do?

CHARLES

I think the women had better go right away where Simmonds has gone with the hounds.

MVY

Oh come, I am not going to miss all the fun.

(Then outside down the hill come deer galloping and when in a line they have swept down it as if drawn by something they turn right-handed and gallop on and into the lake all except one which has tripped and

lies with a broken leg at the foot of the hill. All the others have vanished in the lake.)

EDWARD

Charles the deer have galloped into the lake.

CHARLES

God damn.

HUMPHREY

I observe that the wings of his nostrils dilate and contract at regular intervals which correspond to the movements of the windvane.

HUGHIE

He is breathing.

CHARLES

If Wickham has no success I think I shall go and have a talk with him.

TINY

Would he be amenable to reason?

MAGGIE

Oh dear, do nothing so rash.

MVY

If Charles goes, we must all go. The family must stick together and die with their boots on.

EDWARD

There is Wickham.

(And indeed Wickham is setting out in swallow tails and a dark-grey tweed cap. Suddenly however, as if picked up by an invisible hand, he rushes on and disappears in the lake.)

EDWARD

Well, well.

HUMPHREY

Charles, Wickham has been precipitated into the lake.

CHARLES

Wickham was a good servant.

MVY

This inaction is getting on my nerves. Why can't we do something?

(Charles jumps up and goes to the window which he raises and goes through. Standing on the terrace he waves at the distance.)

CHARLES
(Crying.)
Go away, damn your impertinence, go away, it is not Sunday.
MAGGIE
Charles do remember there are ladies in the room.
(But while a gale had been blowing into the room, a moist hot wind, this now changes into a draught going the other way and if Edward, Humphrey, MVY and Tiny had not seized hold of Charles he would no doubt have disappeared into the lake.)
EDWARD
(Closing window behind him with difficulty.)
Suction.
TINY
My dear Charles we must act.
CHARLES
(In a scream.)
God damn.
MVY
Charlie do take care of yourself.
HUMPHREY
How very extraordinary. Now Charles, were you drawn away from the house or were you blown away? I myself favour the latter, it seems to me a very good hypothesis. And was no resistance possible?
TINY
It would seem that he is very strong.
EDWARD
Yes Charles, this is very interesting. Was it suction as I said at first or an unseen agency? I myself felt a very strong inclination to go in that direction but fortunately I caught hold of the window frame and thus prevented myself from following you.
CHARLES
No one must now leave the house. If necessary we can retire to the beer cellar.
VIOLET
But Charles, Wickham had the key.
CHARLES
It is impossible now to find a servant who will not keep his

keys on him instead of putting them on a hook where you can get them. I have told Wickham dozens of times.

TINY

Charles we must act.

MVY

Tiny I am completely with you.

(Meanwhile Humphrey has produced a pair of race glasses.)

HUMPHREY

I observe a man talking to him. Why, it is Lambert.

(They all see the giant hold his breath and put a hand to his ear. Then his huge voice comes to them while he puts his hand carefully over Lambert so that he may not be blown away.)

GIANT

I can't understand you my good fellow. Why do you talk like that? Be quiet, I want to listen to the people in the house.

MVY

This is hardly decent.

HUMPHREY

It is very interesting, how can he hear us?

EDWARD

They are credited with having a very acute auditory apparatus.

CHARLES

(In a scream shouts.)

God . . .

(And is then cut short by the giant's huge voice saying:)

GIANT

I have come and now I see that my breathing has put you to some inconvenience so that I shall now leave you not wishing to impose myself unduly upon your magnificent leisure. But you must understand that mine, being a comparatively modern race – for we date only from 2000 BC – is singularly lacking in the dignity of everyday conversation and having heard that at Petworth was to be found the phrasing of a golden age I came and have learnt much to my own profit even in so short a space of time. I hope these words of mine testify to it. So I am departing and would only remind you that good manners have occasionally to yield to some pressing need and while I return all the deer and the one man that my breathing drew into the pond I fear that this will be a poor return for my lack of savoir faire. I see a deer is hurt, but there, do you see, it is well again. *(And it was, and he was gone.)*

MONSTA MONSTROUS

(Unpublished, c. 1923)

Giant fell from sky into the sea and made great splash and great
wave went out on all sides from where he had fallen and damaged
many towns where land met the sea. But he first swam then
waded, and soon came to coast of Wales though he had fallen in
the middle of the ocean. Mountains are in Wales but he strode
over these and often knocked over the tops of them, till he came
to where they fell before plains and sat down on the last mountain
and let his feet rest in the plain, resting the toes in a river to cool
them (and they were hot with knocking) and sat there looking
at the smallness before him. Toes made floods immediately.

He was naked. Hair grew over body and out of his nose came
hairs and swallows came fearlessly to perch on these and birds
of all kinds came to rest among hairs thick about his body, for
they were not frightened at him. But men were frightened.

Men hid when they saw him and village was by heel under
where he sat and all were hidden in the village except an idiot
and he poked at the heel where it came out of floodwater. He
was whistling. Giant bent head down towards him. The idiot
whistled and he was known in the next village for his whistling
and in the next after that and I was told when later I went there
he whistled so well that if he was by the mountain rocks came
down from the top that they might be near him and tracts of
earth came down the slopes such was his whistling. Rocks fell
this time down the giant's legs and bounded off them but did
them no harm and only disturbed birds that sheltered among the
hairs about his legs and these circled round then went back again;
the rocks buried themselves near the idiot. But their fall down
the mountain past his legs might have been from the giant's
breathing, which was like storm, or he had moved perhaps. Yet

[21]

the idiot whistled. And giant bent head lower and smile came on his face and his mouth opened. This time, I think it was the giant's moving, many more rocks came down and cloud of birds was circling round his legs from it, and they rose, circling, then settled about his belly so those who saw it told me, and some rocks went on into the village and made great damage there. Then idiot stopped whistling.

But giant sat very quiet and his eyes looked about by heel for the whistler. Then he bent down and those who watched said he did it carefully so that there was no landslide and he reached down and put nails of the fingers of one hand into the ground and took up all the earth round the idiot to a great depth with all that was on it and on that handful were six oak trees, twenty feet high each one and many bushes, and made pit and I have seen it there, a monstrous hole he made. He raised handful close to his eyes and peered at it for some time then rose up, and in doing this moved so much earth and rock that it was a happy thing he did not bury whole village by it, and threw plot of land away carelessly then and it came down twenty miles off and made hole where it fell and I have seen it, a monstrous pit. No one knows what happened to the idiot, whether he was dead when first he stopped whistling or whether he fell from the ground when it was in air or was killed when it fell twenty miles away, no one knows, but somewhere he lies dead.

This was late afternoon. And sun down shining shone on water of Severn river which was in flood and was bright. And giant squatted down where he stood over it and turned his face to it, licking lips. The floods went off again but as his feet sank into earth from his weight water filled in round them from river and as he squatted his shadow fell over town fifty miles away. Women with child brought forth dogs when they saw him. He was over the water and looked into it. He put down finger and finger was so big it hardly fitted into the river, though that is twelve yards across where he was, and splashed the water and laughed at it. Panes of glass broke in windows. He laughed and two hundred miles away they said it was like thunder. (What for did he come and ravage the land?) He played and scooped up with finger sheet of water and in a curve sparkling it rose into the air and fell on cottage not far away and crushed this, and six died there that day. Perhaps it was in anger he scooped it for soon he plucked an ash tree full grown and chewing it in his mouth rose up and went away. They were glad, the people there, when he was gone.

He went southwards along hill range, striding great distances, and train had then come across the weald and was near to the hills when he saw it and evening sun caught in train windows and flashed red at him. He squatted down near the line. When driver saw him he first put on brakes but went on again immediately for he said after he had not believed in what he had seen. And no one in that train believed in giant, only children cried to look at him and their fathers and mothers said it couldn't be and not to look and said the police would not let it be about, nor the government. So the train went on. And giant scratched his head and smiled at sight of it. Children then had no more fear and waved to him and fathers and mothers said not to be silly, though they told me after they were not then so sure, but children said he had a nice smile and was nice man and waved to him and train went on and into tunnel. Driver said after, he had been glad to get into the tunnel. They stopped inside, thinking it safer, for the driver thought now it was a real giant and guard thought so too (all knew it very soon) and one old man had pulled the cord which is in carriages to stop train. Giant outside watched hole of tunnel and shepherd that was hidden in a bush on hillside said he looked disappointed then. But he lay down and put his head on the rails and sniffed at the opening and then blew down it and so pushed the train out the other side. But he did not know this and it was a happy thing he did not or no one knows what would have taken place. Driver then made train go faster than it ever went before, and engineers are very proud of this, till it came to another tunnel where they stayed for a long time.

Giant rose up and went on and in his walking came to a house on fire and fire engine was playing water onto the flames. But all these ran away when they saw giant coming and one jet of water was left playing straight up into air like a fountain, a stem of water, and giant squatted down and put finger into it and broke up stem of water which scattered while finger was in it

[23]

and dropped in all colours from the sun. The fire burnt higher and it was fanned by his breathing. Then he blew on it and the flames leaped up and he laughed at them and the house fell in and clouds of smoke went up from it, no more flame. Soon after, he went away.

And it was night for black clouds had come over the sky (they say this was from his laughing which troubled the air) and he came to port by the sea, a great town. The streets in it were lighted, there were many miles of them, and liner was coming in, all lighted up over the dark sea, and cone from searchlight circled across round edge of the sky from a tower on shore. Men and women in that port said they first thought giant was thundercloud, he was so big against the sky. But when he saw the liner coming with bright shining inside it he stepped forward into the sea and knocked over warehouse in doing this and those who saw it thought he was going to the liner when he was picked out by cone from searchlight and stood there, and the light seemed to daze him they said. When they saw him then all cried out and moan went up from the town for many holiday makers were on the beach. Indeed he was vast, I saw him then, as I live in that town and my wife had called me to the window. He stood and gradually all the birds that sheltered among hairs thick on his body were drawn out by the light and circled round him, rising in spirals round him, and circled round his head, high high up, and then went off towards the light, drawn towards it which was like a lane through the dark. And he went too and in one stride he was before it and the waves his walking made in the sea came near to swamp the liner and when he was by the light-house tower he bent down, he took it in his hands and swayed it this way and that and snapped it off and the electric cable burst and he took the full force of this and was killed there. Those birds which had not been killed or stunned by its bursting circled round above for some time and then went away, and giant was in the sea and the shock had burnt him up and what had been so great was then cinders washed out to the ocean then back to our island by the tides. When they went to look afterwards they could find only foundations of the lighthouse.

★

What had been so great was then cinders washed out to the ocean then back to our island by the tides. What had taken many lives was then dead itself. And what had seemed to be full of a love of bright things had ended in darkness and what had appeared in the guise of a giant the Insurance Companies held to be an act of god.*

* This ending was later deleted by Green. [Ed.]

ARCADY OR A NIGHT OUT

(Unpublished, 1925)

The text was sent to Nevill Coghill, and is described as 'a lyrical titbit for N.C. from Henry', At that period Green was finishing his novel *Blindness*.

We were in the car swinging through the traffic, & the air inside drooped with folded wings at the shut windows & the scent she used, sweeping through the streets that swirled in eddies of changing light, talking nervously she & I of what was coming. Then down into the dirty brick of Swallow Road, & the chauffeur of her proud car incredulous at first, then anxious for her safety, yet not so anxious as she was. Up the stairs, & in through the glass door, & her involuntary cry of 'Henry', for she was nervous while the chauffeur thought dark things of me below, & my voice reassuring her. At our table, groping through the names of Spanish dishes, wrestling with the faulty English of our waiter. She saw someone she did not wish to see, & was that because my reputation had outdistanced me? Then our modest half bottle of some Spanish wine & her account of how she took Wingarnis [sic] as a tonic, & of how her daily dose inebriated her, of my fears that our waiter & myself should have to carry her downstairs to the proud car & the chauffeur's face when he saw what had been done; of my trip to Africa to give Society leisure to forget.

Perhaps we were substitutes for each other, so that her young man was not myself but someone else who in her imagination was toying with the Spanish omelette in my place, while I began to know that it was not her at any rate whom I would have sitting opposite me, but someone else perhaps.

The bill paid, & in the car again with no mishap, thrusting on to the theatre. And my fears, for it was a Music Hall at her request, & the jokes there might prove difficult to face. The programme seller with a face of enamelled paint, a man & a woman on the stage singing of love in a back garden under a flowering tree. Hysterical laughter when the curtain came down to cover the emptiness that was left. She saw more people she knew, & they looked anxiously at me. Then a scene with a bed upon the stage with the tumult of my fears storming within me. More laughter when the curtain fell. Next the chorus dancing with gnarled legs, waving boneless arms in harsh mauve and carmine lights. And so on to the end.

Then sentiment in a taxi, for the chauffeur had gone outraged to bed with his proud car, how we never met, how this must be repeated, what an adventure it was, what fun it had been.

And adventure it was, for we had deputised for each other's dream.

MOOD

(Unpublished, c. 1926)

In 1959 (see 'An Unfinished Novel') Green was to describe 'Mood' as a second novel which could never be completed. Judging by its prose style it clearly predates *Living*, though correspondence with Coghill would suggest that Green was still working on 'Mood' in the early thirties. 'Your new book *Meretricity* [the original title for 'Mood'] is very ambitious,' he wrote, 'and if you succeed in it, as you have in *Blindness* and *Living*, it will have been worth all your depression about it.'

I

She walks down Oxford Street.

When she heard that high, loud, educated voice she saw the Blue Train where it was so much in evidence, then the boat where was no sound of it throughout the crossing, and the English Pullman where again it triumphed, crying: My dear I went to sleep before the boat started and didn't wake up till my maid told me we were in. My dear, that same voice said, what people want is to lie naked in the sun and that drives everyone further south to where it's all unknown. There was that same kind of voice, here in Oxford Street, this time proclaiming: The most lovely sponge. She looked and there was that same kind of woman coming out of a shop. – A most lovely sponge which – and then several buses cut short its price and the story of how that sponge was bought. She wondered where that woman bought her sponges. One shouldn't go just anywhere for one's sponge. For what is a sponge, – and this she felt but did not think. Why it is picked from the sea, it is cleaned and dried, perhaps a lot of things are done to it perhaps nothing very much.

Perhaps a little salt is still left in it. Here she sailed. For, when she heard that woman talk, so she remembered the clatter of knives and forks, the absolute roar of chasses and good living and she remembered how, in the Pullman, she had longed to be in a restaurant again where it was famous and lots of people you knew. She said no I will never go abroad again unless I go with a thousand people, it's really too squalid there being just three or four of you. The sea and everything, it just won't do, she said, if there isn't a whole crowd one knows. It's like going when you're by yourself and turning on the gramophone. Or like a sponge in the water in an empty bath.

Where did that woman buy her sponges? When you saw her kind get into the Pullman with just the right sort of shabbiness in their clothes, then you thought of her lying in the sun, clean, clean, clean to the last little bit. Why had she herself never considered sponges? It was because you didn't have to buy them often that you were rather haphazard about it. Everything else had the right shops and places but she'd never heard of there being one place for these. She looked at the stockings in the window. She accused herself. It was squalid, dirty in her not to have been more careful about her sponges. Absolutely filthy really.

That was what older women did to you, they made you feel rather squalid. Except when you went in bathing dresses, the blue sea and you and they being cadaverous on the sand. Even in the hotel afterwards when you were all dressed up and when they could afford to be so much better dressed than you was still the echo of the sea and your bathing dress round you, like it might be you had nothing on at all. So merely from being young, and your body being more or less naturally thin and not just skinny, you felt you were better than all the older ones in the place you were. Till you got into the train and there were hundreds with those voices. You hadn't seen them on their beaches nor had their men seen you coming out of the sea. And at once their experience put you at a disadvantage, made you feel dirty.

As a botanist knows the best place for his flowers and he will set out and go straight to where he has found that sort before, there he will find them again, under that bank or by those stones on the hill, so they knew so much more about shops. If a man was fond of flowers as a boy and grew up in that fondness, so, as the years went by he would learn more and more where he would be likely to find some particular flower, on a slope looking east or out looking west, and also what combination of shade or wet was most favourable to its growth. As he grew older so he would know more and more, and it wouldn't be just book learning. So, because they had been so much longer at it, older people knew better where to look for things. And as an older man might be more careful where he looked, more knowledgeable about his flowers and everything to do with these, so even in their sponges, she felt, older women were more expert, they showed a greater choice.

She laughed. They had more need of them than me, she said of older people and their dresses, but then they have no real need for better sponges. And then she saw everyone in the world, as the years went round and they grew older, becoming more and more careful in their choice, always refining, that is the nice ones.

There was mother for instance. Being an only child she'd been the chief person mother had lavished on. And as she walked down Oxford Street and saw all these provincial women in their mauves and browns she felt in a blaze her own position, where she was.

She sees where she is.

For the way she had been brought up was quiet, quiet. Where they lived in Kent no noise came to them but it was softened by distances and by the trees and the wind: when any noise came in by their tall windows it no more than murmured round her room. Where their house was in London a drumming noise was all they faintly heard: in Oxford Street the traffic clamoured but where they lived not far away nothing was left of it, only a buzz of what went on there.

In Kent their house was Queen Anne, in London Adams. Her mother came up to London in February and left it in July to go down to Kent again. Weekdays her father was a city man, weekends a squire. All through the year he stayed Monday to Friday in his Adams house, Friday to Monday in his Queen Anne.

In the gardens at their house in Kent were hot-houses, and, when her mother brought her up in February, flowers were sent to London for them. It was only when her mother was in town that Mr Igtham had one vase of flowers in his room. Their name was Igtham. But Mrs Igtham was most fond of flowers and her room was crammed with them, in banks up against the green-blue walls. Constance, her name is Constance, did not have so many. In her room they were put in old-fashioned silver vases, and they were put separately about, were no great masses of them.

Always, wherever she went, Mrs Igtham had blocks of flowers tightly packed against the walls, she was devoted to them. All round the year, whether she was in Kent or in London, her room was full of flowers so when you came in you were in a smother of them. She would be sitting plumb in the middle, not quite unlike a beetle. But Constance was not like that. If Mrs Igtham, with all her rings and jewels – not that she ever looked to have too many, if Mrs Igtham made you think she might have been a beetle, all sparkle in Garden of Eden, then Constance, to see her in her own room, looked like really a silver lance sunk in the blue sea, in her blue-coloured room.

Mrs Igtham was a small dark blackish woman. She wore as jewellery mostly red stones and put more jewels about her than is usually done now, but, in her case, without its ever seeming odd. Having such a deal of stones glittering suddenly here and there about her, and being so dark, so with her it was like that glittering armoured sheath above a beetle's wings: she might, when you saw her in the middle of her flowers, suddenly burst out flying, that sheath might suddenly burst open on her sharp and iridescent skin – she constantly wore black, she might at moments ride a broomstick.

Not so Mr Igtham. Their name was correctly pronounced only by those who said Eyetam, not Iggetam or Iththam. He was fat and cared very much for shooting. Also he was a good business man and served on boards of many companies. Everyone knew him and his wife, and these two did not go out of their way to know anyone. Constance was most of their link with other people, she went everywhere and was everyone's bridesmaid. Constance was utterly charming. This book is about Constance. When you have read it you too will say how charming Constance is.

As it was like saying Bellevoir or Burkeley to lisp Iththam so you will appreciate that for centuries Igthams had lived in a delightful ease. In the eighteenth century they had been a great family in the church, three of them had been bishops at that time. Before then England, in the larger histories, in a historian's deep research, had cause to thank the Igthams. They had been a great landed family. Nor were they in that position now when a man might point at someone in the public baths and say: That boy's family once ruled this island when England was most prosperous of all, five hundred years ago. For the Igthams had stayed prosperous. They had gone into commerce. They were now rich, but not too rich. They had a butler and a footman, a good cook – yet she was not too good a cook – and these two lovely houses.

Her father, Mr Igtham's room looked to be what he was, comfortable and prosperous, also a country gentleman. The walls were done in a brown paper and on them hung pictures of horses which might be by Alken or Sartorius. There was a big desk on which were many papers and that one yellow china vase of flowers. It had flowers in it only when Mrs Igtham was in London. That vase was very ugly and faded, chipped and old, but he held it in a great affection because he could remember where it stood when he was small and his nurse was washing him, and tickling him. Was no telephone in the room, that was outside, in room of its own. These two things were Mr Igtham. His work he kept so to speak at an arm's length away from him and he worshipped his childhood and his parents in that vase. If a maid, in dusting, knocked it down and chipped another fragment off it, then he was always very angry. His wife used to say that she had never arrived at making him throw the thing away, and she used to threaten him she would break the horror but as things were she was proud of him that he still kept it. If now, this moment, he had thrown that vase down on purpose and smashed it then she would have felt that he was not much longer for this world. She would have had to eat all her flowers then to keep a balance in the home.

When you came in by the front door there, in the hall, were flowers only from February to July of course, vast bowl of them on the hall table where lay two or three bowler hats of Mr Igtham's. Was a glass tray also, in which were cards. Then, quite often, under the staircase on a huge table, were large cardboard boxes. From these a sweet sticky smell came. They were boxes of flowers sent up from Kent and waiting there for Mrs Igtham to unpack them. She would unpack them, marshall and mass them, make them form fours, execute a great flanking movement round the corner of her room with them, and here they would be, freshly cut, ready for her lily hand. When she had done she would find Constance and give her what was left over and tell her to arrange them for her own rooms.

Constance had had no education in needlework or looking after babies or counting. She could talk French well. But she had never been to cooking classes or young conservative unions, Mrs Igtham had never sent her and said go there and learn. And Constance would never have gone on her own. She chose her own dresses and arranged her own flowers, but she did not choose the decoration of her room. She had never ordered dinner. Mrs Igtham thought, and who'll say she was wrong? thought that girls wanted no more than that, that need be all their accomplishment. Constance could read any book she liked and there you were, cultured, arranging her own flowers and dressing herself, why more? said Mrs Igtham.

Her sitting room, then, was Mrs Igtham's doing. Constance had no hand in it. In this room were four plain white pillars which went from floor to ceiling. On the blue walls were a number of old paintings, not good, not bad. Was a lot of yellow furniture about. On one side two long great windows lit this glittering room and by one of these, the nearest to the fire, was her writing table. The fireplace was Adams with two fluted marble pedestals. In front of this was a deep bearskin rug, the head left on. Mouth open it had a dry, red ink-coloured tongue and gums and dull blue eyes but huge fangs, gloriously white and it was a Polar bear. On the fireplace a great many invitation cards were propped up against the back and some letters, was a shining brass clock, old and Dutch, two Delft candlesticks and on the right-hand edge of it what was really Constance, two small bright painted aeroplanes in wood.

Lord when you came into that room and looked round and cried out, as you couldn't help doing, Lord what a fine room, then, when you saw those aeroplanes you might sing those are her pets, that's what is most hers in here. When you came in and saw them it might be like you came into a King's rooms and saw a local paper there. Or, more like, the other way about. You came into a common sort of room and then you saw two Kings seated by the fire.

These aeroplanes were old now, they were stained, and they'd never been any better than a child's toys. But Constance had bought them when she was no longer tiny, she'd bought them when she was nineteen. She had never played with them but she had put them there, she would have no one move them. And as she walked in Oxford Street, while her fancy walked like a blue cat about her room, the bright shining silver vases, her Dutch painted yellow chairs with flowers painted on them, the Dutch candlesticks, blue, such a lovely blue, then, standing on the Polar bear, then again she met her aeroplanes and it was like where every year she'd gone since she was nineteen, the Mediterranean sea.

As you came down the beach so when you got into the sea it was like you had a halo round you, where the sun had been and now the warm sea lapped you you felt you could roll like dolphins for that round fat feeling. Oh she had gone plunging out, her wet rubber cap had shone like any god, there were no waves nothing but this blue sea, she rolled on it, the sun played like cymbals on her flanks and on one breast and then from a surfeit of all this she'd lain on her back and floated. She'd closed her eyes. But then was a hum like thousands cheering miles away and she looked and up above in that tremendous blue there was an aeroplane, aluminium painted, all along its wings winking blinding light, high, high above, ever so slowly moving quite straight, like a queen.

So when she came back to England she'd bought the model

aeroplanes, aluminium painted, because she'd been alone the time she saw that one from the sea, and because each time she was alone that was how she wanted it, how she'd always like to be.

She walks in Oxford Street.

Nobody would ever know, she sang as she looked about her in Oxford Street, no one, not one of these, not even mother, nobody would know about those aeroplanes. And when mother had had the walls done that gorgeous blue then suddenly she'd seen she could bring her Queens down from where she'd put them, in a drawer in her bedroom. But when she'd brought them down and put them on the mantelpiece, (she'd put them on the same side one with the other because they looked nicer like that – one just poking in front of the other), when she'd stepped back to look, then she saw they weren't Queens any more, but where they were now they were Kings.

Oxford Street blazed with the sun. There had been long drought and grass in the Park was khaki coloured, which made leaves on the plane trees look blue. The Marble Arch was white, white. From wooden blocks which paved the roadway oozed tar in which these blocks had been steeped, so, as a drunkard breathes out the smell of what he has been drinking, so the smell of creosote lay over where she walked. But as a drunkard, when he walks about, may be withdrawn into himself, so she, filled with the heady wine of Kings, stepped as though she had divinity about her, as though heat, tar and the crowds were nowhere near her, in her companionship with mighty things.

As she slowly walked the people divided. Everyone made way for Miss Igtham. She went between mothers and their children, between sisters, between friends. Any men there were about took a look at her because she was beautiful, particularly now. She wasn't very tall but she had a most lovely body. She walked exactly like herons fly. She was lightly dressed and as she walked it was the balance, the assurance of movements which made you watch her. For was nothing much about her face, and she was far lighter coloured than her mother. Her skin was creamier, it was a good face to draw being fat and round but was nothing remarkable about it except her eyelids were turned up at the outside corners. So all the people were not merely looking at her features, it was the majesty she had just assumed whilst walking, it was her tread, her magnificence which marked her.

She walked absorbed. And if you had passed your hand over her skin it would have dragged at your fingers. The sun, in crashing down, had opened her pores, each one had opened like it might be flowers to the sun. So for a time she walked, as when in the warm sea the water is exactly at that heat where you forget you have a body. Also she had these dreams I have described.

But she came back. The sun became too hot for her before she had gone far and, as a good diver will dive into the flat sea to come up again and break the surface with less than one quiver over the water, so she returned. Immediately she thought about her dress. And at once she turned back, immediately thinking she must go to the Park and sit there, under a plane tree.

This morning she had no ploy, no shopping, nothing to pass the time. Suddenly she was depressed. She crossed over to other side of the street, into the shade, and begged that her shoes might not be ruined by the tar.

Everyone she passed she hated now, and she felt her dress was not sitting right. She longed for nothing more than to get quickly to the Park, she'd have given anything for someone to offer a lift. It was not far enough for a penny bus ride, it wouldn't take a minute to walk, but still why couldn't that idiot Eddy be close by with his Lea Francis. Oh, she cried out to herself, it made you frantic, this useless walking.

II

She sees what she used to be.

When she sat down not far from the Marble Arch, under a plane tree she arranged her dress. She pulled at it at her hip and spread it out to her knees, then at last she felt comfortable again. The damp heat of the day grew over her and then once more she was dreaming. And as in the warm sea the water is sometimes exactly at that heat where you forget you have a body so she might have been floating in the Mediterranean sea, lain on her back.

She swooned. People were riding about on those pneumatic horses made of rubber, the pink rubber whales, and unicorns, on the water. Their cries as they played had faintly reached her, all softened by the expanse. And she thought of when she was small, when as children they had been playing in the hay-meadows.

In those days, when she was nine years old, another girl of her age, called Celia, was educated with Miss Igtham. This girl lived with them in Kent, her parents were in India, and shared the French governess hired for Constance.

In those days, every afternoon at three, they had gone out walking. This day their governess took them down to the hay-meadows.

Mademoiselle wore white stockings and white kid shoes with high, high heels. On top she had a vast straw hat. She held a big black bag close to her. Except for these she was very small, not so very much taller than they, and she walked in tiny steps. One on each side of her, each of them holding one of her arms in their two hands – she had white cotton gloves to her elbows, they shouted across her to each other, never in French always in English, and she was always away in her thoughts. She did not hear what they said because she would fix all her attention onto keeping clean her shoes, and on her balance, which was precarious on those heels like stilts.

When they left the road it was harder than ever for her to get along. The children would hop and skip while they held on to her arms and she felt the grass was crawling with what she loathed more than any living thing, ants. But they had persuaded her to let them watch the hay being made because she had seen an opportunity in it to sit under a hedge at her ease. Even sitting on an ant-heap was better than the walk along these enervating roads which went meandering like streams, monuments to waste. And while she sat they could play and as they ran while they played so they would get so much the more exercise than if she had walked with them. And then again her heart at that time was heavy for Dreyfus. She longed to be back in France while this case was going on, to be at the centre of things.

When they reached the meadow men there were carting the hay, sun was so fierce that there was a danger the hay would be burnt. The children were sad that they were taking it away so soon. But they planned a game where it still lay as it had been cut and afterwards turned, in great concentric rings, in golden dykes with the blue grass like flowing in between.

Mademoiselle went to the near corner of this meadow into the shade of an ash tree. Graciously this tree reached out olive-blue branches and poured shade on the ground. Here were two horses harnessed to an empty farm waggon. The sun, striking down between the leaves in tubes, hit their coats in little egg-shaped patches. Flies bothered them. Every now and again one or the other would half kick out and so rattle the chains, and they kept sawing their heads and so jingled the harness.

Mademoiselle took from her bag a copy of *The Times* and opening this out she sat down on it as far as she might away from the horses without leaving the shade. She did not rest her back but sat erect, hands folded on her lap, and then, once she was settled, she disappeared completely. For the horses had deep-coloured coats which bayed like tigers from the deep shade out at the sunlight, and she was nothing beside the heavy waggon painted a low, crude blue.

Constance and Celia went to where the men were working in a knot about the other waggon, loading it. Two men stood on the hay in the waggon while the others pushed hay along with their forks till they had a sufficiency before them. Then they dug the forks in and with the one movement they heaved their fork-load to the two who waited to receive it on the waggon, and these packed that hay in. As the waggon was filled and became stacked up with hay so these two rose higher and higher on it: Constance and Celia watched their red faces and red arms, and listened, as one of them was singing. But they soon wandered off, tired of watching.

Mademoiselle was nodding and was soon quite lost in a doze.

The children couldn't decide at first what they would play. So they sat down and plaited hay into pigtails till they should think of something. They laughed and giggled. And meanwhile the waggon had been filled and stacked, and those two men on top had roped it. Each taking hold on one of these ropes they had slidden down, and now all the men went to shade of that ash tree where the governess was and that other waggon. The noise of their coming woke her and while one of them was finding the cider she passed the time of day with them. Then they offered her a horn-full of cider and she drank the clear yellow, thinking of their farm at home. It was bitter to her taste. It made the back of her neck burn, and she laughed and thanked them. She forgot ants. She lay back even and propped her chin on her arm. The heavy sweet scent of the hay came like honey to her and the smell of these men's bodies made her homesick. The horses were strong too, the whole summer's day was reeking and she was most deliciously overcome, clinging to consciousness as to the last firm thing on earth. The men sat near by and one was so amused he lay shaking on his back, hands pressed to his belly, while another wanted to give the children cider, but the rest would not let him.

Constance next found a short stick among the hay and began playing with it, first putting it about her body. At last she suddenly put that stick to her head. She put it flat with her forehead, so it stuck up above her hair like a horn. And at once she thought of unicorns. In lessons they had come upon them, on the pages of their book, pacing along a ride trampling the flowers. Celia remembered. And so they played at being unicorns.

Celia found a stick and first they walked on the new grass between the golden dykes of hay and then they ran along these long concentric rings. Each round they made, one following the other, brought them nearer to the middle of this piece which had been mowed in a round.

The horses harnessed to the full waggon followed them with their wide eyes from where they had been left not far away. The children ran shrieking round and then, as they neared the centre, they grew more quiet. The horses shifted, they would turn their heads away and yet always come back to the children. The men, sitting low in shade, lazily watched them, only the governess paid no attention. And as they came nearer and nearer in to the centre, in ever-shortening circles, those two horses, hidden from the men by their waggon, grew more uneasy. They snorted through their wide nostrils, distended and red. The children came nearer and nearer in: each horse struck at the ground, their quarters trembled, they were thrown into a sweat. And when at last the centre was reached and the children fell down there both of them with what came to the men as a faint cry then those two horses, with a scream, bolted. They careered away, the waggon pitching, crashing behind them.

Then the men surged out of the deep shade and ran after them in a fumbling group, running and shouting. Mademoiselle also came out, she wavered out towards the children. They, for their part, sat terrified and Constance could remember now how she had thought that they were blameless, she could remember reminding herself then that Mademoiselle had only told them to be sage, or wise.

Sitting near the Marble Arch she opened her eyes. The world struck white at her, for two moments she was so dazzled that everything appeared like wraiths, or as an image of what was real. People simmered by, walking by on the path she was close to. But when at last everyone took on their true shape and all the rumble of the traffic reoccupied her ears, – before it had been the surf on her seashore, – then she fell to watching.

Listless, she watched them pass, young and old, old and young, children, soldiers, beggars, dogs, a monkey, nurses with prams. Young couples went by, today was a holiday, and only these had that glaring look of Kings in all their gentleness.

And then she thought of couples why in a moment, she cried to her heart, they might break out and play, any second now for their own amusement they may take on the parts of unicorns or Kings. And perhaps that was why so many people kept dogs, who can never have enough of your love if they are yours, who will always play with you, for food and love you are Queens to them, Kings.

A woman will take a walk with her dog and it will keep her pleasantly distracted. As they walk their two perceptions will be allied, when she stops to turn something over with her stick he will come back from where he has run out in front to examine it with her, when he turns in to the long grass and brambles she will cheer him on and watch after his efforts.

So two people who love each other can go out and as they walk there is no need for them to put anything into words, having expressed everything long ago. As they walk, and the countryside meanders by, they need not be looking at the same things, one may be looking to her right the other to her left, but still their thoughts are most curiously joined and what they both see says but the one same thing to them.

When Constance and Celia had walked on either side of Mademoiselle they had said always what first came into their heads. They had no withdrawals one from the other, any whim, any little thing, anything whatever they immediately told. Then when they had grown up there were a very few they hadn't told each other, each had just one or two reservations, but they had already said so much that when they went out walking it was in a great lassitude of silence, a delicious boredom. Constance laughed. For now Celia was married Constance had lost her, when they were together now they avoided silence and said easy things rather quickly to each other.

Your dog dies and after a little you buy another, your friend goes and if you are lucky you find a new friend. And all the time you are learning to walk alone. When Celia married she had gone the way of all other friends. When you have been two you can't be three and now Constance was alone. Celia had married Eddy two years ago and now Constance had no one so to speak to play with. Everyone ought to play she thought. She looked at the beggars, the soldiers, the young and old, and there was a woman with that same high voice. If she played ever she would cry from nerves. And yet she would put her legs over a rubber unicorn, better than no unicorn at all only it was a kind of sacrilege, and go bobbing out on the sea. But Constance had no call to use rubber unicorns. And that woman would not go far out, she would be yelling and shrieking like any nursemaid, and she would soon be back under that vast umbrella she had had pitched for her. She thought, and drew comfort from it, how that woman's life was too full, how she would never be able to walk down Oxford Street her fingers about his horn, her unicorn, arm along his neck, for she would never in her thoughts be alone enough for him.

And Celia also had lost all semblance of what she had been. Constance laughed and thought if they were to go back together now to the Mediterranean again as they had done before Celia married, Constance thought how different it would be. Although she had been alone when that aeroplane came overhead yet she had bought two aeroplanes, one loneliness for each of them. She had not told Celia about it. They had often swum out together, she had been glad to draw Celia away from the beach, they had lain side by side dazed by the sun and delight out on the sea. So Constance had bought one for herself and one for Celia as a celebration in honour of those occasions. And Constance, who had looked on the aeroplanes as one and the same and had held neither in preference one to the other, had chosen one of the two for her very own when Celia married, a secret one.

So she was now in the position of someone whose friend has gone and who goes walking alone, gleefully swiping down grass at her side with her stick. And now that reserve which had, in one or two things, been between them, now that also was gone since Celia was no longer with her. Now she was completely alone there was no restraint at her heart and she could walk proudly.

For sitting in the heavy night in the gardens of their hotel, over the sea, every foot of ground quivering with the shrill cicadas, the heavy night where every tree breathed on her and drooped down from where it had reached up back down to earth and the low noise of the sea, from the cackle of lights she saw through the leaves, she heard Celia laughing.

Once Constance had walked across the School Yard at Eton, and it was deserted, when she had heard such another laugh and had turned round in joy, singing, isn't that gorgeous in a place built in fear like this. So when she heard Celia laugh she remembered.

And she had felt Oh how can she laugh like that, why should she bring the playing fields here, and she had hidden her eyes in her warm fingers.

She had stayed on that seat it seemed like hours, not daring to move in case she came across them. And why, she thought with even now a small pang, why should things one has enjoyed come flying back like a bent withy and strike one and hurt, why should things turn inside out.

She had heard Celia laugh again then, and for a moment she had thought they were coming straight down on her and then she'd heard her laugh again, this time half way down the rocks and to the sea. She had cried, nothing had ever been so bitter, cried and cried till she lost all count, while the earth shrilled and the trees moaned with the weight of thick leaves on them.

That had been the last time they had been together to the Mediterranean for Celia had married that man. And now Constance could laugh at all that, only the way she laughed it made hardly any sound at all, being like a soft neigh at the back of her throat.

For before that last year they had gone out under the moon, under the trees, the palm trees with thousands of birds sleeping above in them so it seemed because they were never altogether still, in the beating night with the earth crying out in the cicadas, where the trees heaved down in the night air which was like bed, they had sat there in a trance when they were younger than they were now, three years ago.

They had gone to the outmost edge of the garden and lights over that porch which led to the hotel were caught in a tiny reflection in their glasses on the marble table which gleamed like skin in the dark. They sat on a bench which had been made to encircle a tree, when they leant back the bark, which was not hot or cold, pressed into their backs in long furry tongues. The marble table kept a hoard of coolness and their glasses of the dark wine looked like huge soft eyes, the pair of them, marvellously soft.

In those nights, hand in hand, they had gone silently sailing and voices from the veranda way away and the low noise of the sea had come faintly like a small wind to take them further out on dreams. They had gone slipping out and once Constance had stumbled on Celia's pulse and had gone beating out on that into a smother of dreams, a glorious obscurity.

[43]

Or again they had climbed from the beach up in the evening by the path which was cut out of the cliff, it went in large flat spirals, and while they were always chattering when they began to climb it by the time they were half way up they had never any breath left for talk. Constance had come in the day time, so she remembered, to hope that this bliss they had then would be renewed each night. For when darkness first showed in the sky after the sun was gone it was then every evening they began their climb.

When they had to stop they flung their arms about each other and would turn out over the Mediterranean to see that shadow coming in over the water like a sleep. Constance laughed as she remembered. She held Celia tight and in her she embraced that enchantment, all the colours marching night made on the sea and what it is to stand on a cliff and watch. But at the first chill that reached them of that shadow they turned again and slowly climbed up till by the time they had set foot on the lowest terrace of the gardens night was rushing by above them, flying with the speed of the world and with the speed of the sun.

At that moment a girl laughed as she went along on the path in front of Constance. No one could laugh, in the mood Constance was now, without her looking up, for as she was now laughter ran like blue threads in her blue tapestry, the fabric of her dreams. But this girl sounded like she must be tired and Constance marvelled again at how little the English love heat, for all they talk about it, and decided that they preferred sharp, frosty weather. Certainly this ticket collector did, she said to herself, and followed him with her eyes as he came towards her. He came slowly along, walking splay-footed, dragging his heels, and he had his uniform cap pushed onto back of his head, and the curve of his forehead showed many bumps in it. He was fifty, his eyes were grey, and he was a very small man. Constance thought he did look so ill.

This man longed for the night. Then, when the shadows came flowing out of trees again all over the ground, and the grass opened its eyes, when the lamps were lit he would soon be able to make his way home then. It was the uniforms that did it and he spent much of his time in hoping that the man who designed his uniform and the tailor who made it might one day have to wear the lousy thing that was more meant for a fireman than a man that had to keep moving. It would be all right for one whose job let him stand on a ladder with the flames licking round him and play a hose onto it and when he got down everyone saying hero, hero, but was none of that talk about when he got home, with his feet feeling like he had been walking on embers all the long day. Not much. Yes and you felt dizzy too with it, nor you didn't dare have a sit, they were down on you so sharp, or an old man wrote to the papers. And why should people pay for sitting, wasn't it mean of them that charged it, for the Parks did ought to be free, or they should put more free seats about. Yes, he said, it made you kind of miserable to be always doing a thing which went against your nature but then why there was some you didn't mind dunning, there was that piece over there, she was so rich she ought to pay. You didn't mind taking her pence, nor nobody wouldn't as you could see from here she filled the eyes: and he slowly bore down on Constance.

Constance opened her bag to look for her purse. In the end she had to take out her handkerchief and pay more attention to what she was doing. Standing above her he held the ticket in his fingers and Lord love us he thought if women don't put a lot in there. But he found his eyes followed the line of her left hand which held the bag while she fumbled in it with her right, and if, automatically almost, he kept exclaiming within him at the magnificence of that blue cigarette case and God help us look at that holder, yet the major part of him yearned to an exquisite transparency, like a seashell in the sea, where her thumb branched off from the palm of her hand. Save us, he cried out in his heart, if I couldn't bury my nose in there, such fine hands, never a day's work in their lives and the nails, like a quartz.

Can't you find it miss he said hopefully and she said oh dear and took out that cigarette case out of the way. Let me hold it miss and she said yes do, giving it to him without looking up. He held it and now he was lost, for he began to wonder what it was like inside as he held that case all of a glisten in his hand. His eyes turned from her and he put his two hands to the case so that it lay on his two palms. And so closely did he watch it

[45]

that when at last she held out his pennies to him she had to say I'm so sorry before he knew she was ready, so that he all but dropped the thing from embarrassment as he gave it back to her. So stupid of me, she said, I'm so sorry, she apologised again, but he had nothing he could find to say. What a pair of eyes, he was laughing inside him, what a grand pair of blue eyes for a man to see he laughed.

He had looked into her eyes. She had looked into his. She had seen a light of mockery there. As she had seen that monkey go careering down along the path in front of her so Constance, being like she was this day, had invested that collector with another life, a new agility. Being so lovely she had brought him out of himself like the night would do which he longed for so: that light in his eye was almost as she had been with Celia on their rocks on the Mediterranean sea. But he was a man. She felt he had been half mocking at her for being a woman. She had a small creepy feeling at that, like her senses were coiled up inside.

These things coming to her about him made her petulant with the collector who, so it seemed, had mocked at her King. Spitefully she watched him move away. What was so shocking in monkeys was that they were nearly human, what was dreadful in men was their similarity to apes. He had been very insolent, she thought now, and would have liked to wake him: if he had tried one thing too much, if he had exceeded in any way at all, then she would have dropped on him. Instead she had apologised. She laughed. It was too squalid, she kept thinking, squalid saying I'm sorry to him when it was so really lucky for that man to see me and so to refresh his eyes.

For when he had come up to her she had shared her glory with him. Part of the time his attention had been taken up with the things she had about her, that was true, but it was no less true that when their eyes met his eyes received that glare of Kings. Even though he'd had to stand away and mock he'd had it. But it was as though you took up that flat spiralled path and you turned him to face out over the sea, and then he cared for nothing but eating. Looking out over the Mediterranean he would see no food, but feeling you beside him and that you cared for what you saw there, then a mocking light came out in his eye because

[46]

of you. And this collector, when he had seen her happy, had thought if he'd been luckier he might have had a bit then, – that was her opinion of his look now she thought of it.

People are most of all indulgent when they are happy and she had shared her glory with him when she had caught his eye. When he'd seen it he must have thought why shouldn't I come in under the wing of that, damn him. He had felt she was so occupied by Kingship that anyone who put himself forward just then she would mistake for Kings, that the majesty she had on her was so great she could see nothing small or mean, that a mercy had made her infinitely indulgent since she had climbed so high and was so majestically detached.

She watched a couple pass before her. They had on them a mood so gentle that everything was brother, sister to them. They had that in the way Kings could be proudly apart and yet near to the people. But it was the loneliness in high places which was the great memory you could have, those secret walks with pets where there were no men to ape cheeky monkeys, that was what counted.

Oh being a King was really for when you were alone, for that was the only kind that lasted. You could promise, you could swear, but friends nearly always changed as the years went round. They married, or one might go to Africa to shoot big-game and then stay there drinking, or another was sent to Mexico, and there were convents. Everywhere you looked were graves for friendship, love, and tombstones on everyone's tongue.

Of everyone you met was only you you would be with always and she thought that's how it is, don't let's have any monkey business with other people, the issue ultimately is with ourselves. As my two eyes are coordinated so let me have myself as my friend, may I have that glory where I draw on no one, lean on nobody. May I learn to be alone.

TEST TRIAL AT LORDS

(Unpublished, c. 1927)

This piece, and the three that follow, 'Saturday', 'Fight' and 'Evening in Autumn', are all fragments which survive in longhand only. A letter from Green to Neville Coghill suggests that they may have been intended as part of a series of 'sketches' which were to be compiled in a volume.

Early, before the game started, people still coming in went out onto the field. A square part in the middle was roped off from them and as they came in all passed by and went along those ropes, looking inwards at the pitch. Two policemen stood at opposite sides of the square and these fat men collected some about them who stayed to talk but mostly the others went to find places on the other side of the ground, though many went to the players' pavilion. Standing in a mass there these watched for favourite players. So there were two movements. One of those who came in and were attracted to the pitch and then in eddies went to their seats or to outside the pavilion. The other, a lateral movement where the stands all round the ground were filling up.

Above the green grass low cylindrical blue clouds rolled along the sky.

Gradually these movements of people were intensified and no longer now were so many crossing from one stand to another, no longer did there seem any purpose in where they were going, only more people stood by the policemen and more still at the pavilion.

Noise of talking went up, so many voices were raised, an aeroplane went by overhead and turned and circled, children began playing in twos with balls before where I was sitting and about. One would throw the ball, the other caught it and would throw it back. Neither stayed in the same place for people now were continually walking between the two of them, and this movement was repeated all over the field covered with people and with boys playing. Now the ball would bounce and he would misjudge the rising ball, missing when it bounced above his head he would have to run back behind him for it. As they played these boys cried out and I thought in a moment I shall be looking at a sea bird, this is so like the sea.

Now, as I was saying, every minute were more people on the ground. At opposite sides of square in the middle was now a thick line of them, three deep, and by where the professionals change a big crowd of people. All dark clothed. And those who walked in their dark-looking clothes walked in eddies, now and again large curves, they seemed to follow one another.

A bell rang and from opposite side to the pavilion twelve men pulled out a roller taller than they, eight of them pulled, the rest pushed at it, bent forward like the others only a little more upright. They went slowly through the scattered walkers who closed in again behind and the line of those standing three deep at our side of the square parted for them, reforming again as soon as roller was through the ropes. Then slowly the roller went up and down with those dozen of men, a sort of study for the Prix de Rome, and now stumps had been put up at the wickets. Now, generally, all over the field, people were converging on that square to watch the rolling, only those in that crowd that waited for their favourite players stayed where they had been, dark, still.

Then, a little late, England's captain came in, walking onto the field he went like the others had done, coming to the square he put umbrella under the loose rope and threw it above his head as he walked under it with his friend. He walked up and down the pitch. His friend held away his umbrella in his hand that the point might not spoil the turf. When they went down again he made that throwing up of the rope, and the crowd parted for him. As he walked away all that side of the square he had gone through turned faces back to watch him go – so was another movement, three sides of square looking inwards at the pitch, one side their faces turned back from it to watch him go. Soon crowd at the pavilion hid him from my sight.

[49]

People on the stand by where I was sitting read newspapers, some of them talked, but when a loud bell rang they began to fold these away. Many got up and putting their newspapers on the seat they sat on them. Boys came round to sell cushions, more hurried than they were before now that the second bell had gone. And now those two policemen began moving up and down and the crowd, in slow centrifugal motion, drew back from the roped-off pitch, back round the outfield, to find seats. As they drew thus from centre of the field they left one groundsman at each corner of the square, these four went to take up the rope. And as the crowd thinned on the ground, except by the pavilion where many people stayed yet, so boys in pairs were left still playing ball. The four men began to roll up the ropes, the boys left off two by two and went to find their seats. The policemen also were walking in wider circles away from the pitch. Now, as each of the four groundsmen drew out the post he was by and made to go, were very few people left in the outfield, now there were one or two only, and these running. Third policeman was clearing away those who stood yet by the pavilion. Boy who sold match cards ran across and then a fat curate in black was running across a corner, and then, as the policemen came in to stand at gate where the crowd had first been coming in, and the sparrows flew low over our heads in the stands to take possession of the outfield again, then the whitecoated umpire came out from the pavilion by where the crowd had up to now been standing. The crowd, once seated, was a murmur. The game began.

SATURDAY

(Unpublished, 1927–8)

'I am still busy experimenting with the definite article – this sort of thing "lights of town danced on water as gnats do" – and I don't know what it will come to', Green wrote to Neville Coghill.

Morning.

Life was in her. Life was in her and beat there. Her bed was next theirs. Their beds took up the room. Her father and mother slept now in that bed. No blind was over window. Sun came by it. And she turned head over from sun towards them sleeping and did not see them. She smiled. Head on bolster was in sunshine.

Life was in her belly. Life beat there.

Morning. Thousands slept. Town was over miles round. Thousands of houses. In each they slept.

Under blanket hands were pressed to her belly. Her fingers stuck out round. With them she felt the beating there. She smiled. Sun came in over her. She was just out of sleep, just in sleep. All of her was under sunshine, in that life beating under her fingers stuck out round.

Thousands slept. Were thousands of houses. In each they slept.

Morning.

Her mother sighed in sleep.

And water dripped from tap on wall into basin and into water there. Sun. Water drops made rings in clear-coloured water. Sun in these shook on the walls and ceiling. As rings went out round trembling over the water shadows of light from sun in these trembled on walls. On the ceiling. She watched.

She got up then. She dressed. She passed comb through her short hair. She bent head to looking glass. She painted lips. Hair in shade then was yellow silky. She sat on bed. She rolled silk

[51]

stockings on her legs and her legs shone. She put small red hat over the hair. And went away.

Thousands slept. She went away, through streets. Yet from houses came smoke from chimneys. Beginning. Thousands of houses. But those living in them were getting up, but slept early sunshine over town. She went through streets. Then she came to the garden of the people. Masses of flowers, heavy wild-headed, masses of them. Man sat on bench there. Sparrows were in and out between his feet on ground. He threw bread to them and some perched on his hat. Fluttering on ground and another one rose up to his head in low curve up through air. Three were on brim of his hat. Sparrows were in and out between his feet on ground. He threw bread to them. And this one fluttered by the brim of his hat then perched there. He held bread up in fingers for them there.

She came. And sparrows like as in handful thrown into the air were off and came down and waited near. She sat down at other end of bench. She folded hands on lap.

He threw bread on ground. One sparrow came back. He threw bread. Another came. And a third. He threw bread and soon all were back and some on brim of his hat.

She sat there. Life beat in her belly under hands on her lap. She did not see.

He threw bread towards her. Sparrows were in and out between his feet on ground. He threw bread towards her. It fell near. One sparrow went towards her. He threw bread further. Another went. And a third sparrow. Soon all were by her. And one rose up to her head in low curve up through air and fluttered by the brim of her hat and there perched then. She did not see.

Soon the man went away. And all the sparrows were by her, in and out between her feet on ground, and three now were on brim of her hat. She did not see.

Masses of flowers, heavy wild-headed, masses of them.

He went out of garden for the people. He went through streets. Smoke came in plumes from chimneys of the houses by them.

They were getting up who lived in houses. And shouting children from streets came out and into the garden. They shouted. Sparrows flew away then from all about her. The children played. She did not see them. Child bowled round hoop along. Now sparrows were right away.

Sunny morning. Everywhere the children shouted. One little girl came then and sat on bench. She swung short legs. She sucked finger. Then she pointed hand at them playing and laughed. She swung legs. Little girl gathering pebbles shouted to her 'Emmy, come on.' 'No' she shouted. She looked then at other end of bench. She watched her sitting quiet. She watched her. She looked. She got off bench. She went away backwards, sucking finger, watching her quiet there.

Soon children went all of them away to breakfast. Soon none was left in the garden for the people. All were gone.

It was quiet then. She was quiet on bench. Noise came from streets but only murmuring. Sun shone on flowers. Dew was on some of them. She did not see. And sparrows came back near, one by one. They waited by her feet, in and out. They watched, leaning heads sideways.

She moved head and sparrows were gone. She got up and went away, head bent. She did not see. Child was in her womb. She left the garden for the people. She went along streets. They were very quiet. But people were about. She walked slowly.

And she came to square. Years back they had been richer who had lived in houses round. They were poor, now, those who lived round in houses. Two drains went across, making four quarters. On right was coffee stall drawn by white horse. Sun made shadow with block of stall, wheels, and the spokes, and horse bent kneed, and three men standing by door at back of stall. Children shouted and played opposite across square. Church steeple came up above houses in further corner.

She saw coffee stall. She yawned. Slowly she went towards it. She yawned. She went slower.

Man standing in door of coffee stall said: 'Ough-to be goin' – was making for 'ome – but seeing you wants tea – seeing it's Tom 'ere – and the urn 'ot still – ough-to be going – but I'll pour you some tea.'

She came towards them. Her face was white in sun and puffed. She came slowly to coffee stall.

He said: ''Ow do wench, 'ave a cup o' tea – sleepy are yer,

[53]

yawning – 'ere it is then – and yer welcome – ain't yer got no use for it then?'

And another: 'She's agoing to drop – now sit yerself down my gel and I'll fetch yer a drop o' something.'

And he said: 'Well, tea's all I got – take a sip o' this.'

She sat on step of coffee stall. She drank tea. Hot.

Another said: 'She's right as rain now – or will be.'

And each had cup of tea and the men talked of football. She sipped. She clasped hands round burning cup, then unclasped them, then again clasped them round. The men talked of football. She sipped. Sweat came out over her face. Each had cup of tea. The men did not look at her.

Then she looked up into sky. Pigeon were there. They flew together. They turned. They were rising higher. They wheeled in the sky. They turned all at the same time in sky, wheeling, wheeling higher. She watched them. Sun flashed on them.

Whistle came from railway station. Pigeons fell away from it and climbed quicker. The men looked up. One said it was racing pigeons. They talked of football. She watched pigeon.

She put down cup then. She tidied herself. She got up. Coffee-stall man, that had been talking over her head from inside stall to those outside, smiled at her then. He asked if she was all right. One of them outside said she needn't hurry. She said she was all right. She asked how much tea was. He said 'Penny.' She took out purse. Pigeon flew off straight. She paid him. She went away. Another one of them outside said she was neat. Coffee-stall man said she was and getting near her time. He poured them more tea. They talked about football.

She left the square. She went along streets. Men were beginning to go to work. Their women leaned out of the windows, some of them. They called to each other. Town was awake now. Motor went by. She walked slowly.

And she came to where town ended. Factory was over beyond rubbish dump. Line of trees with bare branches, dead, were across it. Stream went between town and this. She stood on bridge where road leading to factory crossed the stream. Leaves. Leaves floated. Leave floated down it. Yellow. Houses along one side of this stream were very poor.

She leant against parapet of the bridge. Leaves. Few yellow leaves floated slowly down. And more pigeon were now in sky, in one flock. They turned. She saw them on the dark water and looked up. They wheeled, rising higher. Sun was behind cloud now. They were like white paper.

Across bridge came workers going to factory. One by one. Two by two. Three by three then. Pigeon flew straight suddenly and over great chimney of factory and were gone. After a time more and more workers crossed the bridge. Lines of them. Leaves. Yellow leaves floated. Leaves floated down the stream. They talked, few of those men, crossing the bridge.

'Did you see the racers?'

'Today's the day.'

'Look at them leaves on the water, it's autumn comin'.'

As she left house, who went to garden for the people, to the square, to bridge over stream, man came to window of floor above where she had been sleeping (in bed next to theirs, her father and mother). Skin was dark under eyes in his pale face. He pushed hair back from forehead where it dropped over down. Window was shut. He leant against it. She was walking slowly down street. But he did not look at her. Then he came back into the room.

Bed was in corner opposite to corner where sunlight jutted from window into. Child lay in it, his face grey on dirty pillow. He hardly breathed. Woman sat on chair by bed. She did not move, her face bent over thick hands resting on knees. Over her shoulders woollen shawl of mauve.

He went from window over to his coat hung on door. He took out evening paper and pencil. He sat on chair at foot of bed. In football coupon he wrote in names of teams. Soon the paper slipped. He was looking with mouth open at his ill son.

Pencil slipped. It fell. It clattered on floor. He stooped down and wife came in. Her eyes were dry, dry. That woman got up from chair and the women whispered to each other. Then she went away and mother sat on the chair.

Father went out of the room. He was barefoot. He made no noise. He came back again. He sat in chair again.

[55]

Next door.

Sun came touching Maggie's head which was under window and waked her, and she turned over and slept again.

Later woke baby on floor above and howled for milk and away tried to push ellipse of day which came through hole in blind and fixed on bed. Man next door jumped up at the noise. He went out. Mother sitting by her ill son moved on chair. Father came back again. He looked at the wall, his mouth wide open. Baby howled till mother there lifted it from bed to breast and sighed half asleep in darkness. Gluttonously baby sucked and drinking choked for a moment. Then baby slept. Mrs Craik held baby and slept again.

Later Maggie beneath got up. She dressed. She leaned out of window at the sun smiling. The sun, the sun. Now the street was getting up and children came out into backyards and onto land beneath to play. Shouted the children.

Now sun was higher in sky. Now smoke was coming in plumes from chimneys of the houses.

Next door.

Jim Cripps standing before bit of looking glass oiled hair. He whistled. He made it stand up over forehead in high curl. He stroked it with brush, stroked again. He winked at himself in glass. His brother Alfred watched him and admired. Time passed and Jim was fixing curl still and now it was hard like celluloid. He began to make other curls, one over each ear. Albert said he looked fine. He whistled. His cheeks were round and red and shone. Over his head red hair in curls like celluloid glistened. He winked at himself in glass. He went off.

They ate breakfast all of them. The men went to work.

Her man gone then Mrs Green took chair from kitchen and came to back door with her youngest, Peggy. She put shoulder against the lintel, leaning there. Sun obliquely came down on the small yard and made shadows from washing on the line. Walls and the outhouse were between yards on each side with more washing. Land beyond went down to where more streets were again for miles; and shadows were blue. These – from the five bars of the gate in wall at the back and in pentagon from outhouse and those from shirt, drawers, two sheets, pants, socks, the vests, the washing – went back to the house. Shadow of tree outside was over the wall. Certain of these met in sharp masses joining. In sun brick was orange and shirts and things were like cream if they were white. She went by the washing then. She put chair outside the gate. She sat looking over town in sun. Peggy stood by her, thumb in mouth, holding fold of her skirt.

And Maggie came out into yard next door and asked how she was feeling today and was told she couldn't do the work and Maggie said she would be in directly to give her a hand. Mrs Green asked how that Grant boy was that was ill there. Maggie said he was weak and doctor was coming soon she said. She went in then. And a sparrow came up to them outside and Peggy tugged at skirt but Mrs Green did not see. Her eyes were closed in sun. Peggy laughed at sparrow. It flew away. She sucked thumb again. Children shouting rushed by, was no school that day.

Carrying baby Mrs Craik stepped out of kitchen and fingered her washing. Wind came and sparrows flew from yard to the tree over by wall where light fluttered on the leaves moving and flew on beyond for cat was with Mrs Craik and went across her yard and through the gate and cleaned itself in sun against wall and Peggy stretched out hand to cat and laughed and cat looked up and head bent watched Peggy. Mrs Craik came through gate. Mrs Green opened eyes. Mrs Craik called out to her how she was feeling. Mrs Green asked how that boy was that was ill there. Mrs Craik said she'd heard Mrs Apps that had been with him all night had said he was sinking. Mrs Craik came over and they talked whispering of this.

And car was driven up street. They watched from windows round. Man inside got out and went into house carrying black bag. And he came to the room where father and mother watched by bed.

It was the doctor. They whispered. Then he said to open window, and father did this.

Doctor knelt down by bed then. The boy hardly breathed. Doctor worked. Mother watched, biting back of her thumb. Father stood up and sat down, he stood up and sat down. Always they were sending him back from by the bed.

[57]

And was clatter of wings and pigeon was sitting in open window. Father looked at it, mouth open. He plucked at his woman's sleeve. She saw. Her face went red. Then she knelt to the pigeon, mouth open, and father stood and did not look at the pigeon then. But doctor looked up and seeing it, waved, and pigeon was gone. He said racing pigeon were everywhere now. He said: 'Get me hot water.' Mother made haste. Later he said: 'We'll pull him through.'

FIGHT

(Unpublished, 1927–8)

This fragment survives in longhand. It is not known whether 'Fight' was part of a longer work or whether it was a sketch, a series of which, letters to Coghill suggest, Green intended to compile in a volume.

Sang birds. They lay, arms round each other. Waved ferns in the wind and they were among them, lying silently. Above trees hung a cloud against blue sky and leaves clustering from branch above and tall ferns hid these two deep in the wood from anyone and the sky. Soft the air.

This was on a hill thick-grown with trees and down where was short grass before another wooded hill some men were playing cricket, coats for stumps, and their women sat watching. Beyond were couples sitting, lying in each other's arms, and groups played laughing in sunlight, on grass deer-cropped, along on the valley. More were on either side hidden under branches, in the ferns, and the deer had gone and had hidden for so many people in their park.

They were lying together, then drew he himself away from her and lay on his back as a leaf swayed through air down towards him so that as he was turning from her caught he that leaf coming to rest and looked at it, sleepy, sleepily. He said leaves were falling and she sighed eyes shut and he said leaf not even brown was yet, dried only, when she, not opening her eyes, groped a hand for his and it fell on his face, and she ruffled his hair, already very ruffled.

She sat up then and opened eyes to smile at him then closing them again, and all fingers of both hands went about her hair. Afterwards she lay back and both looked at the sky through green leaves above.

Another smile went through her and propping head with fore-arm up from ground she watched him half asleep again and said he was nice, and it was nice here now.

And he began talking, speaking slowly, saying it was a fine lunch they had had at the inn and if she would be a good cook when they were married. A man, said he, came in tired from day's work in evening and he liked his food. But houses were hard to get. All this long while had they been engaged and she must wait for him, he could see her running off with someone else. Then she rolled over into his arms and he whispered in her ear.

Sun was now behind this little cloud but moving came out and light searching down found holes between the many leaves, cutting holes between here and there through violet shade when often sun-stick found leaf, turning brilliantly green, and melted, dripping to find more green below till there was no more. Deep, deep in wood sun-stick caught deer, quivering, listening, and in his coat was held for an instant but he leaped from the touch and deeper hid in purple shade, but even there came shouts to him from cricket players. Laughter too was in air, from the women looking on at games, from couples nearer in wood low chuckling from them, giggles. They were amusing each other and she on neck was being tickled by him, gently with bit of fern and on and on until she couldn't no more and rolled away. But leaning over he reached out and tickled again and shoulder coming out of dress tickled he lightly there. Laughing she caught at bit of fern and they fought over it till dragging himself nearer he caught her hands and tickled her powerless where shoulder left dress. She was squirming, giggling at it, and a sun-stick they had rolled to broke over them and sweat came through her skin. On and on till she was fighting with him, both laughing when he stopped and made to pull dress off. In silence they struggled when she got free, sprang up, looking at him for a moment, then ran and he after her while flew a bird from them.

She plunged through ferns breast high and he after her till he was catching hold when she slipped to one side and he tripped over legs of couple he had not seen lying there arms round each other, and fell, while she ran on. Getting up and saying no word to them he ran again but she was now come to edge of wood, and laughter came to him from where he had fallen over the legs. He broke through last ferns and she was on the short grass, panting, hands on hips, looking over shoulder to him. He snatched her arm but she said it would be a slap in the face he would get if he touched her and she would scream. In front of them a man was bowled out and all of that party laughed and shouted. Silently then went they together and sat with the others in tree-shadow.

Sun in light was over grass (where shadow of those playing moved with ball) and was over shirts white with blue in them and faces red with playing in the sun. In tree-shadow bright colours of women's dresses shone through shade lit here and there by sun-sticks breaking, melting by the leaves and falling, while a woman had taken off her hat and in her hair was one entangled as she sat beneath. Beer-bottle winked out from under tree to sun.

It was hot and some slept under tree from the heat. There laughed they between themselves when a man would leave the game and sit with them for a time and drink to quench thirst and their voices rising, their laughing was most shrill as he joked with them; then when he went back to play would they whisper again and giggle between themselves while the men shouted before them.

But she was not watching the cricket, looking rather at trees beyond and all the time his eyes glanced towards her and then back again. Said they nothing to each other or to the rest of them there, but soon hand went across grass to hers but she turned her shoulder to him. So for a long time were they like this.

So it went on when looking at her again he caught her half-smiling at him and he moved nearer and she did not seem to mind. Speaking quickly he said they had only an hour or two now before going home and it was a pity to waste a fine day like this. The woods were fine, said he softly, and you were alone in them, not like here with too many about, – you could not talk at all they crowded on you so. And what he always said was to let bygones be bygones and there was no use worrying your head over what had happened when it would not happen again. Getting up they walked closely together to the wood and those who had been looking on at cricket followed them with their eyes till they were gone in between ferns.

But the players were tiring of their game and came all of them to rest in shade except one who by himself went off. In it they rested and fell asleep some of them while others talked and four men began a game of cards. But laughter came from edge of wood and those who looked saw a new couple coming towards them and when they were near these told how they had seen another couple some time back, she running away and he pursuing her, and he had tripped over their legs and gone on and how they had just seen them again but with nothing between them now.

Deep, deep in wood, growing used to noise, the deer bent his head to nibble at fernleaf; quiet his gentle eyes.

EVENING IN AUTUMN

(Unpublished, 1927–8)

'Evening in Autumn' was later typed and dedicated to his
friend, Mary Keene, in 1943.

Warmth. Grey sky. Here the soil was good for trees. Starlings
came. They came in thousands, planing, black across grey sky.
They came to tree and some went to the right. These fell turning
like leaves and darted up into the tree. Rest of them went in eddy
curling round it and fell turning like leaves and darted up into
the tree from other side. When they were there they began
singing.

Another flock, black against grey sky. They came to tree and
some went to the left. These fell turning like leaves and darted
up into the tree. Rest of them went in eddy curling round it and
fell turning like leaves and darted up into the tree from other
side. When they were there they began singing.

And again, were thousands of them. And again.

With noise like wind then came they out of one tree and curled
round and were like eddy of the air and with noise like wind
came others out of their tree and curled round and passed in eddy
under other flock sweeping, and both fell turning like leaves as
they came then darted up each flock into another tree. When they
were there they sang and their singing was joined to all others
that had come and were singing.

Then others left their tree with noise like wind, black against
grey sky, and swept through air curling towards another tree
and swallows came by and then perched on telephone wire and
starlings fell turning like leaves and darted up into their tree, and
again, and again.

Warmth. Then night came.

EXCURSION

(Unpublished, c. 1930)

'Excursion' contains the seed of *Party Going*, written between 1931–8. However as early as 1926 Green wrote to Coghill, describing a work in progress, in some letters entitled *Terminus*, in others *Bank Holiday*. That the idea for *Party Going* was born sometime in the mid twenties is therefore indisputable; though exactly when 'Excursion' was written it is impossible to determine.

Trams came up to the station. They were painted yellow. Black and red letters on their sides read: THE GAY GIRLS DANCE NIGHTLY, LAST WEEK. THE WORKERS' DAILY HAS LARGEST CIRCULATION. DOES IT HURT? TAKE UNCLE'S PILLS THEN. Brass on them caught the sun, and windows on their sides. They were full up and all got out when they came to station, black lines of people coming down the winding stairs and from inside. Else left tram and stood by lamp standard. She waited for Conn and Jim. She had run along street and caught one up when it was moving and Conn and Jim had waited for another. Else pouted. Those who had come by tram and those who had walked went up the steps into station in waves. Like the tide coming in.

Lamp standard was black with swelling black leaves cast on it. Glass shade above hung like ugly flower and caught sun and flashed. Over steps leading up into station were big rounded letters in gold, MIDLAND HOTEL. More and more people came and passed up into station. Else bit finger. She tidied hair at side of hat. She did not see Conn and Jim. Then she left lamp standard and ran up steps and into station dodging people, slipping through them for they moved slowly.

Mr Healy and Mrs and small daughter went up steps and into entrance hall. Stairs in corner went down from it and over those was painted: BOOKING HALL – PLATFORM I. But they began to go across station by the bridge. Sun came through glass roof above and engine shunted underneath making great noise. This passage across station was broad, but so many people were on it you could only go slowly. All along stairs went down to different platforms. And their daughter was separated from them and when Mrs Healy knew this she called out but she could not be heard above noise and she looked down staircases with Mr Healy. On bridge were so many people you could hardly move for them going along. But their daughter was in doorway of fruit shop with her nose flattened against glass of it which was on this big bridge. Pressed against each other crowd went by, some to entrance hall the rest to other side, slowly moving by her and she looked in shop window. Oranges were in pyramids and apples, all in tissue-paper covers. Tins of pineapple in columns. At side of the shop bananas were in clusters hanging like fingers. And tomatoes were put about in the window. Tins of pineapples in columns. A melon. On one side of it pyramid of oranges, one of apples on the other side. Melon was down in centre of the shop window. In corners two cyclamen and by each one, tomatoes and so two reds in corners and about. For shop window rose in three steps, in terraces, covered with pink tissue paper and these apples, oranges, tomatoes, tins of pineapple, cyclamen, were put differently above this melon on the other two steps. And when Mrs Healy and Mr moved with crowd along bridge to look down staircases beyond – Mrs crying 'seen my Ellie?' and not being heard – Mr all at once said he saw her there by the fruit shop and Mrs said she felt faint and they pushed their way there and Mrs rested for a time by the shop behind bananas. Inside fat woman slept behind counter. And Ellie said nothing but pointed to the window with greedy eyes. Mr Healy sweated and wiped forehead. It was no use speaking as you couldn't hear.

The two Miss Weekses came down the stairs at further end of bridge and stood away from crowd coming downstairs into booking hall in a corner and one said to other she had been killed nearly in the crush and other said the company ought to treat you decent when you had paid. First one said were the tickets safe? and other said yes she had them in her glove and it was a good thing they had taken them beforehand and she'd never thought it would be like this, last year it hadn't been like this, or she'd have come round this side by the streets though trams did not run this side. First one said they should have walked even though it wasn't easy with the feet their mother gave them. Lines of those waiting to buy tickets stretched out of booking hall into street. And Else and Conn came into that corner and Else said what had happened to them? and she'd been so nervous their having her money and her ticket and everything. And Conn said why couldn't she have waited instead of running off and she might call herself lucky to have found them in this crowd, and she'd lost Jim a good place in the queue by losing herself and keeping him looking for her when he might have been buying ticket for himself. Else said who had bought their own tickets yesterday anyhow, hadn't she herself gone right to the station to buy two tickets and spent sixpence on trams before they knew Jim was coming. Conn said she'd kept the change anyway and they saw Weekses then just by them and went off and past Ticket Inspector onto platform. One Miss Weeks said to other it was shameful the way Conn Finch lied for she'd heard Conn Finch say to Jim Cripps as they were going up steps into station how glad she was they had lost Else. And other said to first one everyone knew it was Else that saved and Conn that spent, buying scent to make herself smell, and it was Else's money that'd bought her ticket probably. They went past Ticket Inspector onto platform.

Mr Healy bought tickets and he and Mrs Healy and daughter went past Ticket Inspector and onto platform. Hotel was opposite, beyond many platforms. Crowds were on all of these. And windows of hotel faced all this. Friend came up and spoke to Mr Healy. Mrs joined in. And their small daughter saw boy in window of hotel. He saw her. He was smart and rich. She looked at him.

On trolley nearby were eight milk cans in two rows of three with two laid on top on their sides. On trolley was painted L M S. Above, on cylinders, Ws were painted which curved round and were part hidden by other curves beginning and ending other

[66]

curves with Ws convex. Grey metal on round black wheels and trolley with handle, black with using.

Eddie had bit of wood in his hand and was beating empty cylinder, making noise. He began to beat much quicker and was more noise, but mother ran at him and he gave up.

She looked at him. He waved to her from hotel window. She looked. He smiled and waved again. But she just looked. And Mr and Mrs Healy moved away and took her away. She looked over shoulder. People came between her and him. Mr Healy said he would take a nip of something before the train came in and Mrs said not to be late then.

Fewer people were coming now across bridge but most platforms were full and most of all this furthest platform. Jim had bought ticket and was making way for himself towards station clock where he was to meet Conn. Man with Inspector written in gold on his cap went along and shouted and you couldn't hear what he said for the noise. And word went round that train was coming in, and turning all moved, those behind forward to platform edge, those in front back from it. They met in thick line, dark but lighted by faces all looking one way. Across bridge people ran and their steps thudded. Behind barriers the lines of those waiting to buy tickets heaved for Mrs Pendleton could not find purse, and she was buying ticket for herself, husband, one son and half tickets for two children. Husband stood by and said she had purse when they left home and he didn't know what she was after, he said. Those waiting in lines behind cried out and heaved. Policeman came up. Clerk behind window tapped on the counter with his fingers. They all shouted behind. Suddenly Mrs Pendleton wept and policeman led her to seat where husband, knees bent, violently searched her pockets. Helpless she wept. The lines moved on again and bought tickets and went past Ticket Inspector and onto platform and took no notice of her.

Bell rang. Those behind surged forward again to platform edge and a woman was pushed over. She fell onto the rails. Great cry went up. People on next platform waved and their mouths opened then shut but none of their shouting could be heard. Coil of men and women struggled round where she had fallen off.

She was pulled up again then. Porters ran along platform edge and pushed the crowds back. They heard something had happened and out of refreshment room hurried men wiping mouths with backs of hands and a few women. But word went round it was nine minutes yet before their train and Inspector said this again to those round refreshment room. So they went back. Crowd spread out again over platform. They collected in groups.

Train drew in to the next platform and crowd there fought and climbed into it and soon it went off.

Meantime Station Master in black frock coat and top hat had come out through door with STATION MASTER painted on it and was walking about. He was very fat. Each group he passed twisted their heads round to watch him going, so it was like slow wind over grass – the light faces turning. The girls giggled. Conn and Else giggled till they gasped for just as he was by them Jim had winked and he must have seen as he had gone red and puffed cheeks out. But Mrs Pendleton's son was talking to policeman and saying he had his own money, and as mother had been at head of the line he could go there now to buy ticket for himself but policeman said not and that he would have to go to the beginning and start again. He asked the crowd but had no answer from them. The two children, holding hands, watched pa and ma on seat doing nothing, looking at boots.

In refreshment room attendants in black and white, fat women, gave out tea and little glasses to the crowd there. Men had flasks and bottles. They poured spirits out of these into the little glasses. Mr Healy took out flask and said to Mrs Eames if she would have a drop. She said she didn't mind if she did. Her woman friend had cup of tea. Tea urn was rubbed up and shining. Under bell-shaped glass covers on the counter were three-sided pile of sandwiches, one pork pie, stack of sausage rolls, three eggs, apples, small cakes – stack of sausage rolls, small cakes, three-sided pile of sandwiches, six eggs, three packets of biscuits in tissue paper bags, one pork pie, three apples – small cakes, three-sided pile of sandwiches, one sausage roll, one empty stand and bell-shaped glass cover, six apples, cylinder of three pork pies standing on end on each other. Up wall on shelves many bottles with many colours. Everywhere red and blue packets of chocolate, rectangles. Mrs Eames, in hat with three great feathers, leant over marble counter top holding little glass in one hand. Now it had whisky in it. Little finger, crooked, made three sides of square with hand. She said a marriage was in her street that day, in No. 27, and there would be fun there that night, there would said she. She chuckled. But she said she did not think it neighbourly in those two women. She had seen them on platform now, those two sisters Weeks that lived next door in No. 25, it wasn't right in them not to go to it. Neighbours were neighbours and they had been invited, Mrs Clark had told her. They didn't behave Christian. They made a nice profit out of that shop those two, so much that they were selling it now, Mrs Apps had told her. Bleeding money out of you, then not going to the wedding.

Outside on platform two coons, faces black painted, red lips and white eyeballs, walked up and down with banjuleles under arm and grey straw hats on head. Everyone in each big group again twisted head round to watch them going so it was like slow wind over grass – the light faces turning. Many children followed behind in path made for them by them through the crowd and they pulled long noses and shouted behind and man or woman here and there cried encouragement to the children. Soon everyone on platform was laughing at the two coons, then they took no more notice of these two, and children went back to fathers and mothers.

Publican's daughter, Mary Jones, was with Henry Simmons. They stood where platform was least crowded. She said nasty smelly people, why did we come? He was silent. She was silent. Then she said nasty smelly dirty people, why did father make me come? He was silent. She was silent. He fiddled with button of his coat. She said then oh Henry don't fiddle with that button, why did I come? They were silent. She said, look at the Weekses, how surprising to see them here.

Poorly dressed man went to Station Master in top hat who was walking up and took off his brown cap and bowed before him and said what made all near by laugh at Station Master. This one turned red and walked on up. But the children did not mock at him.

Train drew in to the platform next but one and crowd there fought and climbed into it and soon it went off. Next platform was filling up again. Two met there on it shouted and waved to man in front of Mary Jones and he shouted and waved to them. Mary Jones took Henry Simmons away then to end of the platform.

The Misses Weekses stood close by Ticket Inspector who looked at tickets and made holes in them as in lines people still came past Booking Office onto platform. They were looking at Mr and Mrs Pendleton who looked at boots. One Weeks said to other it was a hard thing on them that they had lost purse and to think of it coming all this way and then to be losing it, and this a Bank Holiday. The other said she couldn't think where Mrs Pendleton had put it who was sparing enough with it when she was in the shop. First one went over to Ticket Inspector who was looking at tickets and making holes in them all the time and said she had lost her purse that poor woman behind barrier there and her name was Mrs Pendleton. Ticket Inspector said he was busy. Then the other saw Mrs Healy with small daughter and both went over to them and first one said to Mrs Healy how Mrs Pendleton had lost purse and now she could not go on trip to country and how hard it was on husband for wife to be so careless, and other Weeks said she had always known her careless. Mrs Healy said it was not like her to do something like that and what she always said was that if you couldn't keep your purse what could you keep but she did not say much more and after two minutes the Weekses moved back again to barrier and watched Mrs Pendleton again. Mrs Healy said to Mrs Smith she wondered Weekses weren't after giving Pendletons something to buy tickets with what with all the money they had from Street 37. Mrs Smith said that was so.

Sun came through glass roof. Then a cry. Shouting. Then murmur stopped which had been from the crowd all over station like lathe working under roof and by milk cans on the trolley man cried 'Thief' and 'Thief'. On each side turned they all of them towards trolley and closed in towards it, straining circling white faces. At back they stood on benches, some jumped, all closed in round the trolley, pressing. Here and there cried they asking what it was and policeman who had been by Pendletons and had come past the barriers made way for himself through them to centre. Woman right in centre by trolley talked very high and fast. Station Master also was making way for himself through them and some porters in a bunch but crowd pressed thick, very silent. In centre by trolley man waved his arms and began to shout. Everyone began to laugh at him and when policeman reached him some went away and stood round in circles at a distance and looked round and talked of it. Several had climbed onto trolley in centre but policeman moved them off. The Station Master was there now and was talking and was holding top hat in hand and was wiping red face. Someone shouted 'I'm H-O-T,' and all laughed again. Station Master turned red. And the group which had come out of refreshment room when they heard shouting hurried back in to have a last one. They could not tell Mrs Eames what it was about. So she said Weekses had been getting too gay with some man probably. They all laughed.

One by one from behind door with THIRD CLASS WAITING ROOM painted on it a few men and women, wives and husbands – these were real travellers, they were so dirty – these came out huddled, dusty with travelling. But they went back yawning for policeman was leading man away followed by woman who had talked high and fast and Station Master who led two children and an Inspector and two porters with woman's husband, worried-looking man. The crowd made way for them and broke slowly up into thick groups again.

Weekses had been parted by first rush in towards trolley but with crowd breaking up they met and one said to other it was terrible, pickpockets even on a holiday and you didn't know where you were with them and other said she always held purse in hand and, let them try to take it from her, they could not, and it was what Mrs Pendleton had been done to most likely. Then Conn and Else Finch came up and Jim Cripps and Conn said to first one it made her nervous it did people rushing so so you might get knocked down and walked on and Else said she didn't like to have money now on her and Jim whistled, hands in pockets. Then Conn said to first one she wondered they didn't get nervous in the shop with all the murderers there were about now and Else said to Conn to look at Mr Healy there who had had a drop too much and Conn asked Else what it had to do with her and couldn't Mr Healy do what he pleased on a Bank Holiday. Weekses went away and one said to other it was disgusting, disgusting and in public too and other said she knew now about Conn Finch and she'd never cared much about Finch twins before and now she knew. First one said they hadn't spent a penny in the shop for twelvemonth now, it wasn't neighbourly, and other said they was immoral.

On furthest platform next to hotel walls train drew in and crowd there fought and climbed into it. People went by behind hotel windows above and looked out down on it here and there. Soon the train went off, everyone cheering in it.

Mr Healy came from refreshment room with no collar on now and with shirt open across chest. He asked Inspector when train would be in. Inspector said any time now and would be another after to take those left behind. Mr Healy wiped neck by open shirt with handkerchief. He said to Inspector had he seen the wife and daughter? Inspector smiled and said what did they look like? Then Mr Healy said he'd never have done it if the wife hadn't been so keen for he remembered travelling between Swansea and Malvern, where the wife's people were living then, on Bank Holiday nine years ago it must be now and it was a day hotter than this. Inspector said 'go on.' Mr Healy said yes it was, it was something fierce, but still you couldn't really say it was bad as now. And what had that chap done, he said, what had been taken away. He'd never seen nothing like it before in railway stations he said.

Boy in dark uniform and cap pushed refreshment barrow past Weekses and they stopped him. One fingered banana and said to other she could not understand how money could be spent on things like those picture Society papers next to buns there. She asked boy how much bun was. Boy said tuppence. Other said it was a shame. Then first one said she supposed bananas would be three ha'pence. Boy said not, they were tuppence. She said why you could get better for a penny each in Cornwall Road. Boy said but this was Station Road. Other said it was a shame and shameful the way they spoke to you.

The two Pendleton small children held hands and watched refreshment barrow and then looked back at pa and ma who sat on bench and looked at boots. Mr Pendleton put hand into coat pocket and drew out pipe which he put into mouth and with other hand took out something and looked at it and looked at it again and said here it was and Mrs said what and then when she saw it why it was the purse. So she said all the time she'd known he'd had it and he said he couldn't say how it came to be in pocket and she told him to go and buy tickets now and to be quick as was not much time now and she told children to stay by ma. Mr Pendleton went but policeman who had been there had gone now with the man in the crowd so he began to say to those at top of line to let him in before them as he had been first so should be first again – he had waited hours he said, whole hours, but he did not get much answering out of them. But those in front by platform edge began all of them to look up rail lines, and those behind pressed forward. They met in thick line, dark but lighted by faces all looking one way. It was the train. Mrs Pendleton shouted to Mr to hurry as train was coming in now and Inspector walked down and was saying another train would be in after this one to take those left behind. You could not hear him for noise. People waiting to buy tickets were quite few now but they would not let Mr Pendleton go before them so he went to the end and moved up with them. Fat woman sweating under green faded parasol came in behind him. Ticket Inspector looked at tickets and punched holes in them quicker and quicker and shouted as everyone was beginning to shout. Train slowly came in making great puffing noise and those at platform edge drew back as it came by. Line of those waiting to buy tickets heaved and those on platform heaved forward again when train stopped and they shouted and rushed up into the carriages. Weekses ran up and down behind, one saying to other, here Mary, and, no Agatha this way. Soon train was full and every window filled with faces lozenge shaped one on top of the other which all looked and shouted at those left on platform. Mr Pendleton was buying ticket now and Mrs cried to him holding child by each hand. Inspector walked up and was saying another train would be in after this one to take those left behind. One Weeks said to other it was a shame the way they fought to get into trains, those others, and then train drew out – porters ran down it shouting to stand clear and everyone in carriage windows cheered and it went quicker and was gone.

Station Master turned and slowly went back to door with STATION MASTER painted on it and shut it behind him. Porters went across the rails to next platform. Train drew in there and crowd fought and climbed into it. Soon that train went off, everyone cheering in it. Mary Jones said to Henry Simmons nasty smelly dirty people she was glad they hadn't got places on the first train and she would have gone straight home now if it wasn't that they had bought tickets. One Weeks ran up to Inspector and asked what they were to do now with their train gone and he said another would be in directly to take those left behind. These stood about in groups and circles. Mrs Eames came out of Refreshment Room and waved arms and went back again. Mrs Pendleton blamed Mr at platform edge and Weekses went up to them and one said to her well she saw they had found purse after all and Mrs Pendleton said yes, they had, and would say no more. So Weekses moved further down and other said to first one it was not a thing to get angry about when you had found it but a thing to be thankful of. Not so many people were in station now. And all looked one way along rail lines curving and upright signals and were blue sheds in sun with roofs shining and nothing to be seen but one shunting engine and balls of smoke going from funnel into other blue of sky.

FORTIES

Green said of the fire fighting: 'It was four hours on and four hours off, even when there weren't raids. When there were raids of course we were out the whole time.' On rest days – every third day – he continued to manage Pontifex which was being run by a skeleton staff. With *Pack My Bag* published in 1940, and the first chapters of *Caught* completed, Green wrote several short stories, and submitted the first, *A Rescue*, to John Lehmann in 1941. *Caught* was published in 1943, followed by *Loving* in 1945; *Back* in 1946; and *Concluding* in 1948. In 1949 *Loving* was published in America, where it featured briefly on the bestseller lists.

A RESCUE

(Published in Volume 4 Penguin New Writing, March 1941)

One evening in the third week of the blitz on London, that is after fighting fires every night and all night, my crew was ordered to relieve another pumping out the basement shelter of a store which had been burned down the week before. We were glad. We could look forward to a night spent in one of the deepest shelters, very little work, a good supper and better breakfast provided by the management of the store and, above all, no fire fighting. When we got our orders at evening roll call we were greeted with cries of 'blue eyed' and 'you lucky bastards'.

The sirens had already gone, the night was soft, there was a moon and, across the way, over a street made unreal by thin mist, three searchlights joined at one point to create a slowly-moving giant tripod with nothing, nothing in their beams. The guns were busy and the shell-bursts, like fireworks a mile or more away, did not follow the slowly swinging apex those searchlights threw up of more than moonlight, its essence, that was projected in three paths to the shifting point the gunners did not follow with pink stabs. The noise was accidental in that it seemed to bear no relation either to gun flashes, vast quick semicircles silhouetting roofs, or to the bursts, or, more rarely to those long two-second rosy glows made by a high explosive bomb. Only the steady drone, an interrupted drone, overhead made all of it threatening, gave it that meaning which caused every man in this station to laugh and talk louder than he need, as he put on his gear in readiness for the fire call that might now be only a question of minutes.

I was in charge of the pump and tender. I was anxious that we should get away for there might soon be enough fires started to lead those in authority to abandon for the time being the basement in which we were to work. If we could get out of sight we might be forgotten. There had been no gas at our station for several days. There were no electric cookers in our kitchen such as they used where we were going. Two hot meals and a night in dry clothes looked too good to be true.

Then I could not find the crew. The station was a doorless garage so that at night it was badly lighted. I went here and there shouting and in the end came round to the back. With the men yelling to each other in the half dark as they put on their gear, and the gunfire, the crew had not heard me from where they were already seated in the pitch-dark tender, as keen as I to get away.

I had to go to the watchroom to report out. They booked it and phoned a certain control to say we were going. When this control accepted our departure I knew that nothing short of a bomb could stop us. But things were getting rather hot outside. So much so that when I got back to the tender a voice called out from within, 'Let's get on out, Henry.' And then a fool ran up just as we were moving. He shouted, 'Have you got a tool kit?' Because it was part of my job to know this I shouted back, 'How the bloody hell should I have any idea?' As we drove away it was to these words of his, drifting behind us between two crashes, 'I only asked a civil question.'

We had not far to go and, once outside, it did not seem so very heavy up above, only, as always when on the move in a bad raid, there was that added awareness, you sat forward, you waited for a bomb, for a crater not marked out with lamps, for wreckage, for glass to cut the tyres, for anything, but not on this particular evening for what was coming to us.

As we went the thin mist was like a light over the street, broken by black shadows caused by the moon behind tall buildings; in the square one white building stood out in this watery light that was a kind of tinge of blue, only a colour because of that white block of stone ahead. On the ground everything seemed entirely deserted, dead, but the sky was alive still. We were almost there when a torch flashed on and off some thirty yards in front from the height of a man's thigh straight at us, but in the unsubstantial glow beyond our hooded headlamps it was not possible to see who held the torch until we were right on the man. He was a policeman.

He said in the hurried voice men use when they have a lot to say and no time, yet they hesitate in their speech, 'There's someone fallen down a manhole.'

'Over this way,' another called from the right and flashed his torch. I realised it was this I had dreaded all evening. As we pulled over I called to them behind to get ready, out of its locker, the long line, that is the 120 feet of rope we carry.

In the shadow right under a building three men were kneeling by a hole. This turned out to be one of those manholes, about six feet by four, to a sewer, of such a kind that the cover is usually hidden until some major disaster requires it to be raised or broken open. The store had been severely damaged by fire, the site was not yet handed over by the Brigade and this cover, which had been removed at the time of the fire and never put back, was not marked in any way, that is to say there were no lights round the opening in the blackout. The individual I now saw, as I knelt in my turn, the long line between my hands, had simply fallen down it.

By the cinema light of our electric torches we could see fifteen feet down this opening another cover swinging on a shaft or pivot through the centre of its length, half of it pointing to the sky and half to the smell thirty-five feet beneath where muck in the flooded sewer rushed past, glimmering with solids. Draped over this cover edge, looking flat in the light given by our shrouded torches, grotesquely caught up, dreadfully still, most like a rag doll made full size he was so limp, lay this unfortunate it was now our job to get out. The sweet sickly stench, cloying, hanging about like a taste, like decaying hay, was so thick you expected his image to shimmer where it lay in its sort of box. Through the silence in which we watched we began to hear faint regular groans.

One of the policemen called out, 'You are all right now, old mate, the Fire Brigade's here to get you out.' Then I realised, feeling helpless, that it was up to us.

Now there was a ledge four inches wide running round the sides fifteen feet down and on which, presumably, the lower cover was meant to rest when shut. We carry two ladders, one short, one long, and I saw we should have to get one of these and stand the end on this ledge. In that way a man could climb down to put the line round the poor devil's shoulders. I told the crew to bring the long ladder. Charlie, as he ran back to get it down, called out the short one would be best. I wanted to argue. Then I thought there was no time. While they were fetching it I tried to make the appropriate knot, a running bowline, on one end of the line. The first I made was a slippery hitch. I began again. I had finished it by the time they brought the ladder up.

A short ladder is in two halves. One half has on the base two elbows, or inverted U-shaped pieces of iron, which fit on to any rung of the other half. It is so designed to enable a man to put both halves together against a building and slide the top one up to the required height. Then all that has to be done is to clip one to the other by those bits of iron, and the ladder is safe to climb. But to lower a short ladder the two halves must be lashed together with a line or they will drop apart. The crew was laying the ladder out, a policeman was calling down, 'They won't be long now,' another shone his torch for us and I could not find the other end of the long line. I kept on saying as I fumbled, 'Give me the other end.' Meantime the crew was making a hash of laying out the two halves. They were talking about it. They had got the iron pieces jammed when I found the free end of my line. I began to lash the two halves too soon. I made a clove hitch. Then I had to untie it until the ladder was straight. They got it straight at last. I made the knot again.

But in less time than it takes to read we were shipshape and lowering the ladder down, having to take care not to touch the injured man as we did so. He was too badly hurt to hang on. He balanced.

I was still sure the ladder would not extend far enough to reach the ledge. As we lowered away I blamed myself for not insisting on having the long one. But I was wrong, it did reach after all so that everything just did nicely.

Now that we were working on it, his mid-air tomb looked very bleak, there was no room to move, and the idea of the cramped climb down to him was not attractive. But it was my place in the crew to do so, and as I stepped back to get the other end of the line on which I had made my running bowline one of the policemen said, 'If you don't want to go down I'll do it.' But he made no move. In any case I meant to go. I went. It was simple to get to him. While I did so I said 'I'm coming.' When I stood on a level with his shoulders as he lay absolutely motionless I saw he was heavy, thick-set, and noticed that he had stopped groaning. Someone called from above, 'He's crushed his left side.' I slipped the noose over his shoulders. I said, 'You're all right now, cocker, we have got a line round you, only don't move. It will hurt though, when we pull you up.' He spoke. He said, 'I don't care,' in a level whisper, 'so long as you get me out of this bloody 'ole.'

I had made a big noose and as this lay round his shoulders, with the lower part by his outspread hands, he could just move these a trifle to get them over the rope, so that when we tightened the knot it should come up under his armpits.

I told them above to take up the slack. They did this. I crept round the ledge, holding on to the noose, in order to tighten this as much as possible from behind. I got into the far corner and pulled the rope tight. Then they hauled away. He was drawn up without a sound or a movement from him, slowly. In the end they laid hold of his coat, they dragged him over the edge with their fingers. Then he was safe.

To steady myself I put out my hand to the cover off which he had been raised. It swung slightly on its pivot. I had not realised that it was loose. I was at once, for the first time, aware of the sewer twenty feet below though I could, I know, no longer smell it.

The ledge was four inches wide. The rubber boots we wear are clumsy things, heavy, and as wide as that ledge. I had no hold on anything, dare not touch the cover, had my back wedged into a corner with one foot at right angles to the other. I was stuck.

I called Charlie to come below with a line. As he came into view climbing down he said, 'Hullo, Henry.'

I said, 'I'm stuck, Charlie.'

'Well, hang on to this, then,' and he gave me the line. But he had to reach over to give me his hand before I could shuffle back.

I walked to the station to report and heard the barrage, which had been incessant, for the first time since the policeman had flashed his torch. In the watchroom the light was blinding. They rang up local control. Local control said to the telephonist as though she had done it all, 'You should have stayed put and called us on with the BA,' that is the Breathing Apparatus. What we had forgotten, and what I had not had, because perhaps the manhole was so big that it could get away, was sewer gas. But if we still don't know what this can do to you, at least the four of us know how it smells.

The injured man was taken away in an ambulance. We have not heard anything of him. He may have died.

MR JONAS

(Published in No. 3 Folios of New Writing, *1941)*

Green wrote to Lehmann: 'I have just let a girl read this and she laughed herself into a state of tears she thought it was so bad. . . . In fact she laughed so much at the first page that she put it into her mouth as you can see from the lipstick. . . . Anyway I thought I'd put some commas in this time. I've tried to do it in a more spectacular way to suit the more spectacular blaze. It's true, of course, as the other one ["A Rescue"].'

Above us, in the night, as we drew up, in the barrage, the sky, from street level, seemed to be one vast corridor down which, with the speed of light, blue double wooden doors as vast were being slammed in turn. From outside the fire station, at which we were waiting to be ordered on to a particular address, that is to the next blaze on the list, we could see three fires, one of which was unattended yet.

The raid was in full swing. Already it would have been possible to read in the reddish light spread by a tall building sixty yards away, the top floors of which, with abandon, in recklessness, with fierce acceptance had exchanged their rectangles for tiger-striped hoops, great wind-blown orange pennants, huge yellow cobra tongues of flame. Three thin, uncoloured, plumes of water were being played on to the conflagration by firemen in the street. The extremities of these jets were broken into zigzags, moving up and down as the force of gravity overcame the initial pressure at the nozzle. This gave the effect of three flags of water rippling in a breeze. The plumes, when all pressure was spent, dipped weakly to those flames in a spatter of drops. It was as though three high fountains which, through sunlight, would furl their flags in rainbows as they fell dispersed, had now played these up into a howling wind to be driven, to be shattered, dispersed, no longer to fall to sweet rainbows, but into a cloud of steam rose-coloured beneath, above no wide water-lilies in a pool, but into the welter of yellow banner-streaming flames.

Accustomed, as all were, to sights of this kind, there was not one amongst us who did not now feel withdrawn into himself, as though he had come upon a place foreign to him but which he was aware he had to visit, as if it were a region the conditions in which he knew would be something between living and dying, not, that is, a web of dreams, but rather such a frontier of hopes or mostly fears as it may be in the destiny of each, or almost all, to find, betwixt coma and the giving up of living.

Violence was there in so strange a shape as to appear a lamb, and danger also, but, in the extravagance by which this was displayed, it seemed no more than a rather deadly warmth we could feel, and which, at the distance, was all that remained of that heat, which turned those fountains into steam.

The breaking pattern of rings which rain, lost in colour, can form on the surface of water, was no more likely than this other, blasted white into clouds. But the black goldfish, gulping at the drops, were more conscious than firemen, unafraid, seated hands on knees, silent beneath that awful, the wide magnificence of that sight.

Not many minutes had gone by before one of our crew had criticised the way in which these three jets were being played, so far below the fire that there was no force left behind them. He said they should have been taken to a neighbouring roof from which they could be directed down in a torrent into the flames. He pointed. Looking up again, we saw the writhing mass, the pointed tongues had leapt still higher, huge sparks now flew out in showers and there was more black smoke than steam. This, as it rolled away, was coloured on the under side a darker red, the purple of a fire momentarily beyond control.

More pumps drew up. Those who manned them began, in the half dark, to look about for friends. Then, from out of the fire station, some five or six came trotting. These were the number ones, those in charge of each unit, coming back to their pumps with the address to which each had been ordered. Not able to distinguish crews quickly in this light they were calling out the numbers of their own sub-stations. It was hard to realise all the noise which was made by those pumps already at work, the roaring of the fire, and that continuous battering up above until we had noticed how difficult it was for these men to make themselves heard, shouting, as they passed, into the backs of the tenders.

When he found us our man shouted the address, then climbed in front with the driver. As we drove off, we asked each other which street he had named, but no one behind had heard. And taking, as we did, the first turn to the left, then right, we were far enough from the blaze to lose all sight of it. We did not know where we might be. We had drawn up no more than ninety yards away, but the only sign of what we had left was in the pink roofs of an office building opposite, glowing in the reflection. The noise was so much less.

We had come to a very different problem.

There was almost quietness as we got down. It was very dark. All I could see was a thick mass of smoke or steam, it was impossible to tell one from the other, surging heavy from a narrow passage. We were told to run hose out, up this alley. One man took a length, snapped the coupling in, laid out the fifty foot and went back for more, while another snapped his coupling in where the first had ended, went on, and, while he in his turn was back to get a second length, yet another went on from where the second had finished. The hose was laid without the men taking in their surroundings.

Some living things turn to the light, we went by instinct into the deepest dark. I hurried, stumbled, into this pall of smoke and steam, when suddenly, after my boots had crunched on grit, I came to the debris.

What I saw, a pile of wreckage like vast blocks of slate, the slabs of wet masonry piled high across this passage, was hidden by a fresh cloud of steam and smoke, warm, limitless dirty cotton wool, disabling in that it tight bandaged the eyes. Each billow, and steam rolls unevenly in air, islanding a man in the way that he can, to others, be isolated asleep in blankets. Nor did the light of a torch do more than make my sudden blindness visible to me in a white shine below the waist. There was nothing for it but to go on towards voices out in front, but climbing, slipping up, while unrolling the hose, I felt that I was not a participant, that all this must have been imagined, until, in another instant, a puff of wind, perhaps something in the wreckage which was alight below the surface, left me out in the clear as though in, and among, the wet indigo reflecting planes of shattered tombs deep in a tumulus the men coughing ahead had just finished blasting.

It was impossible to work fast. The number one was shouting for that last connection, into which he could snap the nozzle, long before we could get it to him. In the struggle, with the directions we yelled at each other, the scene came real again. But when everything was laid out, and word had been sent back to turn the water on, a vault quiet fell once more as we stood waiting in smoke which came by waves, hot, acrid, making the eyes run, and bringing on a cough that hurt the lungs.

Water is never got quickly, perhaps because it seems so long to wait before the fire. This I could not see yet from the place I had reached, on top of the wreckage, beyond the steam at last but into smoke, and, as I could now realise in the intervals of sight, on a mass of rubble about fifteen foot up from the road-way. Below, to my left, a Rescue Squad was silently getting into the escape shaft of a basement shelter, climbing one by one into the earth, as it might be into the lower chamber of a tomb. On my right, the steam, which had bothered us as we climbed, was still belching out. There must have been a gas main alight beneath the debris for whitish yellow flames were coming out, as I could now see five yards away round a great corner, in darker blue, of sculptured coping stone, curved in an arc up which this yard-high maple leaf of flame came flaring, veined in violet, then died, then flared again.

In the quiet, I could not believe. The guns had given up firing. There were no aeroplanes. Another few moments drowned in smoke and then I could make out, forward, a concentration of torches in an archway five foot above where I stood, in what might have been a door when the ruins had been an office build-ing, and figures that moved, but were too flat, too indistinct to seem real. I was wringing wet with sweat. At that minute there was absolute silence. I struggled closer. Broken gas pipes caught at my rubber boots, wires at my helmet, jagged spars of wood lunged at my flanks, and, at my lungs writhed briars of smoke. I heard a man steadily coughing. Then I could see the top of him. He was sitting in that archway, in battledress I thought, a mug between his hands, and coughing, coughing. In everything but sound it was too vague. He seemed, by the light of the torch on his belt, to be sitting on a taut sheet of steam.

The number one took it into his head I had a message from the pump. He wanted to know about the water, why it still had not come. We both had a fit of coughing. When he could, he told me the Rescue people had a man in under there, pointing to where the smoke was a rising wall. I was sure the individual sitting on his sheet, still coughing hopelessly, on and on, while every now and then he retched, was someone who had been brought out. Then he spoke. With difficulty he said they would have to have oxygen breathing apparatus, that it was too thick without. I realised that he must be the leader. Again he began to cough. My number one went back to order on the oxygen. Taking his place, I came up to another member of our crew. He told me, between his spasms, that this man was trapped at the bottom of a small jagged hole at our feet, and that before the Rescue Squad had been driven out, they had just been able to see him.

There was a shout of 'water' behind, the hose kicked once or twice and then jumped tight, the jet sprang out solid, white. The leader got up. He stood. His legs were still hidden but I could now see they were in steam which was drawn in by the draught of the doorway, steam running compactly like a swollen brook. He said, 'not too near or you'll drown him, he's just below you there, play it over here against this wall, the fire's creeping along from behind. Come on, he's alive.' We played the water where he said and then were blotted out immediately in more than night, a forgetting, a death of black, the thick smoke, it let no air in, of a fire smacked out below, but which, we knew, would be up again if we did not almost flood it. 'By Christ, you'll drown him,' he shouted. But we judged, at the depth that man must be lying, that we should get more steam and smoke than he would get water. Now everything became too real in our fight for breath, too solid in the heavy river pressing without

[87]

weight, in the enemy that seeks out to weaken, to dam life out from the source.

When we had had enough we raised the nozzle. We played our jet farther away. In under a minute we were breathing air, a little more and the leader was visible again, attended by three others. Smoke is in a hurry to get away, all we had to contend with now was steam, the smoke was whirling off that wreckage and coming back above our heads, we were clear. He asked us to keep our water still farther off while he got down to find out if he could still hear the man below. It was plain he did not think that he would get an answer. He got into the hole and the smoke. He disappeared, it was deeper than I had thought. His companions crowded round, shining their torches down on the rising well of smoke and steam. He called out, incongruously, 'Can you hear me, Mr Jonas?' We waited.

'He's all right,' he called back to us, 'but we've got to be quick.' The others climbed half way down. The torches made it seem as though these men were fighting, half drowned, against a source of water, the smoke came up so solid there.

They began handing back single pieces of wreckage to others by me whom I had not seen come up, bits of wood, slats, part of a chair. They talked about where to shine their torches. They were all coughing again. They worked in silence for some time. Then the leader said, 'here, here.' Then he said, 'careful now, up here.' Then he said 'towards that light.' Another man said 'a bit to the left, take it easy,' and I saw a bald head, then khaki shoulders. He was not coughing. He was getting up alone. Then I saw he was smothered in dust. He was bone dry. It was Mr Jonas. As he came up and out, almost without assistance, we all began talking to him, telling him where to tread. He said absolutely nothing. He climbed right into that archway and disappeared. Coughing, the Rescue men climbed out. They thanked us. There were no more victims below. They also went out through the arch by which we could hear, but not see, others getting Mr Jonas off. Then we were alone.

Then the firing began again overhead. And then we settled down to the next four hours we reckoned it would take us to put the fire out, or, if not to extinguish it, to leave the job in such a state that it would not break out before we could be relieved. But in spite of anything we could do it spread. In half an hour the deep corner, out of which they had got this man, was a mass of flames. By morning forty pumps were on the job. After twelve hours we were relieved, at half-past nine in the morning. When the other crew took over we had fought our way back to exactly the same spot above that hole out of which, unassisted once he had been released, out of unreality into something temporarily worse, apparently unhurt, but now in all probability suffering from shock, had risen, to live again whoever he might be, this Mr Jonas.

APOLOGIA

(Published in No. 4 Folios of New Writing, 1941)

No discussion of the best, that is the magnificent in written English, is complete without reference to a master of the language, the genius Doughty.

In 1888 C. M. Doughty published *Arabia Deserta*, the story in 250,000 words of his travels alone in that country. In an introduction, dated 1921, T. E. Lawrence writes: 'I have studied it for ten years, and have grown to consider it a book not like other books, but something particular, a bible of its kind.' He goes on to praise the knowledge shown, the distances covered, and the courage with which Doughty met his difficulties. As the greatest expert on the country, Lawrence continues: 'When his trial of two years was over he carried away in his note-book (so far as the art of writing can express the art of living) the soul of the desert. . . .' And towards the end of the introduction he adds: 'It begins powerfully, written in a style which has apparently neither father nor son, so closely wrought, so tense, so just in word and phrase, that it demands a hard reader. It seems not to have been written easily, but in a few of its pages you learn more of the Arabs than in all that others have written, and the further you go the closer the style seems to cling to the subject, and the more natural it becomes to your taste.'

Part of the object in quoting Lawrence is to place the way he put his sentences together in direct contrast to this, the opening passage of *Arabia Deserta*:

A voice hailed me of an old friend when, first returned from the Peninsula, I paced again in that long street of Damascus which is called Straight; and suddenly taking me wondering by the hand, 'Tell me (said he), since thou art here again in the peace and assurance of Ullah, and whilst we walk, as in the former years, toward the new blossoming orchards, full of the sweet spring as the garden of God, what moved thee, or how couldst thou take such journeys into the fanatic Arabia?'

On the five hundred and thirty-ninth page, two paragraphs before the end, we read:

When the sun was going down from the mid-afternoon height, we set forward: a merry townsman of Mecca, without any fanaticism, and his son, came riding along with us. 'Rejoice,' said my travelling companions, 'for from the next brow we will show thee Jidda.' – I beheld then the white sea indeed gleaming far under the sun, and tall ships riding and minarets of the town! – My companions looked that I should make jubilee.

This at the end of one of the great journeys and great escapes of history. He has no word of relief or even of farewell. His last line simply reads:

On the morrow I was called to the open hospitality of the British Consulate.

In considering Doughty's writing, it is necessary to examine his circumstances. He started with no more than two large saddlebags, in one of which was a little money and a stock of medicines which he sold. He went into the heart of a country in which it was held a merit to kill Christians for their faith and fair sport to murder any traveller, whatever his religion, for loot. He set out with no other protection than a revolver and to the last retained a fixed determination, amounting to mania, never to say the few words, no more than 'There is no God but Allah,' that would have spared him from this people's fanaticism. His money he spent, or had stolen from him, before he turned homewards, and while he was yet some weeks away from the safety of the coast, he was destitute, being offered work as a herdsman.

'"Abide with me, Khalil, till the Haj come and return again, next Spring." "How might I live those many months? is there food in the khala?" "You may keep my camels." "But how under the flaming sun, in the long summer season?" "When it is hot thou canst sit in my booth, and drink leban; and I will give thee a wife." Hearing his words, I rejoiced, that the Arab no longer looked upon me as some rich stranger amongst them!'

A man's style is like the clothes he wears, an expression of his personality. But what a man is, also makes the way he writes, as the choice of a shirt goes to make up his appearance which is, essentially, a side of his character. There are fashions in under-wear, for the most part unconscious in that we are not particu-larly aware of how we dress. It is possible to date almost any paragraph within fifty years by the use and juxtaposition of words in it. The more mannered the way of life, as in the eigh-teenth century, the harder it is to break through the convention to the man beneath. But with Doughty the man's integrity is such that he writes on his own, if the dates were not available it would be hard to say when. What might be held affectation, his pleasure that he was no longer taken for a rich stranger amongst them, is found to be the expression of a great need he had to get away unnoticed, for, unlike almost any traveller, he had no love for those whose company he chose, so far from the habitation of those others whom, sitting before their coal fires in the month of June, although he never says so, he liked no better, this monu-mentally lonely man.

After twelve months, half starved, he gets to Hayil, the strong-hold of the Prince Ibn Rashid. No professing Christian had ever reached it, he was the first. Inside the castle building he finds the Emir 'lying half along upon his elbow, with leaning cushions under him, by his firepit side, where a fire of the desert bushes was burning before him'. After a while the prince desires him to read from a book: '"Where shall I read?" "Begin anywhere at a chapter, – there!" and he pointed with his finger. So I read the place, "The king (such an one) slew all his brethren and kindred." It was Sheytan that I had lighted upon such a bloody text; the Emir was visibly moved! and, with the quick feeling of the Arabs, he knew that I regarded him as a murderous man.' At a later interview when, as he says, 'full of mortal weariness, I kept silence', Ibn Rashid was offended, he 'spoke to me with the light impatient gestures of Arabs not too well pleased, and who play the first parts, – a sudden shooting of the brows, and that shallow extending of the head from the neck, which are of the bird-like inhabitants of nomadic Nejd, and whilst at their every inept word's end they expect thy answer'.

Here is none of that adulation with which lesser travellers seek to enhance the extraordinary in a visit to the ruler of the country they have reached. But, with words that exactly describe the awkwardness and the scoundrel in this presence, he gives us a living account of a call on a savage. This use of words is even better illustrated by his version of how he explained telegraphy to the Prince:

'It is a trepidation – therewith we may make certain signs – engendered in the corrosion of metals, by strong medicines like vinegar.' Emir: 'Then it is an operation of medicine, canst thou not declare it?' – 'If we may suppose a man laid head and heels between Hayil and Stambul, of such stature that he touched them both; if one burned his feet at Hayil, should he not feel it at the instant in his head, which is at Stambul?'

In as miraculous a way Doughty puts words together which, entering by our ears if they are read out loud, or slipping by our eyes if they are scanned in print, express their meaning in our bones. And this is not so much by conscious art as by the constraint of his adventure, and is thus created by the character this adventure, this finding of himself, built up in him, who, as a sort of second thought, was the composer of great prose.

At first sight Doughty's style seems to be habit. But in his preface to the third edition, in 1921, he says of Arabia:

We have some evidence, that it was peopled by men even from the beginning of the world, in paleolithic flints chipped to an edge by human hands; which have been found in the flint gravel, at Maan, in Edom.

The fall in rhythm of the last sentence he would never have attempted in *Arabia Deserta*. Thus, more than thirty-three years later, he had not lost the idiom of his genius. In this fragment of a hundred words he has added to it.

Much may have been due to his study of Arabic. But there is little in the writings of others who knew the language to suggest this. T. E. Lawrence, Gertrude Bell and Wilfrid Blunt have an elegance that is too easy but which has in it some notes of that noble phrasing of which we catch echoes in almost any translation from *The Arabian Nights*, even if it be in eighteenth-century French. We shall not know until we have learned the language. But this much is certain, that Doughty had read deep in the Bible. At the same time he might be writing in Latin. Also, when he passes on a tale, he treats it as a man will granite that he has to fashion.

There was an holy man who passed the days of his mortality in adoration; so that he forgate to eat. Then the Lord commanded; and the neighbour ants ascending upon his dreaming flesh, continually cast their grains into the saint's mouth and fostered him.

He has no elegance, that is, no ease with which to treat of a universal theme. When he mentions women, which he does but seldom, it is with little more than the same reverence and wonder with which he will treat camels.

She went freshly clad; and her beauty could not be hid by the lurid face clout: yet in these her flowering years of womanhood she remained unwedded! The thin-witted young Annezy men of the North, who sat all day in their skeykh's beyt, fetched a long breath as oft as she appeared – as it were a dream of their religion – in our sight; and plucking my mantle he would say, 'Sawest thou the like ere now!' This sheykhess, when she heard their wonted ohs! and ahs! cast upon them her flagrant great eyes, and smiled without any disdain. – She being in stature as a goddess, yet would there no Beduwy match with her (an Heteymia) in the way of honourable marriage.

Of camels:

The bereaved dam wanders, lowing softly, and smelling for her calf; and as she mourns, you shall see her deer-like pupils, say the Arabs, standing full of tears.

It is impossible, in a short notice, to give sufficient examples of the richness of his prose, its variety, the way he rings the changes, or to dispel a suspicion that his style may have been habit, as with George Moore it did so become in later years.

There are many who read less for the story than for the mind and feelings of the being who created the book they have chosen. It is not hard to break through Doughty's convention to the character of the man beneath, indeed his style is so perfectly the expression of his personality that he stands out as though in the harsh sunlight he describes. When Lawrence was out there he found that Doughty was remembered. Writing too easily, he says:

> They tell tales of him, making something of a legend of the tall and impressive figure, very wise and gentle, who came to them like a herald of the outside world. . . . He was very patient, generous and pitiful, to be accepted into their confidence without doubt.

The question is, why did Doughty ever go to Arabia, in other words, what founded the style, the great edifice of prose which is his mausoleum?

He was an untrained archaeologist. One of the merits of his book is that he finds almost nothing, certainly nothing of any value if we except, perhaps, the stone at Medain Salih. There are no petty discoveries in his travels, no *objets trouvés*. The answer must be that he had such a quality in him that he had to get away. And once he was well into the country he could not get out. The last part of his tale, and the most absorbing, is one long recital, between the lines, of growing exhaustion.

'I am slain with weariness and hunger,' he writes to a friend Kenneyny when stranded at Aneyza, that town outside which, half dead from fatigue at the journey, he had 'heard then a silver descant of some little bird, that flitting over the desert bushes warbled a musical note which ascended on the gamut! and this so sweetly, that I could not have dreamed the like'. Earlier he had praised 'the high sweet air of the Nefud', but he was soon too tired, even by his long halt in the fever-ridden Kheybar. It was in that place that he was befriended by Amm Mohammed en-Nejūmy, of them all the one Arab he respected.

Amm Mohammed – endowed with extraordinary eyesight – was more than any in this country, a hunter. Sometimes, when he felt himself enfeebled by this winter's (famine) diet of bare millet, he would sally, soon after the cold midnight, in his bare shirt carrying but his matchlock, and his sandals with him: and he was far off, upon some high place in the Harra, by the day dawning, from whence he might see over the wide vulcanic country.

Surely Doughty, impatient at the perennial hypocrisy in England, did in his fashion as that Arabian did, and in so doing built himself a prose all writers must venerate. He is harsh, simple to a point of majesty, and not clear, that is his sentences meander. After living many years with the book a suspicion is borne that it was intended to be read aloud. If this is so then it is a fault, for Doughty had so much more than eloquence. There is in it what Henry James has called 'The effort really to see and really to represent, [which] is no idle business in face of the constant force that makes for muddlement.' For this reason he makes no heroes of his Arabs, indeed he treats of them as treacherous, fanatical, and light headed. Yet they and their country made him, because they satisfied a need he had, and the combination made this the great book he gave us.

His style is mannered but he is too great a man to be hidden beneath it. It does not seem possible that future generations will be able to date one of his paragraphs, he seems so alone. His style is constant throughout, seems to be habitual, but, on analysis of this last, is found to vary with his subject. He is often obscure. He is always magnificent.

A question is asked us by his work. Now that we are at war, is not the advantage for writers, and for those who read them, that they will be forced, by the need they have to fight, to go out into territories, it may well be at home, which they would never otherwise have visited, and that they will be forced, by way of their own selves, towards a style which, by the impact of a life strange to them and by their honest acceptance of this, will be pure as Doughty's was, so that they will reach each one his own style that shall be his monument?

Then, if they do learn to write in the idiom of the time, as Doughty without doubt wrote in the idiom of the real Arabia, and not of Araby, can we at last have the silence of those Sunday reviewers to whom, of his generation, we can almost certainly lay the charge that he was not reprinted for thirty years, and from whom, in our own generation, we resent the patronage they extend to us in phrases which, like those sung from the minaret on the last page of the *Seven Pillars of Wisdom*, have, from constant repetition, only a limited meaning even to those so deaf as to be able to hear, and none at all to those who, on reading the words, sigh recognition of the old trick it was on the part of Lawrence to close his book in that fashion, remembering how there is not one such in all Arabia Deserta?

THE LULL

(*Published in* New Writing and Daylight, *Summer 1943*)

I

There was a bar in this fire station. On the bar was a case of beer. A fireman was taking bottles from this case, placing the full bottles onto shelves. He was alone.

Another came in. This one was minus his tunic. He wore a check shirt. The barman began to take him off, without looking up from what he was doing.

'You – you – you fool,' the barman said. The way he spoke you would have thought one or the other stuttered.

'Ten Woodbines, thank you.'

'Ten,' the barman said.

A bell in the cash register. Then silence. These two men stood in silence.

'Cigarette?'

'No, not just yet, thanks all the same, Gerald. I don't smoke such a lot these days.'

'Not like you used to, eh?'

What lay behind this last remark was that Gerald, the man in the check shirt, was echoing an opinion widely held in the station, that this barman often put his sticky fingers, which were of the same length, into the till. But it was said without malice. The barman let it pass. He knew the personnel expected to be robbed, within reason. He lifted another full case onto the bar. After a pause, he said: 'They don't get any lighter. Is there anything on tonight?'

He asked this pleasantly, to get his own back. He was referring to the fact that Gerald, because he did odd jobs carpentering for the officer in charge, was excused the tactical exercises held every evening to keep the men out of bed.

'Not that I know of,' the other replied. His tone of voice was to show, elaborately, that he did not care.

'We want another blitz,' remarked the barman.

'We do,' he was answered.

Neither of these firemen stuttered.

'I saw old Sambo today.'

The other did not make a move.

'Why d'you wear that bloody shirt?' the first man went on. He kept his eyes on the bottles he arranged. 'Has your Mrs got such a number that she can't put your dusters to the proper use? Because we could do with one or two at 'ome. Yes,' he broke off, 'I seen Sam.'

'That fellow with a squint.'

'That's right. Sam Race.'

A short silence.

'You know the last time I seen him?' the barman went on.

'On a working party?' This was a reference to the fact that, because he pleaded he had to check his stock, the barman was excused fatigues.

'On a working party! No! Along Burdett Road the night of that bad blitz.'

'Really?'

'I've not seen 'im since the night Willy Tennant got down under the pump, when old Ted Fowler moved up one. It was surprising it didn't break his leg.'

'The wheel went right over?' the man in the shirt asked, as though enquiring whether the blackbird had got the worm.

'You're telling me. I was there. Yes, from that day until this morning I didn't set eyes on Sam. That's a strange thing, come to look at it.'

They stood, in silence again, leaning each side of the bar. They pondered at the linoleum which covered the counter.

'Sure you couldn't do with a drink?' the barman asked at last.

'Quite sure, thanks.'

At this a third fireman came in.

'Well brother?'

That is to say the barman and the third fireman were both members of the Fire Brigades Union.

[99]

'I'll 'ave one of them small light ales, Joe, please. Will you try one?'

'No, thanks all the same. Been out on short leave?' He called it 'leaf'.

'Yes, I 'ad a drop of short.'

A bell in the cash register.

'I was just tellin' Gerald,' the first man went on, 'I seen Sam Race as I was on me way round to the brewer's this morning.'

'Wally Race you mean, Joe.'

'No, Wally Race is the brother.'

'Wally Race 'as no brother,' the third man stuck to his guns. 'What'll you bet me, Gus?'

'Wally Race 'as no brother. 'E's lived at 'ome ever since I can remember. With 'is mother and 'er old man. No, he's an only child, Wally Race is.'

'Come on, Gus, what'll you bet?'

'I wouldn't want to take your money, Joe.'

'What if you do, that's my business! It's my money, ain't it? Come on now, just for a lark, how much?'

'What, on three fourteen and six a week?'

'Some of you chaps just won't 'ave a go. Forgotten what it's like I suppose.'

The barman pretended disgust. He lifted two empty cases down. He began to polish glasses when Gerald, in his check shirt, turned all at once, and hurried out of the room.

'What's 'e making now?' the third man asked.

'Bedside table. Bloody marvellous the work he turns out. You can't see 'is joins, only with a magnifying glass.'

'Yes. The Boy Marvel.'

Silence yet again. Then a fourth man entered.

'Quite busy, thank you, this evenin',' the barman remarked in greeting. He meant it. 'Bloody awful quiet it is in behind this bar sometimes. What can I do for you, brother?'

'Wallop,' the fourth man demanded.

'Now then, Ted, you know there ain't none. We can do you light ale, in quarts or 'alf pints, ditto brown ale, or a nice bottle of Guinness.'

'What, at eightpence 'alfpenny. Not likely.'

They looked at each other, amiably.

'What's become of the Bar Committee?' the fourth man enquired.

'What's become of it?' the barman Joe echoed. 'It's still in existence.'

'Then it's time it 'eld another meeting.'

'These small lights aren't bad, Ted,' the third man said.

'I don't want none o' that. I like it all right, but those lights don't like me. Too gassy.'

'All right then, mate, but make up your mind.' Having said this, the barman began to polish glasses again.

''Ow much a week, now, is this job you've got behind that bar worth to you?' the fourth man went on.

The barman ignored it. Instead he remarked: 'I seen Sam Race this morning.'

'Well, I think I'll risk a brown, Joe. Out of the large bottle.'

'Pronto. Yes, 'e looked very queer, did old Sambo.'

'Sam who?'

'Sam Race. Why you must remember him, Ted.'

'Wally Race you mean.'

'No, Sam.'

'What station?'

''E's moved,' the barman replied, nonplussed for the instant. 'I disremember where exactly,' he went on rather lamely. This attracted the third man's attention, who asked: 'What station was 'e at?'

The barman had pulled himself together. He knew what to say to this.

'Where d'you think, Gus? Up Goldington Road, at 4U of course, with Matty Franks.' He was improvising.

'With 'oo?' the fourth man objected.

'Old Matty Franks,' the barman answered irritably.

A bell in the cash register. A pause.

'Never 'eard of 'im,' the fourth man announced. 'Good 'ealth,' he said.

'God bless,' the third fireman replied.

'Never heard of Matty Franks?' the barman went on. 'The

rottenest old bastard in the Service. Up Goldington Road just past the Ploughshare?'

The two men looked at the barman, ruminating. The fourth man was about to object he was not acquainted with a pub of that name up that road when they all heard a sad cry of 'Come and get it,' from below, from the messroom.

'Already?' the fourth man asked aloud. He gulped his down. He left.

The third fireman finished his half pint, and went.

The moment he was alone the barman poured himself out a light from one of the quart bottles.

A bell did not ring in the cash register. Joe had his drinks on the house, when no one was looking.

Silence. He let a lonely belch. He pondered the linoleum which covered the counter.

After five minutes, a kitchen orderly for the day brought the barman up his supper.

'Fred,' the barman said, 'it's getting very slow in this bloody dump.'

'You're telling me,' Fred replied.

'I've 'ad Gus and Ted on about Sam Race.'

'Oo?'

'Sam Race.'

'I don't seem to recollect a Sam Race, Joe.'

'No, nor there ain't never been. There's only the one Wally Race, who squints something 'orrible. Yet they wouldn't 'ave a bet on it. Not one o' them. What a game eh?'

'You've said it,' Fred replied, uninterested. He went out.

The barman began to eat his supper.

2

Another evening. The same bar. Five or six firemen sat around. Two were without a drink. A fifth man held the floor.

'Yes,' he said, 'a great big woman, my aunt was, twenty-two stone she weighed. And a real wicked old lady. My dad wouldn't allow us kids to have nothing to do with 'er. I'll tell you what she did once. It was a Sunday morning, on the way to church.'

'On the way to church?' another fireman asked.

'Yes, yes mate, that sort are churchgoers, very often. I'll never forget. Just as she came up on a sheep she put her umbrella right into it. "Err," she said, "you horrid thing." Went right in, the point did.'

No one accepted this. He realised it. He had to go on.

'Terrible she was. Used to kill cats for the enjoyment. She was well hated. D'you know the manner she used to despatch 'em. By strangilation.'

'Strangled them, eh?' another asked.

'Yes, mate. She put a cord round the neck with a slip knot. Then she'd pass the end through the keyhole. She took the key out first of course. Then she'd take a turn round her body with the free end. To finish up she just leaned on that door. With all her weight it didn't take more'n a minute.'

'How d'you mean, a turn round 'er body?'

'Well, she'd entice the cat in first, see. After that she'd put a slip knot round its neck,' and this fifth fireman went on into an involved description of the method favoured by his aunt. No one was wiser at the end. In the pause which followed two of the others started a quiet argument between each other as to the performance of a particular towing vehicle.

The fifth man began his last attempt.

'She was hated, real hated she was in the country thereabouts,' he told them. 'My dad always said she'd come unstuck at the finish. And so she did. It was remarkable the way it come about.'

'What was that then, Charley?' someone asked, from politeness.

'The way she died, mate. It was to do with a duck for her supper. Eighty-six years old she was. She couldn't manage to wring this duck's neck. So she got out the old chopper, held the bird down on the block and plonk, the 'ead was gone. Well, this head, it can't 'ave fallen in the basket. When she bent down to pick up the 'ead, she let the carcass fall. And it fell right side up, right side up that bloody carcass fell, on its bloody feet and all. And did it run! Well she must 'ave taken fright. She must 'ave started runnin', with the duck 'ard after. She run out into the garden. The blood from the stump left a trail behind. It followed

[103]

'er every turn, that decapitated duck did. Until in the finish she fell down. Dead as mutton she was. 'Eart failure. She'd took a fright. But credit it or not, that duck landed on her arse as she lay there, stretched out. That's where my first cousin, the nephew, came on 'em both. Cold as a stone, she was, already.'

'Damn that for a bloody tale, Charley.'

'You don't believe me, ah? Well, I tell you, it's the bloody truth. It's the nerves or something. You'll see the same with chickens that's had their heads cut off. If it's done sudden they'll run around.'

'Not that distance.'

'I'm sayin' to you, this 'appened just like I told you, Joe. All right, disbelieve me then.'

A game of darts was suggested. All joined in.

3

But it was noticeable that, whenever a stranger came into the bar, these firemen, who had not been on a blitz for eighteen months, would start talking back to what they had seen of the attack on London in 1940. They were seeking to justify the waiting life they lived at present, without fires.

A stranger did not have to join in, his presence alone was enough to stimulate them who felt they no longer had their lives now that they were living again, if life in a fire station can be called living.

These men were passing through a period which may be compared with the experience of changing fast trains. A traveller on the crowded platform cannot be said to command his destiny, who stands, agape, waiting for the next express. It is signalled, he knows that it will be packed, it is down the line. The unseen approach keeps him, as it were, suspended, that is no more than breathing, but more than ready to describe the way he has arrived to a man he does not know, waiting in the same disquiet, at his shoulder.

4

It was an evening session in this bar. They had all had a few beers. The stranger, posted to this station for the night because it was short of riders, stayed bored, expressionless, without a hope of comfort. They were sitting back against the walls, in a rectangle. A silence fell. Then the sixth man began. He asked: 'Joe, remember the night we were called to Jacob's Place?'

'I'll likely never forget that, mate.'

'Nor me.'

Silence. But everyone listened.

'What was that, then?' a seventh man enquired.

'They called us on to Number five Jacob's Place,' he began again, consciously dramatic.

'Number seventeen, Alfred,' the barman said.

'You may be right at that,' the sixth man answered, unwilling to argue because he wanted to get on with his story. 'It's of no consequence,' he added, already beginning to be put out, 'the point is some geezer in the street tells us there's a job in the roof, so of course Joe here an' me gets crackin'. The rest of the crew set in to a hydrant, while the two of us run upstairs with the stirrup pump in case we can put it out easy. It turns out to be one of them houses where there's just a caretaker, like, an' all the furniture is covered with sheets be'ind locked doors. Ghostly. You know the kind, a smashing place, but 'aunted. There must've been fifteen or sixteen rooms. Well there's a lot of cold smoke choking us on the top floor, but we find the old trap-door to the roof all right. It was quite a pleasure to get out in the air again, it certainly was, wasn't it, Joe?'

'It was that,' Joe said back.

'We begin taking a few tiles off,' he went on, 'and we find a place where it's a bit 'ot, but we still 'aven't come on the seat of the fire, we're rummagin' about, like, on top of that bloody roof when all of a sudden there's a bloody blubbering noise up in the sky over'ead, yes, like a dog bloody 'owling in a bass voice, and coming down out of the moon though we couldn't see nothink. Was I scared. I thinks to meself it's another bloody secret weapon. I called out to you, didn't I mate?'

'You may 'ave done Alf. I was too busy tryin' to get down out of it.'

'Yes, we had a bit of a scramble. Joe 'ere was nearest, so he goes down first. Well, there was no point in that "after you" stunt, was there? Yes, and as I was coming last down through the trap-door, I looks up, and I sees what had put the wind up me to such an extent. Know what it was?'

Everyone in the room, bar the stranger, could have told him. They had heard this story often. And the stranger was not interested.

Alfred answered himself.

'A bloody barrage balloon,' he said. 'The shrapnel had got at it. The blubbering noise is occasioned by the fabric rubbin' together as it comes down, or the gas escapin' out of the envelope, one or the other. I couldn't rightly say. But it didn't half put the wind up me.'

'And me,' said Joe.

Silence fell again. Each man drank sparingly of his beer. Knowing the story had not been a success because it had been told before, Alfred tried to get some response from the stranger.

'What station are you from?' he asked.

This man awoke with a start from a doze of misery. He replied obliquely, saying: 'I'm a C O you know.'

'A conchie? Well, why not,' Alfred generously said.

'I've never been out on a job,' the stranger answered. 'And I don't know if I should put out fires,' he went on, desperate, 'I don't rightly know if I ought.'

A heavier silence followed.

5

Hyde Park on Sunday. It was hot. A fireman in mufti and a young girl were, of an afternoon, by that part of the Serpentine in which fishing is allowed. They had put themselves back from dazzling water, on deck chairs.

A girl of eighteen went slowly by, dressed in pink, a careful inexpensive outfit, one of thousands off a hook. From her deck chair the other said, rapid and sly: 'La petite marquise Osine est toute belle.'

He had been admiring the calves and tender ankles that girl dragged through thin, olive-green grass. He laughed. He was caught out. He turned to his companion.

'Henry,' she went on, bilingual, speaking only a little less fast, 'surely you remember?'

He was sleepy. He shook his head. She recited, quick and low:

'Oui, certes, il est doux,
Le roman d'un premier amant. L'âme s'essaie,
C'est un jeune coureur à la première haie.
C'est si mignard qu'on croit à peine que c'est mal.
Quelque chose d'étonnamment matutinal.'

He said, 'Yes.' He did not turn away again. He admired her nose, which had caught his eye, as it always did.

'Verlaine?' he asked.

She wondered what he was looking at so particularly about her.

'D'you think my hair's too long?'

'No, I don't,' he replied, 'it's lovely. That was Verlaine wasn't it?'

She thought, of course he's the one who likes my nose.

'You know you're the worst-read man I've ever met.'

'Worse than Archie Small?'

'No, not quite. I like Archie because he's not read anything at all. That's probably why he dances so well.'

What lay behind the remark was that this man Henry could not dance. Before he had time to take it up she began again, lying back in the chair, looking at him with half-closed eyes, almost in a sing-song,

'Ses cheveux, noirs tas sauvage où
Scintille un barbare bijou,
La font reine et la font fantoche.'

She was worried about whether her hair was right.

'Ah,' he said. He stretched. She was wearing an olive-green bow of velvet in it.

She shut her eyes, gated them with eyelashes. It was very hot. After a pause she went on, thinking of his youngest sister, her friend.

> 'La femme pense à quelque ancienne compagne,
> Laquelle a tout, voiture et maison de campagne,
> Tandis que les enfants, leurs poings dans leurs yeux clos,
> Ronflant sur leur assiette, imitent des sanglots.'

'Me, with you, I suppose,' he remarked. 'Go on,' he said. He shut his eyes. 'I'm enjoying this.'

She wondered that he could see himself as a child with her, when he was old enough to be her father.

Both were sleepy from a good lunch. After a while she added slowly, in a low voice:

> 'Bien que parfois nous sentions
> Battre nos coeurs sous nos mantes
> A des pensers clandestins,
> En nous sachant les amantes
> Futures des libertins.'

'Henry,' she said, when there had been another silence. 'You don't know where that comes from, do you?'

He did not open his eyes. 'Verlaine,' he said. He was smiling.

'Yes,' she answered, and shut her eyes. 'It's called "La chanson des Ingénues".

> Nous sommes les Ingénues
> Aux bandeaux plats, à l'oeil bleu,
> Qui vivons, presque inconnues,
> Dans les romans qu'on lit peu.'

'How sweet,' he said, rather dry. At that moment the syrens sounded. Everyone looked up. It was cloudlessly bare and blue.

'Goodness,' she remarked, without conviction and not moving. 'How worried Mummy will be about me.' They sat on. They did not close their eyes again. It was awkward.

Then he suggested they might go to a film, saying it was waste to spend a leave day in the Park. She jumped at it. They hurried off, arm in arm, to the USA.

6

The ninth fireman said: 'A 'ornet? No, I can't recollect that I ever met with a 'ornet. But crows now. I remember the first time I seen a crow, to really notice, like. Yus. I was out on the allotment. On the previous leave day I'd put me beansticks in just lovely. But this mornin' when I comes to see how the beans was shapin' there's not a bloody beanstick stood in the bloody soil. They was by far too 'eavy for 'em. I couldn't make it out at first. But just as I'm bendin' to 'ave a look, there's a bloody great bloody black think that comes swoop at me out of the sky. I thought it was the blitz all over again for a minute. So then I puts me 'ands up and 'as a peep. There was seven of the buggers in the oak tree there at the bottom, where the road goes along by our allotments. An' can't they 'alf 'oller. Kraa, kraa. A chap come with a gun and killed three. Bloody great things they was. The rest never came back. No, we never seen them no more.'

7

Two firemen were walking back to the station from the factory in which they made shell caps for the two hours during which they were allowed short leave, every second day.

The tenth man said to the eleventh: 'I'm browned off Wal, completely.'

The eleventh answered: 'You're not the only one.'

'Wal, d'you think there'll ever be another blitz?'

'Well, mate, if he doesn't put one on soon we shall all be crackers.'

'You're telling me.'

'And they are going insane, in every station, every day. Have you heard about the patrol man over at 18Y?'

'What was that, Wal?'

'Well it seems that the officer in charge finds something to take him out of his office, and as he comes out he sees no one on guard on the gate. So he looks around, and still he can't spot the patrol man. Till something tells him to look up. And there is the chap that should have been on the gate, sitting across the peak of the roof, hauling on a long line (120 feet of rope) he has between his hands. So he calls to 'im, sarcastic, "'Ow are you gettin' on up there?" And this is the answer he gets: "I've saved five."'

'No.'

'It's as true as I'm here. So this officer in charge he climbs as far as he can get inside the building, till he comes to a window across from where his patrol man is sitting. He's one of those fat bastards, and he's a bit out of breath with the climb, you understand. He doesn't know what to make of it. So he calls out: "You've saved five, 'ave you?"

'"Yessir. And I'm about done up."

'"'Ang on there, then, and I'll be with yer," the officer in charge sings out to him.

'"You can't," is the answer he gets. "I'm surrounded." Surrounded by fire he meant. In the finish they had to call out the turntable ladders to bring him down. To anyone not acquainted with this job it seems hardly possible, do it?'

'They'll be bringing the plain van any day for me,' the tenth man replied. They walked on, silent.

The passers-by despised them in this uniform that, two years ago, was good in any pub for a drink from a stranger.

THE OLD LADY

(Unpublished, 1943)

This story was shown only to John Lehmann, who did not like it. Some of the images in this story recur in *Caught*, published in 1943.

I had been reading *The Arabian Nights* at the fire station. At the turn of a peg in his side, no, with no more than a cut with a golden chain over the neck this marvellous black horse would rise to take his rider into the skies. His manger was filled with well-winnowed sesame and barley, his trough held fresh water perfumed with roses. As I read these words I heard two heavy explosions close by. It is hard sometimes, as hard as it is easy in the Tales on my lap, to tell between friend and enemy, between the old lady who brings trouble and the one who is to lead the storyteller to unimaginable delights, between high explosive and the concussion of a heavy gun. On this occasion it was impossible to mistake the way we were shaken in our shelter, as though, by incurring displeasure, we had been changed to walnuts from Damascus rattled in an iron box.

A fireman remarked ironically that the bombs must have been two of ours.

Three minutes later we had the call. As inevitably as any young man is wafted away from delights to trials which he is able, later, to recount between sobs in those fables, I was carried not long after, in charge of a pump and tender, as near as we could get to where the bombs had fallen.

I found we were next a statue which stands in the centre of a London square. Two great streets came in ahead, they converged so that we could see up both, and were like twin approaches to the Sultan's palace. As though at the word of an angered ifrit a gas main had been set alight up each street, one hundred and twenty yards away. The two forty-foot high flames were out of sight up side turnings, but on the face of ornate, tall blocks at the corners, we could pick out details of brickwork and stone facings more easily, in colours more natural, than would have been likely through full spring daylight.

Now, against a livid light, an incandescence of white hot lemon, this old pitch-black warhorse stood, his bronze rider up, both, as always, facing south to Mecca.

I knew the officer in charge. His orders were that, for the time being, my crew was to be in reserve. We stood aside by a surface shelter, waiting.

Then we helped another crew lay out a line of hose to one of these fires. As we came along over small debris, which lay like a vast slumped-down load of coal, I could see wreckage burning up the side street, black hacked-out house fronts flickering above mounds of broken wood and stone, all of which looked much as usual except that the damage was on a larger scale, and also, because of the lighted gas main, easier to seize, that is to apprehend. But, most deadly, the glare was wide enough to attract more bombers, as though summoned, such was the expanse of light, by a secret word to which they answered, the 'creatures of King Nasr'.

Having laid out the hose there was no more we could do. We went back to stand by the surface shelter, among the pumps. One after the other they were started up. They made a shattering, roaring noise. And there we waited.

Having nothing to do was awkward. We had time to feel afraid. The row was too great to hear them, but there must have been a couple overhead. Two groups of searchlights moved steadily along two invisible paths converging at a point above, towards the glare of the gas mains. The guns near were not firing.

A good shot will take a phoenix always at the same angle. I had come to know the point at which I must expect a bomb from a plane, the fatal angle, within about ten degrees. The minute or so the bomber takes to cover that distance is unpleasant, and it was worse this night because the pumps were so close that I knew I should not be able to hear the tearing silk in time to take shelter comfortably. It would have looked silly to lie flat before anything had come down. To go into the shelter would have been cowardly. So we stood it out, and waited.

All of a sudden there was a tremendous burst of fire, every battery kept it up, the venom was almost inspiring, the belch hate, and I looked up and I saw three jewels that swayed down, white diamonds that barely dropped, offerings brilliant but aloof, perfect (pink rocketing shell bursts all about), three drops of a necklet on the cloth of velvet, three more than gems the ifrit in a roll of drums was letting a breeze carry us, three that now outshone Zubeidah's eyes, three 'whose fires eclipsed noon in the springs at Shereef', three stars the djinn had plucked down from heaven, three flares.

This was more than unpleasant and I went in to the surface shelter. As I did so I made an excuse that I wanted to see how many firemen were already hiding. The place seemed to shake, the one light to flicker with the concussion, as that great building had with flame. And in the near corner a girl stood between a soldier's legs. He had been kissing her mouth, which was now a blotch of red. He held on to her hips and had leant his head back and closed his eyes. They were motionless, forgotten, and as though they had forgot. They were alone.

I went out, abashed. Also I resented their being inside. I saw one of our officers I knew. I went up. Cupping my hands to his ear I shouted 'Have you looked in there?' An expression of distaste came over his flat face because he thought I was telling on some fireman who was too frightened to stay outside. But he went in. He stayed longer than I had. When he came out he had a soft, serious look on him. He cupped his hands to my ear. He shouted 'More power to his elbow, mate, more power to it.' He might have come from seeing the Princess Fatimah and the poet Murrakish.

He moved away. The police brought past a looter, two of them holding this man spreadeagled, his clothes mostly torn off him. He might have been the Tripe Cleaner, he who has no name in *The Arabian Nights*.

I moved a few paces to the left. A man was dying in his blood by the corner of the statue, attended by two more policemen.

Alarmed, I remembered and looked up. The flares were gone, the firing was less, perhaps they had been shot out.

Then, alone, carrying a music case, holding a handkerchief to her mouth, an old lady came by, walking past everything, never looking up. She went straight on until she was out of sight.

And then the soldier came out. He proved to be drunk. He shouted in my ear, 'Would you boys like to have a whip round to raise me a shilling to have another go?' I pushed him away and to comfort myself began to repeat the story which, in the French edition, begins 'It was holiday time in Damascus'. It is the story of King Nasr's beautiful daughters. In the guise of doves they fly to a pool where, taking off their feathers as three women might discard their clothes, they bathe naked before the eyes of Janshah who ruled over the Banu Shahlan and was King of Afghanistan.

THE WATERS OF
NANTERRE

(Published in Horizon *No. 60, 1944. From the* Souvenirs, *published 1834, of Madame de Créquy (1710–1800) to her grandson Tancrède Raoul de Créquy, Prince de Montlaur. Translated from the French by Henry Green.)*

Green translated two passages from this particular work, seven volumes of which can be found in the library at Forthampton Court; the other passage was used in *Back*, the novel in progress at that time.

Madame de Marsan, Princess of Lorraine, with whom I often went on little pilgrimages, proposed that we should take the waters at Nanterre, at her patron saint's well. So we set out one day in the gilded coach, part of the time saying paternosters and the rest of it amusing ourselves with what was before us. Because, so she said, you must not wipe the lip of the cup which is chained to the parapet and which you have to drink from; and above all you must not leave a drop although it holds at least half a pint. I cried out at this but the good Princess underlined the duty we owed not to scandalise simple people and in the end I agreed to do as she asked.

I must tell you that the water in question is a sovereign remedy for the eyes, from which neither of us suffered. But when we got within sight of the place we found it surrounded by so many peasants and farm people that we could not get near. As a result we left the coach and with a charming modesty stood away to one side.

We then saw, guess who, coming up to make their devotions? No less a person than Madame du Deffand, who was a rabid atheist, and for whom the Chevalier de Pont-de-Vesle, assisted by several servants, was forcing a way through. She was practically blind at that time, as was also her companion, and because of this the water, for them, was not merely a precaution as it was for us. But we had the satisfaction of watching them drink a full cup each. We did not flatter ourselves that these two old people, who had lived together in sin for years, would boast afterwards to their agnostic friends of what they had done, but we determined to say nothing of it ourselves. The last thing in the world we wished was to promote a story which might encourage jokes about such a subject.

It was at this moment that Madame de Marsan's servants, who were wearing the livery of Lorraine and of Jerusalem, became highly indignant at our humility. They suddenly discovered that they were shocked to see Madame du Deffand precede us. The Princess's first coachman suggested that a way should be made for us through the rabble. We replied that we had no house work nor anything to do in the vineyards as had all these good people crowding round the well, and we ordered him and those under him to let us be.

This very much upset the servants, so much so that at one moment I almost thought they were going to disobey the Princess, their mistress. And this is where I must tell you about Madame de Marsan's first coachman.

The fact is the man wholly disliked me, dating from the time some years previously when coming to me for a place, he had refused to join my household.

'Who was your last employer?' I asked him, naturally enough at this disastrous interview.

'Madame, I was with the Abbot Duke de Biron, but he has gone to meet his Maker.'

'If that man ever got before the Eternal Father he didn't stay there long,' I could not help remarking half under my breath. This seemed to annoy the coachman. He told me he was of gentle birth, as were most of the Duke's servants. I replied that there was nothing beneath him in wearing the Créquy livery, and suggested he should go upstairs to settle his wages with my secretary.

'But, Madame,' he said, 'before engaging myself in your service I must know whom you give way to.'

'To everyone! I give way to everyone except in the streets and the courtyards at Versailles.'

'But surely Madame, you would never expect your first coachman to give way in Paris to the wives of Cabinet Ministers?'

'Certainly. And all the more so because I dine every Thursday in the district where these people live.'

'But really Madame is never going to give way to the wife of a Chancellor of the Exchequer? Why, if one of his servants had anything to say I'd sort him out with my whip.'

'Oh, well, those people usually know whose livery it is they have to deal with, but in any case I do not for a moment intend to knock passers-by over or endanger my carriage just to keep up a position vis-à-vis the middle classes, nor even to injure my horses.'

'It's quite right that Madame has only twelve carriage horses in her stables, and besides I am not accustomed to make way except before the Royal Princes. As a result I'm afraid I shall not give you satisfaction, Madame,' and he went off perfectly furious. Madame de Marsan had taken him on, and it was he who was now urging the coachmen to revolt, saying that we were dishonouring them. What particularly exasperated him it seemed was that de Pont-de-Vesle's servants had taken up a position in front; and, so he said with scorn, the gentleman was only a bourgeois.

Monsieur Girard was the name this proud coachman went by, and it is worth noting that thirty years later, at the time of the Revolution it was Citizen Girard, the same man, then known as one of the most enthusiastic revolutionaries as well as one of their best speakers, who was finally guillotined by his friends for being an Orleanist, or Federalist, I forget which.

While he sat there, growing old without knowing it for a glorious destiny, and while he egged our servants on to disobey us as he held the reins high above the seven-windowed golden coach, we managed to make our way at last up to the well, and there I drank my draught of the water in peace of mind and in submission. Then we went to render thanks in the parish church in which lie the relics of the Saint for, as you will have guessed, this was the real object of our little pilgrimage. Accordingly we

[117]

made our way to the church on foot with, on my part, that sentiment of confidence and tenderness which all my life I have felt for the Patroness of Paris.

But when we tried to get in, the church was so full to overflowing that we sent for the sacristans to ask if we might not be allowed to take our places in the private chapel where the relics are.

'No one is permitted to enter the chapel any more. We have been forbidden to let ladies from the Royal Court go anywhere near the relics. You must surely know that Madame de Créquy last year stole a piece of the True Cross.'

'Madame de Créquy, you say?'

'And no other. She stole a piece of the True Cross from off the altar.'

I burst out laughing while Madame de Marsan was asking how they knew it had been me.

'There was no mistaking her, Madame,' they replied. 'She came in her carriage with six horses, her servants were wearing the yellow livery with red braid; two other servants from Paris were in the church, and they told us who it was. She was at least twice the size of either of you ladies.'

'You see if I'm not right,' Madame de Marsan said to me in a low voice. 'It will be Madame the Marshal de Noailles, she is always doing it.' This was the more likely in that the liveries of our two houses were the same.

Of course Madame de Noailles was insane, and certain steps had to be taken not long after to restrain her, steps in which your old grandmother took a prominent part. Nevertheless that was the end of our little pilgrimage. But while I am on the subject I must tell you one last story of mistaken identity.

On a Sunday evening in Paris I was outside the church of Saint-Sulpice waiting for one of the attendants whom my servants had gone to fetch to open the chapel for me, and conduct me through the crowd. There I was sitting in my carriage when a young priest came to the door. He was very thin and very pale, and his hands were so dirty and he was in such rags that I could almost have taken him for a beggar. He held a piece of paper, which he gave me, and which said he was from the late Duchess of Orleans, wife of the Regent. He went on to speak of the admirable way she had died, according to the rites of the Church. He used such unpleasant expressions that I had no difficulty in recognising that he was one of that hateful sect of Jansenists which had got hold of the Duchess as she lay dying.

This piece of paper, he said, contained a legacy from the Duchess, which he then qualified as an act of conscience on her death bed. It was no more and no less than a recipe for making red cabbage soup. Take two handfuls of Reinette apples, it said, an onion stuffed with cloves, and two glasses of red wine to each average-sized red cabbage. 'I wanted to send you this as I had so often promised to do,' the Duchess had written in her own hand on the other side, 'and I do so now as a mark of my full and sincere reconciliation with the Faith.'

As I was reading this the sacristan was waiting for me to leave the carriage, and my servants were ready to escort me with my cassock, the bag with my prayer books, and the cushions which were emblazoned with my arms, but no more extravagantly than was the custom at that time. All this upset the young priest, who began to call on me to show a more Christian humility and to flee Satan, on account of my velvet bag with gold thread embroidery. 'Vain sinner, learn the way of God,' he wound up.

'Father,' I said, 'first things first. Now who do you think I am?' (For I had read the recipe.) 'Who do you think, tell me? First of all I am not Madame de Mouchy, and I would advise you another time to take greater care when you deliver the last wishes of the dying. Here it is back so that you can give it to Madame de Mouchy, who is exceedingly greedy. Also I shall never forget what a dying woman's conscience pricked her to do under your ministrations, because I am very fond of red cabbage, Father, and have always wanted this recipe.'

At this moment Françoise de Chauvelin, a distant cousin of mine, came up.

'Good heavens,' she said, 'what on earth are you doing talking with my idiot of a nephew?'

'Watch your step as you go into the House of God,' he cried out, most unpleasantly. Then he turned to the servant who was carrying Madame de Chauvelin's bag and her train. 'Don't you tremble at what you are about to do in the Presence of God?' he shouted, and he struck the train out of the man's hands with one blow of his fist. It fell in the dust on the church steps.

'The madman,' she said. 'Does he want me to drag my dress through all this filth so that I'll get as dirty as he is?'

'Now then, now then,' her servants said to him, very indignant at the way he had spoken to their mistress. Particularly the first coachman, who went on, red with fury, 'if it wasn't that I'd be excommunicated, seeing that you're in holy orders, I'd break every bone in your body for speaking to Madame as you've just done.'

You should know, because you are too young to remember, that Madame de Mouchy was Marguerite-Eugénie de Laval, a lady in waiting to the Regent's daughter, the Duchess de Berry. It was not so extraordinary, therefore, that the Berry's mother should think of her at the last, even if only for a recipe, although it could not, at such a moment, speak to the credit of Madame de Chauvelin's nephew. But how he could ever mistake me for a Laval passes all understanding.

THE GREAT I EYE

(Unpublished)

There is no evidence to suggest that 'The Great I Eye' was ever submitted for publication. Clearly dated 1947, the manuscript survives in longhand, and was found carefully preserved amongst other papers. The characters in this story have little in common with those in the novel *Concluding*, written concurrently, but resemble more closely those in *Nothing* and *Doting*.

He lay in full dress on the unmade bed.

The stomach he had begun to have began to hide his knees, the waistcoat through an open jacket swelled to blot out his thighs on which black hairs were laid by tweed.

Head on two pink pillows let his two halcyon eyeballs rest comfortable along his length, to let the potbelly obscure his legs, but the pupils, lenses like a pushbutton always pressed, rang chimes and changes in the brain, allowed his mind to pierce the clothes, to count what he owned in the pockets and see his nakedness.

A stuffed owl regarded him from out a dome of glass.

His wife entered with a cup of tea. She placed it smack on a bedside table next the telephone. She seemed to take care not to look at him.

He called her darling. In reply she said he had been too drunk last night, and waited, eyes averted. He said he knew. She went out. Careful of his head he then leant down and switched his telephone on. Now let the bad news come, he thought.

He thought there was never an excuse, for drink or anything. And one's body that did not forgive. Always the same. The feeling it couldn't go on like it; misery, anxiety, death death death.

When drunk the trouble one caused spread ripples, several dry

[121]

walnuts thrown at the same time into a water tank hung with green ferns; and where the ripples met, leering faces of his green friends mirrored in the base over and over again in the repeated olympic bracelets; linked arms for false amity, a symbol of old games.

And now it rang. A voice he knew asked for his wife. When he answered she said it was Elvira and how did he feel, then laughed. He laughed in turn, enquired whether he had been dreadful the last night. Elvira explained she felt terrible herself and wanted to know how much she had done?

He realised, with relief once more, that people think only of themselves, that anyone who gets ashamed is a fool because his folly must be a thin man no one notices; the fellow guests ignore him in their preoccupation with themselves except when insult or embarrassment is offered. This time he could remember little, or rather, because he remembered visually, he could picture almost nothing of last night, he was almost sure he had behaved, had not affronted anyone. So that when Elvira went on about Maud, he wondered how Maud had interfered with Elvira.

She said Maud (who, as a girl of seventeen in 'Seventeen got engaged to a boy afterwards killed in that war and who had continued faithful to the memory since then, right through the next war, not long concluded, of nineteen thirty-nine) had been seen to languish under the protracted gaze of Harold Arthur, even to lay her face on his; and had he remarked, Elvira demanded, that they left early as a couple, in that way marooning Esther whom Harold had squired to the party? He said he did not think Esther could have minded. But while Elvira went on at him on the line he invented the picture of Maud with this fellow because he could not remember.

He built up a cartoon of the party last night, he imagined he had come upon Maud, and Harold with her stood before the seated man, the fingers of one hand thrust into his tight collar, her palm to Harold's throat, the heel of the hand holding up his chin while Arthur murmured down his nose to the blood pumped through her wrist. And, apart from this couple, in the other corner which he himself did not dare regard, a naked woman lay humped on a sofa, the nudity in wait.

Meantime, and he was able to listen through his daydream, Elvira continued, these two had left early, so early dear, no one had seen them go, they seemed to have melted off into air. Upon which he saw himself sitting in Harold's shoes, looking at Maud's wrist where it came out from under his chin with one bar of wrinkled age there already across her loosening bone-stretched flesh, and his embarrassment as he murmured to it, 'darling, oh darling, go.' Becaus˃ he acutely imagined himself conscious of the naked woman he knew was over to the right, with a camel's hump of thighs.

This time he remained quiet to Elvira's flow so that she broke sharply into her account to ask where his wife could be. He replied he could not tell, he was in bad odour. And so he should, she said at once, quite right. She laughed, but did not add she wished to speak to Angelica because she wanted to celebrate, to praise what was for Maud a unique departure, to mark with soft, wondering approval this first sign that Maud might be in the way to forget as all her friends had prayed she should; nor, of course, did she explain the attitude she had adopted towards Maud in this talk with Angelica's hungover husband, hero Jim on his bed, although it gave her guilt to be so disloyal about a friend. The fact was, Elvira knew it well, she could not now be fair to a woman in a discussion with a man.

Faintness swept over him as Jim lay, he shut eyelids and became, in the sun, a man in a world of thick pink through which white spots were quickly rising, his palm sweating on the receiver. Would she not speak to him then, Elvira enquired, and went on that he must tell his wife he was truly sorry. From out of sickness, the chill over his forehead now broken into sweat, he chose to misunderstand. He replied he wished Maud well and was not on those terms with her in any case. At the other end the voice nagged at him, called him a chump, believed that he had not followed a word of what she was saying. Did he feel very bad, then, Elvira asked?

Upon which he pictured himself at the party again, still in the chair, but this time it was his own girl Jane who had both strong hands either side of his neck round the trembling jawbone. He could even feel her ring on his left cheek. And he was staring into her speechless eyes to promise without a word that he could not even glance at the nudity over on the right which, if he once looked he knew he would find to be his wife Angelica, to his dread.

Did he feel really bad after all, Elvira asked? She had better ring later perhaps, she said, then wished him goodbye, rang off. He fumbled the receiver back on the stand without opening his lids and fell into a doze, the shut eyes in the head communing with Jane's eyes, and no word said.

He snored. The telephone rang to bring him out of a dream which he forgot at once, although he knew it had been as horrible as he now found the dryness of his mouth. His tongue rattled like a box of matches against the palate. 'Let it ring,' he said to himself. 'She'll answer.' He scraped at the tongue with a forefinger. But still the bell went on, double tugging till he could have yelled. 'She must've gone out,' he said of his wife, and the dread was renewed until he lifted the receiver to answer into immediate silence.

A voice he recognised asked for Angelica, said it was Mary speaking. He explained as unnecessarily this was Jim, and that Angelica must have run out. What was he doing home, then, she enquired? Truant player he replied. He thought, 'Isn't Mary the best friend of Harold Arthur's wife, poor Florence?' But he said aloud he only dodged the office once in a blue moon. She said there had been a man writing in the paper to announce he had seen three blue moons in six months. He did not reply. She asked if he wasn't ill. He found this unfriendly, wanted to know why he should be. Her direct answer was to tell him she had rung his wife because she was so worried about Florence. What was it this time, he asked? She said there was nothing in particular, hummed and hawed a bit. When he did not press this woman he got the story. It appeared that Harold Arthur had been receiving presents. Well, there might be nothing to it, her voice went on, but they had been so expensive. He visualised a shaving set in solid gold in its violet silk upholstered case. At first, Mary explained, Florence had been worried because she thought it was Harold's extravagance again, tickets for the Big Fight, two twenty-guinea ones. And now it was almost worse, did he know,

[124]

she asked? Because they could not possibly afford what the man had been getting. Why not, he asked? Because they could never hope to cope on such a scale; Florence and Harold couldn't, Flo was half out of her mind. Such as, he wanted to be told. Various things, she answered, and oh, just recently, she could not say, she couldn't be sure it was the last, they'd been simply raining, but a pair of ivory-backed hairbrushes with what must, only no one could read them, be his initials on the back, in diamante. 'Yes of course,' Jim said to himself. 'Bedroom stuff.' And visualised more clearly that wide, luxurious shop window with the latest watchmaker's masterpiece of a razor to work off any current, dry, to skim his tongue as it was at present; the facial; a tongue reviver maybe?

As his custom was he now began a scene in his head, vivid and sharp, the imagination louder than this Mary's uninterrupted flow of talk. He saw himself up, the front door ringing, and, when he had opened it, a postman who wanted him to sign for the registered package. 'Why does a man have to sign for his wife?' he asked because he thought it must be something Angelica had had repaired. 'There's a deal we have to do without we know the reason,' the man replied. Back in the house he saw the parcel was for him. Then Angelica came up to ask questions. Accordingly she was present as he undid the string, parted brown paper, raised the lid off a box to find bedded in tulle a pair of pink rubber false breasts so hinged together at one lip as to form a soap holder, or a tiny sponge bag, with pink tapes to close the mouth. 'A hoax,' he cried aloud. 'And no note?' Angelica demanded. 'Not a sausage,' he said. 'Then that's the beginning of the end,' she laughed. 'If you don't throw them away Jane might use those. You drink too much,' she said.

Too much and too soon, he suggested to Mary down the line to keep her occupied. She answered, tart, it could hardly be too little and too late. He wanted to be told why not, went on to say he could do with a few things of the kind himself. After all, he pointed out, Harold Arthur could always pawn them. At which he immediately saw himself with his own imaginary present in front of a pawnbroker who, even to the eyebrows, was billiard bald.

'Little bit of something here I'd like to hock,' he was saying to the man. (He expected to get 4/6.) 'Bit unusual naturally, sentimental of course. Value to me, that is.' 'Why, yes sir.' And did one sell or lease to pawnbrokers. One didn't know, one couldn't tell. Meantime there was Mary.

At which there was a click from somewhere in the house below. He said at once would Mary excuse him just a moment dear, but it was, he felt sure, their burglar: upon which he left the instrument, wallowed to his door on the stairs, and listened. Nothing. Then came a long ring at the front bell. He rushed the stairs, yelling in his head 'a copper's seen the basement window forced.' He saw no one. But, when he got the door open, there, much as he had imagined, was a postman with a registered package. 'Of course it's for Angelica,' he thought, and did not bother with the label while his name was mumbled at him. He signed, parted with his own pencil without a word, dropped the parcel where they laid their letters, and hurried back to Mary.

Was she still there, he asked? Should she dial 999 she said, at the same minute? He reassured the woman, a false alarm he explained, just a registered box from Angelica's jewellers. But if it was what he had seemed to think would she have had to dial for him, Mary demanded, and how terrible to have to listen to all the fight through her receiver. Yet she'd have had to hang up to get the police number, he pointed out. She agreed she'd not thought of that. But then, she went on, perhaps a good burglar was what poor Harold Arthur needed, to spare his embarrassment in simply cleaning him out. If the man did not take all Flo's things, he objected, to leave them both with only Harold's adulterous presents. How awful, she agreed. They laughed. To tell sweet Angelica she had rung, Mary sighed, and his line went dead.

He went down to the mass of letters, unopened because he never looked and mixed with folded daily papers for he did not read these, nor did his wife Angelica except casually once about each three days; he went down at a grave pace as there had been something about that package. He looked. It was indeed addressed in his name. He broke off string and brown paper. Then because it was for him he hid these wrappings behind their electric fire, oval, pink in a black, square grate. He was left with the cardboard box which had once held a well-advertised brand of silk stockings. He opened it in disbelief. He found a notecase of alligator hide: no note, no nothing. But he always kept his cash loose in a breast pocket for fear of sticky-fingered gentry. He was much embarrassed. His initials, he saw, were on the thing in gold.

In spite of all, he realised, the present must be for him. So he hastened to his bedroom, hid it away well at the back of some used ties writhed into a knot like adders in the dark midden of discarded clothes. Then went cold himself. The exertion on top of his stomach. He lay down again, was careful how he placed his head. Cold sweat. He wondered if he could bring it all up. And slept.

FIFTIES AND SIXTIES

With *Nothing* published in 1950 and *Doting* published in 1952, Green turned his attentions to drama, reviewing, and broadcasting for the BBC. He continued to manage Pontifex, which had enjoyed a post-war boom but which was now in decline, making twice-monthly visits to the Birmingham and Leeds factories, until his retirement in 1958. After 1960 he seldom left the house.

HENRY GREEN

(*Published in New York* Herald Tribune,
Book Review, *8 October 1950*)

I was born in 1905 in a large house by the banks of the river
Severn, in England, and within the sound of the bells from the
Abbey Church at Tewkesbury. We lived at ease and because in
those days there were plenty of fish in the river I spent much of
my time with a rod and line. Children in my circumstances are
sent away to boarding school. I went at six and three quarters
and did not stop till I was twenty-two, by which time I was at
Oxford, but the holidays were all fishing. And then there was
billiards. My father played this game to win, and until I got good
enough to beat him I minded losing.

I was sent at twelve and a half to Eton and almost at once
became what was then called an 'aesthete', that is a boy who
consciously dressed to shock. I stayed that way at Oxford, where
the athletes reacted violently against my clothes. By that time I
was playing billiards for the University so that when the howling
mobs came round to throw me in the river I was able to warn
them not to hurt my hands or we might lose the next match,
and this invariably saved me.

From Oxford I went into the family business, a medium-sized
engineering works in the Midlands, with its own iron and brass
foundries and machine shops. After working through from the
bottom I eventually came to the top where for the time being I
remain, married, living in London, with one son who is almost
seventeen. I no longer play billiards because I haven't time and
my fishing is just my fourteen days holiday a year when I help
my son catch fish, already much better at it than his father ever
had been.

I write at night and at weekends. I relax with drink and conversation. In the war I was a PFC fireman in London, the relaxation in fire stations was more drink and conversation. And so I hope to go on till I die, rather sooner now than later. There is no more to say.

EDWARD GARNETT

(*Published in* New Statesman, *30 December 1950*)

Edward Garnett, about whom Mr H. E. Bates has written a short memoir, was a publisher's reader, that is to say, he read several novels in typescript every day for, I suppose, something over forty years. I only knew him towards the end of his life but always imagined this prodigiously boring task must have left its mark on his character and person.

He was not unlike his contemporary M.R. James, the finest writer of ghost stories ever, who became Provost of Eton and the first hagiologist of his time, and who also seemed to read all day and half the night. James smoked a pipe, he had seven in a rack, one for Monday, another for Tuesday and so on; Garnett always a herb cigarette which poisoned the room. When James came to stay he had, he was so fond of them, to be provided with a cat; Garnett, so far as I can remember, never gave a second glance at any animal, yet James looked like a huge blue Persian, and Garnett was really rather a bedraggled St Bernard but with a cat-like wit. James had such a contempt for day-to-day affairs that he tossed all incoming mail unopened into a large trunk; Garnett was the reverse, he wrote endless letters encouraging young men to write – young men, not girls – but he also had complete contempt for every publisher, reviewer, or member of the public who bought or borrowed novels, in the world.

Here we must leave James, who was a magnificent man, and concentrate on Garnett, who was a wizard. You met Garnett like this. You submitted a first novel, out of the blue, to the publisher of your choice after, in my case, my parents, knowing John Buchan, had sent it to this writer who replied, probably rightly, that Henry would never make an author; then you waited in some agony for weeks, until at last you got a letter inviting you to call on his reader, a Mr Edward Garnett in Pond Place, Chelsea, London.

You went at the time appointed and rang the bell. There were, I think, three steps up to his door. In those days he did not take his own stairs quickly, so that he kept you waiting. When he did open, he had that accursed Bloomsbury disability of not being able to greet you, nor, when you left, to say goodbye. You were just confronted by a huge old man, his buttons undone all over the place, who stared you down with pale eyes behind deep spectacles and whose white hair was combed over his forehead in a fringe – a pale-faced, menacing, wordless object, immeasurably tall.

You had arrived with an idea that 'they' were determined to make you rewrite your book (indeed 'they' still sometimes do), and you had made up your mind that you were incorruptible because you were twenty and you believed. It was with a sinking feeling you told him who you were. In my case all he said was just 'Come in.' And when he toiled over the stairs to his first floor, I began to dread.

There was worse to follow. When we got to a landing he paused by a photograph framed on a dingy wall. He paused by it and asked with great malice 'What do you think of this?' The subject was, I think, a bas-relief of Leda and the Swan, treated with what I remember as great indecency. It was the second time only that he had spoken. Completely broken down now and ready to run, I answered with the phrase then current, 'Oh, very amusing!' At which he snorted disapproval and I all but fled.

Once seated in his chair, however, and having put the rug over his knees, it was all different. He began with the most delicious praise. He had not only read your work, the stuttering work, but he had seen in it more, far more, than in your dreams you had dared to claim. Better still he had an intense curiosity about you, which is perhaps of even greater importance to young writers. His line was 'How did you come to write anything so good?' That your first book, which was all he had seen, was inferior and poor, proved his particular genius. Like a St Bernard he could smell out the half-frozen body which, if encouraged, might yet be able to wrestle with words. The bottle of brandy hung round his neck was flattery, and at the next meeting with him it was blame. Afterwards he bullied you with a mixture of blame–flattery, nearly always to your good.

He had, I think, the defect of his generation, that with writers young enough to be his grandchildren, he made mistakes about the characters of their own age of whom they wrote. He would insist that this or that girl in the typescript was wrong. There must be several men of my generation who regret the revisions in character drawing which he imposed on us. But what he did know how to do, and yet – why is this? – could not do himself, was to write dialogue and narrative. In that field he was supreme.

He would take out a blue pencil and he would never go through more than one page. The words he struck out were magically unexpected; the result, when one had time to ponder it, was alchemy. He had a unique genius to show what could be done, and that, with his exquisite taste, became an inspiration which still, I am sure, remains with many of us now. He used to say the finest realisation of moonlight in prose that could be found was in Chekhov, the reflection in broken glass bottles cemented to the top of a park wall.

For about forty years he had a hand, and a very powerful hand, in most of the best that was written in England. A most retiring man, he spread his influence far and wide. And he was able to do this, as far as I could see, not only because he was almost always right and the publishers recognised it, but above all because, after his distinguished wife and son, the great love of his life was the craft.

A NOVELIST TO HIS
READERS: I

(Broadcast by the BBC. Published in The Listener, *November 1950)*

Anyone who reads out aloud an essay at home in front of the fire or here, as I am, in a sort of tomb, cannot fail to underline certain words by an emphasis in his voice or by a pause or even a laugh. This I believe to be wrong, especially all reading aloud from a novel, that is to say from narrative. But I mean to deal here with the unspoken communication between novelist and reader in narrative and not about that which may exist between a speaker and his audience, or even between husband and wife, in life.

When infants we learn to speak by listening. Later on we learn to read by looking and listening. We then have to make a conscious act of imagination, whereby we associate the collection of symbols, that is, the collections of letters which go to make up the various words, with the spoken words we have already heard; and by the time we have learned to read we have forgotten the now unconscious act of imagination that is still required. Although this is now in the background, in the sense that we do not have to whip up our imagination any longer to be able to read, it must be the purpose of the novelist to excite this imagination anew in his readers without the crippling aid of speech.

What is the further aim of the novelist? What is the painter going for? What is the sculptor trying to do? I say they are all meaning to create a life which is not. That is to say, a life which does not eat, procreate, or drink, but which can live in people who are alive.

Art is not representational in the sense that the painter, even if he thinks he is painting from nature, does not paint life-size and in any case he is doing his best on a flat surface. But the sculptor does work in three dimensions; his figures have a back and side to them as well as a front, yet they are still; they do not move. While some sculptors have done abstract designs that move to every draught in a room, called 'mobiles', except for the moving elephant to carry children on the front at Margate, I cannot now think of any other animal or human figure to which a sculptor has yet given motorised movement. Art therefore remains non-representational. But, if it exists to create life, of a kind, in the reader – as far as words are concerned, what is the best way in which this can be done? Of course, by dialogue. And why? Because we do not write letters any more, we ring up on the telephone instead. The communication between human beings has now come to be almost entirely conducted by conversation. Must plays be the medium, therefore, by which creative artists in words should communicate with their audience, if any? I say not. Because the artist then, unlike the painter or sculptor, is subject to the interpretation of an actor, who in turn is under orders from a producer. There are thus at least two men or women between the playwright and his audience. Not so with the novelist who, when he is printed, has the typesetter to put down his symbols exactly for him, so to communicate direct with the imagination of his readers.

If, then, you and I are agreed that dialogue is the best way for the novelist to communicate with his readers, this will be non-representational, that is to say it will not be an exact record of the way people talk. Conversation in life is at so many different levels, ranging from the intimate to the unfriendly. To give an example of what I mean, supposing a husband and wife live opposite a pub: at nine-thirty any evening when both are at home, he may say, 'I think I'll go over now.' She will probably answer, 'Oh,' and there may or may not be a wealth of meaning in that exclamation. And his reply to her will probably be, 'Yes.' After twenty years of married life any couple will talk in a kind of telegraphese of their own which is useless to the novelist. It would take too long for the novelist to explain. For if you want to create life the one way *not* to set about it is by explanation. No, it is in the various ways the same thing can be put that lies the power and wonder of dialogue, the glory of the language, your language and mine.

To get back to my illustration of the situation between husband and wife discussing going across to the pub, there are more than 138 ways she can say, 'Will you be long?' Here are some of them:

'Will you be away [or out] long?'
'Will [or shall] you be long gone?'
'Will [or shall] you be gone long?'
'How long will you be?'
'How long will it be before you are back?'
'Will you be back soon?'
'How soon will you be?'
'Back soon?'
'Off for long?'
'Are you going to be back soon?'
'Are you going to be long [or late]?'
'Are you going to be away long [or long away]?'
'Are you going to be gone long?'
'When will you be back?'
'What time [or hour] will you be back?'

And so on. There are almost endless variations on this theme.

It is a good thing that this should be so, for here we have one of the beauties of my language. In the examples I have given there are words to cover almost any shade of acquiescence or even bad temper, or both, or again of moods between the two. For there are reasons why we should use combinations of words with the widest possible range of meaning in dialogue. That is, dialogue should not be capable of only *one meaning*, or mood, as I shall now try to determine.

Art, as I hope we are agreed, is not representational. But novelists have taken to explaining what they think is going on in their dialogue. They will put down the wife's question and then write a paragraph in explanation, perhaps like this:

'How soon d'you suppose they'll chuck you out?'

Olga, as she asked her husband this question, wore the look of a wounded animal, her lips were curled back from her teeth in a grimace and the tone of voice she used betrayed all those years a woman can give by proxy to the sawdust, the mirrors and the stale smell of beer of public bars.

Writing in this sort of way the novelist speaks directly to his readers. The kind of action which dialogue is, is held up while the writer, who has no business with the story he is writing, intrudes like a Greek chorus to underline his meaning. It is as if husband and wife were alone in the living room, and a voice came out of a corner of the ceiling to tell them what both were like, or what the other felt. And do we know, in life, what other people are really like? I very much doubt it. We certainly do not know what other people are thinking and feeling. How then can the novelist be so sure?

The moment the novelist does tell his readers, he enters into a pact with his audience. He is telling a story as a casual acquaintance in the pub might. Whether the audience knows it or not it is in himself, the narrator, that he is trying to create interest by his comments. What he tries to do is to set himself up as a demi-god, a know-all. That life has been so created in novels, in the past, is not for me to argue for or against. All I say is, the time has now come for a change. For how do we, each one of us, find out anything in the lives we each lead? Very little by reading, still less by what we are told. We get experience, which is as much knowledge as we shall ever have, by watching the way people around us behave, *after* they have spoken. As to other people telling us about what they have found in life, about what others have told them, or even about what they have said themselves upon occasion, it may be personal prejudice, but whenever I can check up, I find they are only giving their own version of whatever it may be. Thence, I suppose, the old saying, 'There are two sides to every question.' Presumably the reason for this is that the moment anything happens which is worth while – you could say memorable – one goes over it verbally after, and because conversation comes into almost any experience, in going over it one adds favourable interpretations, favourable to oneself, which colour and falsify the account one gives. If the experience is particularly damning to oneself one can go to the other extreme, shame can make one exaggerate the unfavourable side. What *actually* may have happened probably lies somewhere, east or west, of what one is told of an experience.

In other words, we seldom learn directly; except in disaster, life is oblique in its impact on people. And if this is so, then how can the novelist communicate obliquely with his readers and yet retain their interest, let alone do for them what I regard as indispensable, namely to quicken their unconscious imagination into life while reading? Certainly not by reading out their work aloud, or having it spoken for them. That is to interpret a work of art, it is to give the speaker's interpretation, as if each member of the audience were so immature that he or she could not make his or her own interpretation, or were too lazy to try.

If then we are agreed that novels are for reading to oneself – and please remark by that I by no means imply reading *aloud* to oneself; no, reading is a kind of unspoken communion with print, a silent communion with the symbols which are printed to make up the words; if that is so, then how is the reader's imagination to be fired? For a long time I thought this was best lit by very carefully arranged passages of description. But if I have come to hold, as I do now, that we learn almost everything in life from what is done after a great deal of talk, then it follows that I am beginning to have my doubts about the uses of description. No; communication between the novelist and his reader will tend to be more and more by dialogue, until in a few years' time someone will think up something better.

But, then, it seems almost impossible to write entirely by unspoken dialogue – and that, naturally, is one of its fascinations – but what I should like to read and what I am trying to write now, is a novel with an absolute minimum of descriptive passages in it, or even of directions to the reader (that may be such as, 'She said angrily', etc.) and yet narrative consisting almost entirely of dialogue sufficiently alive to create life in the reader.

To create life in the reader, it will be necessary for the dialogue to mean different things to different readers at one and the same time. In discussing with a friend something which we both may have witnessed the other night, how often have we all of us said, 'Was she angry when she said "Oh" as he went over to the pub?'

And our friend may say categorically, 'No, not at all, she was glad to be rid of him for a bit.' At which we may disagree and say we think she was furious. In life only she knows how she felt, and we may be sure she will never really tell; people never do. It is only by an aggregate of words over a period followed by an action, that we obtain, in life, a glimmering of what is going on in someone, or even in ourselves.

The fascination in words is that by themselves they can mean almost anything; dictionaries get longer every day. It is the *context* in which they lie that *alone* gives them life. They should be used as painters use colour, to give tone. For it is the tone in dialogue which carries the meaning as, in life, it is what is left unsaid which gives us food for thought. How to communicate all this to the reader then? Let us return to the example of a man going over to the pub of an evening. If you agree that the telegraphese usual between husband and wife is too obscure – something like the example already given, 'Well, I think I will go over now', 'Oh?', she says, 'Yes,' he finishes – then how should it be put in narrative? How about this?

He: I think I'll go across the way now for a drink.
She: Will you be long?
He: Why don't you come too?
She: I don't think I will. Not tonight, I'm not sure, I may.
He: Well, which is it to be?
She: I needn't say now, need I? If I feel like it I'll come over later.

Notice that very often one question is answered by another, that the whole passage can be read in various ways, that the man is exasperated or bored, also that she is in one of several moods, *or even in three or more moods at the same time.* It is, of course, necessary to establish whether the man is a drunkard or not, but this is necessarily done by the action in the novel, in other words the man is previously shown to the reader drinking heavily, moderately, or hardly at all. – These three alternatives will colour that bit of dialogue quite sufficiently to bring it alive and, as already shown, there are enough different ways of saying 'Will you be long?' to cover any general inference required by the writer in the reader, while leaving enough latitude for the reader to bring the passage alive in himself. How then does this bit of dialogue come out in finished narrative? It cannot be left as it is; there must be some description of the movements made; the reader must at least be told who is speaking. Perhaps it would go something as follows:

At last he looked at the clock, laid the newspaper aside, and getting out of his armchair, wandered to the door. 'I think I'll go over the way now for a drink,' he said, his finger on the handle.

'Will you be long?' she asked, and put her book down. He seemed to hesitate.

'Why don't you come too?' he suggested.

'I don't think I will. Not tonight. I'm not sure. I may,' and she gave him a small smile.

'Well, which is it to be?' he insisted, and did not smile back.

'I needn't say now, need I? If I feel like it I'll come over later,' she replied, picking her book up again.

Note the 'seemed to hesitate'. If you have 'he hesitated', this seems like a stage direction, and is a too direct communication from the author. Where then have we got? I have tried to show that the purpose of the novelist is to create, in the mind of the reader, life which is *not*, and which is non-representational. This has nothing to do with the theme of his work. We are all individuals and each writer has something of his own to communicate. It is with communication that I have been dealing here. We have inherited the greatest orchestra, the English language, to conduct. The means are there; things are going on in life all the time around us. What I have tried to do here is to show one means of creating life by communication in the hopes that this may be of interest to the reading public, rather as if a mechanic were to open the door of his workshop.

A NOVELIST TO HIS
READERS: II

(Broadcast by the BBC. Published in The Listener, *March 1951)*

One day this winter I was on the upper deck of a bus, in London, held up by traffic lights at Hyde Park Corner which, because I was going east, is, as most Londoners know, bounded to my far side, and to the right, by St George's Hospital. Acoss the aisle, in front, there sat a middle-aged woman waving her handkerchief slightly behind and away from me, that is towards the hospital. At that moment, as she was again to do later, she gave up. She turned round upon her fellow-passengers, who, so far as I could judge, had paid no attention, and gave us all collectively a shy, warm smile. I did not let her catch my eye. She seemed to be encouraged by this lack of interest, for she then turned back, and once more began to wave. At this, I, in my turn, swivelled round to see if I could find what she was at. Up to a point, I did. By following the direction of this woman's eyes, I discovered another handkerchief within a dark window half way up the hospital wall – another handkerchief being waved in return. I gazed again. I was just able to make out a second lady, presumably propped up in bed, but so much higher than what I took to be the level of her floor that she almost seemed to float in space above her ward, a woman waving, in her turn, to what may have been her daughter, a relative, or just a friend.

What I have just told you is a good example of the sort of gift always being made to writers by people living their own lives round writers. Anyone with imagination should be able to make a lot out of it. I propose to give you later two complementary ways whereby this scene could be written up. But on the bus, at that moment, in the actual incident – in life that is – something further occurred. The bus was still held by the traffic lights, they stayed green for all the cars trying to get into Hyde Park from Victoria, the kerchief within its hospital window was still being agitated with a kind of sick, weary movement, minutes passed, and the lady inside our bus gave up a second time. She put her handkerchief down and again turned slowly round on the other passengers, but with what, on this occasion, seemed to me to be a guilty, please-excuse-me smile. It was obvious that she had had to wave too long. No one appeared to pay the slightest attention and I myself again took care not to show that I had seen. For, after glancing briefly over us, she gazed ahead, it seemed full into the red eye which had halted us. She had given over, she had had enough, one thought.

So I looked once more at that ward window and saw the other kerchief still being waved, not so vigorously, rather less now, it is true, and to the back of my lady's rather rigid head. Upon which, all at once, all was changed, our lights turned green! The waving became urgent two floors up, and, as we moved forward, I looked in front, the way we were going, and there was my lady waving back once more, but with violence now. Yet once we were past the lights she finally gave up. Nor did she ever look round on us again. Her face was reflected in the bus window. It was grim. And that was that. That is all there was to it, nothing more.

A trivial affair, you say? Perhaps, but I maintain, first, that this thing seen holds in it the essence of all communication between a writer and his readers, and, second, that his possible treatment of it, the way the writer describes this incident, as I have just done once, and will do twice more before I am finished, is, in itself, what may be the whole essence of how a reader can be brought by the description, by the treatment, to a deeper realisation of what is being described.

If this scene then may be a double 'gift', the first is, here was I, a novelist, seated on the top deck of a bus and handed a situation you might almost say 'on a plate' which was not only suggestive of a story in itself, but which also had in it the essence of all reading, that is to say of communication between two people without the spoken word. Before we can proceed to the second, we must pause here briefly to analyse the first gift. In a talk I broadcast some time ago on the subject of communication between a writer and his reader I made the point that words, out of their context, had no precise meaning; that it was the context in which he placed them that was the first deliberate act by the writer in communicating with his reader; and that the arrangement of the context of the words was to the writer what the tones of his colours are to the painter as he lays these down on a white canvas.

Similarly the point I am trying to make, here and now, is that where and how he places his characters in fiction is for the writer the context of his story. In other words, just as the composition of a painting gives it meaning, so the way in which the writer places his characters in the shifting scenes of his book will give the work significance. Now if it cannot be the purpose of the novelist to create in his books a life which isn't and which is non-representational, that is to say to create life in the reader which cannot eat, drink or procreate, but which can die; and if the arrangement of words and the 'placing' of his characters are the only means whereby he can do this, then the superimposing of one scene on another, or the telescoping of two scenes into one, are methods which the novelist is bound to adopt in order to obtain substance and depth. This may seem obscure at first, but at the end of this talk I am giving two examples of dialogue which will, I hope, make the point clear.

The difficulty before the novelist is to determine how much to describe directly to his readers, that is how much description to give which does not come out of the mouth of his characters. Now since conversation in these days is the principal means of communication between people in everyday life, I for one maintain that dialogue will be the mainstay of novels for quite a while. But obviously even in a script there must be stage directions, yet, as we are dealing here with narrative which is not on the stage and so is not subject to the disadvantage of the actor's or the producer's interpretation, the novelist has in unspoken dialogue at least to make plain who is speaking, and then so to order what he is putting down that, by evocation, by memory, by the mysterious things we all share, which is another set of words for the lone word 'life', he may create life in the mind of the reader.

And what, after all, is alive in a book? Surely something in which we, as readers, can all share. Though again, as in life, we must be able to share it in different ways, in opposites perhaps. Because we are all different. Thus we can all share the idea of a hospital. Yet it may mean death to some, healing to others; it must, I imagine, include to all the notion of pain and of the people inside not being able to get out, to leave, because they cannot walk; some may like nurses with their starched cuffs, others may be frightened of these angels; you may regard doctors as saviours or you may consider that they take the credit when, in spite of their treatment, your wonderful constitution pulled you through. All this and much more can be what the word 'hospital' means to any one of us. Yet, beyond everything, there is the sense we all have that anyone detained inside may be badly up against it.

It is this fact which begins to make the scene I witnessed significant. And it was to increase the significance that, on purpose, I did not describe how the two ladies looked. It is, of course, implicit in the scene, and one of the innate advantages of what I saw, that the figure inside the hospital could be too dimly observed to be seen. Nevertheless it is a lucky chance in a talk like this, not to have to give the age of these two ladies, as one would be forced to in a novel. If I have told the incident right, and I would prefer to be judged by the two examples I am just going to give, then each generation could claim this lady in the bus for their own, from teenagers to grannies. And yet again, to begin without dialogue, to start on a coloured description so often leads to an attempt to write down the shape of a nose, or those wonderful rosy lips, which, while almost impossible of accomplishment in any case, only leads back once more to the variations in individual reader's tastes. For how can one, as a novelist, cater for those estimable men who only admire girls with black hair and pale blue eyes? The answer is, of course, by not describing them.

I want to give you now the first of my two examples, a way of putting the scene I have already described, but in dialogue. If you have followed my argument you will appreciate that it was entirely against my principles, as these are at present, that I gave this example direct from me to you. No, I prefer the oblique approach which follows. Then in my final and second example, I hope to show you why the first is not good enough, and why one of the young men, in the coming dialogue, must telescope into the scene I witnessed on the bus a part of his own history.

Treating the scene in dialogue, therefore, it could go something like this:

'Look at that,' a young man said to his companion on top of the bus.

'What?'

'Waving out of the bus window!' the first youth exclaimed, it seemed in disgust.

'Well, why not, Peter? Or d'you mean she ought to be doing it up at us from the ground. As if we were riding in a liberation army?' He paused. 'No, I've seen people wave before from vehicles,' he ended.

They spoke together in low tones as men do in public transport.

'Traffic doesn't get any better, Harry,' the first young man said.

'We seem to have been stuck here for hours,' his companion agreed.

'Always like this at Hyde Park Corner. I say! D'you know who she's still waving at?'

'Who?'

'Why right up inside the hospital. There's somebody there signalling back. And now ours has stopped and is turning round. Pretty ghastly sort of smile she's got on too, Harry.'

'What's wrong with that, Peter?'

'I don't know. Wait, she's back at her waving again.'

'Well, why shouldn't she?' Harry demanded in what appeared to be a bored voice.

'D'you suppose they do this every day on the way to work, Harry?'

'Well, of course,' this young man said. 'They must have met

before, or how would they have found each other now?'

'Yes, I suppose she couldn't see into that hospital window without she knew who was inside. It's too dark,' Peter agreed. 'Now our one has stopped again. And the other is still waving.'

'I still don't see why not.'

'And ours is looking round again, look out, with a particularly ingratiating beastly sort of smile this time.'

'Well, I wish we could get on. I'm going to be late,' Harry complained. 'All clear,' his companion announced. 'Only our dame has given over waving and is keeping her eyes strictly to her front.'

'Can you see what's holding us, Peter?'

'Lights have stuck, I suppose. But the other one's still waving, getting a bit weak at the last though. Hullo, we're off. And now they're both at it, like mad. Now ours has stopped and we're past and it's over. Now, what d'you make of that, Harry?'

'That I'm going to be late,' this young man replied and then he added, 'Oh, she was only telling the other in here with us that she could go now.'

The treatment I have given you is flat to my mind – at the most it is two-dimensional. To make the scene, just described in dialogue, live, we must make it three-dimensional, that is to say, and avoiding the use of pompous words, I think the two young men who have been talking on the bus are dead from the neck down. So I propose in my second example to bring Peter to life by putting him in love and telescoping his story into the scene, that is, into the example already given. I have no time left to deal in kind with Harry, so I am going to bring him to life by means of an outrageous trick much used by short-story writers.

I shall do this in just three words, and, so that you can look out for them, these will be the last I shall use here.

This revised example therefore will go something like this:

'What were you going to tell me about you and Pam?' a young man called Harry asked his companion on top of a bus, halted by traffic lights at Hyde Park Corner, the top deck of which was crowded with men and women on the way to work.

'Oh, nothing really,' Peter answered.

'Come on, get it off your chest.'

'But look at that,' Peter said.

'What?'

'Why, Harry, waving like it, out of the bus window – our bus,' the second youth exclaimed, it might be in disgust.

'Well, why not, Peter? Or d'you mean she ought to be doing that up at us from ground level. As if we were riding in a liberation army? No, I've seen people wave before from vehicles,' he said. There was a pause. 'Tell me about Pam,' he insisted.

'As you know,' his companion at last explained, 'three days ago we had what practically amounted to a break. Well, you must admit, from all I've told you, she's almost impossible.' Peter was speaking in low tones, as men do in public transport. 'We were going to this party together tonight you see. And, of course, naturally when she said she never wanted to see me again, ever, I thought I might take someone else. So I asked someone.' He broke off here. 'I say,' he said in a new voice, 'd'you know that woman, in here with us, is still waving?'

'Well, it's a free country (isn't it?) and we seem to have been stuck in the same place for hours.'

'Always like this at Hyde Park Corner,' Peter countered. 'But d'you know who she's still waving at?'

'Who?'

'Why, right up inside the hospital; and there's somebody there signalling back. And now the one here with us has stopped and is turning round. Pretty ghastly sort of smile she's got on as well, Harry.'

'Go on about Pam, Peter.'

'And now she's back at her waving again. About Pam? Oh I don't know, it was really pretty awful. I say, d'you suppose these two do this every day, wave to each other from the bus and the hospital, I mean?'

'Well, of course,' Harry said. 'They must have met before or else how would they have found each other now?'

'Yes, I suppose she couldn't see into that hospital window without she knew who was inside. It's too dark,' Peter agreed. 'Now our woman has stopped, looks like she's had enough, but the other's still waving from within.'

'I still don't see why not. But tell me about Pam,' Harry demanded.

'And so I was giving Angela and her mother drinks on the Tuesday. They'd just dropped in. As a matter of fact, I'd asked Angela to go to the party with me on Wednesday instead of Pam after our row. Then Pam rang up. Can you imagine what she wanted to know, and in that loud voice of hers which rang out of the 'phone? Only what time I was going to call for her – Pam, mind you – for this party that I'd invited Angela to in her place.'

'Awkward, eh?' Harry seemed to sympathise.

'Now our lady's looking round on us again,' Peter announced. 'Look out! And with a particularly ingratiating beastly sort of smile this time.'

'Well I wish we could get on. I'm going to be late,' his companion grumbled. 'Can you see what's holding us, Peter?'

'Lights have stuck, I suppose. But the other one up in the old hospital's still waving. Angela heard every word Pam said over the 'phone, of course, and waved to me to say don't bother with me, take her out! So I told Pam the time I'd call. Hullo, we're off!' And their line of traffic surged forward. 'We're really off at last. And now they're both at it, waving like mad at each other. She'll lose her handkerchief out of the window if she isn't careful! Now ours, the one in with us, has stopped, we're past and it's all over. So what d'you make of that, Harry?'

'That I'm going to be late,' this young man replied and then he added, 'Oh, she was only telling the other in here with us that she could go now.'

Harry was blind.

A FIRE, A FLOOD, AND
THE PRICE OF MEAT

(Broadcast by the BBC. Published in The Listener, *August 1951)*

Since the last war no more than three things of note have
occurred in the pub I use at lunchtime near my office and these
were: the chimney fire; the time our butcher got upset, dashed
out to fetch his daybook which he read aloud, in a terrible voice,
to give the prices he had been paying back in 1938; and last, most
significant of all, the time the cistern in the Gent's overflowed,
flooding out the floor.

I am entirely serious when I say I hope to show how these
happenings, especially the last mentioned, had, on those present,
an effect similar to that which occurs between a writer and his
reader in a book. I hope also to show what lessons the prudent
writer should draw from such occurrences, and at the same time
I aim to explain my own attitude, because things are getting
more complicated these days and I, for one, feel that it is for the
writer to explain himself, now, a little.

I was a fireman in the war so you can judge of my incredulous
delight to hear the old roar in the chimney, and to realise, as I
entered the bar at midday, that I was to enjoy the most enviable
moment of all to any ex-fireman, a nice little job in someone
else's chimney, with the unimaginable pleasure thrown in of
watching a crew one isn't on, go through the absurd motions of
putting a chimney out. I should, perhaps, explain that chimney
fires are seldom dangerous if seen to by professionals, always
provided that they are not abandoned before they are well and
truly out. And when is a fire out? Only what we used to call a
bull's-eye, that is to say, the last glowing ember, knows.

Well, the guv'nor of this pub, as I entered, was rather white about the gills, his hired help watched with wooden faces, but I knew, and they knew – we didn't have to say anything – that in three minutes he would have to dial the old 999, and the beauty of it all was, I realised, that what we used to call the attendance, which means the particular station to be ordered on, would inevitably be from my own fire station. As, indeed, it turned out; I knew everyone on the crew, had gone along with them on many a moonlit night in London in 1940. Well, they put this small job out. They made no mess, the customers, after a first small excitement, even seemed to grow a bit bored. We, the customers, had not been sent outside, things were not serious enough for that, and my old mates, under the eye of an officer, just recognised me by little nods and winks. It was, the whole show, still intensely enjoyable for me, of course. But the other customers, the beer, the traditional port-and-lemon drinkers, obviously saw nothing more.

A part in every chimney fire is played by a fireman on the roof. He may drop a loose brick down the chimney, or more likely he will play water down it, but anyway one of them always gets up there. It was this man, whom I knew well, who came below and said to the officer in my hearing, 'Would you like to come up and have a look at it, guv, the roof's quite easy.'

Catching this remark fairly made my morning for me, the use of the word 'guv', and the reference, in almost reverential tones, to the roof being safe when I suppose there is no fireman who went through the blitz, as I and all these men had, who could not call to mind at least one occasion on which he had almost been blown off a high one by high explosive. And 'guv' used to be one of our happier jokes. How often in those days did I hear the injunction given by an officer, an old London Fire Brigade man – 'lad, don't never call nobody "guv", not below the rank of – ', I forget the rank which rated this title, but it was more than nice to hear the phrase again.

'Guv,' the customer in a pub may say with a world of feeling in his voice, if the server looks to be that kind of man, 'Guv, a pint of wallop, quick,' and if the server should be that sort of a man, he'll put one up as though he had reason to know you needed it, sympathetically. Not so with the writer when he serves the dish to his reader. Things, for him, are decidedly more complicated. As with the audience in that pub, who did not know you should never call an officer 'guv' unless he was above a certain rank, so, with his reader, the writer cannot use too much material that has to be explained. If he does, I suspect he will bore his audience, just as these people in our pub got bored with our fire once they saw nothing in the officer being reassured about an easy roof.

And now to my second example, our butcher on present-day meat prices. I must here say a word on his audience, that is, about the people who use the pub at midday. They do not seem so well known to each other as do those regulars who forgather in the other house I patronise at night. Possibly this is accounted for, in the daytime in a business district, by there being so many casual customers at noon. And even the morning regulars have to work, so that their jobs may keep them from attending always at the same hour each day. Anyway when I first noticed our butcher that morning, dressed, as he always is, with the apron of his trade and the old straw hat, he was in a dispute, with a man I did not recognise, about today's meat prices. It is a subject I know nothing about and I did not pay much attention, nor, so far as I could then judge, did anyone else. Yet all of a sudden, with a great cry of 'I'll show you, wait till I get my books,' our butcher fairly ran out of the place to his shop next door, and I could tell from the discreet smiles all around that most of us had in fact been listening, and that this someone had been having the butcher on. In other words, if these two had collaborated in a book, they had their readers' interest. The thing was suddenly alive that morning in the saloon bar; there was tension, attention, and amusement. What author could hope, or plan, for more?

The butcher was back in a moment with a ledger open in his hand. It dated back to 1938, he said, and contained a record of his purchases, with the prices he had paid. He began to read these out in a loud voice. Then, at once, the whole atmosphere in the pub changed. Everyone listened openly, and, so I thought, with disbelief. You might say it had suddenly become a semi-political meeting. In a great voice, one hand above his head, as though taking the oath, our butcher read out, 'a side of beef', which he told us weighed so many stone, then he explained how many pounds weight go to a stone, and then with great ease and rapidity he told the company how much a pound that made, and said, 'There you are, then.' A man cried out, 'Go on!' 'It's right,' the butcher yelled, 'all here in my book,' and so brought his hand down from over his head to lick a thumb, to turn another page.

He gave one example after another, he took us straight through the dismembered carcass of an ox. His remarks on how cheap everything had been in those days did not seem to be disbelieved. Rather his audience appeared as though about to give up listening; what some call the good, and others the bad, old days, sounded remote that morning. Perhaps our butcher sensed this. Suddenly he turned to poultry and then, because it was near Christmas, to turkeys. A blind man, if he had been present, would, I swear, have sensed the immediate rise in interest again. Even I knew how cheap the price in 1938 sounded. Encouraged by this perhaps, the butcher, stretching his free hand above his head, no longer extended the fingers into a sort of salute; no, whilst he dealt with turkeys, he closed the four fingers on his thumb while his recitation rose, then opened them again when he allowed his great voice to fall. It was a performance. But at once I was again conscious of a drop in interest, although the guv'nor of this pub began to insert comment now and then, to encourage his very good customer, our butcher. And it was now that the butcher's assistant, a man, he tells us, of seventy-five, but who looks, I swear, a good twenty years younger, came to the glass door, and beckoned to his guv'nor, the butcher, who left at once. This assistant is always calling him away all morning. None of us, officially, knows why. The butcher is always back in no more than the time one would think it would take to serve one customer. He was away on this occasion just that short while. Yet, when he did come in again, what spell there was had gone. And he did not try to start afresh, but fell back on a dignified silence.

The third occurrence in our pub, the truly remarkable one, also concerned the butcher, but not so directly. It was remarkable because it held the interest of all present for as long as I could spend on that particular morning in the saloon bar. It also had the quality of every good book ever written, it challenged the attention at once, held this and drew all the modest drinkers present into a communion of people, each, in his own way, equally interested in what would happen next.

After describing what did happen, I propose to end with a suggestion why it was significant, and why it appeared to me to have a lesson for writers. Because, as I crossed the busy street, which constitutes a peril every time I leave this public house, I had no idea what lay in wait behind those two swing doors through which we, the customers, one and all have to leave and enter. Because, when I pushed through the last one of these, I came on a meandering stream of water all over the floor, the drinkers keeping their feet out, although it was not more than an eighth-of-an-inch deep. There had been a leak somewhere, and in a stream the water was wandering in rivulets not more than six inches across all over the place; you could see them flowing from the specks of dust advancing with them, that only occasionally joined, at a bulge, into the body of the water before.

There was only one dry patch of any size, and this was occupied, at full stretch, by the Alsatian dog. As was only natural, I halted. I came up short on being faced with this extension of the English winter, within doors. To get across to the bar seemed, for a moment, almost to involve paddling. It was at that instant I caught sight of the butcher. In his traditional get up he was watching me intently, a thing, so far as I know, he had never done before. And so was the rest of the audience. When someone eventually came in, after me, I realised this was not personal. We were all waiting to hear what the latest arrival would do, or say, about the flood.

What my own first exclamation was I no longer remember. And it may, or may not, be significant, that I can recollect hardly anyone's spoken reaction to this floor. Instead, I do call to mind, on every face, as its bearer entered, a look of ludicrous dismay. Meantime, the audience in the pub stayed attentive and silent, studying each new arrival's reactions. But when, on my own entry, I had pulled myself together, I did remark to the butcher, who was watching me so intently and whom I had never in my life addressed before, I did say something to the effect that 'I thought at first all this was to do with you,' I said. A flicker of genuine annoyance seemed to cross his face at this. 'No,' he replied with dignity. 'There's a leak they can't manage to stop out there in the cistern, so it's overflowed.'

When I had got my pint, and picked my way over to where I always sit, I watched the Alsatian which lay with pricked ears, head sideways, on the largest patch of dry floor, a dog which was obviously, from its twitching nose, anxiously regarding the flow of water, at eye level. Then the animal got up and sniffed the small flow before lying down again. At that, the butcher's elderly assistant entered, obviously, this time, for a drink, because he did not beckon to his master. He made no remark on the state of the flood. He looked in a grave way at his feet. And the butcher said, almost sternly, in what was a put-on educated tone of voice; he said, 'Have you had your meal?' 'An' very nice, too,' the assistant answered. There was a pause. Then he demanded of the floor, 'What's this?' Upon which we all, as though at a signal, burst out discreetly laughing. 'I thought for a minute it was something to do with you,' the butcher challenged him, borrowing from me, and then someone fresh came in, and got the floor. So it went on, with not a dull moment, until I left to go back to work.

To examine those round us in an experience, is to learn the little we know about human nature. I do not refer to 'crowd psychology', and do not mean to stick my neck out in attempting a definition of what may constitute a crowd. But, the thing about the flood in our pub was, everyone became so enthralled that no one even discussed it, each one was too busy waiting for the next customer to come in. Some would talk it over afterwards, no doubt, as I am doing now; as readers will, after they have read a good book. Yet they had discussed the fire in the first stages of its being put out, while, when the butcher was on the price of turkeys, people had grown quite heated in their comment, but only for a while. Then, when their attention was really engaged, they stayed silent, and the reason behind it is, I think – I do not know – that they became, by the flood, interested in the people round them, and, more important still, were interested in themselves as well.

How much do you, as readers, think about yourselves as you get through a novel? When I was very young, I did. When six or seven years old I of course knew nothing, had done nothing, and identified myself with all the characters. Up to a point I still do. And how many of you come to read novels out of your curiosity in other people's experience, either in the author's experience or in that of his characters? What makes you read? I submit that the act of reading consists very much of what went to make up the flood water scene in my saloon bar. As we, each in our turn, went up to order drinks, we were not comparing this unexpected occurrence with another. It seemed to me that everyone was shocked into an acute awareness of himself or herself, and of his or her audience. And a reader's audience, in a novel, is, of course, the characters that make up the book, that go to make it live, if it does live.

I said earlier there had seemed to exist, on this last occasion, a sort of communion between the people in our bar. And the reason for the existence of this must be, I think – I do not know – just amusement. There can be few readers entirely without a sense of humour, so, let's have more humour. In any case, every-one, as in the pub, has an acute sense of the ridiculous where he or she is concerned, and a sense of the ridiculous does very well for me in novels; in fact, I often find there is not enough of it.

And so what I have tried to show here is, not how to put the mechanics of written communication over on a reader, but rather I have tried to show the sort of experience I, as a writer, have been allowed to witness, in life, by which people would seem to be drawn together, as into a book. All I hope, in life, is that such people may turn out to be readers!

INVOCATION TO VENICE

(Published in British/American Vogue, *1952)*

Venice, where no ice is, and green has never been, at dawn the fishless stinking sea milk white, a pink palace domed into a sky of milk and towards which one black gondola is being poled; Venice where the only horses must be statues and they have yet to put up motor cars in stone, oh Venice with no bicycle bells but with a Bridge of Sighs and Casanova always on a roof – the sun in rising must bring azure to your roads of sea, tideless with a steadily rising stench, Venice where Proust thought to travel and never did, Venice they somehow missed when bombing, Venice which is still here but for how long, and will it be too late soon, the pigeons, St Mark's, a populace standing under colonnades angrily arguing prices, the sun at noon too sharp striking light off marble, the brazen horses hot and dry to touch – up in that dormer window on the lead roof a maid stretched in black, snoring on the bed with skirts up about her mouth, the natives poling spaghetti down, Venice which is too hot because she never freezes – where do they get their drinking water or do they strike this like oil, are there derricks to gush it from the ocean into those old palaces past which the motor boats must not speed in case they bring the places down.

Venice, for the honeymoon, cushions at the rear in a little moving room, the gondolier who does not look back, but no he would be pushing from the stern – we would be stretched out before him – so what, do they have shades on that little backward-looking window through which his envenomed eyes at the corners of which two bluebottles sip brighter than jewels, the gondolier appraising our love-making, can you then draw a blind to exclude him or can he go to the bows to pole and not look over a shoulder, to stare into sun with his wounds of eyes while I wound you, my love, on cushions white like rice to the lap lap of water. . . .

Venice, the lions of St Mark's in stone – did one such lion on a great afternoon swim in from blinding yellow sands every yard from the South, its home – an orange head athwart the azure sea, with salt-encrusted nostrils, eyes red, a white fish impaled on the claws of one forepaw all the sad way from Africa towards which Venice ever leans – did they then who live there catch its sobbing breath, the dark despair of effort a sounding band about the heart oh Venice of marble, my love unvisited, my honeymoon unspent. . . .

Or is it at dusk when each emerald within the sea will rise to take the surface air, when light winds from the Bosphorus, the Golden Gates, waft from the East a cool to pant palace windows even now lighting against dusk and the sky is gold, when pigeons clap their wings to take evening flight in air that now is eyelid pink and the stench subsides, when those blue-stoned walls can breathe and saints in stone do stretch to sigh for another day that is done in five, six hundred years, then, is it then, Venice, time for lovers in that darker dusk within the little room that glides while the gondolier hums. . . .

But wait, the pigeons circling must be doves in Venice, there can be no sea-birds here, no cormorants forlorn on a post, no red-legged cranes – white peacocks perhaps, but certainly doves there must be above the long hoot of a liner at anchor in the roadway, doves for six, seven hundred years, doves of peace dove-soft and with a clap the square before St Mark's is clear; they rise in spirals indulgently followed in the poached-egg eyes of those who sit over coffee and growing smaller below in Venice. . . .

Hanging to his bars the prisoner at his cell will see this evening dove flight, the maid in black and on her bed will yawn at them then draw her skirts down along fat legs, the lovesick girl will weep in Venice to see her hopes' sweet flight, the sky will droop on doves as they find their way, as the sea must fade, the sun set before they roost on an old statue's taut right arm, the marble shoulder, or on bronze imperishable ever-folded wings of angels standing on a corner to await the daily death of Venice. . . .

And the rising moon. Above a sea turned dark as night on which Venice ever leans her tresses the disc emerges apricot gold and every small wave set with diamonds, fanned by her desert breath, takes on an Afric sunshine only cold as death as dolphins come in out of the wide sea to Venice. For she is wedded to the sea. Her rulers the Doges, when each in his turn came to office, had this custom by which he was rowed out on to the main where he let drop a golden ring to sway criss-cross down into the ocean, to gleam a while a sport for dolphins, for Venice is wed to the sea called Mediterranean. . . .

And the dolphins at night drive in from the sea. With their brief sigh as they come up to breathe, they are quicksilver in moonlight over Venice and in their play they do sigh for lovers adrift in that moonlight lane from Venice. . . .

And these lovers, as they are urged by no action of their own into this old enchantment, leave behind as they must in their care for one another, marble with blood in its veins under midday heat, now classically turned blue blooded in the moon, blanched, carved into a living identity with its statues that live for ever on the buildings of Venice which does not sleep at night. Here too the noonday blaze which stunned Venice, which drew her stench up to freight the air with living, has cooled, has turned as cold as silhouettes where the gondola cuts its own outline where no other vessel is and where, in one another's arms, cut off in our shade from the gondolier, we voyage more than ever by ourselves away from the cold marble forehead of Venice in which doves now swoon on statues and the night holds still and we, bereft in one another's warmth by the sheer moonlight, in one another's nyloned skin, each gently haloed in the other's breath, and silenced she and I, are silenced as we draw out from Venice. . . .

For silence is best where we, while idly talking, might disagree under the clear stars, alone, the gondolier forgotten. Nor is it safe for lovers to more than murmur in Venice, even out at sea. For behind them they have the storied pavements, great lives in mosaic, and above those fabled women swathed in marble idleness over great niches set in silken-covered walls, there are ceilings dimmed now by night, unreflected by moonlight through the wide windows, there are heroes drawn over stretched motionless ceilings to vast designs which were painted to show each in his greatest moment and, thus painted, become the thieves of time; these are for us, in the city we have left behind, which our gondola has sunk beneath the skyline, these are the epitome of all love stories, in mosaic, in statues and in great painting to bring us mortals down to little more than ghosts, but warm, off Venice. . . .

So it is perhaps we should be chary of a honeymoon in or off the seaborne city. It may be too much has gone on or is pictured there. There could be frailty in our lives not to be endured under that magnificence. We might be found wanting. How then can the inhabitants live through such a challenge? The answer must be they are so used to riches that they no longer feel, or else they live in cross-eyed blindness. . . .

Can one then have the heart, the impudence to visit Venice? Is that the reason Proust would never go? For, against this, if it might be too hot by day or the stench then too great, by contrast it would seem only too easy to set out by moonlight so that no couple, if given the miraculous chance, could fail, intent on their two selves, to sink Venice, as can be done tomorrow by the gondola covering of a moonlit lane of sea. Yet to leave her thus is but to come back to bed in Venice. The dawn is always chill, better met between sheets. The sun, in first rising, is not warmer than the loved one's arms. So, in returning over the sea, in seeing that fabled city rise out of the ocean under moonlight, first one dome then another, and the gold crosses paled to white, next the roads of water between black shadows – oh here then must be who knows what of the great myths of the world that each one carries within him, Venice by moonlight, all the whole literature of the world that every human being, the heir as we all are to each beautiful line created, is born to and holds in a molten casket in his heart for Venice. . . .

For Venice is everlasting, lives by a life that cannot die except by bombs. It may be she is too strong for mortals, that we could feel too human to submit our will to hers. But sure as day follows night the morrow's sun will rise on Venice, the stench, if you will, return. But the doves must come down from up the palaces, dawn will find her great statuary eyes wide opened. Prisons, palaces and churches will smile again as they have through centuries, and the people of Venice will go on unregarding. And while she is here still, through her and under her will continue to drift brave pilgrims from the West. Then, as day closes yet once more, Venice will clothe herself for the moon. And, when that reflection rises from Africa in the moon's triumph over men, that is the time for all the world's lovers, living their lives over again (their lives perhaps to be) in the photographs and pictures of Venice; a city for ever wedded to the sea that there is no one does not carry by him and which each one of us lives by, despite himself, his inward eye fixed, perhaps it would best be not in, but rather trained upon Venice. . . .

FOR JOHN LEHMANN'S PROGRAMME

(Broadcast by the BBC, 1952)

I want to say a few words about two things tonight, both to do with style. First about journalism. I have felt for some time that journalists cannot possibly go on writing much longer in the style they now use. It may be the shortage of newsprint has cramped them but the way they are, at present, almost every sentence has become a paragraph, or they make a paragraph out of nearly every sentence. They seem so frightened no one will read them that they have almost as much blank paper from the end of one paragraph to the beginning of another, as they have printed matter. And then consider the space they waste with their headlines, headings and sub-headings.

Paradoxically enough, I suppose it will only be when they get more paper, that they will begin to write with long sentences, long sentences in which, as with life, one thing leads to another, consequences follow and through which there is a kind of flow. Not the sort of staccato drum beat they practise with now.

They seem to think that a reader's mind is so confused, as it is, of course, that he can only follow a series of statements in the severest black or white, statements which follow one another, paragraphed out and away from one another down the narrow column. I have made enquiries of my friends. Our minds are fully as confused as the next man's, but we are all agreed that the facts as presented by journalists nowadays are virtually ununderstandable. It is only too true that this may be due to the incomprehensibility of the facts journalists have as their duty to relate, but my point is, they don't relate them rather they rattle their facts out in a stutter, as a machine gun does bullets, until we are dazed, alarmed and deafened every day, until we don't know what is to be feared, what item is more deadly than the next, in each day's news.

The answer must be in the journalist's use of the longer sentence whereby he can gain depth, or light and shade.

I have long held that novels should be written as far as possible in dialogue only. The conventional approach by a novelist in which he presumes to know all about his characters, what they are feeling and thinking at any moment, seems to me as dead as the Dodo.

This leads me on to novels. But novels have to have occasional descriptive passages too, to link the dialogue and here the longer sentence is, in my opinion, just as important. As an example, offered, let me tell you, not entirely seriously, is an extract from a new novel of mine which is at the moment in proof. There are four characters, a father, a mother, a son who is a public school boy aged about seventeen and a girl of nineteen, who has been asked along to keep him happy at a party at a night club to celebrate the first day of the holidays. This extract is offered you on the understanding that I disapprove of my work being read aloud. Incidentally, it is almost the only bit of description in the whole book.

Then, to yet another roll of drums, violet limes were switched on the small stage, a man hurrahed, and the girl bellied the corsage of her low dress the better to see between their elegant-shod toes, the party being seated to supper on a balcony at this night club and hard against wrought-iron railings, – she did this the better to watch what now emerged, an almost entirely naked woman who walked on to scant applause, and who carried with some awkwardness, within two arms thin like snakes, a simple wicker, purple, washing basket.

'Well but just look at that,' the father said and turned his gaze back to the girl, while the son opened his mouth as if he could eat what he now saw.

'Now, who's being stuffy dear, please?' the mother asked.

The boy shushed both, as, following the drums, a dirge of

indigo music rose then sank, or rose, to a single flute with repeated, but ever changing, runs or trills.

'Would you call her pretty?' the mother asked in a bright voice.

'Fairly awful' the son replied. At which his mother smiled her fondest.

'All right by me' his father said to the girl to be snubbed by yet another 'sh'sh' from the boy.

For the lady had begun to dance.

All she wore was a blue sequin on the point of each breast and a few more to cover her sex. As she swayed those hips, sequins caught the light to strike off in a blaze of royal blue while the skin stayed moonlit and the palms of her two hands, daubed probably with a darker pigment, made a deeper shadow, above raised arms of a red so harsh it was almost black in that space through which she waved her opened fingers in figure of eights before the cut jet of two staring eyes.

MATTHEW SMITH –
A PERSONAL TRIBUTE

(Tate Gallery Exhibition, 1953)

Green wrote to Sir John Rothenstein: 'I have never written about painting before and never shall again. It has given me hell. I am much too
close to Matthew to have done this. I have not submitted it to him and
dread to think what the result will be when he sees it. The trouble is
that the piece cannot be knocked about too much and perhaps it would
be a good thing if he did not see it before it was printed if it suits you
to print it.'

Percipience in a painter can involve an oblique or amused approach on his part to his viewers. This Matthew Smith has in an
endearing degree. Indeed the sense of humour in his work is so
vivid that, to see him in the flesh, the fun might lie, above his
painting eye, as just a crease on a broad great forehead. But in
fact what his eye does see, as well as a joke, is beauty pure and
simple.

In his nudes those flaunting women so often stare us in the
face with what seems to be contempt for the effect their chests
may have on us. Arrogantly proud of their soft great thighs, they
seem more conscious and disdainful of our peeping than the
models of any other painter. Even when curled up in bed, eyes
closed, they obviously pretend to ignore their audience. Or, sitting up, a rose impudently placed against a more than naked
breast, the girl just looks past us, pouting.

Nearly always these models are big women and, if as often is,
they are done asleep, and his colours suggest, as only Smith can,
a great drowsy-hot afternoon, then has sleep portrayed on canvas
ever been more secure or deeper? No, there is a sureness about

these women which carries over to us that utter serenity which only great painting can impose.

And then as to his colours which, as we can see for ourselves here and today, are by no means always the red or rose so often attributed to him. He uses, he puts on canvas, colours as varied and vivid as any other living painter, and, in so doing, extends miraculously the content of his work. For it is Smith's colour that can be said to carry his work away, that fuses the whole to greatness. And yet his use of colour could be called purely romantic: indeed, paradoxically enough, it is the only literary element in his work. And while he knows all, of course, about how to put the paint on so as to make colour clothe and create form, it does seem as if he were ambivalent in vision. For Smith is very much a two-eyed man. It strikes one that form (shape) and colour come to him separately and that then, somehow, and this is his particular triumph, he fuses the two together into his own unity, his integrity as a person. This last is particularly true of what can be called those painter's exercises, the still-lives – perhaps of a plate and few rounds of fruit. In these the effect of colour on form is self-evident. On the other hand, many will disagree, he is not so successful with the shape of his flowers: they are sometimes no more than just a glorious fire of colour. But in the nudes and landscapes when he makes form and colour create and breathe life the one into the other and vice versa, it is then that one plus one does not equal two, no, it is great art; in Smith's particular case it can be called painting in the round.

The landscapes of the country about Aix are poems, lyrical poems. Painted towards that moment of fleeting dusk which lasts down there for perhaps thirty short minutes, they have very often an olive tree or two in the foreground, which have the panache but not, to one eye at least, the true shape of these trees, then a middle distance of infinite mystery, and often a line of hills literally swooning on the horizon. They are done, so it appears, almost entirely in a long gradation of one colour, except perhaps for one touch of one other shade always exquisitely placed. They bring one an extraordinary impression of depth or distance which is conveyed with the minimum arrangement of poles or trees in the foreground, or a winding road, to suggest perspective. No, the whole great panorama, these great expanses of the South of France, which stretch from us back out of the canvas, are done entirely by Smith's masterly play on colour. It is here, in these entirely romantic landscapes, that he displays a new concept of the use of colour.

But like all great painters, Smith cannot and will not be tied down. Around 1920 he went to Cornwall and there brought off an astounding series of landscapes which, to some of us, give the fondest joy we have of his work. In these the principles laid down above that seem to rule his later Aix canvases, are totally ignored. In dark greens and blues and, in particular, with mauves of an amazing intensity, he gives us a sombre rain-soaked countryside in his unique midday of a stifling West Country summer. Far from employing gradations of one colour to give him his perspective or depth, these landscapes are criss-crossed by thick horizontal bands, often in yellow, to show a lane or something else which must recede. This series of pictures should be studied to be realised, and are unparalleled in their ominous lyricism.

To step back, to consider the extent of Smith's range, his oeuvre, is an experience in itself. Nor are we less astonished by the lapse of time his work covers. The earliest canvas hung in this exhibition is dated 1909. And yet how much more cannot be on view, if only for reasons of wall space? For instance there are no drawings here today to disprove what some have written, that he cannot draw. Some of Smith's drawings, with their simplicity and roundness of line are the quintessence of the knowledge he has acquired in a long lifetime of work. There are here no crayon drawings either, with strokes never thinner than one quarter of an inch, which are yet as delicate as lace. Many also of his finest paintings are abroad.

It is the fashion just now in Britain to decry achievement. While one can read in any newspaper almost every day how wonderful a nation we are, there is scant praise for any single Briton who is not a politician. Art critics have hardly more than two inches of a column to give to a one-man show. When therefore the Tate grants Smith his accolade, which is so rarely given to living artists, we should pause before all the richness of his work to ask ourselves why, after a lifetime of dedication and endeavour, there is so little to read about the man? Retiring as he is by nature, nevertheless it is strange we should have so little in print about him. All the more honour to the Tate therefore for allowing us to see for ourselves a great cross-section of his paintings, so to speak, in the flesh.

To take only one picture, the *Nude with Pearl Necklace* (47) from 1931. With what loving brutality has Smith painted the model's belly and that thick strong wrist. How proudly she lies, how superb her bent right knee. How gaily she lies, and how little she cares! And that right breast walloping to the couch! The happy fling of her necklace, to the right as well, is all humour and gaiety, while her face (and surely Smith is one of the very few modern painters to fit the right face to his nudes) her face holds just the expression of what must have been the mood in that studio more than twenty years ago, a situation that is now fixed for ever. And finally the whole magnificent composition of this picture is brought together, fused, is made three dimensional by Smith's colours, those colours which cannot and will never be described in words. And that, of course, is one of the great reasons for painting.

This is indeed, therefore, a moment for heartfelt applause and gratitude to Matthew Smith for this torrent of beauty with which he has endowed mankind.

THE SPOKEN WORD AS
WRITTEN

(Review published in The Spectator, *1953)*

Green wrote to Professor Sutherland: 'As you know, I am not a
reviewer and have great difficulty with *The Oxford Book of English Talk*,
and am afraid I did not bring out how much I really admired it. And
of course I was the worst person to review it as I had a bee in my
bonnet on this subject of dialogue.'

The Oxford Book of English Talk, edited by James Sutherland is
an anthology of conversations, that is to say of oral communi-
cations in print between people and extracted from plays, novels,
proceedings at judicial trials, and so forth. Mr Sutherland, in his
preface, believes 'that this is the first book to record at length
how Englishmen and Englishwomen actually spoke from late
medieval times down to the present day'. This may be true. At
the same time it does raise the question of how people speak to
different purposes and on different occasions. Does a man on
trial for his life speak frankly and easily? At a recent murder
trial Christie used sentences of an extraordinary intricacy in his
defence which were not, one would assume, characteristic of his
everyday speech. Similarly, playwrights and novelists, in dialogue, are always writing, that is to say, introducing 'business'.
This must interfere with their rendering of their idea of how
contemporary conversation goes. In other words no anthology
can be as successful as a gramophone record made off a concealed
microphone and possibly nothing would be more untypical or
boring than such a record. Art must intrude. And the question
is, how far art has distorted this recorded talk, recorded in print
of course, from 1417 in this book to 1949.

I saw, with great pleasure, that a piece of mine had been

included. On rereading this, an extract from one of my novels, I found that it came from a moment, for me, of great difficulty in the writing of the book. Of course talk must be about something, but here a landlady is telling her lodger three things he must know and which are vital to him and to the story. To do this she verbally ducks, improvises and sometimes has to wince away from him in her telling. So what, you say? Everyone has to in real life. Very well, but the question with us here is whether such a conscious effort to other things by any novelist is a valid attempt on his part to convey contemporary talk. In other words can he clothe his purpose, which is the story he is writing, with an accurate rendering of contemporary speech?

Another of Mr Sutherland's choices is a broadcast by John Hilton entitled, ominously enough, 'Calculated Spontaneity'. In this the man, well known in his day, and after four years on the air, gives us his idea of the technique of broadcasting. He tries to show how to be natural in written speech. He does not draw attention to the fact that he repeats everything at least three times. Is this repetition endurable in ordinary conversation? It is prevalent of course. But we are on a high plane here, this is an Oxford Book, and on this occasion one doubts the value of Mr Hilton's inclusion. Nevertheless it does raise the whole difficulty, which anyone who writes dialogue knows only too well – that written dialogue is not like the real thing, and can never be.

Yet there are moments, dramatic of course, when the words ring out and we cannot help but say 'this then is how he spoke'. In 'Charles I Faces His Accusers' we have this recorded as having been said three hundred years ago: 'Remember I am your King, your lawful King, and what sins you bring upon your heads, and the judgement of God upon this land – think well upon it – I say think well upon it, before you go further from one sin to a greater.' Even then a doubt creeps in. At that time this text made politics and must have surely been edited by those in power. Are they then the King's own words?

At another trial, and again the man is 'on his life', poor Colonel Turner is interrupted by his wife while he gives his vital evidence. (He was hanged within the week with Pepys watching.) Turner: 'My wife came to me publicly, I did not whisper with her –'

Mrs Turner: 'Nay, look you husband –'

Turner: 'Prythee, Mall, sit down: you see my Lord, my wife will interrupt me with nonsense. Prythee sit thee down quickly, and do not put me out: I cannot hold women's tongues, nor your Lordship neither.'

Lord Chief Justice Bridgman: 'This is not a May game.'

Poignant enough, this, in all truth, with a real ring of speech, but how true we shall never know.

Another gem is Pope's description of Jonathan Swift: 'Dr Swift has an odd blunt way that is mistaken by strangers for ill-nature.' With a friend he calls on the Dr who rather begrudgingly offers them food and then drink. When both decline Pope describes the following.

Swift: 'But if you had supped with me as in all reason you ought to have done, you must have drank with me. A bottle of wine – two shillings. Two and two is four, and one is five: just two and sixpence a piece.' (He is referring to the cost of two lobsters and two sixpenny tarts.) 'There Pope, there's half a crown for you, and there's another for you, sir: for I won't save anything by you, I am determined.'

Here one wonders whether the artist in Pope has not improved on Swift, so taut and sharp are the sentences.

Perhaps the best way with this difficulty, as to whether *The Oxford Book of Talk* really represents talk, is to turn to the few selections included which span our own lives. There is an enchanting and beautifully written broadcast, 'Holiday at the Seaside', by a Mrs Lilian Balch. It is conversational, certainly, although done with extreme skill, describing exactly what the title implies, but it is a monologue. Now monologue is also always with us of course, but surely only as a small part of talk, its poor relation so to speak.

We have also a speech by Mr John Betjeman in defence of the threatened village of Letcombe Bassett. It is a fine thing but it is not, to those who have the privilege of knowing him, at all the way he talks ordinarily. It is the public occasion we are given, when he is speaking to a cause. Possibly the nearest to what Mr

Sutherland calls 'linguistic truth' is the piece with the frightful title of 'Wizard Prang', another broadcast for which, no doubt, the pilot did not choose the name. But this is in just one of the Service lingos evolved by one more war and which by now is already dated. Mr Sutherland then includes a piece of Hansard, of the time after Munich. The several speeches given are all in that unique and horrible jargon of the House of Commons for which it is impossible to find reason or excuse, or its like outside that institution.

Next we have an extract from Al Coppard's *Abel Staple Disapproved*, 1933. This is accurate dialogue which rings true, but is it like talk, is it the way people actually spoke? You must read it and judge for yourselves.

Talk, I suppose, is an exchange between two or more people watching the expression on each other's faces, hearing the tone of voice. Perhaps there is, as Mr Hilton practised, endless repetition. Certainly there are pauses, hesitations, and changes of direction which will never do in print. And this of course we cannot expect Mr Sutherland to give us. Nor could he very well call his work *The Oxford Book of Recorded Conversation* or *Printed Talk* or what have you. What he has done, and that it is learned as well as scholarly goes without saying, is to raise a monument to that great source of our language as we know it, the spoken word, out of which as the language changes from generation to generation the written word springs; new turns of phrase as they come up in speech, being the tools of the poet and the novelist. And if this book will inspire, as it deserves, at least one young man to write out of his birthright, this most miraculous of all languages open to writers, then Mr Sutherland's labours will not have been in vain.

THE JEALOUS MAN

(Unpublished, 1954)

Both 'The Jealous Man' and 'Impenetrability' (see page 188) were rejected by the *New Yorker*. 'We'll keep in mind your interest in doing reviews of books by dead authors,' the letter finishes.

England once had a sculptor who, at the time I want you to meet him, was old and very famous. It had not always been so. When his wife was alive he did not earn much, and stayed poor for many years after she died. The commissions that came his way then were few, he could not afford many models, so whilst his wife was still living he did many nudes of her and of his incalculably beautiful child Corinne and these, now that he is world known, are in every gallery all over Europe and elsewhere.

He lived in London and was a jealous man.

No one was allowed to look twice at his wife or, later, at most of his models. But, unique in some respects, he did not, when the time came, mind about young men for Corinne, his daughter, who, grown up now, was even more beautiful than she had been as a little girl. At the time I am telling you of, long after his wife's death, it was only occasionally, and perhaps more out of habit than anything else, that in Battersea Park, of a summer evening, he would exclaim on seeing a man sit himself down on the grass up to sixty yards off (just as he had said, but in a voice of thunder, to the mother so often in the past) 'Angel, there's another lout peeping up your skirts.'

Both women, one dead and the other living, had by this time been seen naked in bronze marble or clay in galleries all over Europe. But he had no sense of humour. He was a jealous man.

Like most great men, all his life he had been wonderfully looked after. His wife never spared herself whilst she was alive

[174]

free to work, as he went on working throughout
through the hours of daylight every day.

mother died Corinne was old enough to do as much
when things turned better for them she worked,
she sewed, she cooked and made the beds, she scrubbed to keep
him comfortable. Then he began to be able to afford models. If
what I have heard is right, he would enjoy himself with these
girls every day as soon as the light failed. He was very jealous.
But he was a loving father. And when his daughter came to tell
him one morning that she was with child, he did not seem to be
disturbed, begged her not to marry because he did not hold with
marriage, said to bring her young man to live with them, as, he
explained, he could not do without her. And that was that! So
it was the fellow came to live with them. But what Corinnne
did not tell the father was that her lover, who had begun the
third love of her heart, the third love that to her heart's delight
was already turning over in her belly even then, – what the two
of them did not dare tell the old man was that this lover of hers
was also a sculptor.

So she scrubbed for three and cooked for four. She ate as much
as the two men together and stayed slim, as, being herself, she
would for quite a while. And all the time riotously shared the
bed she was glad to make each day for the father of her child.

About now the old man was commissioned to do a bust of the
King. When he used to take his clay along to the Palace in an old
dirty bucket and the royal servants wrapped it up in serviettes,
he made one of his few jokes. Jealous men are very often
humourless. 'I tell you Corinne they must have thought I'd got
fizz in it.'

'But Daddy did the King ask you that?' 'No, I can't say he
did.' 'Then what did you talk about, Daddy?' 'Râteliers,' the old
man replied and looked sad.

Jealousy breeds jealousy perhaps, anyway Corinne's man
began to grow moody. He had found a gallery to let him have
a one-man show. Which, of course, would mean telling the old
sculptor what he was. And Corinne could not have this. 'Not
until after Baby!' she wheedled her lover in the darkness of night.
'For Daddy will want to do Baby, he does always.' 'Well he

hasn't asked my permission yet, has he?' the young demanded. 'He will, my darling darling,' she murmured a hugged her lover.

Then the father made a great Pregnant Woman in bronze of Corinne.

After which the child, in due course, was born as all children ought to be, at home.

Nothing could exceed Corinne's delight in Baby, and her father and lover were both very proud. And so soon as the little girl was weaned the old man at once wanted to do her in clay, as also did the lover, who naturally claimed first choice. Yet Corinne persuaded her young man he must have patience, and, as usual, without apparent effort, her father had his way.

The marble recumbent figure by the old man which came out of this was, with one lone exception, considered the best thing of a baby he ever did.

Afterwards the lover pressed harder. An apartment was falling vacant above the garage he used in secret for a studio. And Corinne, who truly longed to move in, for it seemed more than flesh and blood could stand to love three people all at one time, was afraid for the old man, but agreed to move once she found someone to look after him.

So she bearded her father. He did not say much, only that he could never, on any account, have one of his models to see to him. 'She'd only get under my feet,' he said.

So the search began and it was not easy. For, as Corinne explained to us all, whoever the girl was she would have to be lovely and beautiful and kind. Which is when I interfered and was sorry after.

I am a specialist on West African religions and knew of an Ashanti girl who had come over as nurse to a British family since sent home. Once here that child had died, and, as I knew her language of which her employers knew little, they brought me in to comfort the distracted, heartbroken coloured girl, who had adored her charge. I found her handsome, clean and young with a skin of a beautiful impenetrable ebony. And she knew how to cook English dishes. So it was I introduced this girl to the old man.

As soon as Corinne met her she was delighted, all the more because she was sure her father would want to do a bust of the maid. But this, in the event, he never did.

Then, after a period when both young women waited on him and the old sculptor worked as usual right through the hours of daylight, while Aba, as she was called, cooked entirely to his taste, then Corinne and her lover took Baby off to the apartment over the garage studio. Her father, although he stayed just as affectionate, did not seem to mind. And Corinne came back from time to time. But she found nothing to remark. Aba kept his place clean and the old man seemed content. His work was going well. His fame grew steadily. So Corinne, more and more taken up with Baby, hardly looked in much any more. Particularly as the three of them always dined together in a small restaurant twice a week, once Corinne had found a neighbour on whom to park Baby, on Aba's nights out.

It was then, as Corinne told me later, that things must have begun to happen.

For about now, it became obvious that Aba was soon to have a child.

You must understand the old man did not so much disapprove of marriage, he just ignored it. He had not resented the arrival of his daughter's child, nor saw any reason to blame the maid.

I did make some enquiries, and found Aba's young man was a law student in London, an Ashanti too. So it was arranged that, when the time came, the baby was to be born in the house where Aba lived, as all children should be. And Corinne engaged to come in more often to do what was needful for the two of them who, so shortly, were to be three.

It was thus, then, they peaceably waited for the birth; the old man, as ever, working through the hours of daylight and, maybe, still enjoying one or more of his models when the light failed, with Corinne coming in every now and again to see that he and his maid were all right. It was now, because she disliked subterfuge, that she told her father the young man of hers was also a sculptor.

'Fine to have one more in the family' was his only comment, but it was notable that he did not ask to see the lover's work.

All this time Aba grew bigger. Corinne told me the girl was entirely sweet, serene, kind and tranquil. There was just one thing. She did not understand plumbing. When the waste pipe of a sink in their basement got blocked up, rather than cope with the trap Aba crept into the studio, stole some clay, baked it in the oven, and therewith laid a conduit or trough from that overflowing sink to the main drain in the yard. As Corinne remarked, no doubt the girl had learned how to make bricks without straw at home in her native village.

And when the little girl it turned out to be was weaned the old man wanted to make something of the infant. Aba did not object, she was too happy. So for three whole weeks Corinne's father put away his other work and recreated Aba's baby in wet clay which he covered with a damp cloth every night when the light failed. We were all agreed it was the best thing of a baby he had ever done in all his life. Then one evening he went to a party. When he got back early in the morning the light in his studio was still on. He went to investigate. And he found Aba pushing the wet clay about with her fingers to alter the shape of her baby's nose.

The old sculptor fired Aba there and then and could not be persuaded to reconsider this. He very much blamed me over the whole business. He was a jealous man.

The maid with the child and her lover went back to Ashantiland, Corinne having to sell the bust of her own child to pay for the fares.

Aba's child was eventually cast in bronze, but has never been exhibited. And what has always fascinated me, the old man never altered the nose from the way Aba left it.

And that is all.

A WRITER'S DIARY

(Review published in The London Magazine, *1954)*

Green's accompanying letter to his piece finishes with these words: 'Quite frankly, the book is almost impossible. It is one long agonised cry from someone who was breaking herself with overwork and it should, as she meant it to be, be the basis on which a memoir was written on her.'

A Writer's Diary by Virginia Woolf [Hogarth Press], being extracts from the journal she kept for twenty-seven years, that is to say from 1915 to 1941 when she died, is a selection by her husband. This volume is of as many pages as there are days in the year. In a wary preface Mr Woolf is careful to inform us that what he has chosen, out of twenty-six volumes of manuscript, includes 'practically everything which referred to her own writing'. However much we admire her as a writer, and we do, this strikes a chill. Most of us, as she was, are incurably curious. And when we are concerned with one of the great women of our time, it is hard to be denied. This Mr Woolf seems to acknowledge. For he has added 'a certain number of passages' on what she thinks of what she is reading, which incidentally is only in the classics, for until towards the end of her life she avoided the books of her contemporaries. This appears to be from a genuine lack of interest (although James Joyce's work she admits bothered her). Then Mr Woolf also includes passages of which, as she herself writes 'It strikes me that in this book I practise writing; do my scales; yes and work at certain effects', and he finally offers us certain pieces which 'give the reader an idea of the direct impact on her mind of scenes and persons'.

Whether anyone so close to Virginia Woolf may be the best person to make a choice is open to doubt. To select is to use art. This therefore is the picture we are, so to speak, officially meant to see of her. But then you may object, that is true of any editor. Also, as one can infer, there are the many still living, for whom it would be too frank to be confronted by her wit and comment. Nevertheless, it must be admitted, one is left with a great sense of the unsatisfied. There is so much more that only our children will read, the blessed fortunate creatures.

Because there are few women who occupied the position Virginia Woolf assumed in her lifetime. She says here somewhere that she can't bear what, in her own day, was written about Bloomsbury, and indeed thought, at one moment, to do her own guide to it. But she cannot be blamed if she was singled out as she was. Not so much the brilliance of her husband and friends, as her own genius, isolated her in a limelight all her own. It is to her credit that she seems to despise this. Nevertheless we can, in this volume, watch her fame rise, and then, in her own estimation, wane. She takes a pleasure in both, as is perhaps natural in the self-comforting of a diary. For it appears she can never get away from herself. But then who can?

As Mr Woolf warns us in the preface, she writes of her diary that 'one gets into the habit of recording one particular kind of mood – irritation or misery, say – and not of writing one's diary when one is feeling the opposite'. Here again is the caveat, noticed earlier in this review, that what we have in this volume may only be one side of her. The trouble is, it is impossible to guess how true these extracts are to all but that one side.

For what we are given is a long chronicle of one book after another written in longhand, then the fair copy typed, then her husband's entirely just praise, the real agony of proofs next, and at last publishing day with, after a few hours, the astonished delight and admiration of her friends and relations and finally of the reviewers. And all this in great agony of spirit, with repeated instructions to herself not to mind the criticism which is hardly ever given (or, if so, which she barely respects) and then the girding of the loins, and the starting of what for her is the new nightmare, the next compulsion, the new book. In between whiles she keeps on assuring herself that she is happy. But, as perhaps her nature was in these 365 pages, she does not I think once mention laughter.

The labour that went to all this is stupendous. Her habit seems to have been to write all morning, in the first years as little as fifty words, later as many as one thousand, though it is true she calls this 'Two pages' which, depending on how she filled her manuscript book, might mean still fewer words. After lunch, at least an hour's walk. She is very close to her sister Mrs Bell, and if she is in Sussex, she may visit there in the afternoon, or go over to another neighbour, Lord Keynes. Two or three games of bowls seem to have been the one relaxation. Then more writing between five and seven. After dinner serious reading, planned sometimes, in this diary, for weeks in advance, and often from the original Greek. Then bed at ten-thirty. And always, it seems, awake again between three and four in the morning, when she seriously appraises where she has got to in her work. The only interruptions in all this are the agonising headaches which come again and again and which incapacitate her for two weeks, or the influenza, perhaps twice a year, which drags her down seriously. And she was really happy, these extracts make one feel, only when she was working.

And if the novel she was doing turned sour on her, got stuck, there were other tasks handy such as criticism. She was always 'resting' her mind with other literary labours. That this was successful is shown by the fact that she left twenty-two books behind her, quite apart from the diaries. But it does not lessen the strain understandably evident in the present volume.

Indeed this sense of strain reaches almost intolerable heights during the writing of *The Years*; *Night and Day*, at the beginning of her life's achievement, had been hard enough, but it was as nothing to the tortures she endured in creating the first named. After close on three years' labour at this book she writes, 'I can only, after two months, make this brief note, to say at last after two months' dismal and worse, almost catastrophic, illness . . . I'm again on top. I have to rewrite, I mean interpolate, and rub out most of *The Years* in proof.' And, at that stage, the novel, which many consider her best, was 950 pages long. A record of hard work and guts that is beyond praise and which measures up to her stature.

Then, at the urging of friends, and his nearest relatives, she took on the biography of her great friend Roger Fry, who had died not long before. A harder task it would be almost impossible to imagine. One of the Stracheys told her straight out that it was impossible. And here is Virginia Woolf sketching a small part of the biography in this entry:

> Suppose I make a break after H.'s death (madness). A separate paragraph quoting what R. himself said. Then a break. Then begin definitely with the first meeting. That is the first impression: a man of the world, no professor or Bohemian. Then give facts in his letters to his mother. Then back to the second meeting. Pictures: talk about art: I look out of the window: His persuasiveness – a certain density – wished to persuade you to like what he liked. Eagerness, absorption, stir – a kind of vibration like a hawkmoth round him. Or shall I make a scene here – at Ott's? Then Cple [Constantinople]. Driving out: getting things in: his deftness in combining. Then quote letters to R.
> The first 1910 show.
> The ridicule. Quote W. Blunt.
> Effect on R. Another close-up.
> The letter to MacColl. His own personal liberation.
> Excitement. Found his method (but this wasn't lasting. His letters to V. show that he was swayed too much by her).
> Love. How to say that he never was in love?
> Give the pre-war atmosphere. Ott. Duncan. France.
> Letter to Bridges about beauty and sensuality. His exactingness. Logic.

In this entry she seems to give a glimpse of the technique of construction towards which she was now driving, within three years of her death, with all her powers. Quite apart from the amazing grasp which she displays in the above – the carrying of the complete projection in the head, a capacity, a state of command which may only come from long application – there is what she calls the 'four-dimension' approach. See how she creates depth in the portrait of Fry, or rather in the portrait as it was then, at that moment in her book; by the death, what Fry himself said, then her first meeting with him, then his letters to his mother, then her second meeting and so on. Here, before one's eyes, is built the sure scaffolding of a work of art.

Even more certain are the few sketches we are given, such as the Doctor from Lewes, who, after the consultation, stays to chat and omitting her, invites Leonard Woolf to the local chess club, and she would have so liked to have gone! Again the altogether brilliant account of travelling by night in the train, the Nicolsons and the Woolfs to Richmond, Yorks, to see a total eclipse of the sun, soon after dawn. Anyone who reads this was with them, must feel they were in the same compartment that night and had stood, at the moment, dismayed on the particular moor. This is also true of her setting down of what she saw of the blitz on London. Her command of what she sees can only be called uncanny.

It is for a later generation to guess at the position Virginia Woolf is to hold. It will be another two decades, as with all work done in the twenties and thirties, before any clear idea will emerge as to whether she will continue to be read. All we can tell the very young now, is that she had a profound effect on her time. And that we believe that, in 1941, a great woman and a great writer died, leaving in her work, as true artists do, a great part of herself behind her so freshly set down with endless, excruciating and exhausting labour.

THE COMPLETE PLAIN
WORDS

(Published in The London Magazine, *1954)*

A review of *The Complete Plain Words* by Sir Ernest Gowers
(H.M. Stationery Office).

Some years ago the Treasury asked Sir Ernest to write a guide
to the use of English in the Civil Service. In 1948 *Plain Words*
came out. No fewer than 300,000 copies were sold, an astonish-
ing total. Then in 1951 he followed up with *The ABC of Plain
Words*, which sold 130,000 copies. Now we have the present
volume which we are warned is a combined edition, revised and
rearranged.

He explains in his Prologue that the book is 'intended primarily
for those who use words as tools of their trade, in administration
or business'. In the last sentence of the book he says that the ideal
in writing this sort of English should be in 'thinking as wise men
do, and speaking as the common people do'. For most of his
200-odd pages Sir Ernest can only show how impossible this is
in practice.

As early as page eight he gives us 'A Digression on Legal
English'. It lasts for but six pages and is a brilliant short essay on
the difficulties of Parliamentary draftsmen, in which this most
distinguished retired Civil Servant begs us very reasonably not
to ridicule the verbiage under which so much of our lives is now
led. For instance 'An application for squashing a New Towns
Order turned on the true antecedent of a *thereto*'; and more often
turned against the citizen, no doubt, when it came before the
Judge. He persuades us that it is impossible to draft these legal
documents in any other way, but then that, of course, is what

the lawyers are for; to, so to speak, translate for us, as there are accountants to explain Income Tax.

And so Sir Ernest goes on to tell Civil Servants how to explain why we, the public, cannot always do what we want. How best they can write their usually negative letters is the narrow main theme of his book. At any rate the public, more concerned with the avoidance rather than the evasion of our myriad laws, comes into touch with the Civil Service mostly when it applies for some permission which would only be applied for when there was a danger of it being disallowed.

As any writer knows, it is more difficult to write correspondence in the negative than the affirmative. Yet the Civil Servant has to find how to say 'no' politely and then give the reasons. As he is a servant of the public these reasons must be intelligible to what may be a half-educated enquirer. How easy by comparison the similar task in commerce.

In productive engineering (manufacturing for instance) nearly all the letters must be in the affirmative. To say 'no' to a customer is quite a decision, as it can be to the Civil Servant to say 'yes'. But Sir Ernest must be right when he suggests that much of the obscurity of the language used in correspondence by Civil Servants comes from the wording of the Acts of Parliament which guide them. An analogy can be made in Engineering. The specification, that is the brief description in technical terms of what it is proposed to supply the customer, is often unintelligible to the layman. And this specification really stems from the Patent Specification, a legal document giving immunity for a number of years to the inventor in order to prevent a competitor copying his ideas. The following is an extract from a Patent Specification:

In accordance with one feature of the present invention, the improved mechanism for transferring bottles or like containers from one operating machine to another includes a table having a peripheral slot in the top thereof, a container conveyor moving in a horizontal plane and comprising a sprocket chain mounted beneath the top of the table for driving a number of conveyor sections, each conveyor section having an arcuate recess in its periphery to receive the periphery of the next

[185]

adjacent conveyor section and having a hollow pivot stud extending downwardly through the peripheral slot in the table top, the stud being closed at the top and adapted to slip over the top of a vertically extending elongated pivot pin carried by the sprocket chain to establish a driving connection between the sprocket chain and the conveyor section.

It may well be that every trade is developing a private language of its own. The Treasury apparently thought the Civil Service was beginning to do so. And this is how Sir Ernest Gowers sets out to correct the situation.

There is a great deal that is admirable in the three sections that follow, The Elements, Correctness and The Choice of Words, occupying some 118 pages and much of it elementary but nevertheless exact.

Only when we get to the second half of the book can it be said that difficulty begins, namely, in The Handling of Words.

It is a brave man who enters there. So much is merely a question of taste. But in these remaining 100-odd pages there is much to give one pause.

Thus Sir Ernest writes 'Like must not be treated as a conjunction. So we may say "nothing succeeds like success" but (in English prose) it must be "nothing succeeds as success does".' In this case the author's alternative seems intolerable and what he seeks to alter far preferable.

Again he says 'if the subject is singular the verb should be singular', then gives the following example of how this should be done: 'The Secretary of State together with the Under Secretary is coming'. Would it not be simpler if Sir Ernest had thought of 'The Secretary of State is coming with the Under Secretary'.

As a last example, Sir Ernest writes 'It is usually better not to allow a pronoun to precede its principal. If the pronoun comes first the reader may not know what it refers to until he arrives at the principal.

'"I regret that is not practicable in view of its size, to provide a list of agents." (18 words).

'Here, it is true, the reader is only momentarily left guessing what *its* refers to. But he would have been spared even that if the sentence had been written:

' "I regret that it is not practicable to provide a list of the agents; there are too many of them." (20 words).'

But surely in Sir Ernest's version it could be inferred that the official concerned might be hinting, in fact, there *were* too many agents. Surely something like the following could be better: 'There are so many agents that I regret it is not practicable to provide a list.' (16 words).

Perhaps writers ought not to review books. They only, if interested, see another way of doing it. (And not, Sir Ernest, 'if interested they see another way to do them'.) On reading his book one thinks he might prefer the latter, which was, of course, invented by your reviewer.

And then, when aged fifty or over, some of us have a nostalgia for the old form of words. A letter from a Civil Servant about one of the remaining Defence Regulations would seem odious to many if it were too explicit. And how could it be explicit since no one understands these Orders anyway, tied up in legal language as they are.

There are many who prefer being stopped in a fog by a net with an unbreakable mesh. How much better this than running nose-on into a lamp-post, South Bank style.

Also in commercial correspondence there is a danger if we changed the phraseology, which is admittedly meaningless, that we should not understand what we all mean at all. 'We are much obliged to you for your favour of the 15th inst.' when changed to 'We have your letter of Tuesday last' would read to many an old hand like a threat.

As though two paragraphs further on we should expect to see some such brutal phrase as 'put the matter before our solicitors' instead of that old delightful wording 'be compelled to place the matter in other hands'.

So it is, in the end again, all a matter of taste. But careful, scholarly and often witty as Sir Ernest Gowers's book remains, it is not, one feels, for readers of *The London Magazine*.

IMPENETRABILITY

(Unpublished, 1954)

We go about our daily lives, in great cities, thinking entirely about our personal affairs; perhaps every now and again sparing a thought for our partners, that is, the person we live with, and of course with even greater guilt, of our children. After a time, in married life, it becomes the other partner's fault that they have married one, but the only child, or, as chance may have it, the many children, have had no choice, they are ours, and this is what fixes the guilt on us.

I was in Moscow in 1938 and I saw men lying in the gutter who looked dead and who, my guide assured me, were dead drunk. I passed on. I had seen the same in the streets of Caen, Normandy, France, where as a child my parents took me so that we could taste meat, butter and cream again after the near starvation the Germans had put upon us in Britain in the 1914–18 war. I had passed on again. And when my father sent me to Paris to learn French in 1923 I once more saw a man lie senseless in the gutter. This time I stopped behind a plane tree. At least two priests passed by without it seemed a glance. I myself had gone past as had several other citizens, who had not stopped as I did. Then eventually, while I watched, two working-class women halted in the Boulevard Raspail and gossiped over the inanimate figure. Then one bent down and turned him over. Satisfied, I can only think, that he was still alive and drunk, she moved off with her companion, as I did likewise. One so seldom learns the end of things in life.

Now in London we have two-decker buses, the difference being that you are allowed to smoke on the top deck, which is why I always go on top. And since we have lived in this house I am writing from for ten years, I have had to catch a bus, holidays excepted, on the same route, every morning, every morning for all that time.

And in that time I've had one terrifying experience with a stranger, completely unexplained, and of course without intervention from myself or my fellow passengers. It was, which may be significant, on the outward, that is the morning, journey. I do believe people behave oddly from the pressure of their private, as opposed to what might be called their public lives. The fact is immaterial that the person I am going to tell you about was sober or so I believe, as people almost always will be at that hour. The point is that none of us, strangers, but I suppose Christians, even if not practising, not one of us ever do much about it.

This particular experience hit me not forewarned some seven years ago. You must understand that my bus route passes one of our great hospitals and that there is an obligatory stop there. We were not three hundred yards from it, and I was in one of the front seats on top, when I heard what was between a loud cry or a groan from behind. I turned round with a deep feeling of disapproval, as much as I saw reflected in the faces of all the other passengers but two. These were women and were directly behind where I was seated. You sit two by two on these buses in London, with an aisle in between, and two women next each other were involved. One was thrown back rigid on the seat in a kind of fit, an arm raised above her head as it might be with a sort of threat or defiance. Beside this woman was another, who from her embarrassed expression, did not know the ill one from Eve. Seated as she was on the outside, that is to say nearest to a window, she had delicately put thumb and forefinger round the wrist of this uplofted fist, in case, presumably, it should with force descend.

A fit, I remember saying to myself with some distaste and looking to my front again.

There were no cries or groans any more and no one said a word.

I thought to myself, I recollect, they will put her, so to speak, ashore at the hospital, which, by now, we had almost reached. Indeed I considered how fortunate it had been for this girl to be taken ill so near a place where everything would be that could be done. And when we stopped at this obligatory stop, which I felt

Providence had timed for her so well, I turned disapprovingly round once more. She looked ghastly, was still rigid, but the uplifted arm was lowered and the woman who had held her wrist was looking straight ahead. In looking back I could see several people getting off, queueing to climb down the stairs. I knew one of them would tell the conductor. I wondered whether he could carry her over to the hospital and thought, on the whole, not. That in fact one of the passengers would have to do it. And that it would not be me. I did not feel well enough. Upon which this thought came. I might as well get off, lose the fare, take another bus, for the delay could be all of five minutes, and besides, there might be a call for volunteers and, in the state I was, a woman in one's arms on those narrow stairs would be a job, I again thought.

In the event I sat tight. Let the police do it, I remember thinking.

Of course one of those departing did tell the conductor. There was the pause I had been expecting when we did not leave the stop and then here he was on the top deck, walking not like a bride, rather as one who is about to stop a wedding, up the aisle.

Now I only really know my own county, I can't tell you of elsewhere, but I must explain that down south in England there is no arguing with bus conductors. They have every legal right to throw you off if they feel like it, or to have you arrested if you won't go, again if only they feel like it.

So I felt almost sorry for this girl when the man came up.

'Are you all right, Miss?' I heard him ask as I sat rigidly looking to my front.

'Yes' she managed to reply, but in an expiring voice.

'Sure now?' he gruffly demanded.

'Yes' she whispered.

'Right' he announced, left us, climbed down the stairs and, to my dismay, we were off, still with our load of trouble I had been so certain would be passed over to that great hospital.

It was worse than being left alone, as one always is, with one's conscience. For, in this case everything might start all over again, and conceivably be worse still. One might, at a pinch, have to force open jaws and hold a tongue to prevent her swallowing it, or whatever one does.

[190]

I looked every now and again, and she seemed barely conscious. Then, to my horror, the woman on the far side wanted to get out. The sick one managed to move her legs out of the way and the girl who had held that ominous fist made off fast. But she came back. She whispered to the sufferer. What she said I did not hear. Even if I wasn't very deaf, I am sure I couldn't have heard. At the time, I remember saying to myself 'is this then one of these strange, secret, inviolable female complaints never to be mentioned before strange men?' But the sick one only nodded and the other left.

As the journey went on I looked round every now and then. Her eyes were open and I took care not to look in them. Something else I saw. Everyone was getting off as he or she got to their destinations. Then again it became a matter of conscience for, once more, as always, one was left alone with it. I was quite sure from what I had observed, that the conductor would be worse than useless. And the next hospital on this route was many a further mile distant. What to do? The conductor and I were now the only ones to know about her. And my stop, my destination, was coming up fast. Here was Baker Street. I looked again. The girl seemed barely conscious. Now George Street and my address where I get off.

The conductor saw me go and said no word. And that was that.

On the same route I have seen this same girl once or twice since. She doesn't seem to recognise me, indeed there is no reason why she should. She looks better. She is still not going to have a baby. I suppose, like any other novelist, and she wore gloves, I imagined her unmarried and just having found she was to have a child. Or some other equally fantastic female compulsion.

Or had she simply had a row with her mother? I shall never know. After all I can't very well go and ask.

But thinking it over through the years I do now consider that the conductor I so blamed at the time was quite correct not to take this girl into hospital. Why, they might have done almost anything to her there. Even a stomach pump! While now she is still all right.

Or is she?

FALLING IN LOVE

(Published in Esquire, *1955)*

Accepting 'with a sense of grievance' that he would not receive remuneration for this piece, commissioned by a freelance contributor, Green wrote to *Esquire*: 'Certainly I would not have bothered to answer his letter if I had known there was no question of payment.'

A man falls in love because there is something wrong with him. It is not so much a matter of his health as it is of his mental climate; as, in winter one longs for the spring. He gets so that he can't stand being alone. He may imagine he wants children, but he doesn't, at least not as women do. Because once married and with children of his own, he longs to be alone again.

A man who falls in love is a sick man, he has a kind of what used to be called green sickness. Before he's in love he's in a weak condition, for which the only prognosis, and he is only too aware of this, is that he will go on living. And, in his invalidism he doesn't feel he can go on living alone. It is not until after his marriage that he really knows how wrong or sick he has been.

I am, of course, assuming that love leads to marriage. Unrequited love is to be avoided at all costs. If a married man falls in love with a third party and hasn't the courage to leave his wife, he is like a man who takes off his belt, ties it round the branch of a tree, and hangs himself to death in the loop while his trousers fall round his ankles. If an unmarried man finds unrequited love then there is even more the matter with him.

The love one feels is not made for one but made by one. It comes from a lack in oneself. It is a deficiency, and therefore, a certifiable disease.

We are all animals, and therefore, we are continually being attracted. That this attraction should extend to what is called love is a human misfortune cultivated by novelists. It is the horror we feel of ourselves, that is of being alone with ourselves, which draws us to love, but this love should happen only once, and never be repeated, if we have, as we should, learnt our lesson, which is that we are, all and each one of us, always and always alone.

JOURNEY OUT OF SPAIN

(*Unpublished, 1955*)

Rejected by Associated Rediffusion television. There is correspondence to suggest that a misunderstanding had arisen over the length Green was to write to. On Rediffusion's insistence that the play be cut, Green wrote: 'I am not without experience in writing and am quite sure after thirty years at it that my piece could not be condensed to 20 minutes without hopelessly ruining it.'

Ritz Hotel, Barcelona. Lounge, palms, table and four chairs, alcove at back. Husband and wife, both aged about forty, sit at table in utmost luxury, he with brandy and soda. She with sherry.

SHE

Oh darling what a relief we're here.

HE

I know. But we're not there yet, though.

SHE

My dear we've only got to get on the boat and we'll be over there at nine o'clock tomorrow morning. And it will be a lovely cabin, the travel agent said so.

HE

Well it hasn't been too bad up to now, has it.

SHE

Darling it was so sweet of you to go to all the expense of the wagon lit. Why we've just drifted across Europe in the lap of luxury.

HE

And the Channel crossing wasn't too awful was it?

SHE

Like a mill pond, only with those lovely drinks one never has on real mill pounds.

[194]

HE

I say, have another.

SHE

Oh no, not yet. Promise me you won't drink too much this
trip. If you start now only think how you'll feel tomorrow
morning.

HE

I don't feel too good now as a matter of fact.

SHE

You don't? After those wonderful French railways have simply
wafted us here!

HE

It's a long way my dear. And then of course, and I'm not
blaming anyone or anything, but I've had after all to see to
everything.

SHE

Well you have your other drink then because you've been
perfect. And it is so wonderful of you to take me a room in
this gorgeous hotel just so as I can have a bath. And am I going
to enjoy it when I've finished my sherry. We've hours of time
haven't we?

HE

The boat doesn't sail until nine tonight and it's just three
o'clock now.

SHE

Only that! We did get here so quick didn't we even if we did
arrive by tram.
(She giggles.)
How fantastic to arrive at the Ritz by tram! D'you think the
Head Porter minded?

HE

But as I told you darling we forgot when we left London
that today would be Good Friday. No one at home told me
there would be no taxis on the streets in Spain in Holy
Week.

SHE

It did seem rather extraordinary all the same to carry our bags
off a tram. But of course it wasn't your fault.

HE

Well you can't take the car with you on the train you know, not yet at any rate!

SHE

Still the tram was quite an adventure, wasn't it?

HE

Yes, the first so far.

SHE

Now don't you start fussing darling. They told me over and over in London the boat out of here is marvellous.

HE

Good God a wedding!

(A tall girl in full wedding dress, her short mother and a photographer start to pose in the background. She is first put with her back to the wall, her train is pulled and rearranged diametrically to the right, and then she looks thrillingly over her left shoulder.

In the meantime the following dialogue continues.)

HE

Just look what luck, a wedding.

SHE

Oh no! I can't believe my eyes. And her dress! Have you ever seen anything like it?

HE

I pity the poor bridegroom. Where is he by the way? And does that woman do this for a living. I mean posing brides for that photographer?

SHE

My dear she's her mother.

HE

She can't be. Look at the difference in their sizes. How could that grotesque giant have come out of her?

SHE

My dear, how surprised can you be? Think of Mother.

HE

I was trying not to.

SHE

Now be sweet. This is the start of our holiday after all. I mean don't be serious. Honestly are her children going to own this photo all their lives?

HE

Shouldn't be surprised if they spent the first night of their married life on our boat tonight.

SHE

Now don't be disgusting.

HE

It's the facts of life after all.

(The tiny bridegroom sidles in.)

SHE

Oh no darling it can't be.

HE

Waiter, another brandy.

SHE

Now be careful.

HE

Poor devil. It doesn't seem possible. What a time he's going to have. Why she'll eat him!

(Her husband is rather tall as he rises to stretch himself.)

SHE

Some of those short men are very virile or so I've heard. But did I look like that when we were married?

HE

You looked very old fashioned.

(He sits down again.)

SHE

No but really Henry. I wore the latest thing.

HE

All I was saying was that it was dated within six months, and now twenty-five years later it looks positively antediluvian in the photos. Don't tell me they're going to be taken hand in hand now?

SHE

I remember you wouldn't even take my arm.

HE

I remember I was so dead frightened of falling flat on my face I was afraid I'd bring you down with me when I stumbled.

[197]

Don't forget the friend of your family who married us and tripped over the cassock.

(She laughs. The mother starts a row with the photographer.)

HE

That's life for you.

SHE

(Finishing her drink as his new one is served.)

Well I'm beginning to think about my bath.

HE

Before you go I fancy we'll ask about our tickets. And we'll have to get a hired car to drive down to the dock seeing it's Good Friday.

(To the Waiter.)

Do you speak English?

WAITER

Please?

SHE

What about the tickets for the boat. You've got them haven't you?

HE

(Looking through his pockets.)

Oh just to be sure I suppose.

(To the Waiter.)

Could you ask the Head Porter if he would come here a moment. Do you understand?

WAITER

(Departing.)

Please.

HE

All these fellows can understand is the ordering of drinks.

SHE

Well I don't wonder considering it's the only English they do hear. But why d'you want me for this?

HE

Oh only for a minute. Just in case I suppose.

(Still looking through his pockets.)

Now where did I put them.

SHE

Oh heavens darling if you've . . .

HE

No here they are.

(Extracting a booklet.)

SHE

But of course no Head Porter. Didn't you know they never left their important desks?

HE

The married couple are going back to the reception too, I see.

(Married group depart.)

Well we must give him a minute or two. No, here he comes.

(Head Porter a very fat man in uniform arrives.)

HE

Oh good afternoon.

HEAD PORTER

Yes sir.

HE

We have booked in for the afternoon so that my wife here can have a bath. We are catching the boat for Majorca this evening.

HEAD PORTER

Yes sir.

HE

There don't seem to be any taxis on the streets and we have to get down to the docks.

SHE

We even arrived by tram.

HEAD PORTER

Now is Holy Week in Spain, Madame.

HE

D'you think you can fix us up with something?

HEAD PORTER

Why yes sir. I get you taxi you pay him double, no tip, that I can arrange.

HE

Good. The old boat sails at nine. When ought we to leave?

SHE

Give us lots of time. We don't want to rush, do we?

HEAD PORTER

From here to the docks twenty minutes, Madame. If I order for seven o'clock, all right sir?

HE

Why so early?

HEAD PORTER

Big crowds many people on such boats in Spanish Holy Week.

HE

We don't in fact have our cabins reserved unfortunately. But will you order the taxi then? I have the actual tickets for the boat for the crossing here. Would you like to look at them?

(Produces book of tickets and hands them over to Head Porter who examines them. A look of deep sympathy comes over his face as he leafs through each page.)

HEAD PORTER

These tickets no good sir.

HE

What! But I paid for them.

HEAD PORTER

I much regret sir.

HE

But now look here.

SHE

Don't be ridiculous. They're issued and paid for, didn't you hear?

HE

Look at the name of the Travel Agency. As a matter of fact it's been nationalised, it belongs to the British Government now.

HEAD PORTER

I'm sorry sir. You see this is Spain.

HE

Don't I know it. Oh dear what is all this about?

HEAD PORTER

I much regret here in our country all travel tickets must be controlled. You must register them at the city you will leave on the day you take train or boat.

SHE

But it's disgraceful.

HE

Just a minute darling. Very well, it's only three p.m. now.
Fifteen hours you call it. Send these tickets down to the office
and jolly well have these tickets controlled then or whatever
you call it.

HEAD PORTER

I cannot, sir and Madame. The office he is closed.

HE

On a Friday afternoon?

SHE

When I could go out of here now and have my hair done
anywhere.

HEAD PORTER

It is Spanish Holy Week. Everywhere closed at 12.30.

HE

Not here though in this hotel.

HEAD PORTER

We never close. Even through the war we keep open.
(He hands book of tickets back.)

SHE

(Despairing.)
Oh darling!

HE

(To Head Porter.)
But look we got into this place by wagon-lit train at two-thirty
from Paris, fourteen and a half hours, do you understand. How
could we have got to your office by 12.30 hours? Why, we were
still rolling across bridges and going through tunnels then.

SHE

But what are we to do?

HE

(To Head Porter.)
Now come, my dear friend, just kindly look at these tickets
again. See, today's date is perforated on them, and it says
'Barcelona to Majorca', so what?
(Hands booklet back to Head Porter.)

HE

Are there two services daily?

HEAD PORTER

No sir. One alone.

(Head Porter holds tickets up to light to study perforations.)

SHE

(Whispering.)

My dear this man is slightly rabid. He doesn't want people to get through. Pay no attention. They give him a commission on all those he keeps here.

HE

I'm not so sure.

(To Head Porter.)

Now you've seen those perforated dates on the tickets what is your real opinion?

HEAD PORTER

(Handing tickets back.)

You could try sir.

HE

Try what?

HEAD PORTER

If I order your taxi as was arranged the lady and you may travel to the dock. But I infinitely regret. You understand. Holy Week in Barcelona. And Good Friday too. And yet . . . you can try. Go to the ship, no?

HE

You can get the taxi?

HEAD PORTER

Of that I am certain. I myself guarantee the taxi. Pay double but no tip.

HE

Understood. I'm trusting you, mind.

HEAD PORTER

I go now Madame and sir, and I arrange.

(Head Porter departs.)

SHE

Is it hopeless? What d'you think?

HE

I'm so sorry this has happened.

SHE

My dear it's not your fault. Just wait till I get back to that Travel Agency.

HE

Waiter, another brandy. Oh well this is the first hitch after all.

SHE

Aren't you going to order me a sherry? I've only had one.

HE

My dear I'm sorry I thought you said you were going to have your bath.

SHE

So I did. So never mind.

HE

You are sure? No, about these tickets my instinct is to get down to the boat and see what can be done. There must be an office on board where these things can be arranged.

SHE

I expect so. Well I'll tell you what I'll do. I think I should go up now and have my bath.

(Both stand up.)

I expect I'll feel better then.

HE

I'm so sorry about all this darling.

SHE

Darling, it hasn't happened yet. Don't fuss so and just for my sake don't have another brandy. Change to beer or something. Be seeing you, in about an hour.

(Fade out to London studio: where husband sits alone in armchair.)

HE

Of course you know I was very tired before we started on this holiday to Majorca. In fact my doctor had told me to get away, or else. Didn't tell my wife that though, no point in upsetting her unnecessarily. But as they say I was very tired by the time we got to Barcelona. Granted we were travelling in the most luxurious way which naturally we couldn't afford, yet any travelling exhausts me. I think it may be the vibration. So what with being pretty dead beat before we started, this trouble over controlling the boat tickets began to get me down sitting over my brandy at the Ritz. As a matter of fact, looking back on it now, I fancy I was more dubious about the fat great Hotel Porter ever getting us the taxi. Something my wife said about 'did he get a commission on the guests he kept in the hotel' stuck in my mind. Anyway there turned out to be nothing in this at all. When we stayed there on our way back to England we found the place was always packed, packed to the roof. And that Porter was a really honest man. None of what followed was anyone's fault really. It was just Spain on Good Friday. They all go to several different churches in turn all through that day. Yet there are a few around to do business. Anyway after a short break you will hear about the adventures that befell us in getting onto that boat. And we neither of us had any Spanish either.

(He waves to camera.)

(Break for commercials.)

(Wife in London studio sitting alone in armchair.)
SHE

Well you remember when you last saw me, I was just off to have a bath. And I had it, a lovely one. It was too sweet of Henry to go to all that expense just so as I could have a bath in the middle of the afternoon. Because we aren't really all that well off, in fact to tell the truth we seem to be getting worse off all the time. Anyway it did me a great deal of good, the bath I mean, because I was beginning to get a little bit upset at this idea about the tickets for the boat. You see we had spent such a lot of money already on this holiday, our first for three years, and my husband's doctor had told me strictly between ourselves, that Henry had to get away, in fact the doctor actually said 'or else' so that, oh where am I, well I had a jolly hot bath and felt a lot better, though I still didn't like that Head Porter one bit. All the same he did get us a taxi like he'd promised, and the taximan who hadn't a word of English, no more than we had Spanish in fact, did deliver us to the docks.

Just by where our ship we were supposed to be on was drawn
up. We could see her funnel.
(She gets up out of her chair.)
SHE
And this is what happened. . . .
*(Fade out to an island site café with striped umbrella top, two round
iron tables, eight chairs, dock gates, façade of building and over roof one
ship's funnel. Sitting in front of dock gates villainous old Porter with
number 37 on his uniformed cap.*

*Our married couple walk on, he over-burdened by four suitcases, one
under each armpit, the others in his two hands.)*
SHE
(Pointing off.)
Henry, look at that cat!
(He does not look.)
SHE
I've never seen a cat do that before.
(He casts the heavy suitcases down with a crash. He still does not look.)
HE
Then you've been dead lucky.
*(A very shabby Waiter, much shabbier than the café, and with a black
patch over one eye, arrives as they sit down.)*
HE
You speak English?
WAITER
Yes I understand.
HE
Then bring me a double brandy and would you like a coffee
dear?
SHE
After all this I think I'd like a brandy too.
HE
(To the Waiter.)
One single, one double brandy then.
SHE
Mightn't I have a double in the circumstances?
HE
Two double brandies waiter.

WAITER

Surely sir. But I have one awkwardness.

(He points to suitcases.)

These not allowed.

HE

Why not, good heavens?

WAITER

(Pointing to Porter.)

He has his bread to make so he can eat.

(Porter advances.)

HUSBAND

(To wife.)

To make, to earn he means. The man obviously cannot be a baker.

WAITER

(Not understanding.)

But he is rich.

HE

Rich? How?

WAITER

Don Alfonso won lottery eight years back.

HE

Why's he working now then?

WAITER

He serious man and many daughters.

SHE

You mean you are going to give my precious things into the keeping of this scruffy individual?

HE

Just a minute darling.

(Waiter and Porter have a burst of conversation in Spanish.)

SHE

Oh heavens what are they saying?

HE

How should I know?

WAITER

This man shall have them.

HE

But I want my things here by me.

WAITER

Patron does not permit.

SHE

Darling I'm beginning to feel quite faint you know.

HE

(To Waiter.)

Get the brandies first will you, and quick.

(Waiter leaves. Porter addresses them in Spanish with great dignity.)

HE

No comprehende, Señor.

(Porter replies sadly in Spanish.)

SHE

Oh dear, I don't like this one bit.

HE

What am I supposed to do darling? Let's wait till the Waiter comes back to translate.

SHE

But what do you imagine is under that black patch?

HE

Why a glass one of course. They're touchy out here. The evil eye you know.

SHE

I don't know, Henry. All I do know is I don't like any of it.

HE

Darling I was only joking.

(Porter now beckons up a neat little Spaniard with good English. He is young and well dressed. He is the Fixer.)

FIXER

You speak no Spanish sir?

HE

Unfortunately not.

FIXER

You would like me to interpret?

(Porter fires volley of Spanish at him.)

SHE

Oh dear!

[207]

FIXER

The Porter he says it is his privilege, his living to put your bags into the waiting compartment, the left luggage do you call it? If you leave here the luggage it may vanish.

SHE

But darling you aren't going to, you promised me.

HE

Look ducky, his number on the cap is 37. That was my locker number at my first school.

SHE

So you think that makes it all right? I wonder who's quite OK mentally, you or me.

FIXER

You need have no fear Madame, I have know this man since I was boy.

SHE

But I must have my things and how old are you then?

FIXER

Alas it is not allowed Madame, by the laws of Spain. And also you have not heard, it is ten years he won the lottery.

HE

Yes we know that. I gather his daughters are rather expensive.

(Fixer smirks at this. Porter picks up bags and turns away.)

SHE

Darling!!

(Porter stops with his back to them.)

HE

Now look angel. Everyone knows this Porter, our friend here, the Waiter, everyone. Let him put the bags away and we'll pick them up when we go on the boat. When in Rome do as the Romans do.

FIXER

You must have no fear Madame, I guarantee this man.

SHE

(Weakly.)

Well darling.

(Porter carries bags off at once.)

SHE

So he knows English.

FIXER

Not one word Madame. Like an animal he goes by the sound of the speech.

(Waiter comes back with the two double brandies. He bows to Fixer.)

HE

(To Fixer.)

Will you join us?

FIXER

Thank you, I will take a coffee.

(Waiter leaves. Fixer sits down.)

FIXER

You are then on holiday in Spain.

HE

We were.

FIXER

I do not understand.

SHE

My husband means that we have had troubles on our holiday.

FIXER

Troubles in Spain. I do not comprehend?

HE

It is all a small question of our tickets on the boat. We got in here by train this afternoon after the offices were closed for Holy Week and so couldn't have our boat tickets stamped or whatever you call it!

FIXER

That is most unfortunate.

HE

So my wife and I thought we would just come down to the dock here and see what could be done about it.

SHE

Please do you understand.

FIXER

(To husband.)

Maybe I could fix something. Sometimes I am fortunate. Can I see your tickets?

(Husband searches and then hands them over. Fixer examines them with care, holding them to sky.)

SHE

Oh d'you think he will be able?

FIXER

(Handing tickets back.)

I much regret these things are without value. They have not been controlled.

SHE

(Interrupting.)

In Spain anyone who makes a journey must have his or her ticket stamped in the town they are leaving before they start.

FIXER

Madame knows Spain then?

HE

Madame does not know Spain. Already Madame has this bitter experience. Can you suggest anything?

FIXER

Yes but you must trust me. Also you will have to pay something.

HE

But of course.

FIXER

You see there exists two boats only for this service, one big, one small and they are old these boats. The Company, they never know which boat can make the crossing every night. They do not know therefore how many people they can carry. And in Holy Week in addition.

HE

But there's no one about. She sails in two hours and we might be in the desert.

FIXER

All travellers are inside with controlled tickets by another entrance. There is big Hall with bar, café, music everything for citizens with controlled tickets.

HE

What are we waiting for then?

SHE

Yes indeed darling.

FIXER

But excuse, you are not controlled. You sit on here and be comfortable. I fix this when boat opens in one hour's time. You want to be comfortable no? No crowds or that? So sit and I fix only you will pay a little.

HE

Of course. About how much?

FIXER

One hundred pesetas. One of your pounds. You understand I must out of that pay money myself.

SHE

(Thankfully.)

Oh how wonderful.

HE

Yes that's all right. Thanks very much.

(Reaching into his pocket.)

Would you like it now?

FIXER

No sir. Wait here for me. In one hour just I lead you on the boat and then you pay me.

(Hands booklet of tickets back.)

OK?

HE

OK indeed. Thank you Señor.

FIXER

I will be here in one hour from present. Thank you sir.

(He gets up having finished his coffee, bows and departs.)

SHE

(To Fixer's back who makes no sign of having heard.)

Oh thank you.

(She gets up, comes round and puts one arm about her husband's neck.)

SHE

Oh dear darling you are so clever and you have been so good all through. Of course once we are on the boat we can buy our way into a cabin. It's only the third class will be so crowded. But darling I'm afraid it will be a bit expensive, a pound here and a pound there.

(Kissing him.)

Oh you are good.

(Sits down again.)

HE

I always said it could be fixed.

SHE

Yes you did. It was only me was nervous. And now it's all arranged I don't feel tired a bit any longer.

HE

It hasn't been too bad on the whole has it?

SHE

Of course not. But I've told you, you've been just wonderful.

HE

(Looking around.)

All the same it is a bit empty round about.

SHE

It's Good Friday darling. They're all in church, they're very devout in these parts.

HE

Yes and yet I don't know. . . !

(The Porter returns and sits on step of the dock gate.)

HE

Well anyway he's back. We'll get your bags out of him all right now he's here again.

SHE

Why my dear you're not really nervous are you? That last little Spaniard with the wonderful English gave me complete confidence.

HE

I know but where's our Waiter? I think I'd like to ask him something.

SHE

(Pointing off.)

Over there darling.

HE

Waiter!

[212]

SHE

It's still going to be all right Henry.

(Waiter comes up.)

HE

Where is everyone?

WAITER

How you intend?

SHE

He means the crowds, the evening walk, the lovers.

HE

I mean this boat over there is due to sail in less than two hours
time and where are the passengers?

WAITER

They are in. Big room, music, drinks; they wait.

HE

Then why are we here?

SHE

Yes, why?

WAITER

Because tickets no good.

HE

But where can I get good tickets with the offices closed?

WAITER

Excuse please but . . .

(Pointing.)

. . . office just along street new opened.

HE

Then take me along.

WAITER

One minute. I fix.

(He departs.)

SHE

Oh dear, d'you think?

HE

I think that's where that little Spaniard you like so much has
gone. And in case he doesn't come back I'll go to make doubly
sure.

(Waiter returns with Travel Agency man and two pretty American

[213]

girls. Husband draws Travel Agency man away and the three women get together. Americans come up to British wife.)

MAY

May I make your acquaintance. I'm Mrs Cyrus E. Pfanudler of Waco, Texas. May's the name.

SHE

Oh how d'you do.

MAY

And this is my intimate friend Mrs Fred J. Hoyt of Houston, Emmeline we all call her back home.

EMMELINE

(Shaking hands.)

I'm honoured.

SHE

Well I'm Mrs Britt and my husband's mother called him Henry. Mine named me Ann. We both resent it.

MAY

My but what lovely names. Well Mrs Britt . . .

(She gestures towards the husband and the guide.)

. . . can you get this situation? Us two girls are just confused about that old boat and our chances onto it.

SHE

I know. You're not controlled but then no more are we.

EMMELINE

You're telling us Mrs Britt.

MAY

And yet if you can believe me so far we've paid for two cabins with good US currency.

EMMELINE

And I understood that like all places out east the natives came down hours before the boat or train was listed to depart.

SHE

Oh I'm told they're all inside there . . .

(Waving towards Porter and dock gates.)

. . . where our luggage is.

MAY

Oh gosh ours is on a hand truck somewheres.

EMMELINE
All of them in there? Then let's go, what are we waiting on?

MAY
Now Emmeline let's take this leisurely.
(Pronounced leesurelee.)
Besides Mr Britt may be fixing something.

SHE
I shouldn't exactly rely on Henry, if I were you!

EMMELINE
(To May.)
Well honey we got our reservations haven't us? Are you coming with me or no?
(She strides off to dock gates followed by the other two women. Husband and Travel Agency man watch incuriously. Porter rises to his feet as they come up. Emmeline makes to go by him but he courteously bars the way. Emmeline shows her tickets. Porter after examination makes mock show of tearing them up and points into far distance. Wife turns to beckon up husband who with Travel Agency man does not move.
After some agitation the three women return.)

MAY
My God if I only had this language.
(He comes over.)

HE
I gather we are in rather the same boat, ha, ha ha. How d'you do.
(The three women glare at him.)

HE
Well it seems the office may be open. Perhaps we should all of us drift over there, what d'you think?
(Travel Agency man comes over.)

TRAVEL AGENCY MAN
It is best ladies you come with me and with Señor. The way is short and the office may shut again.

HE
Shut again? Oh Lord come along then at once.

MAY
My God don't give me this Good Friday all over once more.

[215]

SHE

Yes well perhaps we'd better.

EMMELINE

(To May.)

Let's go, honey.

(In the meantime Waiter has come up. He has paid him. And as they go off Waiter points in opposite direction and both Porter and Waiter laugh derisively behind their backs.

Fade out to London studio where husband sits alone in armchair.)

HE

Well then there I was toiling off to the shipping line office with three women in tow, my wife and now these two American married girls. And I was feeling pretty nervous, I can tell you. I hadn't said much to the wife of course but I could see from the size of her funnel that it was a great big ship. And no one at all on the quay round that beastly café. If all the other passengers were inside somewhere like the one-eyed Waiter said, then it didn't look as though anyone meant to get us on board. Or rather, to be fair to them, as though anyone with the sort of tickets we had, could even get us on. So I was in pretty much of a panic leading the party with the Travel Agency man. About the only thing you could say about him was that he did have some English. And when we did get to the office there was the usual long queue all waiting in a line at the one ticket window. But no goats or anything like that, I'm glad to say. Well my wife and the other two girls began to natter a bit of course, and I started to get even more nervous. You know how it is when you are at the end of a queue with a boat to catch. You begin to wonder if the Captain won't sail before you get the tickets. Anyway I don't think I let my wife see anything of what I was feeling. Can't ever tell with women though. See through you every time. And when at last I did get to the ticket window there was a disgusting type sitting behind it. My travelling ticket man took our two booklets and shoved them through the opening with a volley of Spanish. Our friend took one look, laid them flat on the counter and flipped them back at me *(sorting the action to the words)*. He did it with such a look of contempt on his face I almost walked

[216]

out. It was a good thing I didn't lose our places at the head of the queue though because the Agency man said wouldn't I like at least to get onto the boat. As that was what we had been after all along, I said 'of course' and so we bought two third-class tickets. Remarkably cheap too, they were. Only about 4/6d each. And then when we got outside and he was taking the American girls to another office, I've never discovered where, there came the question of how much to tip him! Well in the end I gave him 10/- for his trouble and felt an awful fool after. So then my wife and I made our own way back to the boat. We had a good hour to spare. The old Porter put us into the waiting room which was a huge, enormous place, and after a bit we were allowed on board – as we discovered later as deck cargo.

(*Fade to open-air scene at dusk on closed canvas-covered hatch on board. Husband again carries four suitcases which he lets go with a crash. Both seem very tired. Behind them is squalid opening to stairs to third-class accommodation in bowels of ship. The two American girls come up chattering.*

One or two sailors and passengers go to and fro again and again. An Englishman gets fully dressed into a sleeping bag on the hatch.)

SHE

Oh dear.

HE

Well at least we're on board. Now we can get cracking and fix something and without the Fixer.

(*He nods to American girls who are tipping Porter who has carried up their bags.*)

HE

Look they're tipping too much.

SHE

But darling d'you think you gave enough to the Travel Agency man?

HE

What? For getting us on as deck cargo.

SHE

I meant perhaps if you had given him more we shouldn't be left here all night.

[217]

HE

(Of American girls.)

Well, they're here too now, aren't they?

SHE

Yes darling.

(American girls come up.)

MAY

Well what d'you know?

HE

(Bleakly.)

Not a thing yet.

EMMELINE

(To wife.)

Isn't this the hell of a note?

SHE

My dears and what do we do now?

HE

(Nodding at Englishman in sleeping bag.)

He's got the right idea right enough.

(The three girls shriek.)

MAY

Why that thing's insanitary Emmeline.

HE

What happened to you two then?

EMMELINE

Right after that Travel man yanked us away from you he conducted us to an underground sort of café where he had us meet a little guy!

(Here she describes the actor playing the Fixer, but in uncomplimentary terms.)

EMMELINE

And from what they told us this little guy is just a genius. He has everyone on this old boat in his little hands.

SHE

Does she mean our Fixer darling?

HE

(To May.)

With good English?

(And then adds a further description.)

MAY

That's the very guy.

SHE

He's supposed to be looking after my husband and me.

EMMELINE

Is that Travel guy and this other in cahoots. Oh my gosh.

HE

Yes in double harness. And what if I may ask did you tip the Travel Agency type?

MAY

Two dollars.

HE

Too much.

SHE

But darling you gave him ten shillings which is more.

HE

They're in league.

EMMELINE

In a world series more likely. So what do we do now?

HE

Well he promised us he'd be here and he isn't.

MAY

I saw him go on board by the crew's gangway.

HE

Then he will be looking after your affairs then!

SHE

And why not ours as well too?

MAY

Look Em, we should get cracking. Supposing you and me goes down into the first class and see what we can do with the Purser, on this little ship. Would you two nice people see after our grips for five minutes?

SHE

Of course.

MAY

That's sweet of you. Here Em.

(The Americans go off right.)

HE

(With ever-increasing agitation.)

It's all a plot!

SHE

What is dear?

HE

They're all in league these Travel people.

SHE

But how Henry?

HE

There are no taxis so a guide gets a fat tip for taking us on the tram. Next you have to pay double to a taxi to make it run and tip the hotel Porter to find it for you. Then you pay good money for tickets in London and you have to tip even to get onto the boat as deck cargo. It's a racket.

SHE

Well we can't stay here all night can we dear?

HE

It's a lovely night.

SHE

But darling when we do sail there'll be an awful draught.

HE

It's not going to rain, I'm sure of it.

SHE

No dear, I can't stay out in this place all night wet or dry. You do see that don't you?

HE

(Starting up.)

Where is this infernal Fixer? He promised he would be here half an hour ago.

SHE

Would you like to go and look for him? While I keep an eye on all these bags.

HE

Never find him. I've been watching the gangways all this time. There are thousands coming aboard.

SHE

Oh dear.

HE

This is a question of getting hold of the ship's Purser. And now those pretty American girls are ahead of us. And of course they're in with the Fixer. Or else why did they go off with the Agency man at the shipping office?

SHE

I don't know Henry.

HE

I do. And why are they doing better than us this very minute? I'll bet they are. Why? Because they're women.

SHE

Oh now dear . . .

HE

Yes because I visualise this Purser we've none of us ever set eyes on yet as a lean dark amorous Castilian who will do anything for a woman with a geranium stuck behind her ear.

SHE

(Laughing.)

And I haven't even a daisy or a violet!

HE

No darling but I think you ought to go and at least try.

SHE

Who, me?

HE

Yes, well perhaps you have just a try. After all I've done everything up to now and now I'm beat I don't mind telling you. Simply have one shot at it darling! Please.

SHE

All right then if you insist I'll go. But don't you move now! If I don't find you when I get back, I'll go straight home to England.

HE

I promise.

(He kisses her.

Wife in London studio sitting alone in armchair.)

SHE

So you see I could tell Henry was getting a bit worked up, knowing him as well as I do. We haven't been married twenty-five years for nothing. Even if we didn't receive a single piece of silver at the anniversary. So, anyway, for the sake of his peace of mind I dragged myself up. And of course almost anything is better than to go on sitting in the night on that degrading hatch or whatever they call the thing. But when I did get down below I simply can't ever describe to you the fantastic scenes that met my eye. There were people lying in the gangways already although we were still tied up in dock. And some of them had been sick, yes, just as soon as that. That was in the second class of course. And when I climbed like a mountain goat over all these prone corpses and got at last to the first class, where by right we belonged, and which we had paid for in London, well it wasn't quite so full in the first class but what a scene it was, talk about a stiff upper lip! That chief Purser was a great big fat bully and he had all his servants, the waiters, stewardesses and things, drawn up in a circle round him. If he stepped forward they stepped back. He had a huge list in his hands, and the first-class passengers were led up to him two by two while he shouted and raved and sent them off with a stewardess to their cabins. And then almost as soon as I had forced my way to the outskirts it was the turn of the two American girls you have met. Led forward by the Fixer who was positively cringing, it turned out they weren't controlled, or whatever it is called. And oh dear the scene that followed. You'll hear more about all this in a minute or two!

(Break for commercials.)

(Fixer in London studio, standing alone as if lost, shaking his head and talking to himself.)

FIXER

English people are OK but they cannot understand. Maybe they do not wish. Our thought in Spain to control tickets is to avoid too many people in one train or boat in one day. But English people pay pesetas in England and I think that they voyage by travel carpet. It is not so. Never-less I like English people. I charge them less than any other country. They are stinking rich in their own country but they have no pesetas in

Spain. So I am not greedy with them. I am man of honour. Now this Manuelito, the fat guy, the head waiter, I have known him all my life. Very fierce and difficult on the ship he is, but very frightened at home. His wife very tiny but very angry woman. And Manuelito much like wine. So when Manuelito is on his ship it is best to be very quiet with him. On this Holy Friday the ship is very full you understand. So the young American ladies become very angry with Manuelito when he shout at them about no cabins when we are with him downstairs. And I, I can do nothing. So when the ladies go up with anger I say 'Manuelito you cannot leave these beautiful ladies, and there is a señor who is good, you cannot leave them with no supper.' So he comes up with me to find them although he is very busy man. I still have hope something for cabins can be arranged. But there, when they are all on the deck, there is another quarrel. As you will see. And me I can do nothing!

(Fade back to open-air scene on closed hatch on deck. Husband is sitting there as the three girls come back alone.)

EMMELINE

Hi there!

SHE

Oh darling!

MAY

Isn't he just angelic guarding all our things.

HE

Did you do any good?

MAY

I'll say not!

EMMELINE

And if that fat slob of a Purser ever comes within a hundred feet of me again I'll just go up to him and tear his false eyes out.

SHE

Oh my dear the man's a fiend! Honestly I did feel so awful for the two of you.

HE

And the Fixer was no good?

[223]

SHE

Useless. Worse, he absolutely cringed.

MAY

Let's you and me talk this situation over Emmeline.
(They withdraw to their bags, but not out of camera range.)

HE

(Despairingly.)

Then what are we to do?

SHE

I know darling.

(Then pointing off.)

But wait look there's that disgusting Purser in person and Fixer
too.

(To the Americans.)

See who's coming! I really believe he's here to apologise.
*(Americans move over to the husband and wife as Fixer and Purser
come up to this group. Purser has a great deal of gold braid on cap and
uniform, is very fat and angry looking.)*

HE

I do believe he's actually come to see us right!

SHE

My darling I didn't mean to say this but I really feel rather
sick!

*(Husband in reply merely points to ship's rail as he gets up to fac
Purser. The Americans also move in to confront this man.)*

EMMELINE

What is this?

PURSER

I come to have explanation.

HE

We've been here hours I tell you.

FIXER

Please ladies, sirs.

MAY

Just don't ever give me please again.

PURSER

I have been insulted, no?

MAY and EMMELINE
You sure have!
HE
Now look here! I don't know what goes on but my wife here is a sick woman.
EMMELINE
And if you can't do nothing for us where's the Captain?
PURSER
I do not have to accept insulting words.
MAY
Then just take us to your Captain and will we tell him.
FIXER
Ladies, if you please! Captain on these boats sails ship. This man has command of cabins.
EMMELINE
Then it's a disgrace, that's all it is.
PURSER
Madame I have had bad words. I throw you off this ship with your friend.
MAY
You hear that Em? This slob. When we've paid good dollars for this trip.
HE
But my wife and I . . .
FIXER
Please.
EMMELINE
Where's the Consul of the US?
PURSER
And on this ship we have peace, no, although we are crowded. In Spain on public holiday.
SHE
(To husband.)
My dear I'm really very sorry but I really think I shall be ill.
HE
It's disgraceful.
PURSER
(Furiously to Americans.)

If you two ladies will come with me.

EMMELINE

Why, what for you just tell me?

FIXER

Trust me and go in peace.

MAY

Em, is it safe?

PURSER

Follow me please.

SHE

(Half heartedly.)

Goodbye.

HE

(To Fixer.)

What does this mean?

FIXER

(To husband.)

Stay here please.

HE

(To Fixer.)

And what about us?

SHE

(To Fixer.)

Don't go just now.

FIXER

Stay.

(And follows Purser and two American girls.
Their bags are left behind.)

HE

How very disagreeable.

SHE

I didn't see you doing much about it.

HE

What d'you mean darling? I'm doing my best. No man can
do more.

SHE

You didn't stick up for them much did you? Two girls alone
without a man.

HE

Oh good heavens darling! What is it supposed I should have said?

SHE

You know perfectly well. Oh mercy!
(She nods in direction of Spanish sailor who is shown drinking out of wine skin. He then champs his jaws at wife in a terrible grimace.)

HUSBAND

(Clenching fists.)
We'll soon see to that here and now.

SHE

(Detaining him.)
Darling you are sweet. He's just hungry. Look he's going off to get a crust.

HE

(To back of departing sailor.)
Well never let it be said I . . .

SHE

(Soothingly.)
Calm down darling.

HE

I'm only doing my best as I told you.

SHE

I know dear. But those poor girls.

HE

What about them?

SHE

Well, to be turned off the boat.

HE

Don't you be too sure of that. They're probably being led off to the best cabins.

SHE

(Incredulously.)
You mean you actually think those two, oh it's disgusting oh! . . .

HE

Good heavens look at that.
(Pointing off.)

Coming up the gangway. It is! It's our honeymoon couple from the hotel.

SHE

Where? Yes it's them. And look at our horrible Purser coming half way to meet them, Henry. And the welcome he's giving!

HE

Yes darling.

SHE

Have you seen those two American girls go down the gangway?

HE

As a matter of fact I haven't.

SHE

Oh so they've stolen a march on us. Oh my dear so that's all the use you are in a crisis on a journey.

(He makes a gesture towards the Fixer who is approaching them. He moved forward to meet Fixer.)

HE

What now?

FIXER

You would like hot dinner in first-class saloon.

HE

Why yes.

FIXER

Then here are two tickets.

HE

And we could sleep afterwards at the table all night.

FIXER

I regret you cannot.

SHE

Look darling didn't I tell you?

(She points out sailor who has come into view again, smiling amiably and eating bread.)

HE

Well we've got tickets for dinner anyway.

SHE

Darling you have been clever.

FIXER

But you do not wish to spend all night here, no?

HE

No we don't, would you?

FIXER

Then follow me. Third class but clean. You will pay me one pound.

(Fixer moves off. Husband picks up the four suitcases.)

HE

(To wife.)

Come on, darling.

SHE

Oh so we're going. But where to?

HE

I don't know. But do come on.

(They go off down entrance into third class at back.
Fade back to London studio where wife sits alone in armchair.)

SHE

Well you know what they say that everything must have an end. This trip had an end too, though I must say it made an awfully long night to end it. Looking back on everything I suppose really I'd been a bit awkward. Still the whole journey had been so very tiring. But d'you notice how my husband never even calls me by name now. It's just 'dear' when he's being affectionate and 'darling' when I'm sorry to say he's fed up. Oh well I suppose after twenty-five years. Anyway Henry was getting really worked up poor dear and we were both very very tired. So I went down with him without a murmur into the ghastly stomach of that boat. You've never seen anything like it; though everywhere was clean I must admit, spotlessly clean. But absolutely jam packed with people, crying children, grandmothers, the whole frightful business of travelling. They must have got them on by another gangway, because of course we were only deck cargo. Anyway the Fixer introduced us to a Steward and Henry paid both of them and then I was snatched away from him and put on a little mattress on the floor of a ladies' cabin and poor Henry had to go on the floor of another one but with his head under a washbasin all night. And the men were locked in all the time! But there it is. Everything comes to an end in the end, and I've noticed it usually comes as an anticlimax. The odd part was we both slept extraordinarily well. But wasn't the breakfast in Majorca delicious next morning.

A CENTAUR

Flash and Filigree by Terry Southern
(André Deutsch)

(Review published in The Observer, *1958)*

Green sent *Flash and Filigree* to Deutsch on Southern's behalf. 'He has given us a dazzling performance . . . ,' he wrote. 'If you decide to do nothing with this Ms. I should like to have it back as I want to read it again.' After the successful publication of the book, Green met Southern. They were to become close friends.

The young fellows with flashing heels are now thundering up the course to overtake those sad over-fifties who limp along, nodding like donkeys. For with novelists there is always a fast start and then, alas, before they are dead, very definitely a finish, perhaps even before they reach the post. From his stand a spectator, that is the reader, must have difficulty in following the race. His glasses are trained yet it is all too hard to follow – who has passed who, and who can that be, surely familiar, who lags so far behind? All he knows is the noise, one punter after another, or simultaneously, calling their fancies whilst dark bookies, silent at last, re-examine their boards as publishers do spring lists.

Mr Southern, the young American, living of all places in Geneva, has in this, his first novel, given us a dazzling performance. The setting is Los Angeles with nary a film star in it. A terrifying figure, the foremost dermatologist, Dr Frederick Eichner, is uncovered with a dubious patient he at first disposes of in, for any doctor, a unique way. This fellow, a Mr Treevly, it is best not to be sorry for, though his tribulations are great. Eichner is the man with whom we are immediately involved. He has a kind of crazy logic which, in all his troubles, must support and save, but not console him; he is above or beyond even contemplating consolation.

A brilliantly funny yet, at the same time, a truly frightening character, the doctor has a conviction about everything. He is of Hungarian extraction. He drives his fast car on theory and this leads him to a smash-up. The police come along, the glimpse he gives them of this theory and several others – for he is not a silent physician – makes him suspect. From here on there are hilariously amusing scenes with the constabulary and towards the end with the jury at his trial.

But it is with Miss Mintner, Babs the hospital nurse, that the book soars, gets like all good novels into its own orbit. Of course it can be argued that *Flash and Filigree* is really two books, or even three if the episode of Frost, the 'private eye', is analysed – a fault not uncommon with first novels. But in Southern's work the cement which binds the kaleidoscopic patterns which go to make the whole is the continuing percipience with which he communicates what he sees in his mind's eye; the sinister Eichner, the low-comedy Frost, and the raving beauty of addle-pated Miss Mintner.

Eichner hires Frost the detective to save him from the police and in the course of a whole night's pursuit of some mythical witness they both get drunk. This gives us some of the most riotously amusing scenes in the whole novel. Eichner tipsy is a thing no reader should miss. But it is when, quite early on, we come on Babs, fair haired with huge blue eyes, that a rocket begins to climb, to climb with great elaborated wit and deliberation until it bursts up above in colour, light and beauty to give a reward with which writers so rarely bless the benighted reader who cries out, so often in vain, to be carried away.

The last quarter of the novel is perhaps weakest where Dr Eichner disposes once and for all of the first victim and returns in all tranquillity to his collection of toy racing cars. And yet this may by anticlimax be the fault of the seduction scene immediately preceding it – Babs in the back of a student's car – a quite exceptional piece of writing and something to warm the saddest bachelor heart.

Let everyone salute Mr Terry Southern who with only his first novel already has a winner. He will start odds on for his next.

THE ART OF FICTION

(Published in The Paris Review, *1958)*

This interview may have been conducted in 'the author's fire-lit study', but it was also a written collaboration, the script passing back and forth between Green and Southern. 'No, there is no real trouble over our interview,' Southern wrote to conclude. 'There is some vague and preliminary dissension among the staff over the use of the word "cunty", but nothing concrete.'

Henry Green is the pseudonym of H. V. Yorke, the London–Birmingham industrialist whom W. H. Auden has said to be the best English novelist alive.

Mr Green wrote his first novel, *Blindness*, while still a schoolboy at Eton, and this has been followed by nine more. Of his life otherwise, he has noted:

> I was born in 1905 in a large house by the banks of the river Severn, in England, and within the sound of the bells from the Abbey Church at Tewkesbury. Some children are sent away to school; I went at six and three-quarters and did not stop till I was twenty-two, by which time I was at Oxford, but the holidays were all fishing. And then there was billiards.
>
> I was sent at twelve and a half to Eton and almost at once became what was then called an aesthete, that is a boy who consciously dressed to shock. I stayed that way at Oxford. From Oxford I went into the family business, an engineering works in the Midlands, with its iron and brass foundries and machine shops. After working through from the bottom I eventually came to the top where for the time being I remain, married, living in London, with one son.

Mr Green is a tall, gracious, and imposingly handsome man, with a warm strong voice and very quick eyes. In speech he displays on occasion that hallmark of English public school, the slight tilt of the head and closing of eyes when pronouncing the first few words of some sentences – a manner most often in contrast to what he is saying, for his expressions tend toward parable and his wit may move from cosy to scorpion-dry in less than a twinkle. Many have remarked that his celebrated deafness will roar or falter according to his spirit and situation; at any rate he will not use a hearing-aid, for reasons of his own, though no doubt discernible to some.

Mr Green writes at night and in many longhand drafts.

His novels, by date of publication, are: *Blindness* (1926), *Living* (1929), *Party Going* (1939), *Pack My Bag* (1940), *Caught* (1943), *Loving* (1945), *Back* (1946), *Concluding* (1948), *Nothing* (1950), and *Doting* (1952).

In his autobiographical novel, *Pack My Bag*, he has described prose in this way:

> Prose is not to be read aloud but to oneself at night, and it is not quick as poetry, but rather a gathering web of insinuations which go further than names however shared can ever go. Prose should be a long intimacy between strangers with no direct appeal to what both may have known. It should slowly appeal to feelings unexpressed, it should in the end draw tears out of the stone.

An ancient trade-compliment, to an author whose technique is highly developed, has been to call him a 'writer's writer'; Henry Green has been referred to as a 'writer's-writer's writer', though practitioners of the craft have had only to talk with him momentarily on the subject to know that his methods were not likely to be revealed to them, either then or at any other time. It is for this reason – attempting to delve past his steely reticence – that some of the questions in the interview would seem unduly long or presumptuous.

Mr Green lives in London, in a house in Knightsbridge, with a beautiful and charming wife named Dig. The following conversation was recorded there, one winter night, in the author's fire-lit study.

Now you have a body of work, ten novels, which many critics consider the most elusive and enigmatic in contemporary literature – and yourself, professionally, or as a personality, none the less so. I'm wondering if these two mysteries are merely coincidental?

MR GREEN

What's that? I'm a trifle hard of hearing.

INTERVIEWER

Well, I'm referring to such things as your use of a pseudonym, your refusal to be photographed, and so on. May I ask the reason for it?

MR GREEN

I didn't want my business associates to know I wrote novels. Most of them do now though . . . *know* I mean, not write, thank goodness.

INTERVIEWER

And has this affected your relationships with them?

MR GREEN

Yes, yes, oh yes – why some years ago a group at our Birmingham works put in a penny each and bought a copy of a book of mine – *Living*. And as I was going round the iron-foundry one day, a loam-moulder said to me: 'I read your book, Henry.' 'And did you like it?' I asked, rightly apprehensive. He replied: 'I didn't think much of it, Henry.' Too awful.

Then you know, with a customer, at the end of a settlement which has deteriorated into a compromise painful to both sides, he may say: 'I suppose you are going to put this in a novel.' Very awkward.

INTERVIEWER

I see.

MR GREEN

Yes, it's best they shouldn't know about one. And one should never be known by sight.

INTERVIEWER

You have however been photographed from the rear.

MR GREEN

And a wag said: 'I'd know that back anywhere.'

INTERVIEWER

I've heard it remarked that your work is 'too sophisticated' for American readers, in that it offers no scenes of violence – and 'too subtle', in that its message is somewhat veiled. What do you say?

MR GREEN

Unlike the wilds of Texas, there is very little violence over here. A bit of child-killing of course, but no straight-shootin'. After fifty, one ceases to digest; as someone once said: 'I just ferment my food now.' Most of us walk crabwise to meals and everything else. The oblique approach in middle age is the safest thing. The unusual at this period is to get anywhere at all – God damn!

INTERVIEWER

And how about 'subtle'?

MR GREEN

I don't follow. *Suttee*, as I understand it, is the suicide – now forbidden – of a Hindu wife on her husband's flaming bier. I don't want my wife to do that when my time comes – and with great respect, as I know her, she won't. . . .

INTERVIEWER

I'm sorry, you misheard me; I said, 'subtle' – that the message was too subtle.

MR GREEN

Oh, *subtle*. How dull!

INTERVIEWER

. . . yes, well now I believe that two of your novels, *Blindness* and *Pack My Bag*, are said to be 'autobiographical', isn't that so?

MR GREEN

Yes, those two are mostly autobiographical. But where they are about myself, they are not necessarily accurate as a portrait; they aren't photographs. After all, no one knows what he is like, he just tries to give some sort of picture of his time. Not like a cat to fight its image in the mirror.

INTERVIEWER

The critic Alan Pryce-Jones has compared you to Jouhandeau and called you an 'odd, haunted, ambiguous writer'. Did you know that?

MR GREEN

I was in the same house with him at Eton. He was younger than me, so he saw through me perhaps.

INTERVIEWER

Do you find critical opinion expressed about your work useful or interesting?

MR GREEN

Invariably useless and uninteresting – when it is of daily papers or weeklies which give so little space nowadays. But there is a man called Edward Stokes who has written a book about me and who knows all too much. I believe the Hogarth Press is going to publish it. And then the French translator of *Loving*, he wrote two articles in some French monthly. Both of these are valuable to me.

I'd like to ask you some questions now about the work itself. You've described your novels as '*non-representational*'. I wonder if you'd mind defining that term?

MR GREEN

'*Non-representational*' was meant to represent a picture which was not a photograph, nor a painting *on a photograph*, nor, in dialogue, a tape-recording. For instance the very deaf, as I am, hear the most astounding things all round them, which have not, in fact, been said. This enlivens my replies until, through mishearing, a new level of communication is reached. My characters misunderstand each other more than people do in real life, yet they do so less than I. Thus when writing, I 'represent' very closely what I see (and I'm not seeing so well now) and what I hear (which is little) but I say it is 'non-representational' because it is not necessarily what others see and hear.

INTERVIEWER

And yet, as I understand this theory, its success does not depend upon any actual sensory differences between people talking, but rather upon psychological or emotional differences between them as readers, isn't that so? I'm referring to the serious use of this theory in communicative writing.

MR GREEN

People strike sparks off each other, that is what I try to note down. But mark well, they only do this when they are talking together. After all we don't write letters now, we telephone. And one of these days we are going to have TV sets which lonely people can talk to and get answers back. Then no one will read anymore.

INTERVIEWER

And that is your crabwise approach.

MR GREEN

To your question, yes. And to stop one's asking why I don't

[239]

write *plays*, my answer is I'd rather have these sparks in black and white than liable to interpretation by actors and the producer of a piece.

INTERVIEWER

Do you consider that all your novels have been done as 'non-representational'?

MR GREEN

Yes, they all of course represent a *selection* of material. The Chinese classical painters used to leave out the middle distance. Until *Nothing* and *Doting* I tried to establish the mood of any scene by a few but highly pointed descriptions. Since then I've tried to keep everything down to bare dialogue and found it very difficult. You see, to get back to what you asked a moment ago, when you referred to the emotional differences between readers – what one writes has to be all things to all men. If one isn't enough to enough readers they stop reading and the publishers won't publish any more. To disprove my own rule I've done a very funny three-act play and no one will put it on.

INTERVIEWER

I'm sorry to hear that, but now what about the role of *humour* in the novel?

MR GREEN

Just the old nursery-rhyme – 'Something and spice makes all things nice,' is it? Surely the artist must entertain. And one's in a very bad way indeed if one can't laugh. Laughter relaxes the characters in a novel. And if you *can* make the reader laugh he is apt to get careless and go on reading. So you as the writer get a chance to get something into him.

INTERVIEWER

I see, and what might that something be?

MR GREEN

Here we approach the crux of the matter which, like all hilarious things, is almost indescribable. To me the purpose of art is to produce something alive, in my case, in print, but with a separate, and of course one hopes, with an everlasting life on its own.

INTERVIEWER

And the qualities then of a work-of-art . . .

MR GREEN

To be alive. To have a real life of its own. The miracle is that it should live in the person who reads it. And if it *is* real and true it does, for five hundred years, for generation after generation. It's like having a baby, but in print. If it's really good, you can't stop its living. Indeed once the thing is printed, you simply cannot strangle it, as you could a child, by putting your hands round its little wet neck.

INTERVIEWER

What would you say goes into creating this life, into making this thing real and true?

MR GREEN

Getting oneself straight. To get what one produces to have a real life of its own.

INTERVIEWER

Now this page of manuscript you were good enough to show me – what stage of the finished work does this represent?

MR GREEN

Probably a very early draft.

INTERVIEWER

In this draft I see that the dialogue has been left untouched, whereas every line in the scene otherwise has been completely rewritten.

MR GREEN
I think if you checked with other fragments of this draft you would find as many the other way around, the dialogue corrected and the rest left untouched.

INTERVIEWER
Here the rewriting has been done in entire sentences, rather than in words or phrases – is that generally the way you work?

MR GREEN
Yes, because I copy everything out afresh. I make alterations in the manuscript and then copy them out. And in copying out, I make further alterations.

INTERVIEWER
How much do you usually write before you begin rewriting?

MR GREEN
The first twenty pages over and over again – because in my idea you have to get everything into them. So as I go along and the book develops, I have to go back to that beginning again and again. Otherwise I rewrite only when I read where I've got to in the book and I find something so bad I can't go on till I've put it right.

INTERVIEWER
When you begin to write something, do you begin with a certain *character* in mind, or rather with a certain *situation* in mind?

MR GREEN
Situation every time.

INTERVIEWER
Is that necessarily the *opening* situation – or perhaps you could give me an example; what was the basic situation, as it occurred to you, for *Loving*?

MR GREEN

I got the idea of *Loving* from a manservant in the Fire Service during the war. He was serving with me in the ranks and he told me he had once asked the elderly butler who was over him what the old boy most liked in the world. The reply was: 'Lying in bed on a summer morning, with the window open, listening to the church bells, eating buttered toast with cunty fingers.' I saw the book in a flash.

INTERVIEWER

Well, now after getting your initial situation in mind, then what thought do you give to plot beyond it?

MR GREEN

It's all a question of length; that is, of proportion. How much you allow to this or that is what makes a book now. It was not so in the days of the old three-decker novel. As to plotting or thinking ahead, I don't in a novel. I let it come page by page, one a day, and carry it in my head. When I say carry I mean the *proportions* – that is, the length. This is the exhaustion of creating. Towards the end of the book your head is literally bursting. But try and write out a scheme or plan and you will only depart from it. My way you have a chance to set something living.

INTERVIEWER

No one, it seems, has been able to satisfactorily relate your work to any source of influence. I recall that Mr Pritchett has tried to place it in the tradition of Sterne, Carroll, Firbank, and Virginia Woolf – whereas Mr Toynbee wished to relate it to Joyce, Thomas Wolfe, and Henry Miller. Now, *are* there styles or works that you feel have influenced yours?

MR GREEN

I really don't know. As far as I'm consciously aware I forget everything I read at once including my own stuff. But I have a tremendous admiration for Céline.

I feel there are certain aspects of your work, the mechanics of which aren't easily drawn into question because I don't find terms to cover them. I would like to try to state one however and see if you feel it is correct or can be clarified. It's something Mr Pritchett seems to hint at when he describes you as 'a psychologist poet making people out of blots', and it has to do with the degree to which you've developed the 'non-existence-of-author' principle. The reader does not simply forget that there is an author behind the words, but because of some annoyance over a seeming 'discrepancy' in the story must, in fact, *remind* himself that there is one. This reminding is accompanied by an irritation with the author because of these apparent oversights on his part, and his 'failings' to see the particular *significance* of certain happenings. The irritation gives way then to a feeling of pleasure and superiority in that he, the reader, sees *more* in the situation than the author does – so that all of this now belongs to *him*. And the author is dismissed, even perhaps with a slight contempt – and only the *work* remains, alone now with this reader who has had to take over. Thus, in the spell of his own imagination the characters and story *come alive* in an almost incredible way, quite beyond anything achieved by conventional methods of writing. Now this is a principle that occurs in Kafka's work, in an undeveloped way, but is obscured because the situations are so strongly fantasy. It occurs in a very pure form however in Kafka's *Journals* – if one assumes that they were, despite all said to the contrary, *written to be read*, then it is quite apparent, and, of course, very funny and engaging indeed. I'm wondering if that is the source of this principle for you, or if, in fact, you agree with what I say about it?

I don't agree about Kafka's *Journals*, which I have by my bed and still don't or can't follow.

But if you are trying to write something which has a life of its own, which is alive, of course the author must keep completely out of the picture. I hate the portraits of donors in medieval triptychs. And if the novel *is* alive of course the reader will be irritated by discrepancies – life, after all, is one discrepancy after another.

Do you believe that a writer should work toward the development of a particular *style*?

He can't do anything else. His style is himself, and we are all of us changing every day – developing, we hope! We leave our marks behind us like a snail.

So the writer's style develops with him.

Surely. But he must take care not to let it go too far – like the later Henry James or James Joyce. Because it then becomes a private communication with himself, like a man making cat's cradles with spider's webs, a sort of Melanesian gambit.

Concerning your own style and the changes it has undergone, I'd like to read a sample paragraph – from *Living*, written in 1928 – and ask you something about it. This paragraph occurs, you may perhaps recall, as the description of a girl's dream – a working-class girl who wants more than anything else a home, and above all, a child. . . .

Then clocks in that town all over town struck 3 and bells in churches there ringing started rushing sound of bells like wings tearing under roof of sky, so these bells rang. But women stood, reached up children drooping to sky, sharp boned, these women wailed and their noise rose and ate the noise of bells ringing.

I'd like to ask about the style here, about the absence of common articles – *a*, *an*, and *the* – there being but one in the whole paragraph, which is fairly representative of the book. Was this omission of articles throughout *Living* based on any particular theory?

MR GREEN

I wanted to make that book as taut and spare as possible, to fit the proletarian life I was then leading. So I hit on leaving out the articles. I still think it effective, but would not do it again. It may now seem, I'm afraid, affected.

INTERVIEWER

Do you think that an elliptical method like that has a function other than, as you say, suggesting the tautness and spareness of a particular situation?

MR GREEN

I don't know, I suppose the more you leave out, the more you highlight what you leave in – not true of taking the filling out of a sandwich, of course – but if one kept a diary, one wouldn't want a minute-to-minute catalogue of one's dreadful day.

INTERVIEWER

Well, that was written in 1928 – were you influenced toward that style by *Ulysses*?

MR GREEN

No. There's no 'stream of consciousness' in any of my books that I can remember – I did not read *Ulysses* until *Living* was finished.

INTERVIEWER

That was your second novel, and that novel seems quite apart stylistically from the first and from those that followed – almost all of which, while 'inimitably your own', so to speak, are of striking diversity in tone and style. Of them though, I think *Back* and *Pack My Bag* have a certain similarity, as have *Loving* and *Concluding*. Then again, *Nothing* and *Doting* might be said to be similar in that, for one thing at least, they're both composed of

. . . what would you say, *ninety-five* per cent? . . . ninety-five per cent *dialogue*.

MR GREEN

Nothing and *Doting* are about the upper classes – and so is *Pack My Bag*, but it is nostalgia in this one, and too, in *Back*, which is about the middle class. Nostalgia has to have its own style. *Nothing* and *Doting* are hard and sharp; *Back* and *Pack My Bag*, soft.

INTERVIEWER

You speak of 'classes' now, and I recall that *Living* has been described as the 'best proletarian novel ever written'. Is there to your mind then a social-awareness responsibility for the writer or artist?

MR GREEN

No, no. The writer must be disengaged or else he is writing politics. Look at the Soviet writers.

I just wrote what I heard and saw, and, as I've told you, the workers in my factory thought it rotten. It was my very good friend Christopher Isherwood used that phrase you've just quoted and I don't know that he ever worked in a factory.

INTERVIEWER

Concerning the future of the novel, what do you think is the outlook for the Joycean-type introspective style, and, on the other hand, for the Kafka school?

MR GREEN

I think Joyce and Kafka have said the last word on each of the two forms they developed. There's no one to follow them. They're like cats which have licked the plate clean. You've got to dream up another dish if you're to be a writer.

INTERVIEWER

Do you believe that films and television will radically alter the format of the novel?

It might be better to ask if novels will continue to be written. It's impossible for a novelist not to look out for other media nowadays. It isn't that everything has been done in fiction – truly nothing has been done as yet, save Fielding, and he only started it all. It is simply that the novelist is a communicator and must therefore be interested in any form of communication. You don't dictate to a girl now, you use a recording apparatus; no one faints any more, they have blackouts; in Geneva you don't kill someone by cutting his throat, you blow a poisoned dart through a tube and *zing* you've got him. Media change. We don't have to paint chapels like Cocteau, but at the same time we must all be ever on the lookout for the new ways.

INTERVIEWER

What do you say about the use of symbolism?

MR GREEN

You can't escape it can you? What after all is one to do with oneself in print? Does the reader feel a dread of anything? Do they all feel a dread for different things? Do they all love differently? Surely the only way to cover all these readers is to use what is called symbolism.

INTERVIEWER

It seems that you've used the principle of 'non-existent author' in conjunction with another – that since identified with Camus, and called the *absurd*. For a situation to be, in this literary sense, genuinely *absurd*, it must be convincingly arrived at, and should not be noticed by readers as being at all out of the ordinary. Thus it would seem *normal* for a young man, upon the death of his father, to go down and take over the family's iron-foundry, as in *Living*; or to join the service in war-time, as in *Caught*; or to return from the war, as in *Back* – and yet, in abrupt transitions like these, the situations and relationships which result are almost sure to be, despite any dramatic or beautiful moments, funda-mentally *absurd*. In your work I believe this reached such a high point of refinement in *Loving* as to be indiscernible – for, with all the critical analyses that book received, no one called attention to the absurdity of one of the basic situations: that of *English* servants in an *Irish* household. Now isn't that fundamental situation, and the absence of any reference to it throughout the book, intended to be purely *absurd*?

MR GREEN
The British servants in Eire while England is at war is Raunce's conflict and one meant to be satirically funny. It is a crack at the absurd Southern Irish and at the same time a swipe at the British servants, who yet remain human beings. But it is meant to torpedo that woman and her daughter-in-law, the employers.

As to the rest, the whole of life now is of course absurd – hilarious sometimes, as I told you earlier, but basically absurd.

INTERVIEWER
And have you ever heard of an actual case of an Irish household being staffed with English servants?

MR GREEN
Not that comes quickly to mind, no.

INTERVIEWER
Well, now what is it that you're writing on at present?

MR GREEN
I've been asked to do a book about London during the blitz, and I'm into that now.

INTERVIEWER
I believe you're considered an authority on that – and, having read *Caught*, I can understand that you would be. What's this book to be called?

MR GREEN
London and Fire, 1940.

And it is not fiction?

No, it's an historical account of that period.

Then this will be your first full-length work of non-fiction?

Yes, quite.

I see. *London and Fire, 1940* – a commissioned historical work. Well, well; I dare say you'll have to give up the crabwise approach for this one. What's the first sentence?

'My "London of 1940" . . . opens in Cork, 1938.'

. . . I see.

– TERRY SOUTHERN

AN UNFINISHED NOVEL

(Published in The London Magazine, *1960)*

Coinciding with the publication of Edward Stokes's critical study, *The Novels of Henry Green*, this number of *The London Magazine* was intended as a celebration of Henry Green's work. In an interview with Alan Ross which follows this piece, Green says of 'the actual business of composition': 'I find it so exhausting now I simply can't do it anymore. The older you get, the harder it gets.'

I was in love in the late twenties when I began a novel I am never to finish, called *Mood*. It was about the particular girl and the name given her was Constance Ightam – 'the name was correctly pronounced only by those who said Eyetam, not Iggetam or Itham'. She was about twenty years old and had once a great friend, another girl who had got married, Celia was *her* name. 'Your dog dies and after a little you buy another, your friend goes and if you are lucky you find a new friend. And all the time you are learning to walk alone. When Celia married she had gone the way of all friends. When you have been two you can't be three, and now Constance was alone.' Alone and walking in London down Oxford Street towards Hyde Park when she hears – 'that high, loud, educated *voice*, she saw the Blue Train where the voice was so much in evidence, then the boat where was no sound of it throughout the crossing, and the Pullman where again it triumphed, crying: "My dear I went to sleep before the boat started and didn't wake until my maid told me we were in!"' And now here was that same kind of voice – 'here in Oxford Street, this time proclaiming . . . "the most lovely sponge". Constance looked and there was that same kind of woman coming out of a shop.'

This being an impossible novel to be able to finish, Constance proceeds to dream. Sponges lead her to the Mediterranean. 'For what is a sponge – and this she felt but did not think. Why it is picked from the sea, it is cleaned and dried, perhaps a lot of things are done to it, perhaps nothing very much. Perhaps a little salt is still left in it. And here she sailed.' Sailed that is in her mind (and everything in this book was to have been through Constance's well-loved eyes). She sailed to that tideless sea. 'As you came down the beach for where you got in the sea it was like you had a halo round you; where the sun had been and now the warm sea lapped you you felt you could roll like dolphins for that round fat feeling. Oh she had gone plunging out, her wet rubber cap had shone like any god, there were no waves nothing but this blue sea, she rolled on it, the sun played like cymbals on her flanks and on one breast and then from a surfeit of all this she'd lain on her back and floated. She'd closed her eyes. But then was a hum like thousands cheering miles away and she looked, and up above in that tremendous blue there was an aeroplane, aluminium painted, all along its wings winking, blinding light, high, high above, ever so slowly moving quite straight like a queen.'

For Kings and Queens, my private symbol I suppose for the burning love I felt for the girl in question, Kings and Queens were to mean much to Constance. An only child, her parents had one house in the country and another in London, the one Queen Anne the other by Robert Adam and all the servants to wait on her as was still feasible nearly thirty years ago.

Her parents are introduced. The mother first. 'Having such a deal of stones suddenly glittering here and there about her, and being so dark, so with her it was like that glittering armoured sheath above a beetle's wings: she might, when you saw her in the middle of her flowers, suddenly burst out flying, that sheath might suddenly burst open on her sharp and iridescent skin – she constantly wore black, she might at moments ride a broomstick.'

And then there is poor Mr Ightam, the father, the city man who comes down to his Queen Anne house at weekends. He has a symbol, as Constance is to have one too. His room 'looked to be what he was' 'The walls were done in a brown paper, and on them hung pictures of horses which might be by Alken or Sartorius. There was a big desk on which were many papers and that one yellow china vase of flowers.' Some play is made of this vase, I regret to say because – 'he could remember where it stood when he was small and his nurse was washing him, and tickling him'.

This so-called symbolism, the love for a significant object, is much more strongly brought out in dearest Constance. On the mantelpiece of her room, amongst the invitation cards, the two Delft candlesticks and the old Dutch clock lay or lurked what was really Constance 'two small bright painted aeroplanes in wood'.

Lord, when you came in that room and looked round and cried out, as you couldn't help doing, Lord what a fine room, then, when you saw those aeroplanes you might sing *those* are her pets, that's what is most hers in here. When you came in and saw them it might be like you came into a King's rooms and saw a local paper there. Or, more like, the other way about. You came into a common sort of room and then you saw two Kings seated by the fire.

Nobody would ever know, she sang as she looked about her in Oxford Street, no one, not one of these not even mother, nobody would know about those aeroplanes. And when mother had had the walls done that gorgeous blue then suddenly she'd see she could bring her Queens down from where she'd put them, in a drawer in her bedroom. But when she'd brought them down and put them on the mantelpiece (she'd put them on the same side one with the other because they looked nicer like that – one just pushing in front of the other) when she'd stepped back to look, then she saw they weren't Queens any more, but where they were now they were Kings.

This was written when Professor Freud was still alive in Vienna, and it would be in my bedroom now if my wife had not dug it out of a drawer for a series on discarded work dreamed up by someone in the BBC. Why does one give up something on which one has been working? Obviously because one feels it simply will not do. It is the reason why it will not do, that may be of interest to readers of *The London Magazine*.

[253]

It is of course perfectly true and feasible that people walking up Oxford Street into Hyde Park can be reminded of much by the faces or the tones of voice, if they can still hear these, of those they encounter. It is also true that any such reminder is almost incapable of being rendered in print. A writer is after all at quite a remote distance from his reader, what he has to say to his reader has no tone of voice, his face is unseen, expressionless, as he confers so to speak at second hand through the black and white of print, as he confers with whoever it may be is good enough to use eyes to read him. It is quite hard enough to establish contact or even sympathy with a reader even by the use of the first person singular – I went to such and such a place, I did so and so – but to establish a girl, in this case Constance, in a static situation where nothing is happening to her except her thoughts and feelings, is an impossible project for the novelist and one which only a very young man, as I was then, would try for. Take the following: she is seated in the Park and a tired ticket collector comes to collect his fee, in those days one penny.

He had looked into her eyes. She had looked into his. She had seen a light of mockery there. As she had seen that monkey go careering down along the path just now in front of her, so Constance, being like she was this day, had invested that Collector with another life, a new agility. Being so lovely she had brought him out of himself like the night would do which he longed for so: that light in his eye was almost as she had been with Celia on the Mediterranean sea. But he was a man. She felt he had been half mocking at her for being a woman. She had a small creepy feeling at that, like her senses were coiled up inside.

The effect of a sentence like this, even if it is an obviously incompetent echo of D. H. Lawrence, must be quite fatal to a book. Any work of art if it is alive, carries the germs of its death, like any other live thing, around with it. But in a passage like the above there is already a death sentence, the black cap on the whole projected work inexorably pronounced for a total lack of sympathy or communication with the reader.

A more experienced writer would have introduced some sort

of action, for instance Constance might have been sitting in the Park with one of her young men who could have resented a familiarity on the part of the Collector. A trick of this kind is only too familiar in many a novel and rarely hides the barrenness of situation it seeks to conceal.

Equally disastrous in my abandoned book is a worked-up climax which fails to come off. Constance while she is making her way to the Park is reminded by something or other of when, as a child, she went with Celia and her French Governess to watch haymaking outside the Queen Anne country house.

Celia found a stick and first they walked on the new grass between the golden dykes of hay and then they ran along these long concentric rings. Each round they made, one following the other, brought them nearer to the middle of this piece which had been mowed in a round.

The horses harnessed to the full waggon followed them with their wide eyes from where they had been left not far away. The children ran shrieking round and then, as they neared the centre, they grew more quiet. The horses shifted, they would turn their heads away and yet always come back to the children. The men, sitting low in shade, lazily watched them, only the Governess paid no attention. And as they came nearer and nearer in to the centre, in ever shortening circles, those two horses, hidden from the men by their waggon, grew more uneasy. They snorted through their wide nostrils, distended and red. The children came nearer and nearer in: each horse struck at the ground, their quarters trembled, they were thrown into a sweat. And when at last the centre was reached and the children fell down there, both of them, with what came to the men as a faint cry, then those two horses, with a scream, bolted. They careered away, the waggon pitching, crashing behind them.

Thus the worked-up climax which fails however well written, and thus the old trick by which the novelist, to be dramatic, casts his reader, or rather drags his reader back into that imaginary golden sunny adolescence spiked with simple fears. When my adolescence, for one, was a time of deep depression shadowed by terror of so much that was unknown, and deep terror at that. And when, at the time I was trying to write this novel I was so much nearer my own adolescence than I am now, in fact I had then only just escaped!

How pitiably bad this writing is you must be thinking. And yet at the time I wrote it I had the inestimable advantage of the ear of no less a person than Mr Edward Garnett, the friend of Conrad, of T. E. Lawrence, and the most celebrated publisher's reader of his day. I had submitted my first novel *Blindness* to Messrs Dent whose reader he was, and they accepted it. Now, in the goodness of his heart, Mr Garnett, from disinterested kindliness, was trying to help me over the hurdle of the second novel. And a real hurdle it is, indeed it is more than that to every writer, it is a sort of Aintree fence for horse and rider, which is not a bad analogy for the relationship between the author and his casual reader. I had this vast new fence to jump and this book *Mood* was to carry me over it, and then, you see, the flow, the impetus, began to weaken, to peter out. That this happened was due I now feel sure to the basic weakness of the construction, a succession of moods indeed, just reflections with no action. And so, as the surge of ideas slowed down, I lost heart and several times went to see Mr Garnett for advice and comfort.

Edward Garnett the first few times a young man met him, cut a formidable figure. Tall, gaunt, greyfaced, with large eyes very much magnified behind his glasses, after opening the door in Pond Place, and leading you up the stairs to his room, he sat down in his armchair and put a rug on his knees. I think it was the grey white hair cut low on the forehead in a fringe which particularly intimidated me. But, at any rate at first, he was a shy man, and I can't forget the rising sense of despair in which, all haltingly, I read aloud from the manuscript of *Mood*.

And yet he had a genius for encouraging the young. He would also give up almost any amount of his time, if he thought one was any good. I only wish I had kept the pages of mine which he blue pencilled to show me what could with advantage be left out. He was almost magically successful with his deletions.

Anyway he said he approved of what I had read him of *Mood* and urged me as I got stuck more and more with it, as I increasingly hesitated, he urged me, and this I think may help young writers today, he said vehemently 'Go on, go on and get it finished and then we can knock the lot into shape afterwards. But you must finish it first.'

This is what I was quite unable to do, I don't now know whether to be sorry or glad. All I do know is that if Mr Garnett, in the event of my finishing the book, still liked it then as the greatest book surgeon of his day, he would have shown me how to cut it open, what to remove, what to renew, and how to sew everything up again until it was a Novel.

Even now I can't myself see how *Mood* could be knifed into a book. For instance, take the following – and you will bear in mind that Celia was Constance's great friend before the former's marriage:

> And Celia, since marriage, had lost all semblance of what she had been. Constance laughed and thought if they were to go back together now to the Mediterranean again as they had done, before Celia was married, Constance thought how different it would be. Although she had been alone when that aeroplane came overhead yet she had bought two toy aeroplanes, one loneliness for each of them. She had not told Celia about it. They had often swum out together, she had been glad to draw Celia away from the beach, they had lain side by side dazed by the sun and delight out on the sea. So Constance had bought one for herself and one for Celia as a celebration in honour of those occasions. And Constance who had looked on the aeroplanes as one and the same and had held neither in preference to the other, had chosen one of the two for her own when Celia married, a secret one.

This passage starts a long return by Constance as she sits in Hyde Park, a 'flash back' in her mind to her time with Celia by the Mediterranean. It would read better if carried out in dialogue, the 'do you remember' sort of thing, with Constance's young man also present to act as a foil. Then I suppose one would have to find some drama they would have been moving to out there which would have to have some bearing on a drama threatening them presently in the Park. I don't know what Mr Garnett would have had to say to that if he were alive today, it might have passed. Certainly it might have given body to the following passage which I still quite like. The two girls, by the Mediterranean, but at night, go off out alone, into the night, after dinner.

'They had gone to the outmost edge of the garden, and lights over that porch which led to the hotel were caught in a tiny reflection in their glasses on the marble table which gleamed like skin in the dark. They sat on a bench which had been made to encircle a tree, when they leant back the bark, which was not hot or cold, pressed into their backs in long furry tongues. The marble table kept a hoard of coolness and their glasses of the dark wine looked like huge soft eyes, the pair of them, marvellously soft.'

Oh dear when I think of the long hours it took to write and wrestle with this unfinished unfinishable novel and then when I think what am I doing making a fool of myself allowing it to be in print at long last, well all I can say to the writer who intends to go on is – 'throw nothing away, it may come in useful some time. If only to show how things shouldn't be written,' and thus perhaps, much later, as now, to turn a slightly dishonest penny.

But the lack of animation, which is probably the first sign of dissolution, the seeds of death there is in every work of art and which existed, to me, so strongly in this unfinishable novel, even while it was being written, that, in spite of encouragement I couldn't begin to finish it, occurs most strongly in the final paragraph, that is the last point I got to and beyond which I could not go. Constance is still alone in Hyde Park and it is not long after her meeting with the mocking ticket inspector:

She watched a couple pass before her. They had on them as they walked a mood so gentle that everything was brother, sister to them. They had that in the way Kings could be proudly apart and yet near to the people. But it was the loneliness in high places which was the great memory you could have, those secret walks with pets where were no men to ape uneasy monkeys, that was what counted.

Oh being a King was really for when you were alone, for

that was the only kind that counted. You could promise, you could swear, but friends nearly always changed as the years went round. They married as one might go to Africa to shoot big game – then stay there drinking, or another was sent to Mexico and *there* were convents. Everywhere you looked were graves for friendship, love; and tombstones on everyone's tongue.

Of everyone you met, was only you you could be with always and she thought that's how it is, don't let's have any monkey business with other people, the issue ultimately is with ourselves. As my two eyes are co-ordinated so let me have myself as my friend, let me have that glory where I draw on no one, lean on nobody. May I learn to be alone.

The manuscript of *Mood* ends, for ever here. As I remember it the love I had for the original of Constance died a week or so before those last words were written. And that, perhaps, is the whole explanation.

BEFORE THE GREAT FIRE

(Published in Volume 7 The London Magazine, *1960.*
Also published in The Texas Quarterly, *1960,*
entitled 'Firefighting'.)

A well-structured synopsis of a book, of which he completed only this, a first section, was found among Green's papers. 'The book, to a length of between 65 and 75000 words, is to be autobiographical with the least possible use of the first person singular . . . it will be concerned almost entirely with the men and women of the three Fire Stations in which I served throughout the War. These people came from all classes and from many parts of Britain. Waiters, manservants, shop assistants, stock exchange clerks, petty thieves masquerading as building workers and professional London Fire Brigade men living cheek by jowl, some-times in great danger, more often waiting in acute boredom and nearly all of them more than thirty years of age – all this created a situation which led to every kind of human relationship, unlikely friendships, and obvious jealousies. The title of the book will be *London and Fire 1939–45* by Henry Green.'

My London at war in 1939 begins in Eire in 1938. It was Munich, just upon us. My wife and I had a hired car and driver, travelled south west from Dublin almost as far as Connemara to a fisher-man's hotel run for officers and gentlewomen. The building squatted beside the Atlantic where in great sighing loneliness the telephone cable from the US came up into an untenanted wooden, bleak and apparently deserted tar-black hut.

My wife sea bathed, we sat about, but every night at nine there was the relentless wireless. Always, each day, news worse than the last.

One by one officers were recalled by telegram, two by two, until at last in a group so to speak of the widows they might soon become, the wives these men had left behind to finish the furlough, if indeed furlough it could now be called, gathered each succeeding evening at nine to listen to more wireless screaming menaces and keep a stiff upper lip to themselves.

We two often took picnic baskets to get into the wilds with our car and avoid, turn a blind eye, on officers leaving for home and mobilisation. We did not want to witness any part of it, dreading forward as we were to what might all too soon be for the two of us.

We used to walk out with sandwiches to get away from the lounge where these women were already in wait for each evening and nine o'clock. And almost as soon as we were out of the grounds the coast was deserted, or so we thought. Enormous crescent beaches curved one after the other as wandering forward we shrimped in sea anemone garlanded, limpid emerald pools. Each one of these led to another and so in turn round the next jutted point of sand over which waves broke in shawl after shawl after shawl of whey-coloured lace, advancing, receding, hissing into a silence where no sea birds were.

It was at one of these divisions between one creamy beach and another that we saw a seal come out of the pewter sea as far as black shoulders, in its mouth a flapping sole so bright the fish was like a shaft of white light, violently vibrating.

My wife said, 'Isn't he clever – a wet cat,' and moved on. We had been married for years, were fond, just did not say much to one another, so stayed comfortably quiet.

Thus we did not have much to do with those who were still left in the hotel. It must have been plain from my appearance I was no Army or Air Force man, and that being the case, these almost bereaved women who remained had really no call to say anything to us. Indeed, as so often at such times, their being the wives of officers made it seem as though they guarded secrets with their virtue and that they might report one if, by ill chance, one asked any sort of a question which might seem to call for a knowledgeable answer. So we kept pretty well on our own.

In silence therefore, although alone, keeping ourselves to ourselves, we crossed the point, stumbling through soft sand no tide had reached in weeks, to come upon the next new moon of curving strand and sea. But not this time untenanted.

For, just whiter than the sand and at a certain distance, a couple were lying on their backs over a rug, but naked. Or had they white bathing dresses? We both of us stopped dead on our heels so as not to embarrass what might turn out to be two of the hotel guests trying perhaps to create a last memory, but when he saw us the man got up and turning his half of the rug over, lay down under it so that they both were covered. We went on. When we came up to them we had never seen them yet. Thus we arrived at the next beach which looked as if it had not been visited in ages. Here were some rocks and another, deeper, bluer pool. So, in this priest-ridden Ireland we sat down to rest, but there would be no rest for us that afternoon.

A milk-like sky hid the sun and because out of all that stillness a fitful wayward wind had begun to spread the freshness and tang of the Atlantic, it came over grey, and because sand dunes were ahead like huge soft dead lions with deep green hills rolling up which it would be necessary to climb, we settled down behind a rock, the pool not twenty yards distant, and were so placed that we could see both hills and sea and yet had our backs to the couple on the point's far side. This man and woman could thus never say we were snooping, no peeping toms we.

We had barely settled and had just held hands when we saw, dressed all in black, a minute and aged crone making her way straight at us down over the last swell of land before the sand. My wife said, 'D'you think she'll make trouble for that pair?' We watched. But she came head on for us. My wife took her hand away. It could now be seen the lady was a peasant and very old, nut-cracker nose and chin like a fairy story witch. I said, 'Will she speak to us, for I can never understand what they say?'

But the old woman uttered not a word, came on up to the pool, and began to undress in our full view. My wife coughed to no effect. One black petticoat after another was taken off until in a few minutes she was stark nude. She then, still facing our way, stepped into the water which she funnelled over her faint pink-white skin with her old hands. The belly was unwrinkled, well preserved, the bush of hair black and enormous, but above her waist and below just above her knees, she sagged and folded into rolls of thin flesh. She could have been all of seventy and the hair on her head was the white of well-burnt wood ashes.

[262]

We did not say a word.

After ten minutes she was done, made no attempt to dry, put all the clothes on again and went off to wherever she was from.

My wife told me she would like her tea now and as we went back a bit inland to avoid the other couple, she said: 'With all the dreadful news there is I think we might tell the driver to take us east to the nearest port, I suppose Rosslare, so if we must we can get home quickly, darling. Besides, I'm beginning to find Ireland creepy.'

So next day we were off in the car once more. Meanwhile over in England, unbeknownst to us, committees had already been sitting for years to decide what, in time of war, was to be done with and for civilians such as ourselves.

Meanwhile, in deeper current ignorance than most others, my wife and I were bowling along behind our driver towards Cork, in Southern Ireland, whilst even in England none except at the top knew that a trial mobilisation had been decided for Civil Defence and that those auxiliary firemen in London who had passed their tests (which will be described) were to have their first experience of London Fire Brigade improvisation.

It was raining as we drove along the sea road. Suddenly, there was a gaudy station wagon drawn up on the verge and then, soon after, where a bridge spanned a stream, we saw a parrot-coloured group of rich women and one or two men with rods and waders. The little river dark red with peat tumbled through an emerald field to the slate-dark sea ribboned with white-capped waves as far as a break-out in dark clouds, edged with sulphur yellow, turned a streak of waste waters below to brightest aluminium. A party after sea trout seen blurred through glass striped by diagonally slithering raindrops. And then for two hours as we went on it was nothing but an occasional dark donkey, tail to the wind, or a flock of geese, wings outspread, hissing defiance at an extremity of their ominous chalk-white necks.

We were both perfectly miserable on this drive, as also when we got to Cork. It was one of the three worst moments of the war, for war it was one always instinctively knew. Declaration of war was not to come for another twelve months, the rising anguish during the whole year before Mr Chamberlain declared war over the wireless, was far the worst, it got more and more bad as the dreadful days went by. The waiting for the worst is the worst thing about personal disaster.

And the other really bad time was the chase of our armies through Flanders by those Germans and the collapse of France. Once France fell everyone for no known reason felt ever so much better. 'Now at last we are on our own,' the whole of Britain said, speaking as one for once.

There was a big speech on the wireless advertised from London that same evening and because we felt we must find out whether or no we should push on to try for any boat home from Rosslare, I asked one of the waiters in the bar if there was a wireless. Only in the manager's private room apparently. Could he then be so kind as to present the manager with our compliments and ask leave to listen? He went off at once but was back in five minutes. The manager was sorry but there was a big fight on the radio at that hour, would we mind? On enquiry it turned out to be Jack Doyle, the Irish heavyweight, who was to fight someone in London. The speech we were after was on the Home Service and the fight on the Light Programme at the same time, and so we were done.

We then had a miserable dinner, went back to that bar for more drinks. Judge then my surprise when a waiter came up to say the manager was expecting me in his room. He seemed definitely to exclude my wife. So I went alone, supposing there had been second thoughts of a sort.

Shown to a combined sitting room and office already laced with cigar smoke, a tumbler of neat whisky shoved in my hand, I found five or six powerful citizens of Eire tight round a huge wireless. They had the thing full on, but in their cups they had mismanaged the knobs. It was bellowing out wild deadly cheering and applause which followed as it always did the end of what had obviously been a big speech to some National Socialist rally at the Sports Palace in Berlin. Now we had no German, my wife and I, yet these screaming, shouted, harshly expectorated speeches had drawn us at home to listen in an ever-increasing anguish of terror night after night; in spite of which when we would read the translation in newspapers next morning it was with complete disbelief. It did not seem possible such things could be said. I was therefore familiar with the uproar the Irish were now listening to, therefore it came as no surprise when the German audience broke into its usual chants of 'Sieg Heil – Sieg Heil' each louder than the last, a kind of rising invocation each step higher than the next like a grand staircase to slaughter.

But my drunken hosts were taken in. 'Ach, the fight's ended in a foul,' they said.

I tried to explain they were on a wrong wavelength but they were too far gone. Then, as the fight might still be on, I felt it a shame they should miss their programme, so I tried to get at the machine to tune us on London. They pulled me away. 'Let's hear how they robbed the boy,' they said. On which *Deutschland über Alles* bellowed into the manager's office. This they did recognise and all broke down into laughter. These men now let me reach the dials and I got on to the Light Programme. Doyle had been counted out in the first round not more than two minutes earlier. They laughed again. Doyle it seems was not unknown at that hotel in Cork. They gave me another tumbler of whisky and let me escape around ten.

The next day we set off in haste for Rosslare. Our trouble was we had no one we could ask for advice. The British papers were two or more days old and the Irish press, in an attitude accepted as far as we could tell by all the natives, maintained that nothing could ever happen to the great Little Republic. It was a joy therefore when after a long drive we arrived at this port and were getting into the hotel, to find old Mr Hanks dashing out of the revolving door, an Associate of the Royal Academy of Water Colour Artists, aged eighty, slightly known to me, all his para-phernalia on his back, scuttling crabwise out presumably to get some more done in the last light of evening. His work was one watercolour after another, and whatever the beach he had before him, consisted always of a golden foreground of dry sand, some-where in mid-distance a wet pool with wet brown seaweed and then the sea, blue coloured, fifteen guineas, always the same, each unframed and with a ready sale. He nodded coldly to me, hurried on.

[265]

'What, Mr Hanks,' I called, overjoyed even at an acquaintance, 'more work?'

'Yes,' he said back sideways over a shoulder, 'it's not so bad. Haven't you ever tried?'

My wife laughed. 'Why didn't you tell him?'

'That I worked? Not me. Well we won't attempt to get near him again.'

'Oh, I don't know,' she said, 'I thought he was rather sweet.' But we didn't, and it so happened he was dead of natural causes in a month. Mr Hanks, guiltless, left guilt all round him.

All the long drive through, we had learned the boats would be full of others as panicked as ourselves. However, our hotel porter said no, there was all the room in the world, we could cross any night we liked. So now we were torn two ways. We had our only child, a son, in London, and it did seem right to get back to him. On the other hand we had paid for the car in advance, and had a few days in hand. So, to discuss this, and as the sun had come out, we took a walk over a golf course, empty and brilliantly green except for that long crocodile of priests in black cassocks also apparently promenading. We decided at last to stay overnight although the place looked more horribly like the England we were going back to defend than any other we had visited in Eire, except for the brisk wind swirling black draperies and so many pale hands held to black bowler hats with vast black wings.

Even the food at supper was distasteful and English. Brown soup, mutton, mashed potatoes, brussels sprouts – we could not understand why until we realised it was a railway hotel. And we were disconcerted when the same crocodile of priests came filing in to dine. They sat four by four to small round tables, and, once grace was said, there arose a roar of conversation, which somehow, in some unexplained way, yet seemed discreet. On being asked, the waitress said they were in retreat and were taking all meals here.

We had been late down. It was not long before the nine o'clock news came on. But this dynamo of conversation round about was such that we heard little from London over the loudspeaker like a huge green ashtray in plastic, covered by netting, hung on one wall. No one besides ourselves paid the slightest attention. But my wife thought she picked up something about an important announcement immediately following the news. When something came, as promised, we could hear still less. 'All the same,' I warned myself against rising indignation, 'you can't just shush priests.' Until, after about another ten minutes my wife said she wished we could be allowed to listen. At that, surprised by myself, I turned about and hissed 'Hush' twice, very loud. They one and all immediately stopped talking just in time for us to hear the unknown voice across the now night-dark sea say, into complete silence, 'Goodnight, then, everyone, goodnight.' We thought we recognised Mr Chamberlain.

We decided to get on the boat next evening.

Thus we sailed home, bereft.

London at the end of 1938 was, for intelligent people, an angry divided town, families divided against each other, old friends after a few sharp words not speaking to old friends. When Mr Chamberlain got nowhere with Hitler in Munich, saw him again at Berchtesgaden and came back with a brolly and the famous bit of paper and the slogan 'peace in our time', the House of Commons rose to cheer him to a man while many like myself were well satisfied, hoping at least that he had bought time, as Mr Baldwin did earlier when he was able to postpone the General Strike for a few months in 1926. Against us in a few days we had those who held that the German tanks were made of cardboard, they actually knew a man who had driven his car slap through one by mistake on an autobahn. More seriously there were those, harking back to the Civil War in Spain, who saw stark betrayal in what had been done to Czechoslovakia. Whatever the opinion held, however, there could be little doubt in any mind that our way of life was about to be radically altered, and for the worse.

What between hope one week, despair the next, it was as if Hitler was at an end of the seesaw, with oneself at the other dominated by the eyes of this maniacal genius with a hypnotic stare out of every published photograph; one would be up one moment, down the next, and completely at the mercy of these ups and downs, with nothing to be done except join one of the Services.

Most small- to medium-sized firms fell during 1939 into a coma of suspended animation. Rearmament had got under way by 1937 in the sense generally speaking that the largest factories were looking up. An account will be given later of how material began to reach the Auxiliary Fire Service (AFS for short). But firms such as ours, who were principally brewers' engineers with little repetition work for what machines we had, were left and indeed remained very much out in the wilderness for most of the war. And our customers, unable to tell what demand there was likely to be in six months' time for their product, or indeed should it come to what the Civil Servants called 'hostilities', to tell whether they would be able to get the raw materials they needed, simply, peaceably gave up ordering. My problem therefore, at the top, was to help my father keep our small but expensive organisation going. For, once we let the top men be dispersed, we felt we should never get them back under our roof again.

I was rising thirty-five in 1939 and, while the talk then was that no man older than twenty-seven would ever be permitted in the firing line, it did seem expedient, as it must have done to 100,000 others, to duck out into one of these non-combatant services to avoid conscription, which must mean being drafted overseas. In London, for most of the war, one was kept while on duty close to the regular Fire Station of one's choice. So that when the Board of Directors agreed to my joining the AFS I was able to call in at the office every third day all through the war, for we worked two days on with one off, and if not at a fire was always available, if only in my case, to sign cheques. The company also agreed to 'make up' my wage as a fireman, to what had been my salary with the firm, which, when in another phrase 'hostilities developed', indeed made all the difference; in fact I suffered financially not at all.

To join the AFS in 1938 all you needed was a doctor's certificate to say you were not likely to fall down dead running upstairs so that they had to pay your widow a pension, and, as far as one can remember at this distance of time, a couple of references as well to say you were a responsible person. Forged notes to this latter effect were so unchecked as to be a ha-ha which deterred no one. Why go so far as forgery? Because unlike anyone else, even the British police force, firemen in England are by law allowed to enter any house when in uniform. The Englishman's house is not his castle once a passer-by claims, however mistakenly, he has seen smoke coming from the eaves. And what attracted a certain level of society to the Service was a prophetic vision that, when bombed, householders in fleeing would abandon trinkets, and, if raids were heavy, might even be relied upon to leave valuables behind, easy pickings, windfalls in open drawers. And indeed, when raids began, there was a sense in which it could be felt that these things left in abandoned houses, had become common property even if the owners were still alive, kicking heels in public shelters.

Having armed myself with the needed few bits of paper, I was enrolled and called by appointment one evening after work to get trained. With the others in the class this instruction, for not more than sixty minutes every seven days, over a period of eight weeks was meant to turn us into full Auxiliary Firemen. They handed out overalls, peaked uniformed caps, three-inch webbing belts to each one, and an axe in a holder which fitted on the belt, but the axe had bitten into it by acid a serial number. My number was so early that I was inordinately proud of it. During the blitz, when conscripts were drafted, all these numbers were changed. From somewhere about the seven thousand mark mine was moved to the twenty thousand, and, however absurd, I cannot stop resenting that to this day.

At the other extreme there were many who volunteered convinced that the AFS must be a suicide squad. They did not want to die but chose what they thought was the most dangerous job of all. Many of these resigned in the 'phoney war' twelve months lull period, which ended in August 1940 with the first heavy raids.

All manner of men, therefore, came in for training in 1938 and for a variety of reasons. The London Fire Brigade (LFB for short) received them all at the Regular Fire Stations. These were always Gothic in design. Built of red brick with white stone pinnacles towards the roof, there was invariably a tower rising high above all, a relic of medieval times through which fire watches were maintained. Curiously enough when flying bombs, V1s, started, this watch was set up every night once more.

At street level there was a yard with another tower four storeys high and open on all sides, a series of bare platforms one above the other joined by an iron ladder. This was used by both LFB and AFS for training. Next door was the fire station, at ground-floor level, three huge great sliding doors of red, in one of which was a small wicket gate next a large brass handle marked 'Fire Bell'.

There were those recruits who, not knowing how to get in, pulled this and so 'put the bells down', i.e. set every alarm in the place ringing and thus obliged the Station to 'turn out' in under thirty seconds flat. To miss a pump, or an appliance as it is called, was a minor crime. There were four-inch brass poles to help the men get down quickly from perhaps three or four floors. Their gear was left on the appliances and they dressed as they drove through the streets, ringing warning bells which never cleared the way like heroes are supposed to do.

They played tricks with these poles. One powerful LFB regular used to take a full tea cup on its saucer in his left hand, wrap the left arm round highly polished brass, and climb this thing up through the ceiling with his right hand, a prodigious feat of strength, not spilling a drop.

The regulars were indeed fantastic men. With just over 3,000 in the Force and thirty thousand Londoners about to join the AFS, they were all shortly destined as officers to oversee the AFS. Some were gunlayers in the Royal Navy Reserve, who somehow or other were retained until the blitz was over when they went back and died at sea, others were men who had made the navy or marine corps too hot to hold them. All thought exclusively of the pension they were to get when aged about forty-five. With this they would retire to one of the large stores and there be firemen once again until they died in bed, or, if old enough, pensioned off on what by then would be a double pension. Loot and pension was all they thought of, loss of pension was the preoccupation in all their minds until bombing started when some, who had been resurrected from sedentary staff duties, felt and said loudly that bombs and fire fighting were two different things, that LFB pensions were no adequate reward for dodging bombs. They had a point. The risk had been increased, the pension stayed the same.

On this ground floor in any LFB station, so clean you could eat off it, for fire fighting is a waiting game – the men spend most of their waiting hours as housemaids – stand the three appliances as they are called, the Dual Purpose (DP), the Pump and the 'Ladders'. Any equipment we had in the AFS with our LFB officers, was based on these. A DP had an 'escape', that is a ladder on large wheels, hitched over the whole wagon, on a built-in tank of water with a pump to discharge this, as well as take water from hydrants, and in addition a vacuum pump to raise water from a pond, which they called 'static water'. The pump appliance was similar except that it had no 'escape', or the built-in tank of water. The 'ladders', made in Germany, had a pump and three tubular ladders telescopically folded but joined together, and which, by hydraulic action, could be raised, with a fireman at the top, to a height of 120 feet. All three were painted red, had a great deal of brass to polish, and carried masses of equipment in lockers.

And who sent these appliances out to ring their bells past shoppers? The 'watchroom attendant'. He took all calls by telephone in a large glass box. It was he who put the station bells down. And it was in response to these that the fireman doing out the Super's flat up on the fourth had to hurry down the poles to be last on whatever he was 'riding' before with a roar and a crash of gears they were out and off.

Living at the top the Superintendent was a saintly figure of incalculable guile who twelve months later was to break windows for me with half bricks as I stood with a nozzle before such flames during the first great City Fire around St Paul's. When he was called out he came slow down the poles, gently, to be driven off, a slight man in a little car with his special little tinkling fire bell. Although flames and smoke were his business, 'softly, softly' he made one think, 'catchee monkey', so discreet was he, so important, so quiet, so self-contained.

On the first floor was the Regulars' mess room. Here they sat most of the day, whatever their cleaning duties, drinking tea, and as we were told by our instructors, when they did speak it was to curse the volunteers.

The instructors were a trifle shy at having volunteered as such. Canny men, they were careful to decry the usefulness of those they were teaching while leaving themselves in a position to take full advantage if and when the AFS was used. They were too clever; the war broke most of these. The WAFS (women's branch), dressed in uniformed trousers, tigresses disguised as humans, were too much for them.

And these hard young females, when war did break out, were nearly to destroy our teacher in knots and lines, Fireman Brent. Many another such they slew remorselessly. But this man was saved, in the nick of time, by his courage in the blitz. Handsome, speechless, incomparably brave, he once described to me his exit in peacetime from a fire when cut off by flames, at a warehouse by the river Thames. 'And then Henry,' he said, with truthful calm, 'I slid down me hose away from it all into the old Thamise.' He could have at that, and from the fifth floor.

He got the George Medal afterwards for incredible gallantry; in front of witnesses of course, but he deserved them. It was impossible to get a medal without at least one high officer watching.

A line is a length of rope in these circles, and knots are taught in great variety, they date back to the days of sail. Because Brent was never ready with his tongue he was given 'Knots and lines' to teach. For a whole hour I have known him silently demonstrate the elegant knot with which, if well drilled, one should shorten any line that has slack in it. Over and over again he got it wrong, undid the knot without a word, only to start once more, expressionless, mute, enormously dignified. Imperturbable, beautiful as Apollo. When war came he was of course put in charge of an AFS station. He had seven WAFS sleeping in. They were too much for him. Their jealousy of each other grew to such extremes that it was even said he might be losing his pension. Then the bombs began to fall.

Brent, as they say, then came into his own.

There will be more of him hereafter.

In the meantime, peacetime, there were moments when Brent showed his innate authority. Deputising for another instructor to take hook ladder drill on that hollow open tower in the fire station yard, he got himself in a dangerous position. A hook ladder is made of the lightest construction, bound with wire and is some fourteen feet tall with a two-feet-six toothed curving hook on the end, which is meant to get into windows and grip on the sill. There was a fire in Knightsbridge in the 1930s. It was at night, of two apartment buildings next to each other, one was well alight on the ground floor. Three or four screaming girls were above, making night hideous. A fireman took the hook ladder off his DP, 'scaled', as they say, the unscathed building, put the ladder across a wall between the two, crossed over, went down and fetched those girls up, then led them across his bridge to love, life and laughter. Next day he had to be told what he had done. He'd been dead drunk.

These ladders have hardly ever been used since. They are absurdly unsafe. You are supposed to lift the thing and smash in the first-floor window with the wrought-iron hook, climb it, open the window, straddle this like riding a horse, raise the ladder hand over hand to the window on the floor above, repeat this treatment, and so on until you get where you want.

Unfortunately a hook ladder is of such light construction that, for the man climbing, it is a matter of keeping in the centre of balance, otherwise, if he is three parts up, the foot of it will shoot sideways and he will be a powerless fly at an angle of forty-five degrees, not away from the building, but to the horizontal window sill above him that his hook is stuck into. And the gallant fellow will be in sore danger of falling, ladder and all, to the hard, hard pavement or onto spiked iron palings which abound in London and elsewhere.

Waiting our turn in the yard, backs to a wall, out of the cone of light with which the drill tower searchlight almost hid those four storeys in vanilla cream, and above, visible to us outside the glare, an infinite warm blue sky with stars, warm with a last flush of summer and the glow given by street lighting, each lamp falling far short of that sky but overlaying it with blue, steeping

[273]

in sapphire heavens above between the stars; waiting our turn we saw Brent advance to demonstrate his hook ladder drill, long since forgotten. But, when he muffed it, was stuck at forty-five degrees half across the tower, he did what he would have done for any learner, he let out a great bellow – 'Still!'

This command means stay put, don't move. And, as we stayed not frozen, but warmly inanimate, an LFB colleague casually came out of the Station, hiked the ladder straight and Brent came down. Without a word to climb the thing again.

They were remarkable men, the LFB. They came out of their mess room once on a 'smell of smoke'. I had never seen them together before. Not so much huge as squat and broad with spade-like faces, they ran wordless up and down stairs dashing off sideways to sniff like steam engines at empty fireplaces. False alarm.

But they are still allowed 'wet canteens', that is a basement room in which they can buy and drink beer, not spirits. When they get in too much difficulty with their figures of takings, it is traditional they should set fire to this room and then put the flames out themselves, after all records have been consumed. It may be one of these conventional blazes was expected to drag them from their tea mugs that afternoon, or perhaps anything to make them forget the hated AFS. One thing is sure. They would never have first inspected a place where money was counted till it was well alight. For they would go in anywhere, fire and flame had become second nature, true they far preferred a blaze in the grate but backed up by each other and their equipment they would face anything, any time, grumbling yes but the sooner the better. Always excepted that memory-dulling 'incident' the witless discarded fag end that 'must have smouldered there for hours' to destroy books conveniently left in no fireproof drawer but on carefully empty shelves, books not of words in black and white but pounds, shillings and pence, the columns added.

Our instructors came from the same stable. We are here on earth only, if strong enough, to look life in the face. If some of the 3,000 LFB had curious ideas it was they who, when real trouble came with bombs, when fires such as they had never seen twitted the horizon, it was these men who sent us in, and often recalled us under conditions they felt were too dangerous, double-faced yet an extraordinary race of men. And then not just men, but perhaps even already heroes, some of them perhaps.

In London the supply of pumps was a very close-run thing. By the time of Munich only 99 had been delivered against 3,000 ordered. By November 1938 with 13,500 AFS recruited only 145 appliances had been supplied. But by the middle of 1939 the pumps came along so fast that there was trouble in finding storage space.

Anyone reading this might reasonably conclude that all was for the best in the worst of worlds. Threatened as never before the British, in their hundreds of thousands with all this equipment, were happily busy training to get ready for their finest hour.

Training they were but the difficulty of being taught by an LFB man was that if you failed then he thought he would be blamed – after all he was paid for teaching you, wasn't he? – and if you flunked he was sure he could lose his precious pension. So no one failed.

This may seem inconceivable but it is true, and the fear of losing the pension, not available to AFS, must never be forgotten hereafter, whatever happened, let the blood flow where it may. On this point LFB men were hallucinated.

It even went so far there was an AFS recruit had forgotten how to write and in his written examination Bernie, our chief instructor, wrote it all out in his own hand for him. No one failed, for that was an extravagance the LFB felt could not be afforded. The halt, the lame, the blind got in.

So what then did we learn? How much the LFB hated us, certainly this was explained, almost apologetically, over and over again. How to put out fires? Hardly. Nothing? No, not that. We just all of us began to live another life in which we had an entirely different way of living.

For instance when I had 'passed out', that is passed the examination no one was allowed to flunk, it was part of the contract that I should attend for two hours each week in case there was a real fire. All this of course before the war, in the sort of unreal peace which then existed. Thus one afternoon I came in to find the LFB returned from a basement job. They were not spick and span. In particular their eyes were bright red and they were crying without sobs. Their different world had been the thick hot smoke peculiar to basement fires. Later when things really began happening, we were to find that thick cold smoke was worst, cold but not dispersed, arising from an incident of perhaps the night before. This gripped by the throat. Until you could break a few windows you were throttled, but if you had a head cold it was miraculously cured. You lost so much mucus by the eyes and nose.

The whole point of a fireman is that he is endlessly waiting. And most have lost their nerve. They wait for perhaps six months and then get into a fire at which they are thoroughly and completely frightened. They say stone stairs down to a basement are worst, worse than wood they will collapse with you and one such experience is sufficient. They say the water they use cools the stone which has expanded in the heat so that it shrinks out of the seating and comes down. Or they may have a nasty rescue forced upon them. Anything dangerous or 'bad' is automatically up to firemen. But however frightened, they are hardly ever cowards. Behind them they have the crew, the other men on the appliance. They are like a small pack of hounds, cowards alone they may be but when together ready to take on lions.

Their being brought into action was governed in my day by the telephone. It is wireless now and may be television next. The huntsman who set them on, who said where to go until they could actually smell smoke, was called the watchroom attendant, a man who never went to fires himself.

Not well paid, out of everything really, whose only other job was to record whatever happened over the long sad hours he waited, the day-long task to fill in his log book and the boredom was such that it was read at least twice a day by everyone else, the watchroom attendant on the rare occasion he did get a fire and the address given him straight by whoever it might be on the other end, the watchroom attendant did not immediately as might be expected pull the lever which 'put the bells down'. He had larger fish to fry.

He had to find out how many pumps, that is appliances, to

send. Surrounded by a large card index system, he first looked up the address. The rateable value of what was on fire determined the attendance.

There is no wicked capitalist trick in this, or is there? True that, pre-war, fire insurance companies contributed annually to the LFB, the remainder being paid out of rates. But the rateable value of a building was directly related to its size, or volume, in other words to how much it contributed to the rates. And the building's cubic content of course had a bearing on the sort of bonfire it might make, bonfire, or conflagration 'when well alight' as they pompously term this. So then having determined the value of the structure he had been told was on fire he put the bells down and sent us off, one appliance, two, or three for a big building as his cards told him.

Such a thing happened to me only once in peacetime. Sitting in the watchroom, ready dressed so as not to miss the pump, the attendant on what seemed an ordinary phone call murmured directly to me 'Ready George' and began to look through his card index. 'Fire,' I yelled to empty beating silence in my heart, and all but fainted. And then he put the bells down.

Running like a hare on the ground floor, I was only just on the ladders as the LFB came swooping down their poles. And we were off, crash open doors, afternoon sudden sunlight after naked light bulbs, the steady heavy surge of this seven-ton vehicle which was a mass of hydraulics, and then above all the very much ting-a-ling bell, the LFB men dressed as we went along but I, ready already, had time to look around.

Along what is called a main thoroughfare my hope was we might cause a stir. But no traffic parted, only one child on a pavement stopped at the end of his mother's arm and pointed. That innocent could never have even guessed how much of a child one fireman he saw before him was swishing past.

This call ended as a false alarm, the kind they call 'malicious', which means no one, nothing.

Next time I went 'on the bell' was some eighteen months later, first night of the blitz. It was the opening night and coming back twelve hours later, we used the bell again. Black, wet through, dead exhausted, I almost fell off the pump when we got, to what

[277]

could hardly be called, back home. It was then that a passer-by with a curiously guilty look which may have been and so probably was shyness, came up to announce softly only in my own ear, 'Well, now you are a real fireman.' If i'd had the strength left I would have hit him. Instead, like all who have just been in action, I just got my head down and slept for fifteen hours.

The last few months of peace in Britain was to go back to be a little boy again, however old you were. It was so to speak those last few days of term, but no holidays promised, and the knowledge that having failed in everything, willy nilly next week would fix you a poorer, harsher academy in which all would indeed be different and for the worse.

Working in an engineering office selling food-processing machinery, one found the younger men resigned to war, their war arranged for and chosen. The seniors, however, could not even entertain the possibility of fighting. Orders from customers were few and far between, ruin loomed a year or two on.

Armament orders take a long time to seep through to smaller firms.

We had all in the office said goodbye to that when, on September first, my red telegram came, and that meant mobilisation, it was like being back at school by the pool when the instructor to your regret at last said you can go solo, and ordered you 'get wet, get in'. Alone.

One civilian told my wife he this day went to his bank, cashed one hundred pounds into notes, and bought a bicycle for forty shillings. His idea was that all transport would cease. He wanted to be mobile.

But the wardens' main task had been preparing for the evacuation of children. On this day, shepherded by their school teachers, they began, they who quite often had never seen the countryside, in their thousands and thousands to go out in special trains to homes, and private homes at that, where people had said they would have them.

A book could be made out of the stories about these children. There was one who saw apples growing on a tree and thought these were tied on. Others refused fresh peas, they would eat only out of the tin. From all accounts they were formidable and dauntless. Most were back by Christmas. But they had to get out again by next September.

My wife was with our son at her parents' in Herefordshire. I asked her last night (2–4–58) what she most remembered about this day. She considered and then she said, 'I think the motor bikes. There were so many more.' Everyone was on the move for sure, right enough.

So I was alone in London that dreadful morning, forty-eight hours before war was declared, and dressed alone into the still unfamiliar uniform with prickly trousers, alone, frightened, sickened, sure of dying.

UNLOVING

(Published in The Times, *1961)*

If the writing of novels is for the author a way of clearing his bloodstream of the various poisons being pumped by his poor heart, then the reading of them may be the reverse of this process, or, more usually, a pleasant soporific as one gets older and one's own heart begins to wither and fade.

Of course in adolescence, cooped up in some boarding school, one is avid for any experience and reads everything that lies to hand. And experience is certainly what reading is. Not least in the personality of the man or woman who has written the book you are reading as for the characters they present. To one reader at least – to speak for myself – unless one or other of the characters runs away with the book, then it is the mind and the heart of the writer that matters, and instructs. And, if she who writes is a woman and one happens to be a man, how much more!

The way the author expresses his cast, the way he or she puts it all together in say 70,000 words, the construction, the edifice give one an idea of him or her which could not be obtained in a fortnight's *tête à tête*. People are such liars. But while novels lie, it is not hard to tell where they do so – why I do not know – where they are then, as reviewers say, 'unconvincing'.

This ability to spot the bogus or untrue is mysteriously granted to almost all educated readers, cannibal eccentrics (i.e., most reviewers excluded). Everyone, black, yellow or white, is writing novels now, and even if one has never visited their sun-drenched beaches, after a page or two (and I am a one-novel-a-day man) one can inevitably tell. There are no barriers in narrative, except that of the religious novel to the irreligious. I have just been reading Charles Williams, who to me is meaningless, and I have great difficulty with Antonia White,

Graham Greene and the later Evelyn Waugh. Yet some myths ring true, notably one or two novels by West Indians, and heaven knows what will come out of the new Africa in the form of what is called fiction.

Because fiction, or indeed any book, if good, is not lying, it is a world, a life of its own. Marginal perhaps, but the marginal, or oblique, has great value. Who wants to travel in *Arabia Deserta* as Doughty did? At the same time it is one of the great classics of our age. Hemingway died just the other day. I saw in action two of the matadors, Belmonte and Lalanda, he so admired and have just enough Spanish to have read the reviews of their performances then, the day after watching and feeling the blood, sun and sand, everything stylised. The *aficionados* I knew in Spain did not think much of *Death in the Afternoon* but, if over-romanticised, all the same it was all right by me back home in this misty, steamy, almost Celtic island. Let Hemingway lie in peace, bless him. With almost every bone in his body already broken he drove his car, in the middle of the last war, at night, slap into a filled Fire Service water tank in Sloane Square. The policeman who got him out told me there was a quarter of an inch of blood on the floor. He came out of hospital in ten days. He was a man. Perhaps he should not have been a writer, but fought bulls or huge marlin in the Gulf of Mexico. In any case he makes any contemporary of mine thin blooded. Céline also is now dead, that incalculably fine writer.

And yet there are those who watch and wait, who don't particularly participate, who still merit a reward. True they see everyone, themselves included, getting worse in health. But death after all is a great deliverer. Good writers, if thin blooded, still live after they are dead.

The observer, better than Hemingway, who can tell us, is the man who matters. Chekhov, for instance. When he saw moonlight reflected in jagged glass fixed by concrete on top of an estate wall of stone, he puts the whole thing down for ever in, I think, three lines. In his short story 'The Kiss' he does more than realise and understand, he makes life as the medicos cannot. Living one's own life can be a great muddle, but the great writers do not make it plain, they palliate, and put the whole in a sort of proportion. Which helps; and on the whole, year after year, help is what one needs.

All this means that writers cannot give the answer. Nor do the wolves in full cry after the troika help the wretched writer being chased to death against a ravening pack of very much younger critics. Or the older Sitwells for that matter, though I for one have never written a word for or against them, nor *vice versa*. But their response to any comment they dislike is now positively violent. We, that is the thin blooded, who have been in two wars, have not much left. We had starvation in the first and bombardment in the second. My generation regards with contempt what one can only describe as the social double meanings of Amis *et al.*

Amis and Wain in their novels often put their young men to rise on the backs of women in the red-brick universities of which there are plenty of buildings in Cambridge as well as Reading. So why should one complain? I don't know, except they are both really bad writers. *Lucky Jim* is disastrous because it pretends to make something pretentious out of nothing without a thought that (to quote a title of mine) the whole thing was nothing from the start.

Of course it is no use finding complaint against one's contemporaries, even C. P. Snow. We all put everything in words as best we know. But there is a winnowing, and perhaps Snow and also Philip Toynbee in their comments should now be silent for a while. Snow thinks and writes of power. Toynbee still seems to be in his impenetrable muddle. And yet in spite of them people are still writing. So what? Certainly nothing these two critics could agree on.

Forget therefore the nattering in so-called high places. Remember also that novelists who read and review current work can usually only see how they would do it themselves. Believe that on the whole novelists who use English on both sides of the Atlantic are writing to a higher general standard than ever before. It is the novelist's reviewers who are the curse every Sunday in this island. If nothing were published or written where would they be? What they say should be taken with a great tongue in the cheek. As a rule they have had a success with a novel of their own, good luck to them, and where are they then but in the sweaty grasp of the Inspector of Taxes? So all they can do is to churn out ambiguous reviews for cash. We have, in literature, as reviewed in the press, no standards left. Anyone who joins in now will find himself a flea in the hair of the dog, which is gnawing ignominiously and futilely at its bottom where the tail joins the trunk.

FOR JENNY WITH
AFFECTION
FROM HENRY GREEN

(Published in The Spectator, *1963)*

Jenny Rees was the daughter of Goronwy Rees, a long-standing friend of Green's. It was to Jenny that Green dictated parts of an intended autobiography, 'Pack My Bag Repacked'. This project, his last, was abandoned.

Green lives with his wife in Belgravia. He has now become a hermit. Only the other day a woman of sixty looking after the tobacconist's shop was dragged by her hair across the counter and stabbed twice in the neck. That is one reason why I don't go out any more.

Green can write novels, but his present difficulty is to know quite how to do it. As *Time* magazine says, Green is ailing, which means he has several things wrong with him which, rising sixty, is perhaps to be expected.

Of course, he sees his contemporaries die almost every day, like John Strachey and many another.

Whether you are a man like Kingsley Martin and believe in things is, of course, an advantage. Green tells me he doesn't believe in anything at all. And perhaps that is not a bad thing. Love your wife, love your cat and stay perfectly quiet, if possible not to leave the house. Because on the street if you are sixty danger threatens.

It has always been said as a sign of age that if you don't see policemen with medal ribbons it means that you are getting very old. In other words, the policemen are very much younger. One of the reasons I won't go out is for fear of meeting a policeman.

Yesterday I saw four at the corner and was very frightened indeed.

Louis-Ferdinand Céline, who was one of the best novelists who has ever lived, and is dead now, had such a persecution thing. When Auric, the composer, was walking with him in a fog in Paris there was somebody wavering in front of them and Céline said in a very loud voice, '*C'est un juif.*' Auric was much disturbed because he didn't have a thing about Jews and in any case the fog was too deep to tell.

So the whole thing is really not to go out. If one can afford it, the best thing is to stay in one place, which might be bed. Not sex, for sleep.

A MEMOIR

BY SEBASTIAN YORKE

'The trouble with cats is that they don't live long enough.
This in a way may be fortunate, because they have
pretty well taken over the whole of London.'

HENRY GREEN, 1964

Born on 29 October 1905, Henry Vincent Yorke, the youngest
son of a squire with a large house and an estate in Gloucestershire,
was writing hard by the age of eleven or twelve under the pen
name Henry Michaels.

The house – Forthampton Court – and its estate lie on the
western bank of the River Severn about two miles from Tewkesbury and in plain view of its Norman Abbey. The house was used
by the Abbots as their imposing country residence from as early as
the twelfth century until 1549 when the last Abbot, John Wake-
ham, also Bishop of Gloucester, died there. After passing through
various hands, the house and estate were sold in about 1750 to John
Maddox, Bishop of Worcester. In 1762 his only daughter, Mary,
married Hon. the Rev. James Yorke, fifth and youngest son of the
first Earl of Hardwicke, Lord High Chancellor to George II. With
the succession of their son Joseph Yorke, the long connection with
the Church finally ended and the Yorke family – direct descendants
of Joseph Yorke – still live at the Court and have been landowners
there for seven generations.

Henry's father, Vincent Wodehouse Yorke, was the heir from
the fifth generation and issue of his father's second marriage,
whose first wife and grown-up son, Augustus, had both died
prematurely – the latter in bizarre circumstances. His ambition
had been to be an actor, and on the night of his stage debut, after

[286]

a celebration, he set fire to his nightshirt with a candle, while relieving himself in a chamber pot, and burnt to death. Henry's parents habitually set great store by family precedents. This was the only example, before their teenage son Henry had started to write fiction, of a Yorke being attracted to the arts, and they did not hesitate when the opportunity presented itself, to attribute Augustus's immolation to over-indulgence in drink.

Like his own father, John Reginald Yorke, who was consulted, on a regular basis, by Lord Randolph Churchill about classical quotations for his speeches, Vincent was a classicist by inclination; it was said that he could read Homer in the original as a young child and for the rest of his life this was to remain his staple bed-time reading. Subsequently a fellow of King's College, Cambridge, he had worked as an archaeologist in Greece and Asia Minor. Vincent's mother, Sophie Mathilde, was a daughter of Baron Vincent de Tuyll de Serooskerken, a Dutch nobleman, whose family owned Clingendael in The Hague. Named after the Baron, who had married an Anglo–American, Vincent Yorke had a donnish manner and little small talk; there was also a bullying side to his nature. He married Maud Evelyn Wyndham, a daughter of the second Baron Leconfield, in 1899.

Of the two, Maud was the more remarkable character. Brought up at Petworth House, virtually uneducated, amongst dogs and horses, she had a natural wit and could hold her own in any company. She was born with a curvature of the spine and prescribed a glass of port a day to build her up; she had to spend many hours as a young child lying flat on a wooden board. An uncle was Lord Rosebery, Prime Minister between 1894–5; his horses had won the Derby three times and that may have inspired her interest in the turf. A blunt-spokenness belied her rather slight and bent frame. Maurice Bowra once asked her about one of her horses which had failed to come up to expectations. She replied, 'We had to put him under the grass!'

Henry's origins were a matter of indifference to him. He was rarely to speak of them. After the Second World War, he never visited Forthampton again because he said it was below sea level and 'an unhealthy place', and he complained that relations bored him and made him feel guilty.

[287]

Maud and Vincent had three sons: Philip, Gerald and Henry. Philip, a brilliant King's scholar at Eton, died of lymphatic leukaemia when he was sixteen. Gerald, the second son, was a talented academic like his father and a batsman in the Eton cricket XI. Henry had no scholarly or athletic talents, but he played as one of the second violins in the School Orchestra.

When Vincent, who was a young don and not rich, married, his family purchased the assets of a semi-bankrupt engineering business – The Farringdon Works and H. Pontifex & Sons Ltd – to give him a start in commerce. In due course, this was to provide him with an entrée into the City, where over the years he secured a number of lucrative directorships in banking and insurance. He retained a link with his interests in classical Greece by serving as Honorary Treasurer of the British School at Athens for exactly fifty years.

Life at Forthampton was dominated by field sports: Vincent was Master of the Ledbury Hunt and Maud bred racehorses from a stallion called White Knight. She also hunted furiously, and Henry was to complain in later life that her practice of riding to hounds well into the sixth month of her pregnancies must have badly undermined his health. Henry found refuge in fly-fishing and billiards.

A bleak glimpse of family life at Forthampton is provided by a fragment of dialogue found among Henry's paper, written probably when he was nineteen.

After dinner, Vincent reads the paper:

Vincent, reading	In 1920 there were 4000 less dogs born in England than in 1924.
Silence	
Vincent	I won't speak again.
Maud	Henry, did I ring for coffee?
Vincent	You did dear, I'm sorry.
Maud	Ring again Henry will you? No dear boy, not that bell, it doesn't ring. I'm afraid something must have gone wrong with it.

Henry rings
Silence

Maud	Billy, did you write to Hepworth about the kitchen range?
Vincent	Yes dear, I sent the letter off directly you told me. I do my best.
Maud	The cook is in despair, Vincent. I do not know what to do about it, and this brute of a man Hepworth will not send anyone to mend the range. He can be up to no good in Birmingham, Vincent. What does he do all day? Playing about with the typists instead of doing the work?
Vincent, reading	In Somerset, two boys were drowned in a river.
Maud	Oh Vincent, you do irritate me so. Now do think about the kitchen range.
Vincent	I'm sorry dear, I thought you liked hearing the news. Yes dear, I'm listening.
Maud, clasping face	Well, then what shall we do about the kitchen range? It may break down at any moment. Vincent, are you listening?
Vincent, scratching dog	Yes dear.
Maud	Then do leave the dog alone.
Vincent, tapping his teeth with his nails	Very well dear.
Maud	Do you think it would be best to write again? The cook is desperate you see, Vincent.
Vincent	I have written. I can do no more.
Maud	And did you tell him all that was wrong with it?
Vincent	What do you think? You do bore

[289]

	me so with your questions. Now let me read the paper.
Silence	
Vincent	I wish my sons ever did any work. Here's a boy who died of overwork last Saturday.
Henry	Misguided.
Maud	Died of what did you say?
Vincent	Of overwork, my dear. I am afraid our sons are in no danger of that.
Maud	What a curious thing! I didn't know that boys could die of overwork.
Sees Gerald get up to change chairs.	
Maud	Gerald, as you're up, could you go and see what has happened to the coffee? What can be the matter?
Vincent	Into the sink It fell I think With a clatter
Silence	
Vincent, plaintively	Nobody laughs at the jokes old Father makes.
Henry	No.
Gerald slams the door as he goes out.	
Vincent	I'm afraid the boy is liverish.
Maud	Yes, both of them are.

Henry was educated at boarding schools between the ages of nine and eighteen. He and Gerald were close enough in age to be at Eton together for two years. They 'messed together' and were extremely supportive of one another, taking sides against Maud and Vincent in frictions with their parents. The other senior boys in his 'house' were jealous of the privileged relationship between the prefect and his very much younger brother. When Gerald left, Henry complained that he was savagely flogged by Alec Douglas-Home, later Lord Home. At Eton, several of Henry's short stories were published in the school magazine, *College Days*. His parents were suspicious about his writing and early stories were shown to John Buchan who strongly advised him to give it all up as a bad job.

Henry went up to Magdalen College, Oxford, in 1924 to read English and went down after two years without a degree but with a half blue for billiards. He found it difficult to concentrate on Anglo-Saxon and did not get on with his tutor, C. S. Lewis. He formed a close friendship there with a young don at Exeter College called Nevill Coghill, who read his manuscripts and volunteered advice, most of which he seemed to ignore. Later in London he met Edward Garnett, a reader for Jonathan Cape, who helped him with his first two novels.

The first, *Blindness*, started while he was at Eton, was published by Dent in January 1926, under the pseudonym of Henry Green. Next he started, but could not finish another novel, called *Mood*. Between 1927 and 1928, living in workmen's lodgings and working an eight-and-a-half-hour day, he served his apprenticeship on the shop floor of the family firm in their Birmingham factory. They were, and still are, heavy engineers. 'It's a harder, but in many ways a finer life than I thought it would be,' he wrote in a letter to Coghill. 'Some of the men are magnificent. The words they use even more so.' There he started and finished *Living*, his second novel. It concerned factory workers, and was published in 1929 by Dent. Upon leaving Birmingham, he married a country neighbour and distant cousin. She was Adelaide Mary Biddulph, eldest daughter of the second Baron Biddulph, and always known as Dig.

The couple set up home in Radnor Place and he started work in the London offices of Pontifex which Vincent had by now built up into a thriving concern. Henry's older brother, Gerald, had studied at Cambridge and been awarded a First in Part 1 and Part 2 of the History Tripos. Subsequently, having failed the examination for a fellowship at Trinity, he also joined the family business but detested book-keeping and found he could not work with his father at all.

Their views of Vincent were contrasting. Henry was much in

awe of him; many years later in all seriousness he announced to a friend who worked at Pontifex: 'My father is the cleverest man in the world!' Nevertheless, the sons found him impossible to communicate with. A favourite tactic of Vincent's was to refer to himself, in the third person, as 'the poor old man'. If taken to task by Maud, who addressed him as Wodehouse on those occasions, he would declaim in a high-pitched whine: 'The poor old man is only doing his best – no man can do more!' Although Vincent had managed the affairs of the British School of Athens with great skill and generosity, he was aloof and tight-fisted to his family and his staff. The factory workers – accurate judges of such matters – laughed behind their hands at his habit of alighting from the bus a stop before Acocks Green and so saving a halfpenny on his fare. Because Henry's books did not sell well, his father never took Henry's writing seriously, and this was always a source of deep resentment.

In the event, Gerald only stayed a few months in the firm before deciding to concentrate full time on his hobby – the study of the Occult – although he remained firmly committed all his life to maintaining Forthampton Court and its sporting traditions, shooting rather than hunting being his passion. In 1937, he settled down and married Angela Vivien Duncan, daughter of Major-General Sir John Duncan. They had three sons.

Much later Henry used to say in cruel tilt at Gerald's hobby that he had put his three young sons down on the waiting list for Eton rather too late – but a fortunate series of deaths and suicides which wiped the slate clean allowed the Yorke boys to sail through.

Between their marriage in 1929 and the war, Henry and Dig lived a social life as Bright Young Things. Through Dig, they became friendly with the playboy Aly Khan and moved in his circle, travelling abroad with him. It may be that his third novel *Party Going* is based on a holiday with Aly Khan which went wrong in the fog. Another friend of that period was the working-class writer and merchant seaman James Hanley. Henry lent him money on at least one occasion and pleaded his case for wider recognition with Edward Garnett and Lady Ottoline Morrell. He wrote to the former in 1931 while fixing up a dinner when they could meet, 'I have a genius here, a man called James Hanley. He was until a short time ago a docker and has since written books, which have been published in limited editions, about working men and has got everyone else cold.. . . .' Garnett was not impressed, although he did grudgingly praise Hanley's short story 'The Last Voyage'. Two years later, still persevering, Henry wrote to Lady Ottoline Morrell in similar vein '. . . but I can't help feeling [Hanley] has a great command over words and that is the gift or the enchantment without which a book is nothing and, in that it shows a high attitude of mind, is perhaps what all the rest will follow on. His working-class speech is, to my mind, unsurpassed by anyone writing now.' Lady Ottoline did offer some practical help to Hanley, making him the loan of a room and a typewriter. It was the first and not the last time that Henry was to help a neglected or aspiring author.

These two friendships were typical of his style: he did not generally seek out friends with backgrounds or origins similar to his own and his friendships were short-lived. Nor were his friendships close – he always kept his distance. By the war he had dropped almost all his old Eton and Oxford friends and he rarely saw Gerald and Angela any more.

Henry was a mad soccer and sports fan. In Birmingham after the compulsory Saturday morning shift, he had faithfully watched the Villa every week. In London he transferred his loyalties to Chelsea, and until well into the fifties he would be a regular spectator on the terraces at Stamford Bridge or Craven Cottage when Chelsea were away. During the thirties he became friendly with the boxer Jack Hood, who trained for his fights with a one-legged publican called Wally Weston in the billiards room at Madresfield Court, the seat of the Earl of Beauchamp. He was also an early fan of all-in wrestling, attending bouts, sometimes twice weekly, at The Ring, Blackfriars, where 'Spider' Harvey presided as referee.

In 1934 the couple moved to a larger house in Rutland Gate with servants, and I, their only child, was born. Despite the move and a busy social life, he wrote *Party Going* (started in 1931 and published in 1939) and *Pack My Bag* (published in 1940).

In October 1938, fearful of the war which was imminent and

of being separated from his family and job, he joined the Auxiliary Fire Service as a part-time fireman and it was probably about then that his fascination with pub life started to develop. It was not only that he liked to drink, which he often did to excess – but he loved to eavesdrop on and to chat and mingle with the pub regulars. Later, in the fifties, he could spend up to four hours a day in two different pubs: at lunchtimes he visited the pub near his office, and in the evenings the George IV near where he lived in Trevor Place. Sometimes, having visited the pub before dinner for an hour or so, he would return to the pub after dinner and remain there until closing time. To the regulars he was simply Henry who always sat at the same table wearing his raincoat and hat with a glass of gin and water beside him.

His conventional social life was structured around the two evenings a week the cook had off. Dig and he would go out for dinner every Tuesday and Sunday to the same restaurants, alternately with the same friends or couple. Drinks and talk flowed on these occasions and it was no coincidence that the wives were usually pretty and vivacious, for he loved to flirt and gossip. He abhorred literary gatherings and although his friends outside the pubs were generally other writers, painters or intellectuals, he did not discuss writing or books by choice. If a book came up in conversation with his friends, it was dismissed as 'good!', or 'pitiably bad!' How he had arrived at that judgement was not generally a matter he would go into even if pressed. His verdicts on books were always instantaneous and you felt that they were right.

This disinclination to discuss books was somewhat surprising because reading, for which he had a voracious appetite, was his chief recreation and relaxation. He read all the current English and American fiction as it became available from the Harrods Lending Library, most of which by his lights must have been pretty dismal stuff. The only writers he refused to read were Simenon and C. P. Snow. On average, he must have got through about eight books a week and sometimes my mother changed their two library books daily, to the despair of wide-eyed Miss Clutton who manned the exchange desk at the library. The standard of the novels never seemed to matter. I can only remember a few times when he put a book down with the words 'This is utterly bogus – I can't finish it!' He rarely praised a book; there were some American authors he would admit to liking, but he seemed to admire no contemporary English writers. He never re-read a book or selected one from his small library of 'classics' collected in his Oxford days. Nor can I recall him reading anything by his professed idols: Gogol, Turgenev, Doughty, Céline or Faulkner. He only liked novels – he would not read poetry or biography. He loved thrillers and magazines, particularly *Time* magazine. When as a teenager, I was interested in motor racing, he used to read aloud a weekly article called 'Pit Stop', written by a mad car buff and full of quasi-technical jargon, which he had found in one of my motoring magazines. He would shake his head over this and howl with laughter.

As with the books he professed to admire, he never went back to the passions of his childhood – billiards and fly-fishing. He completely abandoned billiards when he left university, refusing even to play bar billiards in the pub, and he never fished much any more, even with me, because he steadfastly refused to visit Forthampton where I spent my school holidays. In any case, it was impossible by then to fish for chub with the fly because the Severn was so muddy from the barge traffic.

Behind the shouts of laughter and the talk, there was a strong streak of pessimism, even of fatalism, in Henry's nature. Any setback, however slight, was a cause of intense and gleeful discussion about what worse horrors might ensue. It may have followed from this that the humour he loved was black humour – of a very raw kind. I remember when only ten or eleven, staying with school friends where an elderly relative of theirs fell on a landing and the next day a white bone, which was his nose bone, was found on the stairs by the cat. It proved impossible to re-implant the bone; the cat had partly eaten it. My father howled with laughter when I related my macabre school holiday adventure. He cross-examined me in detail about what had happened next, how the cat reacted, what they thought it was, what the doctor said, etc. Eventually he made a wild story out of this and retold it to his friends with gusto.

He was not a mimic, nor did he like risqué stories, but he was a deadly tease, usually of girls. (As he turned the ratchet he would shout in excitement 'Gone too far?') He could be cruel. It is said that Maurice Bowra would never speak to him again after Henry teased him about a poorly drafted fire drill notice at Wadham College in the war. Due to mastoiditis in his youth, his hearing on one side was poor, though he always maintained it was the bombing, and at times the results were hilarious. Gogi Lee Thompson and Henry were talking about animals. Dig left the room as Gogi remarked to Henry how sexy she thought ostriches' eyes were. When Dig returned, Henry said to Dig, 'How extraordinary! Gogi must have been deep sea diving. She has just told me that octopuses' eyes are sexy!' As a raconteur of stories, many of which he must have made up, he was superb. Henry also had the odd habit of making disconcerting remarks. When he was fifty he introduced himself to an elderly and respectable lady with the words, 'Henry Yorke – fifty-five – and I can't do it!'

In the thirties, there were difficulties with the publishing of *Party Going*. Dent would have nothing more to do with his books. Eventually Goronwy Rees made him show the novel to John Lehmann who persuaded Leonard and Virginia Woolf to publish it at their Hogarth Press. Henry always maintained that the Woolfs did not like the book; but John Lehmann was to remain a life-long admirer and support. When Lehmann moved on from the Hogarth Press after the war to form his own publishing firm, my father, in his characteristically cautious way, was unwilling to make a change, which was always a sore point with John.

By the outbreak of war, Henry Yorke was a fully trained fireman, attached to Sub-station 34A5V 'A' Division, 79 Davies Street. In the blitz that followed, there were both short periods of dangerous physical activity and long lulls. Although his station was in a flying column and as a result went to many places outside London – as far as Manchester and even Chichester to defend the cathedral against a 'Baedeker' raid – there must have been many duty days when he was on stand-by. Pontifex did no munitions work and was just ticking over, and he was able to keep an eye on what little was going on there in his rest days. I was evacuated to friends in Bedfordshire and my mother, who did voluntary work in canteens in Bedford and in London, alternated between the two households – they had by then moved into a much smaller house in Trevor Place. His father, too old for both World Wars, based himself at Forthampton. This seemed to suit Henry's writing. *Pack My Bag, Caught, Loving* and *Back* were all published between 1940 and 1946. He also wrote a number of short stories, three of which were published in New Writing. *Concluding* was published in 1948.

Henry often spoke of a rescue he had carried out during the blitz outside John Lewis's in Oxford Street. This he describes in his short story *The Rescue*. His mate Charlie in the story was Charlie Vincent who had worked before the war as the butler at 104 Harley Street. Right up to the sixties he and Charlie, now a greengrocer in the East End, would meet every year to swap reminiscences. Henry was always bitter about this rescue. He felt Charlie and he deserved medals, but they were both later reprimanded for not wearing the correct type of BA (breathing apparatus), and there was no officer present to make the official recommendation in any case.

He had a fierce pride in the Fire Service. He told me once with emotion of a special joint parade held with the army in Hyde Park. He was there with his crew and an appliance. Their job was to direct a jet of water through a high pressure hose over the saluting stand. An arrogant army major strutted over and poked his swagger stick in the jet. To the delight of the fire crew, he suffered a double compound fracture of the arm for his pains.

Henry once entered a burning house, axe in hand, to find a naked girl, oblivious of smoke and flames, making love to a Great Dane.

For the rest of his life, ex-fireman that he was, my father was continually on the look-out for other fires. I remember once in the fifties walking back with him and my mother up Montpelier Street after a good dinner, when he 'smelled smoke'. Neither my mother nor I could smell a thing, yet the fire engines were summoned. It was a false alarm. This was to happen again and again, according to my mother.

In the post-war years, Pontifex flourished like all manufacturing firms but a serious decline had set in by the early fifties. In 1952, an effort was made to improve the situation by buying another engineering business in Leeds. This at least was a step

[297]

forward, since it was a diversification into other markets, but it did nothing to address the fundamental problems of the Birmingham factory, which was operating under capacity and losing money hand over fist. Henry faced increasing difficulties with his aged father, now strapped in a wheelchair and accompanied by a nurse, who insisted on continuing to come into the office every day and interfering with everything he did. Although he made grotesque stories out of these visits, retold to all and sundry, he must have resented his father even more deeply.

It was easy for other writers to assume that the novelist Henry Green had little interest in business and only 'worked' at Pontifex to give himself a comfortable income so that he could write. Certainly his choice of colleagues on the Board, who were close friends without engineering qualifications, appointed by him and not Vincent, seemed to confirm this assumption. One colleague was the Welsh don, Goronwy Rees, a great crony and a wild character. At times the drinks must have flowed and their talk ranged far beyond the finer points of 'jig and tool design', but it would be a mistake to believe that Henry did not take his work seriously. Before the war, very much in face of opposition from Vincent, he had set up a subsidiary business dealing with the sale of food and chemical equipment, quite separate from Pontifex's main business, which was the manufacture of counter-pressure filling machines for beer. He visited Moscow on a sales trip and just after the war, sold a series of penicillin plants to the Russians. I can just recall a wild and riotous party held at Trevor Place to entertain the Russian Trade Delegation, and I can remember him telling me that Russian peasants swarmed over the train carrying the equipment across Russia, scraping the grease off the pump casings for food. He toured Canada on a government trade mission after the war. He became Chairman of the BCPMA (British Chemical Plant Manufacturers' Association), a position of some importance in industry. He also confided in me that he had a secret ambition to emulate his father's career in the City where he hoped to 'inherit' his seats on various banking and insurance company boards. This never happened. Either Vincent was not prepared to push his son's name or the days of nepotism in the City were over.

He was a weak business man, and he was impatient with detail. He could not or would not stand up to his father, and he lacked decisiveness. His prevailing moods of pessimism and fatalism made it almost impossible to move in any direction. In typically blunt fashion, Gerald was to describe a fateful visit he made to the office in 1958. 'I found what I had thought was a glass of water on Henry's desk – it was gin – and he was really incapable of making any decisions. So I had to get him to retire.' Henry's business life, while it lasted, was a key source of inspiration for his novels, but increasingly, as things started to go wrong, it was to prove a drain on his energies for writing.

In 1949 *Loving* had been published in America and for a short time it figured in the best-seller lists. He felt that at last he was going to earn popular recognition and make some money out of his books. In 1950, my parents and a lawyer travelled to New York with the idea of setting up a trust in favour of my mother and myself to avoid paying UK tax on the royalties. Such was his passion for anonymity that they travelled to New York and booked into the Gotham as Mr and Mrs H. V. Yonge, the initials matching the initials on their luggage. It was also about this time that he started to insist on being photographed only from the back. He was fêted as a literary celebrity, attending parties with writers and film stars, and one of the highest points of his trip was meeting his greatest idol after Céline, William Faulkner. It is said that as he booked out of the Gotham for the trip home, the doorman, who had seen all this before, bowed him farewell with the words 'Good-bye Mr Green!' Sadly, this novel had only a brief success in America.

He published *Nothing* in 1950 and *Doting* in 1952. He also broadcast on his theory of the novel and did more reviews and articles than at any other time in his life.

After *Doting*, his tenth book, my father never spoke of doing another novel. He wrote a play for television called *Journey out of Spain* which was never performed. Next he became immersed in writing a stage comedy to be called *All on his Ownsome*. He wrestled with this play non-stop between 1955 and 1956. It was set in 10 Downing Street with a woman Prime Minister and involved sex and politics. The writing and re-writing of this play became a long drawn-out nightmare. He submitted draft after draft to the impresario with whom he was collaborating. They could not get it right. The manager of the Worthing Repertory said he found the subject matter 'in questionable taste'. John Lehmann read it and did not think it a success but added rather hopefully: 'In fact the odd idea came to me that if you made a novel of it, it might be very good indeed.' In November 1956 he abandoned it, ostensibly on the grounds that 'the political side of it has been completely stultified by the Russians' actions in Hungary.'

He started a book about his experiences in the Fire Service, to be called *London and War 1939–1945*. He completed a long section and then abandoned that.

In 1957 his father had at last died. Completely demoralised by the problems at Pontifex, which was now in a serious state of decline, Henry toyed with the idea of getting out altogether as soon as I joined him from university. On doctor's orders he went on a cruise to South Africa to make up his mind. The first night out in a bad swell in the English Channel, exhausted and depressed, he fell against the door knob in his cabin and badly bruised his ribs. He used to recount with sly glee that the captain was so concerned about his near suicidal state of mind that he seated him beside the ship's young and pretty nanny at meals so that she could keep an eye on him for the rest of the trip.

In 1959 he finally resigned from Pontifex on the grounds of ill health. I took over as Managing Director and Gerald loyally served a stint as Chairman. By a cruel irony, it was the Birmingham factory which had finally ended his business career; he could not bring himself to close the works and make redundant those foundrymen whom he had described, thirty years before, as 'magnificent'. Just before his resignation he and Dig had moved to a much larger house in Wilton Place, with a separate study for him – in Trevor Place he had written his novels on his knee in the drawing room. Despite these advantages, his energies for writing seemed to desert him altogether.

There was a vague plan for him to write another autobiographical piece to be named *Pack My Bag Repacked*. He dictated drafts to Jenny Rees, the daughter of his old friend Goronwy, but this petered out eventually. In 1964 he dictated a piece which he put aside uncorrected in a drawer, about his childhood passion for fishing and Forthampton Court, the family home which he had steadfastly refused to visit for twenty-five years or more.

The walk around our garden, hidden at the bottom where it went along what was left of the moat, and nearby the Bishop's causeway, from the sixteenth century, so designed that he could keep his feet dry until he got into his boat to go across a flooded Severn right to the doors of his Abbey, already visible across those floods as though built on one of the lagoons of Venice, our house having been His Eminence's summer residence.

In summer down our way gray days are best because they bring out the incredible green of trees and grass. Best also to fly fish for chub from a boat.

Or even if to fish in sunlight, which was hopeless, one beached the boat at dusk to turn and see Tewkesbury Abbey's Norman tower in Caen stone glowing rose above dying light – the Rose, darling Rose – he did not know it yet but of whom he was to write, never even having met her, written of not until after the Second War, muddled as she was, unthinking but always right, the dear Rose he would love at that time just to lose the agony of air raids.

When the wind was right with not too much sun, the art was to cast one's fly close to where those withies dangled in the water, underneath which slowly rocked the chub waiting for a grub above to fall off those green leaves. It was wet fly fishing and only a swirl would show when the whitewinged fly was taken and it was time to strike. And what harm in that when fish are cold-blooded? None of course, instead there was pure joy. The ache was to walk back less than a mile home imbued, though he did not realise this yet, with his love for red-haired Rose, the very stuff of dreams, the whole of every-thing to him then. Those evenings were magic to a boy alone.

Although he still read at least one novel a day from the Harrods library, he did not leave the house any more, even to go to the local pub, nor did he go out of his way to see his friends, whom he called 'my much hated old friends'. There were exceptions, of course. He liked the young company of my friends, but by then I was working in Leeds and visiting London seldom. Occasional visits from strangers, usually fans, academics or students, were welcomed and, at these times, all his old fire and enthusiasms returned. He watched the television a lot, particularly the sports programmes.

His hearing got increasingly bad. I remember once ringing the house from Yorkshire and getting him. In a hurry and without time to explain who I was, I asked to speak to 'Mummy'. The dour answer was: 'So sorry, I have absolutely no money.'

In 1968, after some persuasion, I took him to see the Howard Winstone/Seki world flyweight championship eliminator in the Albert Hall; he came unshaven and in slippers. He had not been out of the house for several years, and I was terrified that, being so deaf and only accustomed to the background rumble of Knightsbridge traffic, he would find the sound of a hyped-up fight crowd baying for blood too fierce and intimidating. Not so. He loved it, and when it was over, being stopped in the ninth round on a controversial cut eye decision, I took him down to meet the disconsolate Seki in his dressing room. By the time we reached the car a slipper had disappeared.

However, this expedition was never to be repeated.

Two things my father never lost were his love for cats and his gifts for laughter and talk. However ill or depressed he was, I only had to tell him a story about something that had gone wrong, and he would give his distinctive yell of laughter. For me it was his mark.

Henry Yorke and Henry Green died on 13 December 1973 at the age of sixty-eight. When my father was buried at Forthampton Church, Sid Cutter, the grave digger, had dug the grave too short for the coffin and it could not be lowered – in fact it stuck fast. My mother remarked to Gerald at the graveside: 'How Henry would have laughed!'